D1611836

THE SONG OF
WIRRUN

THE SONG OF WIRRUN

Patricia Wrightson

Reissued 1987

C

CENTURY

LONDON MELBOURNE AUCKLAND JOHANNESBURG

The Ice is Coming
First published in Great Britain in 1977 by
Hutchinson & Co (Publishers) Ltd

The Dark Bright Water
First published in Great Britain in 1979 by
Hutchinson & Co (Publishers) Ltd

Behind the Wind
First published in Great Britain in 1981 by
Hutchinson & Co (Publishers) Ltd

This edition first published in 1987 by
Century Hutchinson Ltd
Brookmount House, 62-65 Chandos Place,
London WC2N 4NW

Century Hutchinson Australia (Pty) Ltd
PO Box 496, 16-22 Church Street, Hawthorn
Victoria 3122, Australia

Century Hutchinson New Zealand Ltd
PO Box 40-086, Glenfield, Auckland 10
New Zealand

Century Hutchinson South Africa (Pty) Ltd
PO Box 337, Bergvlei, 2012 South Africa

ISBN 0 7126 1150 9

Printed and bound in Great Britain by
Anchor Brendon Ltd, Tiptree, Essex

Wrightson, Patricia
The song of wirrun.
I. Title
823 (F)   PR6073.R5/

ISBN 0-7126-1150-9

The Ice is Coming

MIMI COUNTRY

Alic

The
Olgas   Ayers
Rock   *   Mt.

The Ice
is Coming

* Ice appears

▓ Rail journey

prings

nner

Mimi's Flight

Wirrun's

Flight

Toowoomba *

Tenterfield *

Emmaville *

Dorrigo *

Ko-in's
Mt.
*

Flight of Wirrun and Mimi

Tilba-Tilba *

Bunyip's gully
Ice Mountain
*
*
*
Battle on Shelf

Author's Note

This is a story of today and of Australia. It is my own story, grown out of my thinking. Its human characters are my invention, but its spirit characters are not. They are the folk-spirits of the Australian Aborigines – not the ritual figures of the creative myths but the gnomes and heroes and monsters of Australia.

I might have written a story about more familiar spirits, the elves and fairies and dragons and monsters of Europe. Then everyone would have known that the story was mine and the spirits borrowed from an older convention. But for that story I would have to invent a foreign setting, an Earthsea or a Middle Earth; and powerfully magical as those countries are I know one as powerful and as magic. It is the only one I know and the one I want to write about.

So every spirit appearing in this and my two previous stories, *The Nargun and the Stars* and *An Older Kind of Magic*, belongs originally to Australia and its Aborigines. Many of them are beliefs still living; some are remembered from only a generation ago; a few have outlived the people who believed in them. They claim their place in an old convention, these even older and perhaps purer spirits of the Aborigines' domestic life. And I claim a writer's leave to employ them in my own stories in my own way.

I

A Young Man of the People

One

The old south land lies across the world like an open hand, hollowed a little at the palm. High over it tumbles the wind, and all along its margin tumbles the sea – rolling in slow sweeps on long white beaches, beating with hammers of water at headlands of rock. Under and in this tumbling of wind and water the land lies quiet like a great hand at rest, all its power unknown.

Along its green margins, clustered in towns here and there, live the Happy Folk with their faces to the sea. They live for happiness; it is their business and their duty. They study it and teach it to their children, debate it, make laws to force it on each other, struggle for it, export and import it. Most of all they buy and sell it. They have no time to look over their shoulders at the old land behind them. Only sometimes, in their search for happiness, they make expensive little explorations into the land with cameras.

The Happy Folk know that they are the land's true people and everything in it belongs to them. Yet between the towns, and inland behind cliffed and chasmed mountains, live other races. There are only a few of them, thinly scattered: the Inlanders and the People. The People are dark-skinned, with heavy brows and watching eyes, and they belong to the land; it flows into them through their feet. The time when they took the land from another people is so long ago that they can forget it and claim the land as theirs; but really it is the land that claims them.

The Inlanders come from the same stock as the Happy Folk, and the two still claim to be of the same race. But the great old silent land that claims the People for its own has been at work on the Inlanders too, and by now they have become a separate race. The Inlanders suspect it with bitterness, the Happy Folk laugh and deny it. Between the Inlanders and the People there is another sort of bitterness: they are both jealous children of the land.

So these races struggle to come together and drift farther apart, while the oldest race of all lives among them and is hidden. This is a race of creatures born of the land itself: of red rocks and secret waters, dust-devils and far places, green jungle and copper-blue saltbush. They are sly and secret creatures. The People have known of them for a long time and said little. As for the other two races, if a man of them ever meets an earth-spirit he is silent for lack of a word and so no word is said.

Among the oldest of all are the Narguns, monsters of rock poured molten from the fires in the heart of the land. Far down the world they live, near the south-east corner of the land, crouched in the darkness of caves or holes in the ground. Long before the white races came to the land the People had learnt to avoid those caves in case death should roll out of them, quick and crushing. If Narguns are old, the Eldest Nargun is as old as the land itself; and because it is the oldest, and closest to the heart of the land, the red fire of its beginning will come when it calls.

For thousands of years the Eldest Nargun lay in the dark of the earth. In time it emerged, the first, the biggest and most powerful. It felt starlight and wind and saw great battles; and when those were over it found a cave and went into darkness again. In later times it took its power into battle against the sea, standing against the sea where it tears at the edge of the land.

The Nargun soon found that the power of fire

12

was useless here. It only stood against the sea as the rocks did. On a rising tide great glassy swells rolled in, exploding in rockets of water or spilling over in sudden flowers of foam. When the tide drew back it left quiet pools where weeds swayed, anemones flowered, and small things made slow journeys from side to side; but still the sea curled long exploring fingers into channels, and sent its puppy-waves licking among the rocks. Sometimes the Nargun lay just covered by water; looking up, the old stone monster saw a rippled sun or washed and wavering stars. Sometimes when deep green swells rolled over, in the tug of water the Eldest moved a little and cried out with its old cry: '*Nga-a-a!*' And there it crouches still, defying the sea.

Far to the north live the Mimi, and no one knows how old they are. Even the People cannot see them, but they have always known they are there. They know by the paintings in the caves.

In that north country the rough cave walls are crowded with the paintings of the People: paintings of late times and long-ago times and the Dreamtime. All the lore and history of the People are painted on the walls of those caves, and the People look and know and remember. But among those paintings there are some that were not made by the People. They are no part of the People's lore, so they know that those paintings were made by the Mimi. From the paintings they have learnt much about the Mimi themselves.

The Mimi are shy spirits who live inside the rocks. When they blow on a rock it opens to let them in or out. They have very sharp eyes and ears; at the first sign of a stranger they slip away into their rocks, and this is why the People never see them.

Their paintings show that they hunt with spear and spear-thrower in the normal way, and dig with digging sticks and cook with fire. They are very tall and thin and frail, so frail that the wind might break them. Because of this they never gather food in windy weather but only when it is calm. But once there was a Mimi who was caught by the wind and carried far away; and perhaps it was the old south land itself that called up that wind.

It was late spring: the time when the trade winds tramp south, when in the north stray winds play to and fro, soft and hard, till the monsoons come down. These uncertain winds had kept this Mimi inside her rock until her food was running short. In the first calm she went out with her digging stick and her bark dish to dig roots and honey-ants in a place near at hand.

She heard the first hissing of leaves in the wind, but her digging stick had caught under a root. She waited only a second to jerk it free, snatched up her basket, and sprang like a spider to a rock. She blew to open it – but the tricky spring wind swirled along the rock and blew her breath away. Then it tugged her legs into the air. Her body strained at the weight of basket and stick – she dropped them quickly in case she should break. So the updraught caught her like a straw, and the wind had her.

'*Wa!*' she cried thinly, whirling and spinning. She twisted her arms and legs together to keep them from being torn off. The wind spun her upward and swung her south in a wide curve.

Tumbling in waves of wind she caught glimpses of her country below: stooping rocks and shadowed gorges and flat green swamps, all the dear known country spinning in corroboree. She was still reaching for it when her country danced north and away.

Strange winds dropped and caught her, passed her from one to another and carried her higher, and still she did not break. She was learning to hold her wispy arms and legs together and to lie along the wind. She came swooping down: a black speck below grew into a grey tree-top that she tried to catch before she was whirled up again. She saw a tide of darkness creep over the land and night come. The stars swung to and fro, and she wondered with terror how she should get back to her country. Already the wind had carried her down the old south land to its beautiful, terrible heart; and there, though she did not know it, something waited.

The centre of the old south land is a place of waiting; of waiting and of age. In the palm of that great hand lies the age and travail of the world, and the Happy Folk call it a desert. Here the ground lies so level that water will not flow, and empty river-courses lead only into clay pans crusted with salt. The sun beats down like a gong on red wind-drifted dunes. Flat-topped mountains, painted red with sand, are not mountains at all but single, enduring, rocks quarried by winds and seas far off in time. Desert creatures hide by day under spinifex and saltbush and slow brave mulga. And under the castle-ramparts of a mountain lies one small lake of dried salt, where one small outcrop of rock leads down to the caverns of the Ninya.

Under the fiery sand they live, men of ice in caverns of ice. No icicles drip from their cavern roofs, for there is never any melting here. There is only the whiteness of frost never touched, and a shining floor of ice, and columns and arches of ice that the Ninya build for pleasure, and a frozen howling wind. The Ninya are men like men of the People, except that they like their caverns are pure and sparkling white. Their eyebrows and beards are needles of ice, and frost falls from them as they move. Wherever they go through the caverns, the frost and ice and the cold wind go with them. They are the makers of ice and their blood is white.

They are green-eyed and beautiful and they live together as brothers, but there is no kindness between them. The frost goes deep. Their voices creak and grate; they often howl in anger; and every man of the Ninya wants all and wants it for himself. So this power of wanting and this power of ice lie under the sun-beaten sand, prisoned and waiting.

On that day when the spring wind caught the Mimi, the waiting had exploded into quarrels. The cold white vaults were beautiful, but it was always twilight there and the sparkle of frost was dim. The Ninya yearned over that. The wind's howl should have widened into a song; it needed a sky. The ice wanted sun to touch it to green and blue fire; they longed to see it. Bitterly they snarled at each other.

'*You* may hide like a black bat in a cave. I – I will go out and take the land.'

'Go, then – and melt. I wait till the Nargun is found.'

'You will crawl out when the ice is built and the frost laid.'

'And without me when will that be? We are few since the days of the Nargun, and all are needed. A frost or two, a little ice to cut the People's feet, and you will melt.'

This sneer brought howls of anger. 'Hear the Great Glacier! He says we are lost without him!' 'The People are gone and we are free, yet he sulks in a cave while the sun burns the land!' But some drew apart from the others and muttered and creaked together.

'We wait till the Nargun is found,' they said at last.

'The Nargun! What is a Nargun? A beast of rock!' 'Can we not freeze rock? Look there!' One of them struck the cavern wall and showered frost into the wind.

'Freeze your own ears – you talk like a fool!' 'We say not a Nargun but *the* Nargun. The Eldest with the power of fire.' 'The one that melted our bones into rivers and sent us under the ground. That Nargun.' 'They have forgotten. They are men without ears.'

There were more howls at the insult, and frosty hands groped for frosty stones. A stronger voice than the others grated through the howl of the wind.

'Stop, you fools! No man can be spared. We are few enough for the work we have to do. You howl for freedom, but when the work begins you waste yourselves in fighting.'

The howls died into mutters. The stones dropped. The Ninya waited to hear how the work might be beginning. The strong-voiced one told them quickly, before the fight could start again.

16

'Some of you say, go now. Some of you say, first find the Eldest Nargun. I say, go now to find the Eldest Nargun.'

They listened. He went on.

'How shall we find the Nargun? By hiding in a cave? It lies in its own country by the far-off sea. We must go there: a long journey in the winding roads of rock. We must find the Eldest and catch it quickly in a fist of ice. *Then* we are free.'

Creaks of argument broke out, but the voice cut through them quickly and began to chant.

'We will build mountains of ice with the rainbow in them. We will sparkle the ground with frost and feather the air with snow, with the silent feathers of snow.'

'Snow!' they all groaned, for they had not seen it for an age.

'Drill into rocks with the delicate needle of cold; fling a net to trap birds from the air and furry things from the forest. Bind up the running waters and hold them still.'

Now all the Ninya howled and sang together. Frost showered from their swaying bodies and needles of ice from their beards. The first singer listened with a cold white smile and sang a new line.

'In a mountain of ice shall the Nargun, the Eldest, be held.'

But this tore the chorus apart into separate howls. 'We build here, we build now, while the People forget!' 'Why should we journey? Let the Eldest wait by the far-off sea while we grow mighty!' 'As we were before, when the Nargun melted our bones! Find the Nargun, find the Nargun!' 'And who will find it?' 'The ice! The ice will find it!'

Soon the two sides had fallen apart again and instead of singing there were bitter snarls. The wind raged on through the glitter of ice and circled by deeper caverns far into the earth. Above, the sun burnt down on the lake of salt. The surface rock, the Ninya's entrance, baked in the heat.

The sun sank. The land gave back its heat to the shining, paling sky. Flat-topped Mount Conner rose like a castle, sharp against the western sky. Its haze, that most lovely and tender haze of the central hills, was lit to lilac and gold. Acacia blossom rippled with gold in the last breath of falling wind, and brittle-dead flowers chattered in the feathers of an emu-bush. Under a native plum beside the lake, a young man of the People unrolled his sleeping-bag for the night.

Although he was one of the People, this young man was a stranger. He lived among the Happy Folk in the east, because there by the sea was his own country. Until lately he had gone to one of the Happy Folk's schools, and now that that was finished he worked in one of their service stations. He knew the Happy Folk well, and liked to watch and think about them, for he was a young man to whom thinking came more easily than talking. He talked only to his friends.

His friends were among the People of the east who lived as he did, and some he had met as he went up and down the country. A few of his friends called him Wirrun, though he had another name among strangers. He talked to them mostly about the land and the People.

Wirrun didn't know that the land flowed into him through his feet. He only knew that he liked to walk on the earth in lonely places. He spent holidays and weekends doing this; and he had learnt from the Happy Folk the trick of saving money to buy easy travel over long distances. One of his friends in the east had come from the great quiet centre of the land. He often talked about it, and Wirrun listened, and wished he might walk on the red sand. At last he saved up a great amount of money, enough for the plane fare, so that his short holiday would be long enough. And when he had travelled over the wide land as far as that fare would take him he talked to People, asked questions, bought a bus ticket, and explored even further on his feet. So now he unrolled his sleeping-bag beside the small salt lake with its outcrop of rock, and hung his canvas water-bag from a branch of the native plum, and camped there for that night.

Darkness came in a soft sweep, with the lemon-sharp twinkle of stars. Like a spider-web dropped by the wind came the Mimi, slipping down between stars and spinifex. She drifted over the salt scab of the lake, saw the rock and reached for it. She blew on the Ninya's rock and slipped inside.

The night drew on a little and grew chill. Under the wild plum Wirrun slept soundly. A round-eyed mulgara whiffled at his sleeping-bag, then veered off after the scent of a mouse. An orb-spider's golden web shook and swayed to the flapping of a giant moth.

There was a snarling struggle in the lake: a man of the Ninya had burst out through the rock. Starlight sparkled on white arms that fought angrily to drag him back. He was pulled in, and the rock shut solid; and outside, spilt on the salty crust, lay the Mimi. She was frozen stiff with cold and terror.

So they lay that night as the old south land had ordered it: the young man from the east sleeping under the plum, the rock-spirit of the north frozen on the salt. In caverns beneath them the Ninya raged and fought for possession of the land; and far down the world the Eldest Nargun crouched on its shelf of rock while the sea swirled over.

Two

By the small salt lake the chill night had grown suddenly colder, for a gush of cold had come forth with the Ninya. The young man burrowed deeper into his bag, the moth stopped flapping in the web. The Mimi lay stiff for a long time; but presently she wove herself into the spinifex and curled up, shivering.

She was far and far from home, in an unknown country whose wandering night-things might find her and be angry. She had never lain before under the prickling stars, and she longed for the soft utter blackness of rock. Yet this rock here had been a trap; her poor wispy wits were in a tangle. What she had seen and heard in the rock had chilled her with fear as well as cold. It reached back into the past, to some old dread that she couldn't remember and couldn't forget.

She lay all night, a long loop in the spinifex, watching with frightened eyes round and dark like a possum's and listening with her large ears. She saw and heard the mulgara eating the mouse, the moth hanging in the web, and the young man of the People sleeping. She saw daylight begin to flow in slow waves from the east, but when it was newly shining she pressed her hands over her eyes and whimpered softly. Not this – she couldn't look at this –

Wirrun woke and sat up to look at the country. Like the Mimi he shut his eyes again quickly. He opened them, stared at the ground beside him, then slowly raised his eyes and looked again.

Yes. The country was hanging upside down and floating in the air.

Salt lake and emu-bush, mulga and red sand and the distant castle-mountain of Conner, all of it floated the wrong way up. Trees and bushes reached down with grey leaves, trying to get back. There was a shimmer at the edges of it, like cellophane. If last night's wind came back now and blew it away . . .?

A quietness came over him and told him not to look because this was not his country. In a moment, surely, it would put itself right for strangers. Because he had been to school and learnt about mirages he knew this must be something of that kind – but he didn't want to look at it.

He turned away to wait, and reached for his water-bag hanging on the branch above him. The bag crackled under his hand, and a thin glassy coating slid from it down to his shoulder. He shook it off hard. This time it was the shock of cold that startled him. He saw that now the floating upside-down country had slipped back into place. The great gold gong of the sun beat down on the saltbush. It was late October – almost summer; and there was ice on his water-bag.

He remembered again that he was a stranger here.

'You'll get funny weather any time,' said Wirrun politely, rubbing the unshaved hair on his round young chin.

He breakfasted, rolled his gear neatly and slung it from his shoulder, took down his water-bag, and walked away from the small salt lake under Mount Conner. He didn't know that the Mimi watched him from the spinifex; he had to reach the road in time to catch a bus. As he walked he looked, far and near. He could not afford a camera as well as a plane fare; he had to trust his eyes and mind.

He saw a flight of green parrots, and the sand glowing red between the saltbush, and the brilliant blue of a small strange flower. He must ask someone about that. He saw the sharp, clear lines of sandhill and mountain against the sky – but this he knew was a pretence because from the plane he had seen the truth. This country had no horizon. From above you could see it spreading out and out till it melted and vanished in purple haze. There was no true meeting of land and sky, no horizon.

A country with no horizon . . . could it come loose and float in the air? And ice in October. . . . What could the People of this country tell him? If they would?

He reached the road and heard the bus: first a tingle in the ears, then a whisper, then a whine, and at last a moaning motor. It stopped at his signal. He found a seat at the back and watched the Happy Folk returning from exploration, their cameras full of happiness. They were building little webs of friendship meant to last a day or so. Wirrun watched them now and then through hours of bumping and swaying. Mostly he looked from the air-cooled cocoon of the bus at the country shimmering in its heat haze. Ice on his water-bag. . . .

At sunset the bus rolled through a gateway in ranges of jumbled rock, and into Alice Springs. The Happy Folk collected their baggage and vanished into motels. Wirrun found an open shop and bought a few supplies. Then he walked out of the town, over dried-grass flats to the ghost gums beside the empty river. He knew where to look for the People.

There were a few of them just over the lip of the bank: two men with their wives and four or five tumbling children, and one much older man with proud dark eyes. The younger men had cans of beer and the old man a pipe. The women sat dark and shapeless, watching the children and waiting for the cool. Wirrun chose a gum that was not too far and not too near, and dropped his gear under it. He nodded to the men and threw oranges to the children, who scrambled for them, giggling. In a few minutes Wirrun went over to speak to their elders.

'All right if I camp here?' he asked.

'It's free here,' said the old man kindly, and the two younger men laughed.

'That's right, boy,' they said, turning it into a sneer. 'All free here.' Wirrun recognized the sneer and knew it was not meant for him.

They were not sure how to accept this grave, lean young stranger. So Wirrun talked about who he was and where he came from, and about his friend in the east who came from this country; and he told them where he had been and what he had seen; and their eyes grew warmer.

He asked about Mount Conner, and the old man said that that was his own country. Wirrun was delighted with this piece of good luck. He told about the swooping wind that died at night, and his camp last night, and the rich blue flower and the golden web, and the sunset behind the mountain; and the old man smiled and nodded. Then Wirrun told about the upside-down country and the ice.

The old man chuckled and puffed at his pipe. 'That's them Ninya,' he said. 'Terrible fellers, them Ninya.' And he looked sideways at Wirrun, but Wirrun only waited.

'They're all ice,' said the old man, puffing away. 'Ice beards, white frost all over. Ice in their caves. Under the ground, they are, and a big wind blowing in there. Quiet nights, no wind outside, them Ninya comes out. Ice falls off 'em. Cuts your feet in the morning. You can tell when you see them trees wrong side up. That means them Ninya's been out.' He looked sideways again. 'No men left to sing 'em back in their caves, put the trees back.'

Wirrun was silent, thinking of the frost-men in their caves of wind and ice. It was a satisfying story, big enough to explain that weird moment of morning; and yet it did not explain. Not quite. 'But it must be a bit late for 'em?' he suggested. 'Near summer. A bit hot for ice.'

The old men chuckled and chuckled, for it was a good joke on Wirrun. 'You camped in the wrong place,' he explained at last. 'That lake, that's right over their home. That rock's where they go in and out.'

All the People laughed, and Wirrun rolled his eyes and accepted the joke. When it was over he tried again, fingering the uneasiness inside himself. 'And now there's no one to keep 'em in order. Any chance they might get real bad?'

The old man puffed comfortably. 'They don't do no harm, you know,' he said. 'No one cutting their feet now, no one shivering. . . . Middle of summer, real hot, the women used to sing them out for a breeze. Good breeze then, nice and cool real quick. But they don't stay out long if it's hot.'

Wirrun nodded, and they talked about other things. The wind, which had died last night, was up tonight and singing in the ghost gums. They built a wind-break round their small fire, and the children curled up behind it and slept like puppies. Soon Wirrun said good night and went off to his own camp.

He wasn't really satisfied with the old man's account of the Ninya. Somewhere deep down, perhaps in his feet, he knew that a loved and beautiful country should not be left alone to battle against age and drought, heat and ice. It shouldn't be left to float upside down when the wind came. Maybe it wasn't. For it was very likely that the old man had told him only part of the tale.

'Not my business,' he reminded himself, lying in his sleeping-bag under the sharp bright stars. 'I told him any rate.'

The wind swooped over the ghost gums, and high over Wirrun it carried the Mimi tumbling in its waves.

All day the Mimi had eaten only seeds shaken from the grass and a few roots dug from under it. She had been sorrowful, thirsty, and distracted; it was too much to remember to be cautious too. So when a small lizard flickered from shade to shade she freed herself from the spinifex and pounced. Then she sat carelessly in a hollow of sand and ate the lizard. She was astonished when a gust of wind reached down and gathered her up.

She was tossed again from wind to wind, whirled high

and circled lower. She had to learn all over again to ride the wind-waves with limbs and body safely held in line. She had her wits back by sunset, just as one broad deep shadow stole across the whole of the land.

For a moment she saw it: the land with no horizon, set forth in red and grey and slate. Empty rivers meandering into broad dry lakes of salt; hills ground down with age or baring jagged, hacked-out teeth; wind-built sandhills fold within fold; all stretching on and on till it melted in purple. The heart of the land as only the wind could see it, set forth with fearful honesty and a truth too plain to be believed. Then the shadow came, and even the Mimi's possum eyes could not see into it from so high.

It was good that she had to ride the wind with so much care; it kept her mind busy, and her terrors stood further back. Yet they stood all around. She saw in the darkness the brooding presence of spirits who belonged here where she had no right. She saw that she was carried always farther and farther from home, and her mind ran in terror from the question of how she might ever get back. And there was that worse terror that she didn't understand and dared not think of: the horror of the ice. The other fears had a tiny speck of hope in them: the spirits of this country might not mind so helpless a stranger blowing by under the stars; some day kind winds might come and carry her home. But she must not think of the ice.

Daylight came and she was wrapped in mist. Through wispy gaps she saw, very far down, the striding feet of dust-devils. All that day she was rolled in the soft white nothing of cloud and felt that she could neither breathe nor see. At night she came out of the cloud and was bewildered – she was between stars! There were white stars above and constellations of yellow stars below.

In the morning she was amazed again: she was passing over green country, and it was all divided into neat angular shapes. There was the shine of water in rivers, there were cloudy green heads of forests. But here and there were dead patches, like a lichen growing over the land; and even these were neatly cut into sections with straight black lines. Along the lines a kind of beetle swarmed and scuttled, shining and many-coloured. It was very strange country. The Mimi had little time to stare at it; the winds grew wayward and troublesome again and she was whirled back and forth, high and low, as at the beginning. She was giddy and weary and hopeless, and could only fight to hold on to her arms and legs.

In the late afternoon a broad band of hills rose gently, stretching away up and down the land. The wind rolled upward in a climbing wave, and she saw that these hills were not gentle; they were cleft deep into cliffs and had shadowed gorges and steep narrow valleys. Over these the wind tumbled and rolled, there was no pattern to it. The Mimi lost all sense of control – and found herself eddied backwards and tumbling down. She had fallen out of the wind.

Like a very long twig she came planing down a steep face of rock and scrub. A rise of warmer air lifted her – she stretched out her hands to a boulder, caught at a ledge, and hung weak and giddy. Now she was afraid of strange rocks and what they might contain – but the wind might loop down at her again, and she knew only one thing to do. She breathed on the rock and it opened its dark heart to her.

The Mimi fell into it and breathed it closed.

For two nights and a day she lay in the thick stillness waiting for something terrible to happen. It did not. The rock held her safely; it was black and still, neither warm nor cold.

On the second day she moved her arms and legs about, learning to use them again. On the third day she ventured out. She found roots and water and caught a bush-rat, and ate and drank. Then she slipped back quickly into the rock.

She was infinitely alone – banished she didn't know where – and at night she wailed for the far, dear country

26

of home. But this one rock held the safety of home.

And only a little way to the south, Wirrun too was at home. He was sitting on the bed in his rented room with a newspaper spread over his knees. The yellow light of an electric bulb spilled over the print, and Wirrun read one small paragraph over and over. His dark face was heavy with astonishment.

It was strange enough for astonishment. The air in the room was warm and heavy, and this newspaper had already recorded the warmest spring for twenty years. Yet this small paragraph, tucked into the financial pages to fill up a space, told of a sudden frost in Queensland.

Three

For a young man of the People, a rented room in the Happy Folk's town was hardly home; but one of the things that Wirrun in his short life had never found was the place, the one spot in all the land, that was home. It may have been this that kept him thinking more than most young people of his years.

At any rate, he was back in the town he had left. He had travelled more comfortably than the Mimi, by plane, and had arrived a day or so earlier. He had pinned his used plane-ticket on the wall to celebrate, put away his camping gear, and settled down to save more money.

At the service station they had welcomed him back with all the proper jokes.

'Got used to living like a lord pretty quick, didn't he?'

'Collar-proud, eh? We'll soon knock that out of you.'

Wirrun had smiled his young white smile and hosed down floors and measured petrol and given change. And at night, because he was saving money for the next trip, he had gone home alone to cook his own dinner in his room, taking the newspaper to read. There he sat now, under the yellow bulb, staring at that small astonishing paragraph.

There was a small heading, PUZZLED INLANDER; and under it:

Mr George Jennings is a puzzled man. While the temperature soars and the summer promises to be the warmest for years, how did a small area of frost develop on his farm near Toowoomba on the Darling Downs? Mr Jennings claims to have discovered the phenomenon when bringing his cattle in for milking on Tuesday morning. After yarding the cattle he returned at once with a camera but found the frost had melted and was unfortunately unable to produce any evidence of his claim. 'It was in a little hollow between outcrops of rock,' Mr Jennings claimed. 'It's a bad spot for frost, but in fifty years I've never seen it this late.'

'Claims to have discovered . . . unable to produce any evidence.' It seemed to Wirrun that the newspaper did not believe the story. He was a student of newspapers. He thought that this one had had an empty space to fill, and had used an amusing story from a country newspaper. Perhaps that was the answer: the frost hadn't really happened. Yet Wirrun found it harder to believe that an Inlander would invent such a tale. A cabbage six feet round . . . a shark in the water-hole or an escaped lion in the scrub . . . a flying saucer landing in the swamp . . . it might tickle a dry Inlander's humour to fool the Happy Folk with tales like those. Frost in a warm October was a different matter, more serious.

He called up a picture of an Inlander face. It would have the settled look that came of never questioning anything it already knew. It was a cheerful face, but it could harden easily. It would harden a little at any mention of the Happy Folk, for the Inlander knew with hurt that the Happy Folk had abandoned him in favour of more impressionable peoples over the sea. But mostly the face was hardened by facing realities close at hand: realities of the land, the weather, and the bank. There was deep bitterness between the Inlanders and the People, but at least you knew their realities were real. On the question of frost on his own farm, this George Jennings had to be believed. Wirrun could only shrug and say what he had said once before.

'You'll get funny weather any time.'

He said it without thinking – but when he had said it the newspaper dropped to the floor. In his wanderings

Wirrun had been north just as far as the Darling Downs. Toowoomba, on the edge of the escarpment . . . it could be cold in winter . . . in a freak summer too, maybe . . . but in the warmest spring for twenty years? *You'll get funny weather any time*; and the great quiet country floating upside down, and ice on his water-bag. . . . He went to bed remembering his night under the ghost gums with the People. Already it was strange to remember.

There was no such quietness in town. The Happy Folk were in more than their usual frenzy, for Christmas was only weeks away and after Christmas there would be the summer sales. The streets were crowded, and there were big bright signs all over the town. GIVE HER A LITTLE HAPPINESS, they suggested, and offered it in a plastic bottle deliciously perfumed. BE HAPPY THE UNITED WAY – 10% ON YOUR SAVINGS, they offered with a gleam in their eyes. YOU TOO CAN AFFORD FUR, they promised while the pavements were melting in the heat. And every night Wirrun, at home with his newspaper, followed the doings of the Folk when they were not buying or selling.

They were a study, these Folk. They dragged themselves, exhausted by heat, through ordeals of running and batting for the happiness of being top. They drowned themselves in pools for the happiness of owning pools. They cheated each other for the happiness of being rich, told lies for the happiness of being important, fought bitterly for the happiness of being right. Young Folk, taught in childhood, took what they fancied from other Folk, used it for an hour or so, and threw it away. One man killed another for the happiness of fifty dollars.

Wirrun read and wondered. He knew his own stern People would not have tolerated so primitive and destructive a happiness. He read his paper with care every night. That was how, within three or four days, he found another small heading: UNSEASONABLE WEATHER IN NEW ENGLAND.

He read the brief story, and his fingers and toes began to prickle. A patch of frost had been seen at Tenterfield. The paragraph was very like the one from Toowoomba; but at Tenterfield, as well as frost, a thin glazing of ice had formed on the drinking troughs of fowls. The news-paper made no mention of the earlier frost. Could only Wirrun have noticed that there were two? Two patches of frost late in a warm spring, and not very far apart. . . .

He put the paper down and went to riffle through his collection of maps. He thought the two places could hardly be more than a hundred miles apart. They were both in the high country, where in some years there might be a frost close to Christmas. Wirrun went back to the paper and checked the weather report. As far as he could tell, 'warm to hot and sunny' seemed to cover both areas.

He sorted through his maps with restless hands, laying them out and putting them together again. His fingers and toes still prickled. *Funny weather*; too funny. And too often. And too close.

'Not my business,' he said uneasily. It made him feel no better – for that too he had said before, in the great quiet centre of the land.

At last he stood up and shook himself impatiently. 'Too much shut up by myself. I should've seen Ularra before this. He'll want to hear about the trip.'

Ularra was the friend who had come from the red country, and whose talk of it had sent Wirrun there. Wirrun tracked him to a milk-bar and was greeted with a joyful shout. Ularra's skin was even darker than Wirrun's. He was tall and loose, not yet having learnt to manage his length. In the same way he talked loudly and laughed a lot, not yet having learnt to manage his feel-ings.

There was a table in the corner of the milk-bar. They sat there with glasses and straws and talked for a long time. Wirrun told about his trip, and Ularra's eyes shone. He laughed so loudly that Wirrun was sorry for

31

his homesickness. But his voice dropped when he started to talk, drawing maps on the table, enlarging the trip and making it come to life again. Wirrun's eyes shone too.

'You know Mount Conner?' asked Wirrun, for the west is very wide. Ularra said of course he knew it, been there often, all down those salt lakes to Conner. Yet Wirrun knew that it was not really Ularra's country, and it turned out that he hadn't heard of the Ninya. So Wirran told of his camp by the lake and his talk to the old man in Alice.

Ularra listened, nodded, but said nothing. It wasn't his business any more than it was Wirrun's.

'Funny thing, though,' said Wirrun; and he told about the newspaper reports of frost in Toowoomba and Tenterfield.

Ularra laughed loudly. 'Cheeky devils!' he said. 'No harm though. A bit of frost won't hurt.' With his eyes on Wirrun's face he shook his head. 'That's a long way, man, from Conner to Toowoomba. Never knew anyone make that trip, not straight across. What would it take walking? Couple of months?'

'Walking straight across you wouldn't make it,' said Wirrun, nodding. They talked about other things till the milk-bar had emptied and they had to go.

They stood on the pavement, Ularra's long arm thrown loosely over Wirrun's shoulder; the red country in the west had made them brothers, at least for tonight. Wirrun's uneasiness had almost gone; but when he felt a flick of its tail he spoke at once. He didn't care if Ularra grinned.

'You know some of them out there,' he said. 'Got a name and address for any of the Mount Conner men?'

Ularra didn't grin. 'I might,' he said. 'There's a bloke in Alice'd know any rate. Want me to see?'

'You do,' said Wirrun. 'I might need to write.' He went home feeling that he had done what was needed, and slept soundly.

And the next evening he found another small strange paragraph in the newspaper: FREAK FROST AT EMMAVILLE.

Wirrun knew about Emmaville and its tin mines: south of Tenterfield, on the western side of the plateau. The two places were so close that the paper had treated both frosts as one, but Wirran noticed there had been a day between them. Only one day and a few miles between two frosts? What were they up to now?

What were who up to? He was suddenly angry, either with himself or with the frosts. Ularra was right: a little frost, a bit of thin ice, what harm could it do in warm weather? The women of Mount Conner would have called it up for a breeze.

But the women were not there now to call up the Ninya. And the men were not there to sing them back. And no one else would know the right songs.

And still, what harm could they do?

Wirrun never threw away his old papers too soon. He found the earlier reports of frost, cut out all three, pasted them together on a sheet from his writing-pad, and put that away with his maps. He did all this angrily, as though someone else had nagged him into doing it; and he found a point that he seized on with an angry 'Ha!'

None of the stories said anything about the country floating upside down in the air. Not one word about any mirage. That was it, then. The Ninya were safe at home and they were having funny weather up north. He went to bed in triumph.

But just as he was falling asleep a voice, maybe his own, spoke in his mind: 'They shoulda got up earlier and they'd have seen it floating.'

The next day's paper gave him no trouble. It was full of the Happy Folk's frenzy, and advice about Christmas spending. At the service station, in the boss's little office, a large plastic Santa Claus and a tinsel tree were propped behind the door, ready to be used for decorations at the first permissible moment. Wirrun turned his mind to Christmas, and friends to whom he might send a card or a gift. It was four days before the paper bothered him again, and this time the paragraph was easily seen. It was nearer the front of the paper and had a bigger heading than the others: SUMMER FREEZE ON TABLELANDS.

The hair on the nape of Wirrun's neck crawled a little as he read.

Mystery surrounds the reported appearance during the week of freak frosts at Toowoomba on the Darling Downs in Queensland and at Emmaville and Tenterfield on the Northern Tablelands of New South Wales. Yesterday a fresh report came from Glen Innes, also on the Tablelands. This year's unusually high temperatures have prevailed throughout the area and the Weather Bureau is unable to offer an explanation. 'These are unconfirmed reports,' said one of its officers. 'We have to consider the extreme unlikelihood of frost in prevailing conditions. You could say that these reports have much in common with reports of flying saucers.' But from his farm near Glen Innes Mr Warren Jones claims . . . .

Wirrun read on. Frost on a rocky hillside, thin ice on a dam. He cut out this story to add to the others on his sheet of paper and stayed for a moment staring at his maps.

It was coming south, then; coming down a route along the high rocky country of the Tablelands. What deep caverns might run through those rocks, and for how many miles? If you were the Ninya you could find them.

He took out some of the maps, and an atlas he had kept from school. He thought there was high rock-based country running all the way from Mount Conner, first north and then east into Queensland, and curving round to the Downs near the coast. But no one had talked about frost along all those thousands of miles; and no mirage, no floating country. The Weather

Bureau was right. It was just the same as flying saucers, and he was as bad as anyone.

But staring at the map he knew he was making excuses, shutting his eyes and refusing to see, like the Happy Folk. Not many people had seen those miles, but everyone knew about them. The Simpson desert, the channel country . . . at night it would be all black, with maybe one dot of light here and maybe another a hundred miles away. No wonder if nobody happened to see a small patch of frost, gone in an hour. And suppose anyone did? He would talk about it by radio to his Inlander neighbours. He wouldn't write to the papers – and if he did they wouldn't print it. It was too far away from the cities of the Happy Folk; they couldn't possibly understand that it mattered. Only an Inlander, any Inlander, would know that.

He put his maps back with the newspaper story and smiled grimly at the thought of four tight-lipped Inlanders reading it. 'Flying saucers,' they would mutter in disgust. 'Typical, isn't it?' Wirrun suddenly thought that if he wanted a white man's help in a matter like this the man had better be an Inlander.

Only he didn't want help. He still didn't see what harm a little frost could do, and it wasn't his business. The most he could do was to send some word to Mount Conner; and what word could he send?

He lay in bed and wondered how many frosts there had been, and where; how far apart, how many days between. How far south would they come, and when? Where were they heading?

He woke up saying, 'But I don't know the songs.'

It didn't make any difference. He knew he would have to go. Maybe he didn't know what harm there was in a little frost – but he knew there was harm. Maybe he didn't know the songs, but he was the one easterner who knew about the Ninya. Maybe he was wasting his time, but how did he know till he started? He had breakfast and set to work.

He took his saved-up money from the place behind the dresser. Only forty dollars yet: it would have to do. He cleaned out the shabby refrigerator and switched off its noisy motor, packed a few supplies with his oldest shirts and shorts, and rolled up his gear ready for travel. Then he locked his room, put the key over the door, and went to the service station to speak to the boss.

He knew this would be bad. The Happy Folk might grumble about their work as much as they chose, but they knew it made their little world stick together. You held a job and pulled your weight or you poled on other people. Jobs were for sticking to, and Wirrun was full of guilt as he spoke to the boss.

The boss was amazed and stern. 'Not good enough. You're only just back, and there's young David off next week. You can't keep a job and go walkabout whenever you feel like it.'

'That's right,' muttered Wirrun. 'It's bad, that. Only I gotta go. Business.' He hoped for much from that magic word, but the boss only snorted.

'Too much money, that's what it is. I've got a business to run, too. You can get into your overalls and get yourself started or you needn't come back at all.'

'Sorry, boss,' said Wirrun; and he was sorry, and acutely embarrassed as well. 'It's a good job here. But I gotta go.'

He took the small final pay that the boss snatched out of the cash register and walked away from his job. It was worrying, but when he got back would be the time to worry. Now he had to find Ularra.

Ularra worked in a factory and would not be out till midday lunch. Wirrun bought more supplies while he waited. He was there when Ularra came slouching out of the factory, straightening up with a grin when he saw Wirrun.

Wirrun explained as quickly and as much as he could. Ularra listened thoughtfully and nodded. 'But what's the harm?' he asked, a little puzzled.

36

'I don't *know* what harm. Somebody's got to keep an eye, haven't they? You can see that. Did you find that address?'

Ularra had found the address of the bloke in Alice and thought he could get word quick to the men of Mount Conner if Wirrun found the word to send. He promised to wait for a message from Wirrun, and to send it on fast if the men were wanted. They said goodbye solemnly.

Wirrun set off for the railway station. His only plan was to take a train as far up the Tablelands as his money would allow, and then to start walking. He would watch the newspapers for news of the frosts, and sooner or later he thought he would see one for himself. He would try to discover and follow the route of the frosts. What then, he didn't know. But when he reached the station the afternoon papers were out and he bought one at once. The story was on page two, with a bigger headline than before.

FREAK FREEZE COMES SOUTH?

The story altered his plans while he read it. It came from the high country near Dorrigo . . . Dorrigo! That was east as well as south! And so much nearer! It would have been a mistake to go up the Tablelands, or to go too far in any direction; he could have overshot his mark. . . . Some ice and a heavy frost, 'more like snow', the farmer had said. And he had added a phrase that Wirrun read sharp-eyed: 'There was a funny sort of shine to it.'

A funny sort of shine: like the cellophane shimmer of the country when it floated upside down?

He dropped the paper into a bin and stood thinking for a moment. The frost had turned to the coast, maybe towards his own country. He thought of places where high and rocky hills came near the sea. Port Macquarie might be too far up . . . somewhere near the Hunter, maybe . . . a quiet place in the bush where he could strike north or west or south . . . with a post office handy, for his message to Ularra. He went to buy his ticket.

37

Soon the train, swaying and beating its song-sticks in the unchanging rhythm of trains, was carrying him on the short journey north. In a little while he would leave it and walk inland, a young man of the People in search of a mountain.

Four

And much farther north a mountain groaned. It was full of a heaviness and chill it had long forgotten. Deep inside it a cold wind howled, freezing the bones of the mountain as it went. There was a stream, never seen or heard, though its sound had silvered the dark for an age of time; it grew silent now, and fretted into ice. There was a lake, cool and liquid in the dark for a thousand years; now it had hardened into ice in a frosty twilight. The wind howled on ahead, and the Ninya walked in the mountain.

They glittered with the purity of frost; crystals like diamonds dropped from their beards; and they snarled at each other for company.

'A wasted search, led by the earless.'

'Truly I am a fool, to lead those who fret like the children of the People. Lead yourselves, then – into the fire.'

'And where is that? We travel as blind as ants in a crack. Who knows where the Eldest Nargun lives?'

'I know, and I lead you there. The Eldest lives by the sea, and south, in its country.'

There was snapping laughter and a chorus of creaks.

'By the sea. And south. And in its country. Now we know all.'

'The sea is long, oh Leader of the Ninya. The south is wide. The countries are forgotten.'

'To walk on and on is not to search. I see a rock: is

that the Nargun? I see a cave: is the Eldest in there? Tell us, Clever One.'

'Look for yourselves – what holds you back? I, who lead you, I think and need not look.'

'Tell us what you think then, Great One.'

'Must I tell you again, like children? If the Eldest were here, would it not have seen the first blooming of frost? And would it hide in a cave and freeze? I tell you it would stand here now, in our path, and these cold rocks would glow red.'

They muttered sullenly.

'Listen again, you who cannot think. If the Nargun were in any country we have passed, if it were anywhere within knowing, it would stand here now and your white blood would trickle in the stream. So do not look in caves like hunters of bats but look at the ice. Feel the air, and the flowing of the wind. If one drop of water gathers on a spear of ice – if the wind only falters for a moment – it is time for work.'

There were creaking whispers and sharp glances all around. The leader nodded.

'Come, then. South by the coast. We hunt no bat in a cave but the Nargun. To ring it with frost and work a sudden wonder of ice. To call down snow and crack the old bones of the Eldest. To see the land white again in the sun, and the glory of sun on a glacier. No changeless frost in a twilit cave but the delicate melting and building again, with the air breathing white.'

All the Ninya broke into chanting, and the wind howled with them, and the leader felt it with care. And far to the south, off the shore of its own country, the Eldest Nargun felt the sea.

The sea flowed over and round it, tugging. The Nargun spread itself a little and gripped at rock. All its senses were sharply alert, fixed on another movement. Somewhere in the water there was a quickness of life, and the Nargun was hungry.

Only five years had passed since its last meal; once it

would have been twenty or fifty. But the old thing hungered oftener now, and the sea could not satisfy it. Life in the sea was slyer, colder, quicker, than life on the land; or it was sly and cold and slow. Nothing moved the ancient monster to love any more; only to yearning. So it hungered often, and seized what the sea brought near.

Something flicked and nibbled at the weeds on its side. The Nargun crouched and waited, with the slow enduring patience of stone. The fish nibbled again – flicked away from a streak of foam – nuzzled back. The Nargun crouched, balancing its weight against the pull of the tide as the sea had taught it.

A wave pushed in and pulled out, and the weed swayed with it. The Nargun moved too: a secret movement, lighter than a leaf. Now it was poised. The fish hovered and stayed.

A ripple flashed in the sun: with that same speed and light the Nargun moved. There was shock and stillness in the water, and a mist of blood and white flesh. Nothing else was left. Nothing flicked and nibbled at the Nargun's side.

With the next wave the old monster rocked back and cried, '*Nga-a!*' It spread its weight again and gripped the rock and rested. A glint of green-gold light wavered over it, and a faint warmth from the sun.

The ancient stone lay still and dreamed of fire.

2

On the Mountain

One

Wirrun found a dusty road and walked inland, hoping he had chosen well. Was he too far up the coast or too far down? Was he right in choosing the coast at all, or in choosing a lonely height behind the coast? Maybe the frost would leave the heights and be seen in one of the towns. Maybe it could travel in a flash and appear tomorrow a hundred miles to the south. Maybe it would pause and stay where it was for a month or a year. He could find no answers to these questions, but as he walked he remembered that there were no answers. He remembered what he was: a young man alone, looking for a mountain.

He found a company of them, standing above a village on a ridge. Their volcanic tops were roughly draped in scrub and their lower slopes hung with forest. For a moment he wavered, uncertain which to choose; but he could have sat and thought for an hour, inventing some reason for a choice. Instead he started to climb.

The slope steepened rapidly. He was stepping on boulders buried in grass and creeper, winding his way up between grey box and stringybark. The upper heights, when he reached them, seemed all rock; but the scrub had found pockets of leaf-mould and clay. He came upon an overhanging ledge of rock. From its nearest end he could look down at the village. He went along its length, further round the side of the mountain, and stowed his gear under the ledge and built his fireplace. It would be hidden from the village.

The sun was low already. He had only time to explore a little around his camp, but he had to find water. He looked for a gully, and found one that at any other time he would have thought too far – he would have had to move his camp nearer. But he liked the camp he had found, and he expected to be walking every day around this mountain; he could always fill a water-bag on the way.

The gully was steep and rockbound with a trickle of water slipping through stones in its bed. A little scrub timber grew there, tallow-wood and sycamore, with tree-ferns and small ferns and moss. It was steep and narrow, shutting out the sun; but it was easy enough to climb into if you went to the right place. He took some water back to his camp and lit his fire.

He slept soundly that night, tired after walking, till the early sun struck under the ledge at his face. It was too late by then to look for frost. He spent his first day walking over and round the mountain, finding out about it and working out a route. Always, like a man of the People, he moved under cover of shadow and rock and scrub. If the Inlanders saw him they would narrow their eyes and watch; then they would judge in terms of their own hard realities.

At first he thought like a bushman, noting the chain of ridges that tied the peaks together, examining faces of slippery rock and slopes of falling stone. He found his way into deep and shady places all around the mountain, climbed over ledges and into the heads of gullies. After a time it seemed that he had stopped thinking at all; or perhaps he was thinking with his feet.

In the afternoon he went down to the village, circling from tree to tree and coming in from the opposite direction. He bought a paper and sat under a tree to read it. There were no more reports of frost, but the Happy Folk were having fun at the expense of the In-landers. ATTACK FROM OUTER SPACE? . . . SANTA ESTABLISHING POLAR OUTPOSTS . . . and so on.

The merrymakers were supported by the opinion of a learned man. Wirrun left the paper behind in a bin and returned by his roundabout route to the mountain.

On the second day he began a round of the mountain in the colourless shadowless dawn. It was cold, but not too cold for an early November morning. He went into all the hidden places, feeling and seeing. He found no frost, but as the sun rose he found the mountain: rock and cone-tree, moss in its damp places, the violet poised, the clematis twining and coiling.

I am Land, the First Thing. Serve me, said the mountain.

'That's what I came for,' said Wirrun. He saw gold of wattle and silver under grevillia leaves, shadow and wind and the heat-stroke of sun on rock. He heard spiders scuttle and owls sleep, felt the lizard twitch under the bark and the snake slither under the stone.

He walked the mountain till late afternoon and lay among ferns to rest. He saw the reflected sunset turn the eastern haze to fire; and at night he sat close to his own small fire and listened to the mountain.

Frost grows by night and melts by day, said the mountain.

'Tomorrow,' said Wirrun, 'I'll sleep first and go about in the night.'

Peering around the ledge, the Mimi heard him. She had seen him much earlier and remembered him sleeping by the saltpan in the west. It made her all the more anxious and she tracked him through the day with great caution, always sliding near rock. She thought Wirrun had the look of a man who might soon see earth-spirits, even a Mimi.

The peace that the Mimi had found in her rock had not lasted long. She had slipped out of it and travelled along the ridges trying rock after rock. She could not be at peace for long in any of them. She was forced to spend most of her time on the outside, nervously sheltering from sudden breaths of wind, ready at a rustle to slip inside; and then as soon as she could she must slip out again.

For when the safe black silence of rock folded close, the Mimi thought there were noises in it: noises too faint and far for even her quivering ears to catch. The deep-down plinking of a hidden stream she knew; and the footstep of a spider; and the falling of dust. She could be at ease with those. But when they were still – what was that tremble of rock, as though somewhere in the mountains something creaked? What was that rustle, dry and cold and faint, *rrsh*, like a mouse-claw in sand? And why did the air stir and whisper a word? Caverns should not breathe. The Mimi lay stiff, straining her ears past their limit. If she did sleep she dreamed of wind, and the rustle of frost, and the creak of ice.

She began to look for some home outside the rock, a hollow log or a hole in a tree. She saw Wirrun and followed him till he slept, then went on with her search. It was hard both to search and to gather food when she dared not go two paces from rock for fear of the wind.

In the morning Wirrun made his early round of the mountain and found only the dawn cold and no sense of ambush. In the afternoon he made his silent visit to the village, then ate and slept. He slept into the night, till the white stars of the Cross had swung far over and the yellow lights of the village had blinked out. He fed his fire and banked it deep in ashes, then started his night round.

The night is not quiet. It pulsed with the singing of crickets, and some tiny insect rang a bell as clear as a bell-bird's, over and over. Lower down the mountain a koala cried. Possums swore and squabbled, or breathed heavily to themselves like asthmatic old men. A wallaby thumped, a bushrat scuttled, a moth beat the air. All the soft scurry of the night was woven into a fabric of sound that hung across the mountain like a curtain; but Wirrun listened to the mountain.

The ice is coming, said the mountain.

'I can't find it,' said Wirrun. He slid from bush to thicket, resting his hands on rock and feeling shadows.

He could still find no sense of ambush or any black cold, but he felt the awareness of the night. It was breathing and waiting.

There was something watching in the night: something larger and quieter than cricket or wallaby. Did the darkness thin and thicken, swirling in clouds? What followed him?

Look ahead, said the mountain, *for the ice is coming*.

And Wirrun went on, fixing his mind on the route that he had to find again by night; but it wasn't the ice he felt. Some tingling in his hands and feet, and at the centre of his forehead, told him that he was followed.

He skirted rock-faces and slopes of stone, feeling his way. He found the entrance to the gully and climbed in and out. And the darkness thickened behind him and thinned when he looked back. At last he drew near his camp-fire again, and stopped to lay more wood on the coals and draw them together. It was warm and safe by the fire; he longed to stay there, but the mountain called. He must go round again.

He started, and the darkness thickened ahead, and he forced himself to walk into it. Step by step, step by step, while his hands and feet and the centre of his forehead tingled. He felt a chill and thought it must be the ice, but it was a sound that did not belong to the scurry of night noises: a clear trilling that came from where the dark was thickest. Wirrun turned that way and stood still. The dark came to him.

It looked like a man of the People, but its eyes were red and it grinned. It carried a great pointed nulla-nulla, too heavy for a man. It held out the nulla-nulla to Wirrun.

'We fight,' it said. 'You strike first.' And it bent its head for a blow.

He knew he must not touch the nulla-nulla. He knew he must run, but he stood shocked and shaking. The shape of dark seemed to gather and thicken over him.

He tore himself free of it and turned and ran for the camp-fire. He could feel the dark shape running and

49

grinning behind, and hear it trilling. He turned his head desperately and shouted: 'The ice is coming!' The thing faltered, and Wirrun bounded to the fire.

He dropped down by it and reached for wood to pile on and make a blaze. He had to keep looking into the dark but nothing came out of it. Then the flames leapt up, and the dark stepped back and stood around the fire a little way off. When the flames sank down it breathed forward, and when they rose it shrank back. Wirrun fed the fire till the dark grew watery because morning was near. Then he banked the fire down and crept into his sleeping-bag. He could see all the shapes near by, and they were trees.

'Bones gone squashy,' he told himself weakly. 'That's a nice thing. You come looking for – things – and when you meet 'em you run like a rabbit.' But he hadn't thought of meeting them. He wondered what had happened to men of the People who had met this shape of dark, who had taken the offered club and given the blow. He shuddered.

These too I have bred, said the mountain.

'Old sinner,' muttered Wirrun. He didn't like what the mountain said but it had to be thought about. He lay while the sun rose and the land grew warm, wondering how many dark earth-creatures the mountain had bred in all the ages of its cooling and weathering. By the time he crawled out to cook some breakfast he knew that however many there were, and however terrible, they had to be accepted. You couldn't choose to have the rocks and ferns and moss and the green shadows but reject the cliffs and the snake. He didn't like it, but the ice was coming. He would walk the mountain again at night if he could, and run if he had to run.

'Any rate,' he remembered, 'that old one didn't like the ice either.' And he wondered what it was that the old thing disliked. That the Ninya were coming out of the west into its own country? Or the ice itself?

He went early to the village for his paper and found

he was too early. He had to wait till a truck had brought the papers in from an early train. Sitting under a tree and waiting he thought that he didn't really need the paper now. The ice was coming: the mountain, or the land itself, had told him that through his fingers and feet and the centre of his forehead. It was settled and known. The Ninya were bringing the ice, bringing it here, and it was not a little thing that melted in an hour. It was a power of ice advancing. He wondered if he should tell Ularra to send for the Mount Conner men at once; but he still didn't know when the ice would come, or where or how long it might halt on the way.

A cloud of dust came along the road with a truck mixed up in it. Wirrun watched it roll up to the shop and waited while bundles and cases from the train were carted inside. Then he went and bought his paper.

More frost had been found, yesterday morning, about sixty miles nearer and still close to the coast. This time the Inlander who found it had left his stock and called out his wife and a neighbour. The neighbour had brought a camera, so the combined witnesses could not easily be dismissed. The Happy Folk were irritated by this, and would soon be looking for someone to blame. Wirrun smiled a little as he cut out the article and dropped the paper into a bin. The Happy Folk seemed to have grown smaller since he left them; from the mountain they looked like children.

The night and the morning had tired him. He went back to the mountain and slept through the rest of the day. The Mimi peeped at him from her tree before she ventured out for food. He was sound asleep.

He woke to stars and the billowing dark and the fabric of noises curtaining the night. He looked down at the village lights and up at the shapes of mountains against the stars, and he felt the land reach for him and take him. His fear of the night tingled like an old nettle-sting; but he ate, banked his fire, and set out to walk the mountain.

It was a long walking, while the darkness gathered and thinned and Wirrun's skin crawled. He listened and felt, and crawled into all the deepest places to test the shadows, and found no sudden bite of cold.

The wind comes, said the mountain.

Wirrun stood still and listened, but the night was calm without any stirring of leaves. There was no wind; yet he felt in his feet the faraway howling of a gale. He went on troubled.

He was on the steeper face of the mountain and far from his fire when the dark gathered and pursued him. It came at him in the shape of a woman with a long horn pointing up from each shoulder. It shook its shoulders, grinned wickedly, and bent over to run at him with lowered horns.

Wirrun ran, but he knew with terror that he could not run far on this slope without falling. He dived through a thicket, hoping that the long horns would tangle in branches, but the woman-shape flowed through it like water, grinning after him.

'The ice is coming!' shrieked Wirrun. 'Why don't you run at that?'

The shape faltered and shook its horns, and he slid away trembling to hide in a cleft of rock. But he went on, and made two rounds of the mountain, finding nothing.

He went wearily back to his fire in the pearl-shell dawn and ate and slept. He woke in the evening, tight with tension, wishing for the first time that he could go away and leave the mountain to itself. Yet when he tried to think of going it seemed there was nowhere to go and nothing to do. All the land was closed to him except this one perch on the mountain.

He made himself a meal and sat over it listlessly, not wanting to move and yet itching and twitching with nerves. For hours after the meal was finished he sat by the fire twisting a straw of grass round and round one finger. The night wore on and the mountain called, but like a sulky child he refused to hear.

The mountain groaned.

Wirrun gave in with a bad grace, dragged his fire together, and went like a sulky child, muttering.

'Shoulda brought a firestick if I had the sense of a rabbit. What's the good of a man that can't even carry a firestick? Cold – cripes!'

The Mimi watched him in terror. She had ventured into the rock an hour ago and had tumbled out quivering. She had been quivering ever since.

As Wirrun walked his mind awoke from sulkiness but the brooding anxiety grew worse. For one thing, as he grew more alert he discovered the silence. No fabric of small noises hung over the mountain tonight. The silence was deep and shocking. It frightened him. For another thing, he found that he was not in fact cold yet still he longed for a firestick. He wondered what terror worse than the horned woman waited for him in this night.

I freeze, said the mountain.

Wirrun searched and searched, but he could not find the cold.

He went into all the deep and shadowed places, and the clefts of damp rock, feeling and testing. He lingered in the gully where the water trickled; his hands and feet and the centre of his forehead tingled, but he could find nothing. He climbed out again, muttering.

He stood like a shadow in a patch of scrub and listened to the silence. He wanted badly to go back to his fire. When the silence cracked into sound he shuddered and shrank back. The sound came closer, *crack . . . crack*, a measured beat like the thump of a wallaby but loud and sharp; and with it came a strange cry, '*Pirralog! Pirralog!*'

He knew it was an earth-creature and shivered. This must be it, the worst thing, the thing he had felt and dreaded. Yet he couldn't run. He saw it gather out of the darkness, bounding like a kangaroo, but in shape and size more like a horse. It had a sort of mane on its neck and its tail was like a long sharp knife. It saw him: its neck reached for him, its fierce eyes cut the dark, and it

53

bounded again. And still his fear weighted Wirrun's feet.

Then – the earth-thing stopped. It shifted restlessly; its head turned from side to side; it pawed at the ground. It had lost interest in Wirrun. It gave its cry once or twice, '*Pirralog! Pirralog!*' Then it turned and bounded off, and the sharp cracking faded.

That was indeed the worst. Wirrun knew it would have been better if the old thing had chased him. But the night lay heavy on it, as it did on Wirrun, and to-night it would not chase a man. He went on his way, pricking and tingling.

He came near his camp-fire again, and stopped to feed it and draw the coals together. The stars were wheeling towards morning. And suddenly Wirrun could not leave the fire – not yet – He crouched beside it watching the red pulse of the coals, and the fresh wood smoulder and catch. He felt the mountain groan and said sullenly, 'Not yet.'

He left the fire when the stars had thinned and trees and rocks were coming out of the dark. He went straight to the gully. It faced east, and the light was stronger there.

The ice lay in it. Its dark rocks glistened silver-grey with frost, and the ferns were silver-green. The trickling water lay in little pools of ice and in ridges of ice between the stones. Wirrun climbed carefully down to the slippery bed and scraped at the frost with his foot. The sun rose, and struck straight up the gully.

And it rose and floated above him, shimmering. Tree and rock and fern reached downward, groping for their proper place. Wirrun shut his eyes for a moment and then began to climb out, for he didn't know the right songs to put it back in place.

Two

Wirrun went back to his fire, and his mind was clouded with weariness and defeat. The Ninya had come and gone, and he knew no more than before. He had seen the ice, the great and terrible ice, and it was a little thing. And still it was terrible, and still he did not know why. He was only Wirrun, alone and not much more than a boy; he had done all that he could and it was useless.

'Not all,' he said bitterly as he crawled into his sleeping-bag. 'I shoulda gone sooner.'

He fell asleep like a worn-out child. He woke in terror, hurling through space with the wind screeching in his ears. He tried to shout but his throat had closed up as if he were choking. Something gripped him: a dark body painted with white markings. When he struggled it held him strongly as though he were a child and carried him on into the wind. There was nothing in the world but the wind and the dark, painted body – until Wirrun looked down, and tried again to give a choked cry. They were flying at eagle height above the trees.

Wirrun stopped struggling and tried instead to cling to the arms that held him. He was helpless in this dizzy rushing of air.

'Don't be afraid,' said a deep voice just over his head. 'I am Ko-in.'

When he managed to look up he could see a strong, stern face, a face of the People. He knew that one of the earth-creatures had caught him at last, and he lay weakly waiting for whatever might happen.

55

A great thickness of trees was coming at him from below. He was falling like a stone, he and the creature together. . . . Treetops grabbed at them, but they slipped between. The ground rushed at them, and while Wirrun waited for the crash they came safely and gently to earth. There was a fire deep under trees and Wirrun was laid beside it, choking and gasping.

He tried again to speak, and again he could not. His throat was closed, though he could breathe well enough. The earth-creature stood beside him, tall and dark, its body painted in a pattern of white pipeclay. It moved away – he should run, but he was too weak to stand. The creature came back, crouched beside him like a man, and laid some leaf on his lips.

'I am Ko-in,' it said again in its deep, grave voice. 'This is my fire. Speak with me.'

Wirrun found that he could speak now, but there were not yet any words to say. Slowly he sat up. He began to believe that this creature meant him no harm. It had none of the fierce and dreadful look of the night-things, and its eyes were like those of the oldest of the People. He found that he wanted to speak, but all that came was his one urgent message.

'The ice is coming.'

'The ice has come,' said Ko-in. 'It has taken its path further on. Why do you hunt the ice?'

Wirrun tried to remember why. 'The land told me,' he said.

'Ah,' said Ko-in as if all were explained. But all was not explained, and Wirrun struggled to tell more.

'You think it's just a bit of frost. It looks small. But it's big and terrible.'

'It has been a big and terrible ice in its time,' said Ko-in. But he spoke as if for conversation's sake.

'It comes from another country in the west. The Ninya brought it. And the People have gone, the ones that should have sung the Ninya back.'

'There must be the People,' Ko-in agreed politely. It

56

angered Wirrun. He hadn't walked the mountain at night and done all that he could to have his urgent message received politely.

'Now it's gone further on, out of your country,' he said bitterly, 'so you don't care. Well, there's others of a night, I've seen 'em. They don't look as good as you, and maybe they can't fly, but any rate they care.'

Ko-in's grave brown eyes lit with a spark. 'You've seen them,' he agreed, 'and they care. Ko-yo-rowen, and Yaho with her horns, and Puttikan who bounds; the old ones of the night. They dislike the ice; and they dislike the Ninya who leave their own country and come into ours. They are earth-things. But I am hero. My care is a different kind. I care for the land when the ice grips it and when the fire scorches it. How do you care?'

Wirrun had never known, but in his fury he discovered now. He looked around him for words. The hills – the sky – the sea – anyone could care for those.

He said, 'There's a dung-beetle by that log. I care for that. And there's a rotten toadstool with a worm in it: I care for both of 'em. I care for that bit of fern, and the little white men by the sea, and the horse-thing in the night. I care for the ice and the fire.'

Ko-in bent his head. 'You are of the People,' he said. 'We have talked very much, very long; we have talked so long that we have said everything. You have said everything, for you have said that the land told you. And I too have said everything, for I have said that there must be the People. Now the talking is over and the doing begins. Put away your anger, for in this country and at this time you must not be angry with Ko-in.'

Wirrun stared at the ground. He was now too embarrassed for anger. He felt as people feel whenever they speak in anger: that he had said too little and too much and had failed to speak at all.

'I give you help in your hunting,' said Ko-in. 'Go to the place where the ice came. There is a cave in that gully, a small cave, a large hole in the rock. A man who

was dying left in it a power of the People. Find it and
keep it with you. Now sleep.'

At once Wirrun slept.

He woke by his own fire in the shade of the mountain,
and knew by the shade that it was past noon. He felt
rested and strong, not despairing, not even in need of a
meal. He started at once for the village to send out his
call for the men of Mount Conner.

As he went he thought with wonder of Ko-in, who was
hero. Soon he would think about Ko-in's help and try to
find it; but first he must do what was right. For this was
a business of the People, and Ko-in himself had said
that there must be the People. His own were not the
right People for the Ninya, and their power was not the
right power. Even if Wirrun found it after its long years
of mouldering in a cave; even if he knew it when he
found it; even if he dared to touch it! For among his
People Wirrun had never been made a proper man.

He did not buy a paper in the village, for he knew
where the last frost had been. He sent his telegram to
Ularra: 'MEN WANTED SEND QUICK.' That was
enough. The post office would say where the message
came from, and Ularra would watch the papers for
later news. He hoped very much that the men would
come quickly. He thought they would come, for it was
their business; but it was a long way to come and it
might be hard for them. They might not have learnt the
trick of saving money and buying speed. Wirrun bought
a few things in the village and went back to the mountain.

Tonight there was no need to walk the mountain.
First, while it was still light, he would look for Ko-in's
help. Then he would think again about his own plans
and what he should do now that the ice had gone past.

He stowed his goods under the ledge and went on to
the gully, pausing on the lip to remember it as he had
seen it last. Now it lay cool and shadowed; evening had
come into it already. The water slid and whispered

through its stones but the ferns were black with frost. Wirrun climbed into it, holding by a creeper here and brushing past a tree-fern there, by the route he had learnt to follow even at night. He went straight to the steep wall of rock at its head for that was where the small cave, the large hole, would be. But how would he know the power?

He climbed as high as a man might who was dying and needed to hide a power. Then he worked his way across the rock, reaching into hollows and exploring with his fingers. He might be looking for wood, carved or painted or fingered smooth – and rotted away long ago in its damp cave. He might be looking for stone, and how would he know this one stone from all the rest? He shut his eyes and let his mind flow into his groping fingers. . . .

When he touched the power he knew it at once. It was round, both soft and hard, and enclosed in coarse net. He drew it out.

It was dark with age and damp, and with dust that the damp had darkened. The outer bag was netted from a strong twine of bark fibre. The round ball inside, both soft and hard, was the size of a cricket ball: a closely wound ball of soft cord made from what he guessed was possum fur. Wirrun slung the net bag from his belt. As he did so he realized that that was what the bag was meant for; but the belt too would most likely have been of soft cord.

He climbed down from the rocks and out of the gully. The evening was spreading. He walked back to his camp with one hand closed over the power on his belt. It felt powerful; and old; but he didn't know what he should do with it. He didn't even know if he should take it out of its bag or unwind the soft cord. He left it hanging on his belt, for that much at least he knew was meant, and sat by his fire to eat and think.

He had done all that he knew: seen the ice and felt its power; sent for the men; found Ko-in's help. Tomorrow,

59

he thought, he would have to leave this mountain and try to track the ice on its way south. That was all he could think of. At least he could mark its way for the men of Mount Conner. But he wished he knew where it was headed, and what its terror was. As for the People's power that hung at his belt, he didn't think it would really help very much. It was a power of this country which he must now leave. And Wirrun didn't even know what sort of power it was.

He put more wood on the fire and dragged the coals together. Then he took the power from his belt and left the net bag hanging in place. He sat by the fire with the power folded in his hands: he could feel in its roundness the swing of the hills, the cup of the valley, the arch of the sky, and the circling of the sea. He felt tall, tall as a tree.

The wood caught into red and yellow flame, and the dark stepped back. Wirrun looked out at it across his firelit space; and there at the edge of the breathing dark stood Ko-in with a firestick in his hand. The firelight caught him and lost him again as the dark breathed out and in.

'Come and talk,' said Ko-in, 'Clever One.'

'That's not me,' said Wirrun a little sternly. 'I'm not even a proper man.' But he got up from the fire to go, with the power in his hands. Ko-in watched him with the People's eyes, grave and gentle.

'And where are the proper men?' he asked. 'I have looked for them a long time. Are they here hunting the ice? I see only a boy who hears what the land tells; and who else is there now to speak and tell? I put the power of the People into the boy's hands.'

Wirrun halted in shock. 'But I can't,' he said.

'The power is in your hands and the land has told you. Will you refuse the land?'

'I've tried that,' said Wirrun. 'It didn't work.'

The firelight wavered, the dark breathed in and out, and Ko-in said again, 'Come and talk, Clever One.'

Wirrun saw that behind him the dark gathered into other shapes. He saw the maned beast that bounded, and the woman with horned shoulders, and the shape of a great nulla-nulla, and other shapes that he had not seen before. But as he moved forward again these shapes fell back. Only Ko-in waited at the edge of the dark, with his firestick in his hand making a point of fire, and the white paint on his body catching the light.

He said to Ko-in, 'But I don't know what to do.'

'And there is no teacher and no time. I am no teacher, Clever One. Unwind the cord and look at the power.'

Ko-in might not be a Clever One, but at any rate he was hero. Who else was there to say what Wirrun should do? Reverently he began to unwind the cord.

It was soft and supple, clean and grey under its outer layer, and it came off yard after yard. Wirrun heaped it coil upon coil like a fishing line. The softness diminished and the hardness grew: a small angular hardness with a sharp point to it. At last this core of hardness lay bare in his hand: a single crystal of quartz, perhaps two inches from point to base and an inch across the base. Its hexagonal shape was precise except on one side where it was flawed by an intrusion of stone. It was skeined with pink if the firelight could be trusted, and it had a frosty sparkle. It held rain and sky and dew and frost and the glitter of the sea.

'A very great magic,' said Ko-in softly. 'A magic that reaches across many countries and covers all the land. A magic that reaches to the sky. Wherever the ice may lead you this magic will have power. All the restless things of earth and night will know it in all their countries. They will let you pass, or help you. I have done well, Clever One.'

'No,' said Wirrun, his fingers busy rewinding the cord. 'I'm not Clever. That's the People's business, and there's more to it. But I reckon if you give me this it'll help me, and after it can go back in the cave. I needn't look at it again.' He finished rerolling the cord and hung the power

61

in its net bag on his belt again. 'You never know, it might tell me something. I could do with a bit more telling.'

'Ah,' said Ko-in. 'But now another will tell, I think. Come and listen.'

He moved along the ledge into the dark, and Wirrun followed. A little way behind the end of the ledge and close to the rock behind, Ko-in stopped. The darkness of a tree-trunk rose and disappeared above into the darkness of leaves. In the trunk by Ko-in's head was a patch of deeper blackness, a hole. Ko-in spoke to it.

'Come out, stranger. You who belong in another country far away, say what you do in mine. You know the law: those who come into a country that is not their own should have permission. Come out and speak.'

The silence within the tree was as deep as the dark. Nothing moved there. Nothing breathed. It was such a silence that Wirrun knew something listened and hid inside the tree. Ko-in reached into the hole and gently drew something out, holding it long and limp in his hand.

'Don't be afraid,' he said. 'Yet.'

He led the way back to the fire, and Wirrun at last could see what he held. A dark female figure, taller and more stick-thin than he would have believed possible; wispy arms and legs twisted together; dark possum-eyes wide with fear.

It was the Mimi.

Three

The Mimi's round eyes shone green in the firelight as she turned her head this way and that. She would have slithered off into the dark, but it billowed and twisted into shapes wherever she looked. The earth-creatures were gathered out of reach of the fire, and they were angry at this intruding spirit. She could not have got far.

She looked at the wall of rock that rose behind Wirrun's camp. She might have tried to slip away into that, but there were worse things in there. Beside her stood Ko-in who was hero, wearing the white paint of the People. He looked stern, but not angry; yet. The other who watched her so curiously was the young man she knew of. It embarrassed and distressed her that he should watch her like that for, though she had half expected it from Wirrun, she was not used to being seen by humans. She turned her eyes away from him, this way and that – and then she stepped close to the fire.

In all her weeks of hiding and fearing the Mimi had not dared to make a fire. That was banishment and isolation indeed; for who is the homeless, the outcast of earth, but the one who has lost his right to fire? The Mimi stood drooping by Wirrun's fire with her dark eyes fixed on the coals.

'Come, you must speak,' said Ko-in not too kindly. 'It will be remembered that you did not choose to come to my country. But you come with the ice and the hunter of ice, a rock-spirit nesting in a tree. There are reasons and causes to be told, fibres of knowing to be joined into one cord. Speak.'

'I can't tell – I don't know – I won't say – ' whispered the Mimi.

Ko-in towered over her frowning. 'And in my country who gives you the right of can't and don't and won't? Are your ears duller than the ears of one who is not even a proper man? Have you lived your long time listening within rock and you do not yet hear the voice of the land? You are ordered to speak, and not only by me. Tell how you left your own country.'

That the Mimi knew and could tell. 'The wind. It carried me here.'

'Ah well,' said Ko-in with scornful pity. 'The wind is no toy for a straw thing. Those who cannot ride it should stay out of its path.'

At this the Mimi seemed to sneeze. She drew her thin body to its full length, standing almost as tall as Ko-in, and Wirrun saw that the sneeze had really been an indignant snort. The Mimi was offended.

'You are a rider of the wind, old thing, and I am a straw,' she said proudly. 'But I have ridden a tribe of winds and yet I am not broken. You have made your little journeys here and there about your country, but I have ridden over every country across all the land from one sea to another. There has never in all time been such a riding of winds, and I still have my arms and legs.'

In the firelight Wirrun thought that Ko-in's eyes twinkled, but he spoke with grave respect. 'Then indeed we need your skill and wisdom, woman. And did you never rest in all that riding? Did you sleep on the wind?'

The Mimi grew uneasy and drooped. 'There is no sleep on the wind,' she muttered, looking this way and that. 'I rested one night.'

'And did you nest in a tree that night also?' asked Ko-in. 'Are your powers too weak for strange rocks?' He watched her restless eyes. 'You rested in rock in a western country and saw the ice.' A shiver passed down her long body from head to feet. 'You saw the men of ice in their own country, and then you rode the winds again to mine. And here you rested in a rock for a while, and ate our food; but later, as Ko-in saw, you nested in a tree like a bird or a possum. Yet the ice had not come here then. Why did you fear it so? What did you learn on that one night in the western rocks?'

The Mimi's eyes shone green as she looked at Wirrun. 'He was there,' she said sulkily.

'That night!' cried Wirrun, staring at her.

'He was there,' Ko-in agreed, 'and has told what he knows. But he did not see or hear the men of ice. That is for you to tell. Why did you fear them here in my country when they were still far off?'

'The wind blows,' whispered the Mimi, 'and the ice creaks. And the frost rustles like sand.'

'In the western rocks. But why do they come here?'

The shapes of dark round the firelight pressed in a little. The Mimi shivered.

'They will take the land again,' she whispered. 'They will build the ice and whiten all the land. As it was before.'

Now Wirrun too stirred. He had known it was a terrible ice.

'But this they do not do,' Ko-in said. 'They walk through rocks and peep out at the sea and make a little frost. What do they seek?'

'They seek the one who fought them before with fire, to freeze it and crack its bones. They will find the Nargun, the Eldest of Narguns, first.'

'The Eldest Nargun?' Ko-in seemed astonished. 'That was another battle, long ago. Do they seek that Nargun now? Where do they seek it?'

'In its own country by the sea. In the south, they say.'

'Well . . . we have joined the fibres of knowing into a cord. I thank you, woman. You are free of our rocks when the ice has passed. You are free of our food and no

65

creature will harm you. But you will come when a great one calls.'

The Mimi crouched over the fire. 'Take some,' said Wirrun, and she rolled her dark eyes at him and watched him lay on more wood.

'Come, Clever One,' said Ko-in. Wirrun shrugged at the title and decided not to argue. He thought that Ko-in had chosen to keep to it, and once he had made a choice he would not easily change it. 'It is full night now, and we must talk at my fire where no ears listen. Close your hand on the power.' He held Wirrun tightly round the shoulders and sprang into the air.

This time, with his hand on the power and Ko-in's arm about his shoulders, Wirrun rose upright through the air as a diver rises through water: above the scrub, with his fire a red twinkle below; above the mountain and forward into the wind. The stars welcomed him. The hills spread out their folds for him, wearing the dark draperies of their forests. A river marked its path for him to read. He was laughing, as Ularra sometimes laughed, with the pain of delight, and the wind in his ears fluttered with laughter too. . . . They were dropping between trees to another red twinkle of fire and Wirrun, falling like a stone beside Ko-in, laughed again with the delight of fear. . . . They were down and Wirrun was tumbled beside the fire, his hand still tight on the power, laughing as he fought for breath.

'I thank you,' said Ko-in, sitting there too with a laugh of his own in his eyes. 'It is a very long time since I last felt flight. I had forgotten it with use.'

'Wish I could,' said Wirrun, shaking his stiff fingers. 'That'd be something, forgetting it with use. And I'd stand a lot better chance catching the Ninya. They'll be a day and two nights ahead by the time I get started tomorrow.'

'And youth goes out of your face with the thought.' Ko-in sat silent, brooding. He roused himself and turned again to Wirrun. 'Tell me your plans, Clever One, now that you have the power of the People and have heard the rock-spirit from the north.'

'Well . . .' said Wirrun awkwardly. 'I gotta thank you for all that, and it helps. Only there's not a lot I can do, see. It'll have to be the men with the right songs that send the Ninya back, and I've sent word for 'em to come. But they'll take a time. There'll have to be a lot of talking to get the story straight, and I don't know how they'll travel but it's a long way any rate. All I can do is what I thought before: just hang on till the men come. Follow up these Ninya, and keep letting the men know where they are and what they're up to.'

Ko-in frowned. 'It is you who know the business of the People – but it is not a powerful plan. We fought more mightily once. You have now a great advantage over these men of ice, these Ninya. For they know only that they travel south, and must go by the caverns in the rocks and look always for the sea. But you know what they seek and can go there straight and fast.'

'M'm . . . as long as they don't change their minds and start building ice when I'm five hundred miles ahead.'

'But you have sent word to the right men. If the Ninya start building ice the men will know of it. They will go to the ice. Now think: if the Ninya keep on their path to the Eldest Nargun? You might reach it first, and rouse it to hold them until the men can come.' He frowned again, and seemed puzzled. 'Well, it is good that they seek it, for it keeps them within their caverns and tells you how to track them.'

'What is this thing they're looking for, anyhow? Where's its place?'

'A Nargun? It is a monster of rock. It lives in the south and the People avoid it with fear because from time to time it crushes and eats one of them. Narguns are born from the fire deep in the earth, and because this is the Eldest it has the power of First Things. It can call up fire, and was the worst enemy of the Ninya once.'

'And that's what you want me to rouse? Well . . . I just hope I don't get crushed and eaten.'

Ko-in laughed. 'You do not know your strength, Clever One. For the land is under you and you have the power of the People.'

'M'm. Well, it should save time knowing where to go. Where's this country?'

'Ah, the countries. Who can tell the People where the countries are? Its name would be strange to you and its People are spread far; but the Eldest Nargun remains. The country is far south, by that coast where the land turns sharply west. You must ask for the Eldest Nargun as you go.'

'But that'll take a time! Finding the People to ask, waiting while they hunt up some old man who still remembers – I won't be much better off than the Ninya! Except I can stick to the coast while they dodge round in caverns.'

'You will be much better off, for you will not look for the People unless you chance to need them. The earth-things will be awake all along your way as they are here, for they sense the ice from far off. They will be as active as wasps, and their memory is longer than the People's; and you have the power at your belt. They must help you. Ask the earth-things.'

'Well . . . all right. *If* I can get ahead of these Ninya, and *if* they're so scared of this Eldest Nargun, and *if* it doesn't crush me and eat me, and *if* the men don't come in time, and *if* the things outside this country know the power . . . A lot of ifs, I reckon.'

Ko-in was looking displeased. 'Mighty battles are fought on ifs,' he said severely. 'You need not fear the Nargun or the earth-things; for I have told you that this power is a very great magic known to all things in this land. I have given you much help and will now give you more. We must return to your fire, for the night deepens and there must be time for sleep. Is your hand on the power?'

They sprang up again through the darkness of trees into the wind and stars. They flew together, youth and hero, an army of two against the ice; and they dropped into the folds of the mountain and down to Wirrun's fire. There Ko-in stared for a moment at the rock-face behind the camp, then turned away from it and raised his voice. It was a strong and ringing voice.

'Rock-spirit of the north, Ko-in calls you. Come and talk again.'

They waited, Wirrun a good deal taken by surprise. Ko-in was about to call again when the Mimi came into the firelight from the direction of her tree.

'So you do not yet trust the rocks, spirit-woman,' Ko-in greeted her.

'Mimi,' she said pettishly. 'I'm a Mimi.'

'Indeed.' Ko-in bowed his head. 'Then you were right. You have come from very far and there has never been such a riding of winds. It needed skill, in one whose greatest enemy is the wind. You have conquered your enemy, woman of the Mimi,' said Ko-in, making one of his pronouncements. The Mimi straightened her drooping shoulders. 'Yet I think you are not able to direct the wind? How will you return?'

She drooped again. 'The right wind will come,' she whispered.

'And carry you over the mountains before it falls. And the wrong one will come again and carry you back here, or over the sea, and drop you again. Will you trust your frail limbs to the dust-devils or the ocean?'

The Mimi shivered and was silent. Wirrun was sorry for her and wondered what Ko-in was about. He was beginning to suspect that Ko-in, hero or not, liked to talk. For one who claimed that the talking was over and the doing should begin he had talked a good deal tonight.

'But perhaps,' he said now, 'you are happy here in my beautiful country. Perhaps you do not wish to return to the country of the monsoons.'

Her eyes shone green as she raised her head, and she gave that snort that was like a cat's sneeze. 'Your country is very well for those who can do no better. It should not be spoken of with my rich and lovely country, my far home . . .' Her voice trailed off, but she summoned it again and hissed at him. 'It will be long before the ice ventures into *my* country.'

Wirrun admired her for speaking so with the creatures of this country rustling and blowing in the dark all around her. 'It's the one land under all of us,' he said quickly, to get in before Ko-in could make an angry reply. But Ko-in did not seem angry with the Mimi and only bowed his head again.

'How will you return?' he repeated. There was no answer. The Mimi drooped. 'Your skill and courage deserve some help,' said Ko-in. 'This one can help you.' He pointed to Wirrun, who stared at him in amazement. So did the Mimi.

'Listen,' said Ko-in. 'This one goes on a journey to serve the land. He must go far and fast, and somewhere along the way there will be winds. With your help and the power of the People he can use the winds. He must talk with earth-spirits on his way, and you will know them better than he. You must travel with him.'

'I won't go,' said the Mimi at once and with force.

'You must go. The land requires it.'

'You are not the land,' hissed the Mimi. 'You do not speak with its voice.'

'But you hear its voice. Listen again. This one goes to find that Nargun that the ice men dread, to call it into battle with them. You will not stay here fighting on the side of the ice.'

'I won't go,' she said again. 'I fight no battles. I am not hero but frail, a hider in the land. I was not meant for battles.'

'Then you must hide in another country, for this one will not hide you.'

Wirrun was angry at Ko-in's cruelty. 'She doesn't have

to go,' he snapped; and the Mimi repeated desolately, 'I won't go.'

'What, not to return to your rich and lovely country, your far home?' The round possum-eyes turned quickly to Ko-in, and he went on. 'At the end of his journey this one meets men of the Ninya's country which is near your own. The winds are steadier there, and men travel from that country to yours. If you have helped the People they must help you. They will send you home.'

The Mimi twisted her arms together. 'I won't go,' she said, both helpless and obstinate.

'She can't,' Wirrun agreed. 'I gotta start off through the Happy Folk's towns, and I gotta get started quick. Unless the right wind happens to come straight off, that means I gotta go the first way by train. She can't do that, with all those Happy Folk looking at her.'

'They will not see her,' said Ko-in. 'No man, even of the People, can see a Mimi unless he carries a great power or the land itself gives him eyes. She will travel hidden as if in rock.'

'Well I reckon you're too tough,' Wirrun exploded. 'She doesn't want to go, and I can get on without her. I'd rather.' He looked nervously at the Mimi's frail limbs. 'It'd be like looking after a mayfly.'

Ko-in smiled gently. 'She has lived a thousand ages and ridden the winds across the lands, and still those mayfly limbs are unbroken. I am no monster of the dark, Clever One. She must go, for it is her only way home. She has courage; she will know the spirits; and her eyes and ears are the best in the land. And if the wind is right and you hold the power between you, then both may ride the wind safely.' He turned to the Mimi again. 'Go to your nest and eat and sleep, and come here at first light. This one will find a way for you to travel.'

The Mimi had been stealing glances at Wirrun and listening sharp-eared. 'I won't go,' she said pettishly, and flounced away spring-kneed.

When they had watched her go Ko-in laid his hand

on Wirrun's shoulder and smiled again. 'It has been a long day since the ice at dawn, but there is still time for sleep. You will rest well and wake well and journey well out of my country. After that you will listen to the land and the power, and journey well to the end. And I, Ko-in, I will go back to watching alone and silent, and my love will follow you. I will talk to no more People till the ice comes again.' He gripped Wirrun's shoulder tightly. 'I never knew a man who was angry with me three times in one day.'

Then Wirrun dared to put his own hand on Ko-in's shoulder. It felt smooth like stone and hard like leather. 'Not three times, only twice,' he said. 'That Clever One stuff, I just know it's not right. Like my cheek, anyhow, when you've done it all for me. Whatever happens, it'll be good to remember you. And thanks, man – ' He stopped, confused. That was no name for Ko-in who was hero.

Ko-in chuckled. 'Goodbye, Man.' Like a diver rising from the ocean he sprang towards the stars and was gone. Wirrun was alone with the mountain in the soft scurry of the night.

Heavy with the need for sleep he glanced over his supplies, packed a few and buried others, laid his gear ready for morning. Then he dragged himself into his sleeping-bag and slept like a stone.

3

Wirrun and the Mimi

One

Wirrun woke at dawn, and in the first moment of knowing it seemed to him that the mountain held him: that this place, this one spot, was home. He sat up feeling sad and comforted in the same moment; for today he must leave the mountain, yet this spot would always be here. And as he sat up he saw the Mimi.

She was sitting by his fireplace staring at the charred remains of his fire. Her stick-like knees were drawn up, and a cloud of wispy hair fell around her large ears to hide her face. It was the first time he had seen her by day and he sat quiet for a moment to look. It was like seeing the half-imagined shapes of night take on the reality of day.

He had seen Ko-in by day and had flown with him; but Ko-in was hero, not earth-thing. As the mountain had bred its shadowy creatures so man through long ages had bred Ko-in: not as mystic as the sky but larger than life; not man but of man, sharing his better self. Ko-in was real enough to be seen by day. To see the Mimi sitting by his fire was to see some darker, secret, older being out of night or the earth. From what Ko-in had said he must get used to such things.

He felt her peeping at him through her hair, so he stopped looking and spoke. 'What's up? Can't you make a fire?'

She hissed at him. 'Only a fool makes a fire in a strange country.'

'That's me,' said Wirrun cheerfully. He climbed fully

dressed out of his sleeping-bag and began to make the fire. 'Want something to eat?'

She shook her head, and he wanted her to stop in case her fragile neck broke. While he ate his quick breakfast he remembered Ko-in's confident promise: 'This one will find a way for you to travel.' He had no idea how she should travel.

'You can't walk, I reckon,' he muttered, looking at her critically over a slice of toast. 'Your legs wouldn't stand it for one thing, and there's the wind for another.'

She said nothing. Well, if she couldn't walk she had to be carried, that was all.

'Tell you what,' he said suddenly. 'If you live in rocks you must like the dark and you don't care much about air. I can roll you up inside my sleeping-bag and carry you that way.' And he brought the bag, rolled it up and strapped it, unrolled it again and showed her how soft it was. 'Of course,' he added, 'you'd have to curl up a bit, but that ought to be easy.' He had realized that the Mimi was a little taller than he.

'I won't go,' she said scornfully. He was not sure whether she was rejecting the sleeping-bag or the idea of being carried or the whole journey.

'Well,' he said, exasperated, 'if I'm not supposed to carry you I don't know what I'm supposed to do. There's the train, for one thing. I don't suppose you've ever seen one – noisy as hell and they go like the wind. You'd be scared stiff.'

'I go my own way,' said the Mimi.

'You do that,' said Wirrun because he had no more ideas. He watched her rise and walk to the rock wall. She blew, there was a gape of darkness, she was gone.

'That's that, then, and good riddance,' grumbled Wirrun. One part of Ko-in's plan had come unstuck already and it wasn't his fault. He had always thought that the whole plan was full of ifs. At least it meant that the rocks inside the mountain were unfrozen and safe again. And that meant that the Ninya were well away.

76

'She would've been handy, at that,' he told himself. 'Like a sort of thermometer; you'd know if the ice was close.' He packed his gear, buried his fire, and took up his pack.

The eastern sky was a cloth of gold promising the sun. He set off down the mountain, and it was like leaving some very old person who had been part of his childhood. He stopped now and then on his way down to look back and up. He had done this two or three times when a sort of wink at the edge of his vision made him turn that way and look.

There was nothing.

He turned back and went on down the mountain. There were many things on it that might follow him, and perhaps they were invisible by day; but Ko-in had promised him safe journey out of that country. He laid his hand for a moment on the power at his belt.

He came out of the forest and on to the dusty road he had followed in. Now he could see all round in the open country; nothing followed him. There was not even an Inlander in sight, and only a few cattle grazed in a paddock to his right. Now too he could lengthen his stride to the long, easy lope that he liked. The road began to wind away behind him.

It was like a holiday. Nothing weighed on Wirrun just now, or called to him through his feet; the challenges were all behind or ahead. On this fresh morning of new sun and high white clouds and light winds, he need only enjoy walking until he reached the town. He began to whistle softly.

The road ran under a bank of rocks and tall grass; and as Wirrun walked under the bank a rock winked at him.

He stopped whistling.

Half a mile farther on another rock winked.

Wirrun began to whistle again thoughtfully. What would happen, he wondered, when the ridges lowered and the valley widened? He thought there were miles to come with no rock outcrops near the road; and at the end of those miles there was the town.

Another rock winked. A spark of mischief made Wirrun break into a jog for half a mile. That was foolish when he had so far to go, and at the end of it he sat on a low bank under a grey gum to rest. He had been sitting there for two minutes when the grass rustled as if a lizard moved, and the Mimi stood over him.

He grinned at her. She hunched her narrow shoulders and folded herself down against the gum, sitting with one arm looped around the trunk.

'It is foolish to go so fast,' she said severely. 'The rocks do not know your road. To follow I must always watch; and to watch I must find the points of rock that rise above the ground. It takes time.'

'It's too slow, then,' said Wirrun. 'And you'll wear yourself out. You'd be better off being carried inside my pack.'

The Mimi cat-sneezed at him. 'I am not a dead bush-rat or a twist of cord to be carried on your shoulders. I have ridden the winds.'

Wirrun was about to answer when the sound of a motor made him turn his head quickly. 'Someone's coming,' he warned the Mimi. 'That's a truck.'

'I'm not deaf,' she retorted. 'That sound is heard in my country too. It will pass, for the tree will keep it off; and it travels too slowly to make a wind.'

'There'll be someone driving it, an Inlander. Do you want to be seen?'

But the Mimi sat calmly where she was as the truck came round a bend trailing its dust. It was the truck that brought the newspapers to the village under the mountain. The driver looked closely at Wirrun with hard Inlander eyes, noting his pack and everything about him. Wirrun knew that he would tell them in the village that the Abo who'd been hanging round had moved on all right. Yet in spite of his close inspection the driver took no notice of the Mimi.

'You were told that I am not seen by men,' she said as the truck passed. Then she turned her dark round eyes on Wirrun accusingly. '*You* –' she said, and stopped.

'Sorry,' said Wirrun. 'I can't help it.' It was hard to realize, in spite of telling, that she was invisible to other people when she was so clear to him. 'Look,' he said, 'if they can't see you and you're going to walk anyhow, why can't you walk on the road with me? It'd be a lot shorter and easier for you and we'd make better time.'

'And the wind?' said the Mimi.

'Oh . . . yeah, the wind. Well, why can't I hold your hand?' He looked uneasily at the stick-thin fingers, but he had to get used to them.

'And has the wind spoken to you? – will it be a small wind all the way? Or will it leap with a sudden pull to break off my hand and carry me over the sea?'

'Cripes!' said Wirrun. 'There's got to be a way, though. Because when this little road runs into the big one there won't be any more rocks for you to peep through. So you won't be able to follow.' He closed his hand on the power at his belt as he thought of the problem. Suddenly his fingers were throbbing and he knew what to do. He unfastened his belt and slipped off the net bag. 'Look,' he said. 'This is the way.'

He unwound a yard or so of the soft fur cord and tied it under the next winding so that it would unroll no further. Then he tied the free end into a long loop and passed it through the mesh of the bag so that it hung outside.

'Now,' he said, 'you can hang on to that while you're walking. We won't both be holding the power, just you, so we won't go flying off on the wrong wind. Only the wind won't take you while you've got a line to the power. Try it and see.'

He could see that the Mimi did not favour the idea. Her dark eyes were fixed on the distant hills. 'I am not a dog to be tied to your belt,' she said coldly. 'You speak of speed; we do not make it by sitting still.' She extended

79

herself upward, sighted along the line of the road, then mounted its bank like a very tall stick-insect and blew on a boulder that looked only big enough to sit on. Wirrun saw it gape darkly; the Mimi slid into it feet first, and the rock winked closed.

'Cantankerous female,' he muttered crossly, picking up his pack and setting off again. If she wanted to make her own way she could; he wouldn't be watching for winking rocks or trying to adapt his pace to hers. He trudged on.

The road ran out of the hills into the valley, and by late afternoon he could see the highway ahead. He could hear it, too: an animal moan, rising and dying but never silent. He was nearing the small railway town by now; and suddenly he decided to camp for the night here on the river. It was better than close to the town. If he went on he might catch a train and reach the city by night; but then he would have to spend a night in the city. It would be expensive, it would not save much time, and he didn't like the idea of it. As for the Mimi, he had no idea how she was going to manage in any case and was certain that he didn't care; for himself, he would camp by the river, sleep and wake early, and reach the town in time for the first trains. He could reach the end of the short southern line in one day, leaving all the city area and the Happy Folk behind.

At a point where the road was out of sight of houses or farm buildings he climbed through a fence and made for the river. Following it along a little way he found a shelving bank overhung by river oaks. There were no grazing cattle to bring a horseman; in fact milking was probably over already. He unrolled his pack on the shelf of the bank. Below it, on the coarse river sand, he laid a few stones for a fire-place and set his fire ready. It was still too early and too warm to eat. He left the fire unlit and went to lie on his sleeping-bag and rest. It had been a long day, and tomorrow would start early.

He lay listening to the quiet talk of the river, and the

wind singing softly in the needles of the oaks. It was the first chance he had had to think quietly over the plans Ko-in had made for him. There was a lot to think about, for Ko-in and his help had changed Wirrun's course completely. He was no longer simply a scout for the men of Mount Conner. He was now an advance party, to harass and hold the ice till the men arrived; and his journey was a race against the Ninya, who must already be far to the south. Wirrun hoped he might overtake them in his day's journey by train, but there was something else to be thought about before that. He must send fresh word to the men.

What word should he send? That the Ninya were headed for some unknown point near 'the coast where the land turns sharply west'? Not very easy to explain in a telegram – or even if you were talking to them. Should he arrange to meet them at some more precise point, say on the Victorian border? But the Ninya might change their plans and begin to build the ice before they reached it. It would be better, as Ko-in had said, to let the men follow the frosts. Yet he needed to send them some message of the Ninya's doings and his own. He worked it out and wrote it in pencil on the margin of one of his maps: 'Going south fast big ice coming send men quick.' That was the best he could do; and he only hoped the men really would be quick for he didn't like the sound of this Nargun, the Eldest with the power of fire.

He did not even know from what direction the men would come, or how they would travel the long and lonely miles. Not by plane, he thought; even if they had the money, they would not like to be carried on tribal business by the Happy Folk. But the People had their own ways of cutting a knotty problem; and all along those miles there would be others, a scattered few of the People here and there, to know the fastest route and help them on their way. They would come. And thinking this Wirrun fell into a doze.

The wind was still hushing in the oaks when he woke, and the river was talking louder. There was soft light from a young moon that would soon be setting, and the red-yellow light of his fire. . . . But he had not lit his fire. And what was that smell of cooking? He sat up and looked over the bank to the sand below.

The Mimi was sitting over the fire eating a fat, fire-blackened root. As Wirrun watched she reached out with a stick and dragged another from the coals. It looked to him like a good big sweet-potato from a farm garden. It lay cooling while she went on hungrily stuffing the first into her mouth; but even while she did this she stared absorbed at the fire. Wirrun stood up, stretched, and came slowly down the bank.

'Good fire,' he said. 'You're always catching me asleep.'

She blinked up at him like a possum, dragged another root from the coals, picked up the second and broke it open, and went back to staring at the fire. Wirrun set a tin of stew to heat. His supplies were running low; he would have to buy more tomorrow. Sniffing the good smell of roasting, he thought he would have preferred one of the Mimi's stolen roots.

They ate together in silence while the moon set and the fire grew redder. Afterwards Wirrun tidied his camp: flattening and burying the empty tin, filling his water-bag for tomorrow, washing his plate and himself in the river. The Mimi began by watching curiously, but at some point while Wirrun was busy she vanished.

He was not at all surprised. He sat and watched the fire go out and held the power between his hands, feeling again its completeness and strength; and he thought of the mountain, and of the dark things and Ko-in, and then of the Ninya and the Eldest Nargun; and now and then anxiously of the train.

When the moon and the fire were both out he went to sleep under the whispering river-oaks and slept to the talking of the water till earliest dawn. He breakfasted without a fire, rolled his pack, and climbed out of the river. By sunrise he had reached the highway and made some distance along it, forging ahead on its wide verge.

It was a little after sunrise when something flickered at the edge of his vision and something flicked at his belt. The Mimi was walking beside him, holding to the possum-fur cord.

Two

'Nice morning,' said Wirrun.

'From here the rock goes only down,' muttered the Mimi sulkily.

It was a moment to talk about something else but difficult to know what to say. It was pleasing to have won a battle with the Mimi, but it meant that the worrying problem of the train was his alone to solve. And he could not help feeling ridiculous with this tall, frail figure walking jerk-kneed at his side and clinging to a cord from his belt.

He said, 'Yeah, well, we'll be in the town soon. You won't like it – I'm sorry about that – but we've got to get through a lot of it to get to the coast in the south. It'll take all day, even in the train, but we'll be right by tonight. The train takes us through fast, just like riding the wind again. Only this time you'll be inside where there's no wind, sitting pretty on a soft seat.'

He glanced sideways. She was looking obstinate again, staring ahead and saying nothing. It was no good. However he might try to encourage them both, in no way could he picture the Mimi travelling by train.

Several cars howled past, and both Wirrun and the Mimi cringed. She had clutched at the possum-fur cord in fear of the sudden wind; he had watched under his heavy brow for a sign of turning heads and pointing fingers. Neither happened: no jerk at his waist and no curious eyes. They glanced sideways at each other, each proved right and each a little smug. Wirrun thought of something he had wanted to ask her last night.

'If you can follow me through the rocks, couldn't you go home that way?'

'Do you not know the law?' she said. 'How many countries lie between me and mine? All with their rock-spirits, angry at strangers. How can I go so far alone in strange rocks full of fear and trouble?'

'The Ninya seem to manage.'

She shivered. 'They send their wind ahead, freezing the way as they go. Who could stand against the ice? But I: I am frail and a hider. I do no harm and nothing fears me. Even the People do not fear me.'

'Don't let it worry you,' said Wirrun. 'You rode the winds, didn't you? You've seen all across the land, and now you're seeing a town, and you're going south and helping to fight the ice. They ought to pin a medal on you.'

The Mimi raised her head and looked fiercely at the town which they were now entering. But she walked very close to Wirrun and he thought it was lucky that her first town was a small one. He could not help feeling strange himself. He was glad that it was still very early and so few people were about. None of them gave him more than a glance or seemed to notice even the cord looping outward from his belt. Their faces showed that they all had something important to do and were grimly intent upon doing it. Wirrun suddenly felt that it would not have mattered if they had seen the stick-figure springing along at his side. Some, knowing no word for it, would not have believed what they saw; others would have run in fear from the frail hider.

'I'd rather have you than any of this lot,' he grumbled to the Mimi; and she cat-sneezed in anger because the comparison was an insult.

'Never mind, their trains are fast. The station's round this corner.'

He led the Mimi on to it. If they couldn't see her she

wouldn't need a ticket; he bought one, for as far south as the coast line went, and asked about timetables and changes. While he was doing this an express roared through, and he felt the Mimi stiffen and quiver at his side. There was going to be trouble all right.

'What was that?' she hissed as he turned away from the window. He didn't answer until he had led her down to the end of the platform where he could talk quietly.

'That was a sort of a train,' he said then, 'but we're not getting in one like that. We'll just stand here and watch a couple so you can have a look at 'em, and then we'll get in a nice quiet one.'

'I won't go,' said the Mimi. She was clutching the cord in both hands, looking desperately up and down the line and at the rough vacant land opposite. Wirrun didn't blame her. When you really looked at it, a train was a rude and noisy fuss to make about getting from one place to another.

A second train drew in and stopped. The Mimi cringed, twisting her head from side to side as she tried to hide her ears. Wirrun talked soothingly.

'The noise is only on the outside, that and the wind. Look there – see the people sitting inside, quiet as quiet? There's seats, see? Trains don't hurt you, they – ' the train whined out of the station and roared off down the line '– get you a long way fast,' said Wirrun winningly.

'I won't go,' said the Mimi. She let go the cord, sprang long-legged down to the line and across it, leapt over a fence, and dived into a tangle of blackberry.

Wirrun groaned. 'Now she's done it – she'll never get out of that! She'll be tangled up and broken into matches.' He turned to run off the station, heard another train coming and hesitated. He couldn't cross the line till the train had passed, and the Mimi was not going to wait for him; the damage would be done. And he had to keep things straight: what had to be done was to start his race against the ice. He wasn't supposed to risk that by being a broody hen to a Mimi. She would have to

86

take her chance. At the back of his mind he had always known that she couldn't travel by train.

The train drew in at his platform and Wirrun stepped doggedly on board. At least he hadn't wasted money buying a ticket for her. The train whined out of the station and hurled itself south, beating its song-sticks and howling its song; and Wirrun stared moodily out of the window.

The Mimi had been an irritating companion, all fears and prickly pride, hating this journey, resenting Wirrun because he was a man but could see her. Yet he wished sadly that he could have helped her safely home. She wasn't far from the coast where there were plenty of rocks; but even if she could disentangle herself unbroken from the blackberry there was nothing on the way to protect her from the wind.

'I never shoulda come by train,' he told himself. 'I knew she couldn't do it.' But what choice had there been? It was his one chance of catching up with the Ninya.

He stared at the Happy Folk who shared the carriage with him. There were not many of them yet, but they all looked as though they had something important to do and must do it at any cost. Well, so had he; the thought became a weight of anxiety. The small towns grew bigger, joined hands and became one; passengers boarded and left; Wirrun no longer saw any of them. He was seeing the men of Mount Conner receiving his message.

There would be a lot of talk and argument before they decided to act. After that they would talk and argue again about who, and how many, should go. Then they would have to raise some money for the trip, and probably round up a couple of cars or trucks. These would be old, and would break down often on the way. Would they take the good road that was so much longer, south then east and north? Or would they risk the shorter road east? In either case it would be a dangerous and terrible journey. For the first time Wirrun felt that the men could not possibly arrive in time. There was only

Wirrun. He must win this race. He must force the Eldest Nargun into battle.

The train reached the city and he had to change to another. Between trains he must find a post office and send his message to Ularra, and he must spend more of his scarce money to buy supplies. Hurry, hurry. . . . He bought a newspaper too, and caught his second train. This one was full to begin with and would empty along the way. It was hard to find room for himself and his pack, but he found a seat at last and opened the paper.

There was no time for thoughtful reading when the whole land and all these busy people depended on Wirrun's speed. He skimmed quickly through for news of the Ninya. There were no new stories of frost but several letters about the earlier stories, an article by a meteorologist, and another by a psychologist. Wirrun had to read them all in case they mentioned some report that he had missed since his last paper. The letters suggested that the frosts were caused by rays from a neighbouring planet, or by a crack in the field of gravity, or by vested interests, and that in any case it was time they were stopped. The meteorologist claimed that the frosts had simply not occurred at all but if they had they must be blamed on something called a Black Spot. The psychologist explained about crowd psychology and the effect of unexpected weather on the emotionally insecure. Several of them mentioned specific areas of frost and Wirrun, after careful checking, decided that he had missed no new reports. He still had no idea how far the Ninya had travelled now.

He tried to calculate their speed, going over in his mind the frosts he knew about and the days between. It seemed that the Ninya had varied their speed very widely, travelling sometimes only about twelve miles in a day and sometimes very much more. The fastest must have been from their own country to the east; at best he had to allow about eighty miles in a day for that stretch. Of course he did not know how far each stretch had been, how the caverns might wind to and fro deep down in the rock, how they might have to find their way from one level to another; but it worried him to know how quickly they could sometimes travel. What hope could he have, with perhaps three hundred miles to travel on foot? One day's journey by train was not enough – he should have scraped up the money from somewhere to hire a plane, or at least a car. If only this line went a bit further south!

So Wirrun's thoughts went round and round, and his body tightened into a knot of worry, while the train rushed south beside the sea. The passengers thinned, the towns dropped hands and drew apart. There were green hills, steep but humped with age, and below the scarp lay the sea. The sun crawled down low behind the hills, and the train drew in to the small town at the end of the line. Wirrun got out, leaving his newspaper behind on the seat as the Happy Folk liked to do. They some-times talked about tidy trains, but if they had wanted them there would have been garbage containers in the trains.

It was late to start walking, but he needed to start. He needed a quiet camping place out of town, and much more than that he needed to feel he had started on his slow race. He took out the right map, shouldered his pack, and began to walk.

He left behind the railway towns and the highway, and found his way by lonelier roads to the sea. When the first stars came out he was striding south, with the yellow lights of a village winking open and the sea endlessly mourning away to the left. By then he knew that all day the train and the Happy Folk had been fooling him. He had come to them too soon from the quiet of the moun-tain, and some of their frenzy had got into him.

He knew again that the men from Mount Conner would come, and that all across the land the People would help them. He knew that the speed of the Ninya was all a matter of guessing and for his part he could only do what he must. He could not have run his race with them in a plane or car or train like a can of peaches on wheels, for he knew only roughly where the country of the Narguns was and not at all where the Eldest could be found. He had to find out from the earth-things as he went. The men could travel after him as fast as they might, but he must find their path; and to do that he must walk the land in its quiet places and trust to it. All he knew so far he had learnt in this way. It was the only way.

He left the track to join a fellowship of banksias and laid down his pack among them. In the day's last light he built his fire and enjoyed the first night's luxury of grilling chops. The dark came down with a sense of companionship in it. He lifted his eyes from the chops and saw the Mimi again, sitting at the edge of the fire-light and eating a lizard with her round dark eyes fixed on the fire.

Three

When Wirrun saw the Mimi he was filled with a sudden delight. It astonished him, but he was careful not to let it show too much. He was sure she would only have hissed or snorted.

'Why don't you come near the fire?' he said. 'Don't you want to roast your lizard?' He took a stick and dragged a few coals to the edge of the fire.

The Mimi looked from the fire, to Wirrun, to the lizard. She had only begun eating the tail. She shuffled closer, laid the lizard on the coals, and used another stick to cover it with ashes and more coals. Wirrun smiled with content. She might be frail and full of fear and prickly pride, but she had kept her bargain with Ko-in in spite of it; and she had trusted Wirrun to send her safely home.

He forked his chops from the fire and offered her one. She ignored it, dragged out the lizard, and began to peel back the skin. Wirrun drew a little water from his canvas bag into a mug and set it near her.

'How did you find me?' he asked.

'I looked for fire in a strange country,' she said, and he wondered if she could possibly be teasing.

'But how did you get down here at all?'

'You said south, and by the coast. There are rocks all the way.'

'But how did you get to 'em out of that blackberry? I thought you'd get caught up in it and break yourself for sure.'

91

She hissed at him angrily. 'I am not a fool. I can find my way through a bramble; and behind it I saw the rock.'

'You fooled me, then; only how did you know how far the train was coming?'

'That noise – how could I lose it? The rocks shook with it; even the rock-spirits of this place have been driven off. When there was no more shaking I began to look for a fire.'

Wirrun shook his head with admiration. 'I don't know why I worry about you,' he said.

The Mimi looked at him for a moment, then drank a little water from the mug. They finished their separate meals, but Wirrun put off the jobs of tidying up. If he turned his back she would vanish into some hiding place, and after that day in the train he wanted her by his fire a little longer. Its flames flickered and sank, and a little way off the sea poured and poured.

'You know what we gotta do?' asked Wirrun.

She answered promptly. 'I help you speak to the spirits, and ride the wind when it is east of north. At the end you find a way for me to travel home. *Not*,' she added, 'rolled up like a cord in a rug.'

'Well, if you'd rather ride the wind home without the power to help you – '

She hissed again. Wirrun saw that if teasing was allowed it must be on one side only and he would have to make it up to her.

'Only it's not just me you're helping,' he said. 'You're doing it to fight the ice, and I don't know how I'd get on without you.' He wondered if that was a bit too much, if she would see through it and cat-sneeze at him; but she only looked a little queenly. 'I been worried all day,' he added.

The Mimi drank another drop of water.

'Wish I knew where these Ninya are now,' Wirrun murmured as if he were talking to himself. 'We've gotta get ahead of 'em and be first to find this Eldest Nargun.

And for all Ko-in says, we haven't got much idea where to look.' He waited for her to shrug, or to give some sign that this was not her affair, but she went on brooding over the fire and he hoped she might be listening. So he went on.

'Just have to keep our eyes peeled for signs of the ice and our ears open for news. Well, you've got the best eyes and ears in the land, and I've got the power. If we stick together and the right winds come we might manage all right.'

'I go my own way,' said the Mimi.

To hide a grin Wirrun reached for fresh wood for the fire. When he turned back she had gone again. He was vexed, for he had wanted to suggest that they travel mostly by night. It was the best time for the earth and earth-things, and the easiest way to avoid the Happy Folk. But he knew now that there would soon be another chance to talk to the Mimi, and tonight at least he needed rest. So, probably, did she. He tidied his camp, banked down the fire, took off his shirt and shorts, and went to bed. His belt with the power fastened to it he took into the sleeping-bag with him. Funny how he hadn't thought of it once while he sat in the train. . . .

. . . Something, a grass-stem or a spider, was tickling his face. He brushed it off and turned over to sleep again. . . . Something fluttered about his neck, and a voice was calling. He sat up quickly and opened his eyes. It was dark, but the dawn was coming.

'Wake up, wake up!' the voice was crying. 'Stupid – log – ' A twig of leaves fluttered in his face with a twig of fingers at the end of it.

'I *am* awake,' said Wirrun crossly. 'It's you.' He peered into the paling dark. As his eyes gave up sleep he could see the Mimi herself. She was wound around the trunk of a banksia, reaching out a long skinny arm to brush at Wirrun with the leaves.

'Get up quickly!' she cried. 'The right wind is coming! Am I to be carried off because a man sleeps like a log?'

93

'I'm coming, I'm coming,' growled Wirrun, climbing out of his sleeping-bag and reaching for shirt and shorts. 'Have you had breakfast?'

She hissed fiercely. 'Oh yes, you will race the ice, if only it will wait for you to eat. Do you think the wind comes east of north whenever you call for it?'

'All *right*. Quit nagging.' Wirrun buckled the power about his waist and bundled his gear together. The banksia leaves rattled and a sigh of wind breathed down his neck. He felt nervous. It was one thing to be seized and carried strongly aloft by Ko-in. It was quite another to trust himself to the wind and the fragile Mimi. And had Ko-in allowed for the weight of his pack? He slung it from his shoulder and closed his hand on the power, standing like that for a moment to get the feel of it. Its old strength flowed into him, and he held out the loop of cord to the Mimi.

'Can we hold it like this? Or will I take it off the belt?'

'A man would let it fall, and we should both be lost. There is no need.' She took the cord. 'Keep your hand on the power and never take it off. Now walk from under the trees, and when the wind comes strong run with me.'

They walked into grey daylight with the wind blowing lightly in their faces. Whenever it strengthened the Mimi tensed and gripped the cord anxiously. Wirrun saw that the wind was a greater terror for her than for him, yet she faced it without faltering. He ventured to say, 'Are you sure it's the right wind? Feels too far east to me.'

'Up there it is the right wind,' she said shortly. 'A wind is not the same all through. – Come now!'

She began a long-legged lope, bobbing a little between strides like a balloon on a string. Wirrun had to race to keep beside her. The wind curled a hand around him and swung him up like a leaf – the Mimi was bobbing on the cord at arm's length above. Wirrun felt himself tumbled in waves and acted as he would have done in the sea, except that his hand was glued to the power. His eyes were tight shut and for a moment he and the Mimi

94

floundered together. The wind seemed suddenly to lose force – they must have failed – he opened his eyes to see.

They were treading water high above the trees, two swimmers in sunlight with the old land brooding darkly below. The wind carried them gently because now they were floating with it. The shadowed land slipped away beneath, with sometimes a higher hilltop gilded in sun. The Mimi clutched at her cord and her big eyes were solemnly amazed; Wirrun could only guess what the wind had been like when she rode it before. He felt it push at his back with a large hand and laughed as he was hurried forward. The Mimi rolled her eyes towards him and turned them away to the left.

To the left was the wrinkled, silken sea which the Mimi watched in fear. Wirrun watched it too, both for pleasure and to be sure that the wind was a right wind. The coast curved in and they were carried directly over a bay. Seagulls glided with them, wind-ruffled and sun-dazzling, and swung off with loud cries and a beating of wings. Wirrun laughed again: he and the sea were both dreaming. He thought he was flying with seagulls and the sea moved like a dreamer. With slow, slow, power its white waves swung in to the beach; the lace of foam behind them was shaped like movement and yet was still. At the end of the bay where the rocks reached out the sea smashed into them slowly like a dreaming giant. Slow fountains of spray hung poised in the air.

Then they were over land again, with low green hills mimicking the sea and the black line of the highway appearing and disappearing through toy forests. It was netted to the coast by smaller tracks, and the wind washed over them all like water.

All that day they rode the wind along the curving coast, sometimes dropping low and sometimes carried high, and the old land brooded below. They hardly spoke; they had no need, and the wind fluttered in their ears and tore their words away. But Wirrun often laughed, turning his head to the Mimi, and she often watched him curiously. They passed over villages and towns, and from the blue-glass sky watched tiny cars and trucks fussing along like beetles. Wirrun laughed at those too, for they nearly always fell behind. The wind was faster.

Late in the afternoon the wind began to tire, taking them slower and lower then pushing them on and up with an extra effort. And it swung more to the east, so that the beaches disappeared and the sea was a field of stretched silk beyond a fringe of trees. A pair of wicked currawongs darted down at them, clacked their beaks and flew off. Wirrun had begun to fear that they were being carried too far inland when the Mimi called some words that he caught as they were blown away: 'Soon we will fall off the wind.'

He began to think about landing. Did they have any choice of where and when? There were hills ahead, smooth and green below a crown of trees but patched with surfaces of ancient weathered granite here and there. They were beautiful surfaces, moulded into the shapes of the hills rather than rising from them: the hills' own faces looking out from grass and forest. Wirrun thought that if they could reach those hills the hilltops might not be very far below – unless the wind flowed upward over them. He did not want to be carried farther from the coast than this. But the hills were coming closer and he did not know how to get off the wind.

The panic of the morning came back – why hadn't Ko-in told him how to land? He tried to steady himself and let his mind flow into his fingers, but he could only feel their aching. Both his hands were aching, for they had taken turns at gripping the power all day since dawn. Well, there could be only two ways to land: either to keep on holding the power or to let it go. If you did the first you must leave it to the wind to put you down where it chose. If you did the second you must fall; but you could grip the power again at the last moment and break the fall, couldn't you?

He shouted to the Mimi: 'Get ready to land!' At once she twisted herself into a complex knot of arms and legs.

The hills were very close now. He thought and hoped that at the level to which he and the Mimi had now fallen they should strike the central slope of the nearest hill. He could see it clearly ahead: a slope of grass, a surface of granite, a rounded boulder or two. Any minute now –

And then the wind surged upward in a wave, lifting them higher, hurrying them forward. There were trees rushing at them. Wirrun snatched his hand from the power.

The wind screamed upward past his ears – he was a falling stone, dragging the Mimi after him – in panic he clutched the power again. His feet were knocked backward – he was on his knees, and then on his face, on the grass. With a light bump the Mimi fell on top of him.

He lay still for a moment, breathing hard. He didn't seem to be hurt. His mind was saying over and over, 'There must be some other way.' He thought of the Mimi and rolled over quickly: funny, he felt stone-heavy, and the ground was rushing at him as if he were still on the wind. His stomach felt like a balloon that was trying to get away. He looked for the Mimi gasping, 'Are you all right?'

She was sitting stiff and erect beside him, still grasping her loop of cord in case the wind pounced, and gazing far off at the view. When he spoke she turned her dark eyes on him as though he might be a toadstool and probably poisonous. Then she looked back at the view. It was clear that she was too offended to speak. Wirrun ran his eyes quickly over her: four stick-like limbs still there, each with its twigs of fingers and toes.

'Sorry,' he said between breaths. 'Didn't know – first try – better next time – '

She gave him the same glance and looked away again. After a moment she spoke.

'Those who do not know would do well to ask.' She

97

lifted her chin even higher and looked at the sky. 'Those who claim to care for the frail should not hurl the frail to the ground from a great height. It is well that I have learnt to save my own limbs.'

Wirrun sat up, blinking and shaking his head at the view which still seemed to be blowing past him.

'Aw, come on,' he coaxed. 'It wasn't a *great* height. That's why we had to come down fast before we cleared the hill. And I couldn't ask – there wasn't anyone to ask.'

If it had been possible for the Mimi to swell he could see that she would have done so. Instead she hissed. 'Why then,' she demanded, 'did the spirit of the mountain send me to help you ride the wind?'

'Well, sure you helped,' said Wirrun quickly. 'But this was using the power, and you don't know about that. It doesn't even come from your country.'

'And did not the spirit tell you that all creatures in all countries know that power? It is of the sky and I am of the earth, but still I am spirit. How should a man know what a spirit knows? I could have told you to loose your hand only a little and tighten it again at once. We should have climbed down from the wind step by step, not hurtling like spears of lightning.'

Wirrun was obstinately silent, staring at the view and forcing it to keep still. The sun was behind the hill and its long shadow lay in front of him. He told himself that he had had about enough of this; Ko-in had put the power of the People in his hands, not in the Mimi's. Sure he was glad to have her around, but he was getting sick of being bossed by a bundle of sticks. Look at her now, hanging on to her cord like a little kid because she couldn't even stand on her own feet in a breeze.

The shadow of the hill reached further. He could feel the strength and thrust of it, the power of the land itself lifting and holding him.

Let children fight over toys, said the surging hill. *Serve only me, for the ice is coming.*

'All right,' said Wirrun, 'next time I'll ask. Come on,

Mimi, I said I was sorry. We'll go across to that rock so you can let go of the cord, and we'll make a fire and have a meal and a bit of a sleep. Then we'll go on while it's still night. That's the best time for us.'

The Mimi gave a righteous sniff and stood up long and thin and severe, like a schoolmarm receiving an apology from the class. Wirrun strode beside her up the slope to a broad bare face of granite that brooded under the hill's crown of trees. They walked across the granite till its grey brow bulged over them; and under this Wirrun took off his pack and laid it on the stone. The Mimi dropped her cord and crouched on the rock.

The slopes below were dusted with purple and the forest rose gold-edged against the setting sun. Wirrun went into it and gathered sticks. The granite was already a safe fireplace. He built the fire's foundation of sticks and went into the forest again for heavier wood. When he brought it back the Mimi had lit the fire and was feeding its flames with bigger sticks.

Even crouched over a fire and on this broad face of rock, she seemed uneasy. She looked from side to side at the purpling shadows. Wirrun wondered if she sensed any coldness in the rocks, or if she could find nothing to eat in this place. If she were half as hungry as he was she might even share his can of meatballs.

A little way from the fire he stooped to lay his wood in a neat pile on the rock. Behind him the Mimi hissed fiercely. He turned his head just in time to see her blow on the rock and vanish into it. Then something struck him hard on the temple and he fell forward over his wood heap.

4

The Ninya

One

Pain thumped and banged in Wirrun's head; he turned it restlessly and felt rock. The thumping came into his head from the rock – it was noise, not pain. There were grunts, too. All around, near and far, a chorus of grunts coming and going: a herd of animals grunting and stomping on rock? He was being tugged and torn – he opened his eyes – closed them again – opened them quickly and tried to sit up.

He was pushed down hard. He struggled against little arms that pushed and tore. No good. They were strong. Strong and hard as iron. A little dark man stood over him brandishing a heavy lump of wood.

A crowd of little dark people swarmed over the rock. They were only about eighteen inches high, but three of them held him easily while they tore at his clothes. They had torn his shirt right off. Others were beating out his fire, thumping and banging at it with sticks. Another hurled his neat pile of firewood piece by piece into the forest. They swarmed like ants and grunted to each other as they worked.

Wirrun fought with the little men near him, but two of them grabbed his arms and legs and dragged him to the edge of the granite. Little iron-hard hands tore at his shorts. Through his shock and daze Wirrun felt a throbbing at his belt. The power – they would take it! He fumbled for the net bag and closed his hand on it just in time. He felt wiry little fingers fastened on the bag. He heaved his shoulders, jabbed with his elbows, and glared into dark angry little faces.

'Hands off!' rumbled Wirrun.

The power was throbbing in his hand. The small wiry fingers fell away. An arm waved; there was quick grunting, then silence. The silence spread. The thumping stopped. They were looking at him from hard dark eyes under heavy brows. Dark-eyed and heavy-browed, Wirrun stared back.

There were one or two grunts, and this time Wirrun thought they held words. 'Back,' he thought he had heard, and, 'Ants.' The hands seized him again and he made ready to fight, but this time they dragged him back up the rock and set him against its bulging brow. One of them dropped his shirt beside him. Then they squatted at a little distance and stared at him again, about fifty small dark men in a half-circle in the evening shadows.

Something rustled down the rock from above, and the Mimi dropped beside him and seized her loop of cord.

'It's all right,' he muttered at her. 'They've felt the power.' He looked at them sternly again and they stared sternly back. He knew he must try to speak to them.

'You hear me?' he asked.

Some of them nodded. One grunted words that sounded like 'Got ears.' The rest went on staring from under their brows.

'The land sent me,' said Wirrun.

They grunted quietly together and again one of them spoke to him: 'No fire.'

The words went all around the half-circle. 'No fire,' they grunted sternly. 'No fire.' 'No fire.'

'You've put it out,' said Wirrun, 'but you might need it yet. The ice is coming.'

They grunted to each other and to him in an angry chorus. 'No ice.' 'Gone very long.' 'Done for last time.' 'No ice.'

'The land knows,' said Wirrun, 'and the earth-people

know. And you know. The ice is coming back. The ice people, the Ninya, are close by now coming inside the rocks. I don't know where they are but they're not far. This,' he showed them the power, 'and this,' he patted the rock, 'say you must help me fight the ice.'

They looked from him to the Mimi and at each other. 'No fire,' they grunted. 'No fire.'

'Never mind that,' said Wirrun sternly. 'Who are you, any rate?'

They replied with a chorus of grunts too many and fast for him to follow. He turned to the Mimi as an interpreter.

'They are the Wa-tha-gun-darl,' she said. 'They live only here, in caves and among these rocks. They do not go inside the rock like rock-spirits, but I think they have felt the ice far off with no real knowing. They say they will have no fire lest it bring strangers; they hunt birds and eat them raw. The big ants, the fierce biters, the bulldog ants, are theirs. If a stranger angers them they place him on the nests of the bulldog ants and hold him there till he dies.'

'Do they, now?' said Wirrun sourly. He could still feel those little iron arms dragging him from the rock. He did not think he would have had much chance against the Wa-tha-gun-darl and the bulldog ants. The half-circle faced him silently, half seen in the soft light between evening and young moonlight. 'Little toughs,' muttered Wirrun, and spoke to them again.

'You'd better hear this and remember,' he said. 'The Ninya will be going through in the rocks somewhere near, some time soon, on their way south. They're looking for the Eldest Nargun, the one that makes fire and fought them before. If they find it and freeze it they'll come out of the rocks and build the ice again. Here, everywhere, all over the land. They'll freeze the lot of you, and your bulldog ants too. So you'd better help me find the Eldest Nargun first. Now then: tell me. Do you know this Eldest Nargun?'

They looked at each other and grunted softly, then began to speak out. 'Know that Nargun long time gone.' 'Very long time not see that Nargun.' 'Don't know now. Not see that Nargun.' There was a background of further grunting that Wirrun could not follow, and he turned to the Mimi again.

'They keep to themselves in their own country,' she told him. 'They see no one, save sometimes the Nyols who are small like themselves and live within the rocks. It is not a thing they would know, for their knowing is small.'

'All right,' said Wirrun, glad to have it over. 'But if you see any of these Nyols you'd better ask them. Keep your eyes and ears open, and if you find out anything about the Ninya or the Nargun you'd better send me a message somehow. If you can.' They grunted together and nodded, but he thought they were not likely to help. They had no way of sending any message that he could understand, and they themselves never left their hill. At least he had warned them of the Ninya.

'Right,' he said. 'Now, we've been travelling all day and we're off again before morning.' Weariness flooded over him as soon as he let the thought of it enter his mind. 'So we're going to eat here, see?'

'No fire,' they grunted at once. He ignored that.

'And after that we're going to sleep till the moon sets. And I don't want any tomfooling while we're asleep, see? No tricks, no ants, hands off.'

In the moonlight the little men were only a dark half-circle of gleaming eyes, but he heard their angry buzzing. 'What's up now?' he asked the Mimi. 'Don't they even want us to sleep on their precious hill?'

'You have angered them,' she said severely. 'They are angry that you think they will hurt us as we sleep. They say that if they wished to hurt us they would do it now or it would already be done. They say they have no need to creep on sleeping strangers and that they too belong to the land.'

'Let's hope they remember, then,' said Wirrun unrepentantly, for death by bulldog ants is a very unpleasant death and his struggle with the little men had left a strong impression on his mind. He stood up and walked firmly to his pack. The Wa-tha-gun-darl had not begun to deal with it at the time they discovered the power, and it lay untouched where he had left it. They squatted where they were and continued to watch while he unrolled his sleeping-bag and prepared to eat his meatballs cold from the can. 'You ought to eat something,' he said to the Mimi. 'Why don't you try a bit of this?'

She had trusted the Wa-tha-gun-darl enough to let go the cord to the power. She sniffed at the meatballs, catsneezed, and shook her head. Wirrun was too weary to think any further and could only draw a little water for her from his canvas bag. 'Have to get that filled tomorrow,' he said, feeling its lightness.

There was a stir in the watching half-circle, and a figure moving to and fro. Then one of the little people moved forward, laid something on the rock with gruntings, and moved back. The Mimi picked up the object and bent her head to the watchers. She showed Wirrun what she held: a small green parrot, dead and limp.

He wrinkled his nose at it. 'Can you eat that raw?'

'It is good food and all they can give,' she said. 'I have eaten raw meat for many days now.' She began to tear out the feathers and eat.

When Wirrun had finished his meal he offered the empty tin to the dark watchers, pushing it down the rock towards their crouching shapes. 'Your ants'd like to clean that up,' he told them.

One of them picked it up cautiously, sniffed at it, and passed it quickly to the next. They passed it from hand to hand all along the half-circle, sniffing at it and grunting with dislike. Then one of them took it away down the hill. While they were doing this the Mimi slipped away into the rock. Wirrun stowed his gear safely beside him, hung the water-bag back on its branch, and got into his sleeping-bag. Though he was so tired he knew it would be hard to sleep with the fierce little people watching and grunting.

While he was thinking this he heard a stirring like leaves, and when he looked the dark half-circle of watchers had melted. The hill seemed empty against the stars; but just before he dropped into sleep it seemed to him that in the moonlight someone was still watching. . . .

He was wakened in darkness by a small strong hand pulling at him. He sat up quickly. The moon had gone; the stars and the sharp coolness of night told him that it was now about two in the morning. Three of the strong little men stood by him.

'Sleep too much,' one of them grunted. 'Moon gone, you go.'

Wirrun yawned. 'Thanks,' he said to the Wa-tha-gun-darl; but he thought they were more anxious to see him gone from their hill than concerned about his journey.

The small men nodded and moved away to the edge of the rock, and the Mimi stood beside Wirrun as he fastened his pack. 'Have a good rest?' he asked; and then he saw that she was quivering.

'I have not rested,' she said softly. 'I have lain outside the rock lest these people think I did not trust them. The cold wind is blowing.'

Wirrun woke up sharply. 'What – in there? Did you feel it?'

She shook her head. 'I was in the rock. It was colder than rock. Deeper in there are caverns. I heard the wind howling.'

Wirrun wrenched at the straps on his pack. At last he knew where the Ninya were. They were here.

'Time we got going,' he said urgently. 'After all that time on the wind I thought we'd be a bit ahead.' He saw that she carried a bundle of leaves tied firmly with grass cord. 'Here: do you want to put that in one of these pockets? You don't want to carry it.'

She hesitated, gave it to him, and watched him fasten it into a pocket. He lifted down his water-bag and hefted

it, frowning in surprise. Its weight told him that it had
been filled. The three little men were watching closely
and silently. He turned to them and gave them a small
bow.

'Thanks,' he said. 'Very good water.' He bowed again.

They nodded and seemed pleased.

In silence, in the dimness of starlight with the Mimi
holding her cord again, they set off down the hill. The
three small men came after them, and shadowy out of the
darkness came more until a little crowd followed them
down the hill. At the foot of the hill they stopped, still
watching. Seeing this Wirrun paused and spoke to them.

'Thanks for having us,' he said; and however odd it
sounded he wasn't joking. 'The cold wind's blowing
now, right inside those rocks up there, so watch out for
the Ninya. If you need any help send word.'

They nodded and grunted. 'We send,' they said; and,
'Good journey.'

Wirrun turned and went on with a lighter heart, for
now he knew the little Wa-tha-gun-darl had done their
best to help. They had given the Mimi that bird last
night, and whatever it was that she carried when he
woke. They had filled his water-bag, watched while he
slept, wakened him at the proper time, brought him
safely to the edge of their country, and wished him good
journey. Fierce they might be, and tough, but they could
have done no more than this. They had spoken truly:
they too belonged to the land.

He and the Mimi walked on and found the highway,
a hard black line in the dark. 'We'll stick to this for a bit,'
said Wirrun, 'till we know where we are. It's near the
coast, any rate.' The Mimi said nothing; perhaps she
knew exactly where they were in earth-spirit terms that
Wirrun could not grasp.

Very soon the highway went over a bridge, and black
letters on a white board could be read by starlight when
Wirrun peered close enough. 'Tilba-Tilba,' he said,
calling the map into mind, and he frowned anxiously.

'Just as well we had that wind, I reckon it took us a hundred and twenty or thirty miles. With that and the train we've come a long way, a lot faster than I thought we could. And still we find the Ninya nearly here.' He shook his head. 'They're going fast.'

'The spirits will not help them,' said the Mimi.

'M'm. They haven't helped us much yet. Still and all, we haven't had the chance to meet many. And maybe we're still a bit far from the right country. The ones that live in the Narguns' country ought to know more.'

He quickened his pace, striding down the highway at his best speed, and the Mimi loped easily beside him keeping up without trouble. It made him remember how she had overtaken him after the train journey, and he thought she might well have raced the Ninya without him to hold her back.

'Ko-in should've given you the power instead of me,' he growled.

She gave her sneezing snort. 'Stiffen your spine, Man. You do well enough when you do not hurl me from the sky like a spear. The Ninya are near but they have not found the Eldest of Narguns.'

'All right, all right, quit nagging,' said Wirrun, but he felt a little better.

'A man looks forward too far and backward not enough,' said the Mimi. 'But the earth needs him. I could not come alone. The spirit knew what he did when he gave you the power.'

In the black wall of trees on their left a cavern appeared and Wirrun looked for the road that turned into it off the highway. It was a gravel road, narrow and dark between trees, and its surface soon became rutted and rough. But Wirrun laid his hand on the power and felt the silent strength of it, and the land around and beneath. He walked surely on the rough track and was glad to be away from the highway. In half an hour they came out of the trees within sound of the sea. The stars lit them again; and in a little while they saw the darkly glinting restless field of the sea with pale stretches of beach and dark shapes of headlands, and it seemed almost as light as moonlight.

For some time the track ran between the sea and a wide sand-locked lagoon. The night was growing pale when they passed it and walked between sea and land: a half-dark movement and a hushed, forever, crying on the left where the stars swept down, and a watching stillness shadowed with hill and forest on the right.

Light and dark, cold and thaw, age on age, all is mine, said the sea.

I am. I will be. I rise out of time, said the land.

Wirrun and the Mimi walked between them by track and causeway and bridge: past a sleeping township while the stars went out and a small wind stirred, across inlets and on while the sun came out of the sea. And in the early sunlight by another sand-locked lake they sat down to rest and eat. Wirrun gave the Mimi her leaf-wrapped package out of which she took a dead wren.

'Do you want that?' asked Wirrun. 'There might be oysters. Or you could try a bit of bread and cheese.'

'The bird is good,' said the Mimi shortly, tearing out feathers. She slipped the loop of cord over her wrist and turned a questing face to the breeze. 'The right wind comes again,' she told him.

'It does?' said Wirrun, cutting a hunk of cheese. 'Maybe that's luck. Only I'm not sure we should take it.'

'You cry for speed because the Ninya are near, and the land hears. The land calls up the wind.'

'You reckon? But we gotta choose. If we ride the wind we don't meet any spirits, and we can't ask our way to this Eldest Nargun.'

The Mimi hissed. 'You think too much and know too little.'

'You said I couldn't help it,' Wirrun retorted; but he lay back on the land with his mouth full of cheese and the sun warming him, and let the sound of the sea pass over. When they had finished, and had drunk some of the water the Wa-tha-gun-darl had given them, he said, 'Come on then, is this wind ready yet?'

'Soon,' said the Mimi; and they walked on a little across the mouth of the lake with the wind coming stronger at their shoulders. When they had walked about a mile she said, 'Turn with me now and run,' and Wirrun closed his hand on the power and ran with her.

They were caught up into the wind and tumbled higher, and rode again above the broken coast; and the sea dreamed again below and Wirrun dreamed that he flew with gulls. But the gulls dropped away and slipped off in a current of wind, and other broader wings beat about Wirrun and the Mimi. There were a dozen great birds shining in the morning sun, birds that Wirrun had never seen before, like hawks but bigger. One of them called to him shrill and sharp across the wind.

'What man rides the wind with a rock-spirit at his side and magic at his belt?'

Then Wirrun saw that these were spirits too, but he was already clutching the power.

Two

The great white bird-spirits swung on their broad wings under, over, and around Wirrun and the Mimi. Now and then one of them diverted the wind so that the two wind-riders went spinning or slipping for a moment. Nervously the Mimi twisted her legs together and pulled on her loop of cord to draw herself closer to Wirrun. He himself was not afraid, for who can watch the flight of birds without delight? He shouted back boldly to the spirit that had called to him.

'I'm Wirrun of the People! Who are you?'

'Yauruks!' screamed the spirit, and the others screamed too so that they sounded as well as looked like a flock of great sea-birds.

'Yauruks! Yauruks! We are Yauruks!'

'Do you come from the sea?' shouted Wirrun.

The bird-spirits swung overhead so that he could see their soft under-feathers ruffled by the wind.

'Land!' they shrieked.

'We come from land!'

'We hunt whales for the People!'

'Whales?' Wirrun was astonished. He turned his head to the Mimi. 'What do the People want with whales?'

'A man should know that,' she cried in his ear. 'A whale is meat for a tribe.'

'Whales!' the Yauruks were screeching. 'We hunt them to land!' 'We drive them ashore!' 'Whales for the People!' They were the loveliest, liveliest, happiest spirits that Wirrun had yet seen, and even when their great wings beat too near they charmed him.

'Why does a man ride the wind?' one of them shrieked, and he remembered his journey and his quest. It was hard to shout an answer through the wind while the great wings beat close and swung off again, but he did his best.

'The ice is coming again!' he shouted. 'The Ninya are hunting the Eldest Nargun, and if they trap it the ice will come! I'm looking for the Nargun, to warn it!'

'The ice!' they shrieked. 'The ice! The ice!' They drew away on each side and flew in silence at a little distance. Wirrun waited for them to come close again so that he could shout his question; but soon they spiralled up and flew at a great height into the sun and away to sea. Wirrun watched them out of sight, hunching his shoulders in disappointment.

'You did not ask if they knew the Eldest of Narguns,' the Mimi hissed in his ear.

'I know. I was trying. Any rate I told 'em. If they'd known they would've said.'

She turned her round dark eyes on him in silence.

They rode high on the wind for about three hours and saw high rugged mountains ahead, reaching across the land towards the sea; and stony-backed hills facing the dreaming sea; and tall headlands of rock standing over it and broad shelves of rock reaching into it; and Wirrun grew restless and uneasy. Where hill and rock stood so near the sea the Ninya might be too, for they were travelling fast. And soon the coast would begin its sharp turn west, and still he knew nothing of the Eldest Nargun.

'We'll go down,' he said to the Mimi. 'We'll find a place to sleep for the day, and tonight we'll walk all night and not just a few hours.'

At once she began to twist herself into a tight protective knot. Wirrun sighed.

'All right,' he said, 'I know. I'm supposed to loosen

my fingers a bit and tighten up again, and keep on doing it all the way down. Right?'

She untwisted again. And when Wirrun tried it he found that this method worked well. If he loosened his hold on the power too much at one time it was like coming down a bumpy staircase of wind and the Mimi glared at him, but when he had it right he could bring them down at a steep or a gradual slant.

They crossed a wide bay with towns around its shores and a busy population of Happy Folk. When these were past Wirrun came sloping down into forested hills with only a lighthouse in sight. He used the staircase method to drop them between trees on a hillside. The Mimi landed twisted up and Wirrun with a stumble and a fall, but it was much better than his last landing. There was only the stone-heavy feeling again, and the sense of the land still blowing past, but even these passed off quickly.

Wirrun rubbed his aching fingers. 'Too soon to eat again,' he said, for it was not yet noon. 'We'll sleep till evening, and I'll light a fire for a proper meal before we start again.'

'Fires, eating, and sleep,' gibed the Mimi. 'It is slow work being a man.'

Wirrun was nettled, for they might have ridden the wind all day and travelled far. Only his anxiety had brought them down, his need to be near the hills with the land under his feet so that he could watch and listen; and he was not at all sure that he had been right. 'I reckon,' he said shortly, 'that by wind and walking we've done around a couple of hundred miles in two days, and I can't help being a man. Do you want to keep going?'

She drooped and shook her head. 'You are the thinker and the pace is yours,' she said; and he was sorry, for he saw that she had been teasing again.

'Will you try the rocks?' he said. 'I'll wait and see if you're all right. There's no wind here in the trees.'

Above in the treetops the wind was mimicking the sea, but in the forest there was warm and summery stillness. The Mimi dropped her cord. It took more courage to try the rocks now that they knew the Ninya were near, but rocks loomed all along the hillside. She went to the nearest, blew on it, and slipped into its gaping dark. Wirrun waited for a while, making a sleeping place for himself under that rock while he waited. In ten minutes she had not come out, so he lay on his sleeping-bag in the heavy warmth of the day and let his mind slip free.

It went backwards, past the teasing Mimi and the Yauruks crying over the sea in search of whales, back to the angry little Wa-tha-gun-darl dragging him to their ants; and then to the cold wind howling in their hill. He thought of the old south land lying burdened again under ice and snow; the great red rocks in its tired old heart cracked and tilted again; its far tender hazes washed into white; its fragile grey shrubs and slender lines of forest beaten in their long fight for life. And for comfort he put his hand on its stony clay.

Sleep now, and dream no dreams, said the land.

So Wirrun thought of Ko-in and the mountain; and in an hour he slept.

He woke with the forest shadowed in evening and coolness flowing up from the sea. The Mimi was beside him, having wakened him with leaves. She laid her twigs of fingers on his face to quieten him and they felt like a spider. She pointed through shadows to the hillside behind. Wirrun rolled over without speaking and looked.

At first he saw nothing but shadows, and then a movement of shadows. As he kept looking there were little shadowy shapes slipping out of the rocks and away among the trees. He put his hand on the power and saw that they were little grey spirits about as big as the ant-people, but these were more spidery in shape and not so fierce and angry. The power throbbed in his hand and he unfastened it from his belt and began to unwind the cord. After a moment of thought he held out the power

116

to the Mimi while he himself held the loop of the cord.

She hesitated with her dark eyes on his face, then took the soft-hard thing in her hands with awe. Her tall thin shape, as silent and shadowy as the others but blending more quickly with trees and grass, slithered away and vanished. Wirrun held his end of the cord and waited for her to lay a trail of it along the hillside and back. He could not see her at all – but he saw two spirits from the rocks suddenly halt in their flight down the hill and turn this way and that. Then the Mimi was beside him again, having waited till the two spirits were in her trap before she closed it behind them.

The two trapped spirits darted here and there along the line of cord looking for a way past, and so came at last to where Wirrun and the Mimi were silently waiting. They would have flickered off again, but the Mimi held up the power and Wirrun said, 'Stop.' Then they stood there, two little grey people with eyes that flashed like tiny stars.

They did not seem at all nervous but looked Wirrun up and down, yet he saw them glance at the power with reluctant respect. 'You wrestle?' one of them invited in a voice that rumbled like stones.

Wirrun was not tempted to accept this offer. The Watha-gun-darl had taught him to respect the powers of little people, and he did not think these two would have offered to wrestle if they had not been sure of winning. He thought he knew what had made them flee in such numbers from their rocks inside the hill, and he came to the point at once.

'The land sent me,' he said, 'and you know this power. You're running off because the cold wind's blowing in the rocks and the ice is coming.'

They looked at him with their star-like eyes and said nothing.

'What people are you?' Wirrun asked.

'We Nyols,' they said. Wirrun thought he had heard that name before and looked at the Mimi.

'They are rock-spirits,' she told him. 'They are the people known to the Wa-tha-gun-darl.' She added, 'I have been in the rocks. The cold wind is not yet blowing.'

'Not blowing?' Wirrun looked at the two Nyols. 'Why are you running off, then?'

'Not yet blowing,' said one, and the other added, 'Soon.'

'Right. Now listen.' Two pairs of bright eyes were at once fixed on him, yet he felt they measured him like wrestlers and not in any awe. They would listen, and then they would do as they wished. He spoke distinctly. 'The Ninya make the cold wind: the people of the ice. They go through here to hunt the Eldest Nargun. You know it?'

They nodded. 'We know Narguns.'

For a moment Wirrun's heart leapt. It was the first time any creature had admitted knowing anything. 'But the Eldest,' he said. 'The one that calls up fire. You know that one?'

They looked at each other, conversing in their rumbling voices with nods and head-shakes. 'Very big Nargun, that one.' 'Very clever, very old.' 'Not see that Nargun now.' 'Not see for a very long time.'

'If the Ninya find that Nargun first,' said Wirrun still with care, 'they'll freeze it and build the ice again. You don't want that, do you?'

They thought about it. 'Build ice on land,' they said. 'Better than in rocks.' They nodded wisely.

'But,' argued Wirrun, 'if *I* find that Nargun first, the Ninya will go home to their own country and build no ice at all. That's better still, isn't it?' They thought again and nodded. 'Now tell me: where is the Eldest Nargun?'

They conversed with each other again. 'That very old Nargun, that first one with the fire,' they told one another. 'Not see that Nargun a very long time,' they reminded each other. 'Gone, that First One. Gone from our country.' They turned to Wirrun, having worked it out between them. 'Gone into the sea,' they said.

'Into the sea? Are you sure?' They nodded. 'Where-abouts, then?' They looked at him with their twinkling eyes and said nothing.

The Mimi said softly, 'They do not know where.'

'In the sea of its country,' said one of the Nyols. 'You wrestle?' it invited again.

'No, I won't wrestle, I got no time,' said Wirrun, nodding to the Mimi who slipped off to rewind the cord. 'And if I did I'd win because I've got a very great magic. Now look, if you want to dodge the ice you tell your people to go north to the people with the bulldog ants. You know those people. The cold wind was blowing up there last night, so it ought to be past by now – finish – coming this way. You can get behind it if you go north.' He nodded to the Nyols, and like shadows they flitted away down the hill.

The Mimi had rewound the power in its possum-fur cord and stood holding it out to him on her two hands. He took it, thanked her, and sat staring at it cupped in his own hands. The Mimi watched him; she could see that he was thinking. She crept off and made a fire in the shelter of a deep angle of rock. Its yellow light broke into Wirrun's thinking, and he got up and went to the fire. He noticed that at some time during the day the Mimi had supplied herself with a root and a lizard.

'Thanks for waking me,' he said, rummaging in his supplies and finding mostly potatoes. 'In the sea, they said. Do you reckon they really know?'

'They know what they have heard,' said the Mimi. 'It is one fibre of knowing. There will be other spirits.'

'They don't seem all that anxious to help,' said Wirrun. 'Ko-in reckoned they would when they saw the power.'

'He said they must help, for it is a great power known in all countries. He did not say that because of it they would *wish* to help.' He stared at her under his brows. 'Man,' she cried suddenly, 'you know nothing! They are small creatures of the earth, in doubt and fear of the ice! Do the ants wish to help you when their nest is broken?

Do the shadows and the streams turn aside to help you? The spirits will help if they must, and if they can they will hide. Have you forgotten why *I* help?'

He looked at her in distress, and she drooped a little under his gaze. 'You!' he cried. She just stood there holding her lightly roasted lizard by the tail. But then Wirrun laughed and shook his head. 'No, not you,' he said. 'You help a lot more than you must. You're an ice-fighter, you poor frail hider, you.'

'I help,' said the Mimi sadly, 'because then you must send me home.' Wirrun laughed again, shaking his his head. 'And because the land sends you.' He laughed again.

'And because you remember the ice,' he told her. 'These little things, I reckon they'd rather forget. Maybe some of 'em never knew.' He broke open a roasted potato and loaded it with butter, but she could see that he was thinking again.

'In the sea . . .' he murmured. 'Once the Ninya know that, they can stop looking. Fire's not much good in the sea.'

She cat-sneezed at him. 'And what is to keep the Eldest in the sea? Since it chose to go there, the Ninya will know it may choose to come out.'

'What's to keep it in the sea? Ice. Ice will keep it there.'

'Must a Mimi give courage to a man?' she hissed. 'You will call it out of the sea!'

'And that's more than I bargained for. A creature of rock . . . and the sea's full of rocks round here. Someone's got to know this Eldest Nargun. Someone's got to show me the very rock – with the Ninya right on my tail all the way.'

'While you sit and eat by the fire like a man, and the night passes.'

She had eaten and drunk quickly, and to her Wirrun's meals were always enormous. But he finished this one, complaining that she was nagging again, and buried the fire and rolled his pack.

The fall of a gully led them down through a darkness of trees. They came out of the forest on a moonlit shore and found a track. The tide had turned and the sea cried savagely, tossing a black and silver net of a beauty so dangerous that Wirrun was almost afraid to look at it. All down the long coast the same sea cried and tossed its dark-bright net; and away to the south it caught the Eldest Nargun.

Around it on the shelf of rock, broken rocks shouldered aside the tossing sea. The Nargun crouched among them and knew itself greater than they. For it was old, a First Thing; it ached and was weary with age. And though it lay in the cold bright sea, yet it had the power of fire.

It was days since the Nargun had crushed and eaten the fish, and sea-things have memories as short as things on land. They had come back to creep under it and shelter from the crashing tide. A crab pressed close to the rock under its edge. At its feet a tangle of weed wrapped close, fanned out, wrapped in again; and folded under this curtain hung the fish. An anemone clung tight closed in a crevice. Triton, whelk, and limpet had locked themselves to the Nargun's sides.

The monster's blind and ancient love was for man moving warm in the sun. There was no love here; but there was the hidden secret of life. The Nargun nurtured this. It spread its weight on the rock beneath. When the tide tugged it cried aloud to the moon, and its cry was as far and as cold as the moon's silver.

And while it cried and fought the sea Wirrun and the Mimi sought it, striding between the sea and the brooding land; and behind them in the forests the Nyols fled north; and on the hill of the Wa-tha-gun-darl a battle was raging.

Three

The fierce little people of the hill had done their evening's hunting at the time when the birds were nesting for the night. Now they were crouching and sitting and lying together in one big cave, pulling the feathers from their dead birds and tearing the raw flesh with their teeth. As they ate they grunted quietly together, about the evening's hunt or in satisfaction at the one meal of their day.

They grunted too about the strangers who had come out of the sky to visit them last night, for this was a big event and the strangers were the first they had seen for many years. Though they had been bound to help these two they did not welcome strangers. Once or twice a year they enjoyed a corroboree with the Nyols, whom they had known for an age or so and who were friends; but even these friends they did not welcome too often. The Wa-tha-gun-darl were a tribe who kept to themselves, as fierce in their affection for each other as they were in defending themselves from outsiders. Men they had always distrusted, and other spirits they kept at arm's length. By day they hid, and by night they would have no fire or light to bring strangers to their hill.

So now they crouched in their tribal cave, grunting companionably together and building up little heaps of feathers between them as they ate. The dimness of the cave hid the brightness of the feathers: rust of swallow, blue of wren, bronze of thrush, yellow of thornbill, green of lorikeet, all faded into grey. Outside the dusk was beginning to blend into moonlight. The Wa-tha-gun-darl watched it in content; later the moonlight would tempt them into games, and perhaps to dance.

A cold breath moved in the cave, and the heaps of feathers stirred. The little men fell silent, turning dark eyes to each other and behind them into the cave. Wind may curl out of a cave when it has first blown in, but outside the evening was still.

The feathers fluttered like injured birds. The breath became a breeze, knife-edged with cold. Silently the small dark men dropped their food and grasped the heavy sticks that lay about them on the rock. Silently they melted out of the cave and vanished.

The sky grew softly bright with the moon and was hung with stars. The cold that gushed from the cave was bitter; the wind carried feathers like the flying ghosts of birds. In their hiding places the little men shivered and grasped their sticks more tightly. They waited.

The dark cave-mouth caught a sparkle from the moon, as if it were quartz instead of granite. Out of it stepped a man, all white, who sparkled too in the moonlight. He stood there, tall as a man and white as a cloud, but sparkling. He looked towards the sea and along the hill; and then he turned to look at the dark forest above.

Small black shapes darted from hiding, sticks swung and smashed. The white man toppled and the sticks beat at him. Broken ice flew in the moonlight. The man lay smashed; white blood came out of him and spread on the ground.

The little dark men slipped back into their places. From nooks and shadows of rock they watched the broken man and saw the ground where he lay whitening and sparkling with frost, and long icicles growing from the mouth of their tribal cave. The wind blew on.

The frost grew. In the ground, hidden spear-heads of ice were forming. Across the mouth of the cave something gleamed and glittered in the moonlight: ice was building there. There were creaks and whispers; the little men watched and listened. Soon they saw that a wall of ice was building fast across the mouth of their cave. Angrily they rushed into the moonlight, grunting fiercely and brandishing their sticks. Frost bit them and spears of ice cut their feet as they ran; that made them angrier. Slipping on frost and struggling up again they beat at the wall of ice.

Ice-crystals flew and sparkled. The centre of the ice wall creaked and cracked – they flew at it with their sticks, but it strengthened even while they smashed. And the wall grew higher. In places it was clear and deep like water; through there they could see white shapes that moved and laughed.

Some of the beating sticks were broken, and small men rushed to find new weapons. Their shouts made the others swing round: a second wall of ice was building behind them, its ends curving in to meet the first. They saw that the ice was walling them in, and they threw themselves at the outer wall.

It was already almost two feet high. When they tried to climb their hands and feet stuck to the ice; they had to pull themselves or each other free. And while they struggled the walls grew, both in height and in thickness.

One of them seized a broken stick and pressed it against the ice until it froze there. Quickly more broken weapons were found and frozen into place to make a ladder. The Wa-tha-gun-darl began swarming up the wall even while those at the rear were building a second ladder.

Green eyes in sparkling frost-white faces were looking over the wall from the cave. The Ninya watched the Wa-tha-gun-darl escaping. Now they could let the ice melt, and sticks and small men slide down, or they could build the wall faster. They built faster.

The Wa-tha-gun-darl climbed and leapt, froze to the wall and tore themselves free, clamped on more sticks as the first were frozen over and buried in ice. The two walls built towards each other. The space between them grew narrower; dropped and broken weapons disappeared under them; there was no more material for building ladders. The last four little dark men could not climb.

Those on the outside screamed and grunted in fury. They laid branches against the outer wall to climb up, tried to lower branches into the narrowing space inside, clamped sticks and stones to the inside and grunted, 'Leap! Leap!' But the captive four were weaker, dazed with cold and the pain of torn skin. They could only run a little up and down the narrow space. And the walls grew and joined, shining under the moon.

Looking through clear ice, the Wa-tha-gun-darl could see a dark blur here and there. They beat at the wall with stones and sticks, froze to it and tore free, cut their feet on hidden spears of ice. There was now a single block of ice ten feet long, five feet high, and seven feet thick. From behind it came a cold crackle of laughter, fading as the Ninya went back into the cave.

The little men fought on while the moon went down, sending powdered crystals flying and sometimes breaking off large chunks. But the great block of ice stood solid, though its surface was beginning to melt and trickle. One by one the fighters fell back, dazed and exhausted. They lay or squatted in despair, shivering and bleeding, staring with hopeless eyes at the ice.

That was how the Nyols found them.

The Nyols fleeing from the coming cold had met it flowing in a tide down the Wa-tha-gun-darl's hill. They had stood for a while, chattering, shivering, pointing. What drew them on was their knowledge of the Wa-tha-gun-darl, the fierce little fighters who lived only on this hill, who would not have been driven off and had no place to flee. Huddled together in a body, watching bright-eyed in the starlight, the Nyols advanced up the hill.

When they saw the hopeless, exhausted shapes and the great gleaming ice they wanted to run. They also wanted to help their friends, and most of all to know what had happened. Their first move chanced to be forward, and after that they forgot about running.

They dragged the Wa-tha-gun-darl into caves, dressed their wounds with leaves, heaped earth over them for warmth, and gave them water and the blood of lizards. They rumbled to each other softly, exchanging news and putting together the grunted words they gathered from one or another of the wounded; and at last, gathering their courage and their curiosity, they ventured by ways of their own into the rocks.

From there they found a way under the ice and, digging and hacking upward, dragged out four small still bodies. These they laid within the rock and stood around them at a loss, not speaking or looking at each other. They had not before known any death among their kind. After a time they went back to their patients, leaving little bodies in the rock, and told those who could listen what they had found and done.

In one of the caves a Wa-tha-gun-darl man stirred and grunted weakly. A Nyol bent to listen.

'Message. Man with magic.'

The Nyol nodded and slipped away.

And inside the hills, deep in caverns where the wind howled, the Ninya rested and laughed. To them it had not been a battle but only a small skirmish, yet they were excited. They had won the skirmish, and they had built their first good ice in the moonlight. Their beards bristled and gleamed in the twilight as they laughed together. Only their leader paced the cavern and frowned. In time their green eyes turned to him and their laughter crackled into silence. He saw them looking.

'We are one short,' he growled angrily.

They creaked with laughter. 'Even one short we built fast. We gave him a grave of beauty. And how it shone! Brighter than the stars!'

He crackled with anger. 'Oh yes, we built fast: there was no fire in our faces. But one of us was smashed by a thing no bigger than a stone.' He glared at them. 'He should have no grave of beauty, for he betrayed us. A man who walks upright from a cave into a stick betrays us all. If you would take the land and build the ice, then watch the man beside you. Let him not betray you with his death, for you need him. We come near the country of the Eldest of Narguns.'

They looked sideways at each other; yet they could not help their grins and hid them in sparkling beards or frosty fingers. Their leader paced among them full of anger and rounded on them again.

'Those small things that were captive, why did you give them to the ice? Why did you not bring them alive to me?'

They only looked at him under their icicle brows, not understanding. He howled at them.

'Where then is the Nargun, the Eldest? How shall we find it in its country? Tell me that!'

They did not tell him for they did not know.

'But the spirits know!' he roared at them. 'The spirits of these countries, they can tell us! And you give them to the ice and waste our journey!'

'They know,' growled a voice, 'but that is not to tell. They will tell us nothing.'

'Not for love, or the ice,' the leader growled back. 'But for fear they might, or for life itself. If you would not live for ever in a cave then bring me a spirit of this country and I will make it tell.'

They crowded together and growled softly to each other. From the crowd one voice creaked out again.

'The mighty leader of the Ninya has said that the Eldest will come of itself: that it will come from anywhere within knowing and stand in our path and redden the rocks with fire. Has the great and mighty leader not spoken truly?'

There were icy titters. The leader glared.

'Was I not right? Have I not led you safely though we searched no caverns?'

'Oh, you were right, great leader. We believe you

even now. Therefore we need not search through the country of the Narguns. If we find a quiet place by the coast and away from men, if we build a great ice and wait and watch beside it, then the Eldest will come to us.'

The leader frowned in thought for a moment. He lifted his head. 'Truly a wonder, a marvel beyond snow: a man who thinks as one of the Ninya and not as a child of the People. This we will do.'

They howled with joy and stamped till the frost flew, and when they were quiet he spoke again.

'Yet still you will bring me a spirit if you can take one. For the caves smother you, and you wait and watch badly, and we will lose no knowing that we can find. Now let us go forward again as fast as the caverns will take us.'

So the Ninya went on fast in the path of the wind. The caverns twisted back and forth, and plunged down crevices and broke into cliffs and narrowed into clefts; they were threaded with streams and floored with lakes and grew heavy with ice; but always their windings turned south again at last, as Wirrun and the Mimi walked south by the shore.

The young man of the People and the rock-spirit of the north walked far that night. While the moon lasted their walking was quick and easy, and when it was gone the sea reflected the starlight and Wirrun kept a hand on the power. It was as well he did, for they might have been attacked by an earth-spirit.

They had just rested for a short time and eaten and drunk. The track had turned some way inland; they were walking between heath and banksia on the left and under a forested hill on the right. They were silent, as they mostly were. There was only the mourning of the sea. Suddenly three loud cracks rang through the silence.

Wirrun turned a startled face to the Mimi. 'It is some spirit,' she said.

They stood still and searched the darkness all around them; but the Dulugar came from above, flying down from the hill. If they had known it he was a sign that the spirits were restless and uneasy; for the Dulugar's place was in the higher hills farther back and its usual habit was to attack women of the People.

It came hurtling down in their path and made a lunge at them – but Wirrun held the power and the Mimi its cord. The Dulugar hesitated and its arms fell. It was a great strong shape like a man with long arms and short legs, and covered with hair like a dog. It peered first at Wirrun and then at the Mimi – peered more closely – and broke into loud rude laughter. The Mimi's tall stick-figure, big-eared and possum-eyed, was not the female shape that the Dulugar was used to.

The Mimi bristled with fury. 'Ask it quickly and order it off,' she hissed.

Wirrun was angry too, for the laughter was coarse and rude and the Dulugar's sudden appearance had startled him. He took a step forward with the power, and the great black shape stopped laughing and stepped back.

'Whatever you are,' said Wirrun, 'you can stop right there and speak. The land sent us because the ice is coming.' The Dulugar looked from side to side in a hunted way. It would have shuffled off, but Wirrun had ordered it to stay.

'None of that,' he warned again. 'Here's one with me not a tenth your size but she rode the winds right across the land to fight the ice. If a great big lump like you can't fight, any rate you can talk. Say where the Eldest Nargun is, the one that calls up fire.'

The hairy thing snorted like a horse. 'That old rock,' it said in a thick voice. 'No one sees that rock now. Went into the sea, that rock did.'

The sea again? Wirrun frowned. 'Whereabouts?' he asked. 'Is it far from here?'

'Off this coast. Off its own country,' the Dulugar said. 'Not far.'

'Off here?' said Wirrun keenly. 'Off this country? Is this the country of the Narguns?'

129

The Dulugar snorted. 'Country of the Dulugar,' it said. 'Narguns live here too,' it added.

Wirrun would have needed a map and daylight to know exactly where they were, but he knew they had probably crossed the Victorian border during the night and were near the place where the coast turned west. If this creature lived in the Narguns' own country it must surely know where the Eldest could be found.

'I want to know which spot,' he said. 'The ice people are after it, and I gotta find it first.'

But the Dulugar shook its head. 'Don't go in the sea,' it said. 'Don't know where that old rock is.'

Wirrun was bitterly disappointed and glared at it for some time, but the Dulugar could only tell what it knew. 'All right,' he growled at last. 'Clear off and behave yourself. And if you see the ice people, the Ninya, see if you can't help instead of hiding like a great loon.'

The Dulugar snorted again and sidled off into the dark. When it had gone a little way it broke into the same rude laughter, and so flew off still laughing to the hills.

'Come,' said the Mimi stiffly. She had to tug at the cord, for Wirrun was thinking again. He broke into his long stride beside her murmuring, 'The sea. . . .'

'You cannot change what is known,' said the Mimi. 'You can only know it, and maybe before the Ninya know it.'

That was both true and comforting, and he needed comfort. Since the Mimi had heard the wind in the Wa-tha-gun-darl's hill Wirrun had felt at every step that the Ninya were at his heels. 'Any rate,' he said, 'we know we're in the right country now. That's something.'

'A country may be large,' said the Mimi; and that was true but not comforting. It spurred Wirrun into a faster stride and made him search the dark with keener eyes; for if they were already in Nargun country he must miss no opportunity to speak with a spirit. He could not wander up and down the coast vainly searching for he did not know what.

The track was dark now that it lay between trees. He saw the Mimi's eyes turn sharply into the dark, and paused to look and listen. There was movement, a black shape low on the track; while he strained his eyes it snuffled away into the heath.

'Some old dog,' he told the Mimi, who had followed it with her eyes.

They walked on. The sky had the shine of black glass; the stars were sharp and the air crisp. The night had passed its peak. It must now have reached the smallest hours of morning. Wirrun felt the Mimi give a small warning tug on her cord. He followed her look and in a minute saw another black shape low down on the path. He thought it might be the dog again, but he saw that it waited for him. In a few more steps he saw that it was one of the little grey people they had caught in the early evening fleeing from their rocks. It was a Nyol.

'You waiting for me?' he asked, and the Nyol nodded.

'Message,' it rumbled. 'From Wa-tha-gun-darl.'

So Wirrun and the Mimi sat on the dew-wet track to bring themselves closer to the Nyol; and Wirrun heard how the ice had come to those fierce little fighters on the hill.

Four

Wirrun sat with a face of stone staring into the dark, and once or twice he muttered 'Cripes!' in pain. He was thinking of the angry little men who had wanted to drag him to the bulldog ants and instead had given him water; the little men who sternly grunted 'No fire'. The ice had beaten them, but he knew it would have been a good fight.

The Mimi and the Nyol, one on each side, watched him with their old spirit eyes. This, they knew, was the curious thing that men were made for: to care. Spirits might care sometimes when something could be done. If they were the right kind they might help when help was needed. They might be and know and remember and do; but men cared even when they could not do. Only the earth itself knew what good that was – some cord that the earth had twisted and used to bind its creatures together. So the Mimi and the Nyol watched and waited while Wirrun mourned; and somewhere in the dark a dog snuffled.

At last Wirrun turned to the Nyol again. 'Four dead, you said?' The Nyol nodded.

'Under the ice,' it said. 'More soon, maybe. Skin off, all cut, all cold.'

'That's bad. That's very bad. You going back?' The Nyol nodded again. 'When can you be there?'

The Nyol's bright eyes looked at the sky. 'By morning.'

'Wish I could travel like you,' said Wirrun heavily.

'No good,' said the Nyol. 'You find First Nargun. Look here, look there, keep looking.'

'Yeah. Only don't you forget to look too; and come and tell me if you hear anything.' The Nyol nodded. 'Well, tell the people . . . tell 'em I'm sorry and I wish I'd been there . . . and we'll finish with these ice people yet. Tell 'em that.'

The Nyol nodded for the last time and vanished into the dark. Wirrun looked after it for a moment. Then he turned aside, and he and the Mimi went their own way. The track was now travelling uphill, and he made himself stride up it fast in spite of his tiredness. The Nyol's news made him feel more than ever that disaster travelled close behind; and in all this night's walking he had met only the Nyols and the hairy man-beast, and neither had known where the Eldest Nargun could be found.

'We might as well have stayed on the wind,' he grumbled, climbing faster to make up for it.

'Only by walking,' the Mimi pointed out, 'have you learnt that the Eldest is in the sea.'

'And about the Wa-tha-people. I could've done without that.'

She cat-sneezed impatiently. 'And I, I learn much about men. Their heads are hollow when their stomachs are hollow, and that is often. You must eat and sleep again.'

'I go slow enough compared to your sort without wasting the dark,' said Wirrun.

'Day is near, and there are white people. See there.'

The climbing track had reached a point where the forest broke and the ground on the left fell sharply. Looking down Wirrun could see a black depth below and hear a quiet lapping of water among trees. At first this seemed only a small coastal lagoon like others they had passed, but as he looked further through the grey dark he saw more distant humps of trees, and beyond them farther stretches of black water. This was a large and winding water threaded with land; and three far-off points of light would be some village on its shores. He remembered that they had crossed the border and thought he knew from the map what place this was. The Mimi was right: there would be more than a village or two here. At this time of the year there would be tents and cars and caravans, and all the anxious pursuit of happiness. It would be hard to find a quiet place to sleep.

'We must go round it, inland,' he said.

'It is far around this water,' said the Mimi.

'Well, we can't stop here. I need a bit of cover from hikers, or they'll be tripping over me all day. And you can't lie up in the deep rocks with the Ninya so near. We'll have to find you a hollow tree, or a big boulder on the surface, or something. We'll just have to go on a bit.'

They went on up the slope, hoping to stumble on a place of shelter and surface rocks. Soon they found they had reached the top of a ridge, and the ground began to fall. The Mimi paused uneasily for a moment, but followed Wirrun down the slope clutching her loop of cord.

There seemed to be some gully below, dark in a thickness of forest. The Mimi hesitated a second time, and this time Wirrun paused too. He could feel a clutch of cold about his ankles. They went on down a little way and stopped again. Wirrun's knees were aching with cold.

He turned and looked into the Mimi's face. It was all eyes in the dark, and he could feel her quivering. He gripped the power in both hands and showed it to her for courage. 'We gotta go on,' he whispered. 'Very quiet.'

They crept on without a sound, for the Mimi's tread was always silent and the power was helping Wirrun; and the dank chill rose around them as they went down. They paused often, and the Mimi listened tensely. Wirrun thought he too could hear a sound: a grunting and blowing down in the gully to the right. They reached the stony bed of the gully and the cold was deep and biting. The power was throbbing in Wirrun's hands; he turned down the gully towards the gasping sounds. As he turned he steadied himself with a hand on a rock and felt the bite of frost.

The grunting and blowing went on – and all at once broke upward into a howling bellow. It brought them both to a stop, for Wirrun had never heard such a sound of terror and perhaps the Mimi had. It died, yet still it seemed to fill the gully as if the forest held it or the stars threw it back.... But the power still throbbed in Wirrun's hand; in a moment he had to go on, and the Mimi followed stiffly.

It was lighter in the rocks of the gully than under the trees that fringed it. They could choose their way among boulders, and past hollows where water should have flowed and that were filled now with ice. They could see that just ahead the gully turned sharply. The grunting and blowing came from round that bend. They went towards it in dread.

Wirrun lifted his eyes from his feet for a moment to measure the distance, and as he raised them caught a glimpse of a black opening in the rocks on his side. He stiffened like the Mimi and turned that way as though he could not help it. He was chilled with cold already, but a new chill was creeping up his spine. He took two steps and bent to look into the rock.

A depth of darkness running back into the hill. Two twilit shapes, silent and still, white with a sparkle like salt. Green eyes glowing under needles of ice – faces of frost with green eyes colder than death. They sprang backwards like spiders into a hole; the rock was dark and empty.

Still stiffly he turned to the Mimi, and she knew from his face what he had seen. She stood and shuddered. Then that howling bellow rose again ahead, and shattered their frozen stillness. The throbbing of the power urged them on. They went unwillingly to what they knew was another terror.

They rounded the bend. There was a large pool into

which the water of the gully should have trickled and splashed. Now it was locked in ice of a strange milky colour, and fringed with frozen ferns. And something was fixed in the ice.

The head was reared up as though it had been climbing out of the pool when a sudden freeze caught it. The eyes were red and rolling. Through the milky ice could be seen the darkness of a great body. Wirrun could not look at the rolling red eyes, even with the power in his hand, but he seized a heavy branch and began to smash at the ice.

It was hard and thick. He only sent a jar through all his body. 'Quick!' he gasped to the Mimi. 'A fire!'

She dropped the cord and stood afraid while he rushed for wood and sticks, and while he laid them from the bank to the ice farthest from that terrible head, and while he threw down more branches from the edge of the gully. But she roused herself and had a fire burning on the lip of the pool when he threw down his second load.

'Another one!' said Wirrun, and laid more branches in place and sprang away; and two fires were burning when he returned. Wirrun heaped them into quick-blazing bonfires. Burning sticks fell and hissed on melting ice. The great head twisted and bellowed, from the heat or the ice or anger, and Wirrun had to look at it in the new white daylight.

It was a thing of many kinds that could not be truly seen, but its red eyes were like death and its bellow was like fear. It was like a calf, like a seal, like a man, it was white, it was black. It was all these things, together and separate, in one fearful beast, and it had haunted the land since the land was young. The red eyes rolled. He knew what it was and had always known. It was Mu-ru-bul, Tu-ru-dun, Bunyip, that seized men and dragged them into water-holes or waited for them quietly in reeds; that killed and ate men, or only held them close to it till they died. Wirrun heaved up heavy rocks and hurled them on to the ice till it cracked across. The ice tipped and heaved; he sprang back with his hand on the power, and the Mimi scuttled beside him.

The monster dragged its heavy body out on the opposite bank and lay half over the rocks. It had heavy shoulders with arms, or flippers. It was feathered, or furred, or scaly. You could not tell what it was except that it was dreadful.

But it lived in water: in lagoons or swamps or rivers or the sea. And it was old and strong and very knowing.

And the Dulugar could not answer Wirrun's questions because it did not go into the sea.

And in Wirrun's hands was the power that was old and strong and knowing too.

So Wirrun spoke to Mu-ru-bul, Tu-ru-dun, Bunyip, dragging his few words out of himself.

'The land sent us to fight the ice. I gotta find the Eldest Nargun quick. They say it's in the sea near here. Do you know where?'

The Bunyip rolled its head and gazed at Wirrun and the Mimi. It did not speak. Its eyes were spirit-old, knowing loneliness and fear, so that Wirrun had to drop his own to the broken ice again. But the Mimi's eyes were spirit-old and lonely too. She looked steadily back, and after a moment whispered to Wirrun.

'The Great One is angry, for I think the Ninya have tried to take it as if it were some small thing. It may be that the Great One will seek the Eldest in the waters.' She paused. 'But I think you need not fear it.' But Wirrun thought that all things, and even the Bunyip itself, must fear the Bunyip.

Mu-ru-bul, Tu-ru-dun, Bunyip, raised its mysterious unknowable bulk and looked upward between trees gold-tipped with sunrise to the sky that had turned from quartz to opal. It turned its head and looked for a long moment down the gully. Then it heaved itself back on the tipping ice and sank.

'It's gone down under the rocks,' said Wirrun in a

dazed voice. He was still shaking with cold and other things.

'Come,' said the Mimi. 'You must go out of this place.'

He was almost too cold and weary and afraid to move, and she had to hiss at him. Then he pushed his smouldering fires out on the cracked ice of the pool and began to drag himself up the farther ridge. The frost had melted and the ice would soon melt too, and the Ninya's cold was flowing down the gully and away to the sea.

They climbed slowly up into the warmth of the morning, to a leaf-mouldy ridge that carried another forest; and a little way on in the forest they found three tall boulders standing together.

'We've been helped,' said Wirrun to the Mimi. 'This is what we want, and I couldn't have gone much further. I'm beat.'

If he was too tired to go on, still he could not sleep yet; and the Mimi too still shivered from time to time. So between the rocks they made a fire to melt away their chill; and when the horror had gone out of them Wirrun felt warmed and rested, and roasted potatoes in the fire. He and the Mimi shared them, letting the fire burn down as they and the day grew warmer.

'First time we've shared a meal,' said Wirrun, burying the fire when they had finished. He expected a hiss or a cat-sneeze, but when he looked up the Mimi had vanished. She must have slipped away into one of the large boulders.

He stretched himself out between them and in spite of his weariness wondered whether he could sleep, for he had seen the clash of two great earth-powers. He had caught only a glimpse of the green-eyed Ninya, but in the heavy warmth of the morning he was shaken to remember their cold. And they were very sure of their power: they had dared to trap the Bunyip as they planned to trap the Nargun. He wondered why they had failed to take it.

Sleep, said the land; and it folded around him the heat of its summer and the quiet of its trees.

Wirrun rolled over on his side. As he drifted to sleep it was not the Ninya that he saw, but the old red eyes of Mu-ru-bul, Tu-ru-dun, Bunyip.

He did not see a black dog that lay in a patch of sun beyond his boulders. The dog too seemed to sleep.

5

*In the Country
of the Narguns*

One

So Wirrun slept above the gully where ice had trapped the Bunyip; and while he slept the day grew, and laid its heat over ridges and gullies of forest. In long reaches between them the sand-locked water lay still.

Yet the forest was astir, full of restless, anxious movement. There were rustlings and patterings and whispers as the small earth-spirits ran and hid. Nyols, little star-eyed shadows, fleeing out of their rocks; Net-Nets, small wild hairy ones from the caves and rock-hollows; Pot-kuroks from the waters, their prankster faces now woeful like clowns; they slid and scampered, driven from their homes and seeking shelter. When they met they whispered to each other before they hurried away.

'Cold wind blowing.'

'Ice comes.'

'Ice here.'

Hidden in leafy places the Turongs watched and listened. So far they were safe; they kept still and hoped that the ice might not reach their trees. And while these little earth-things scurried to and fro in fear, a great and ancient one went secretly searching for another. The Bunyip was hunting for the First of the Narguns.

It was a silent search. When the Bunyip cries it stops your breath with fear, but that is not the moment for fear. When the Bunyip hunts it hunts silently, and fear waits for the last moment of the hunt.

The Bunyip went unseen through weedy swamps and close under the banks of rivers, and where it went the water was clouded, milky. It went underground into darkness along old and secret streams, by channels deeper than the ice-wind of the Ninya found. These dark and secret ways took it from one river system to the next, and to the rocky edges of the sea. For who should know the dark places better than the Bunyip? It had lived in them since the People were scattered.

Of all the ancient spirits known to the People, only Bunyip had been seen by white men too. When the forests first began to shrink and the sheep to spread, only Mu-ru-bul bellowed its rage and pain. And white men saw and heard. They questioned the People and heard its names, but names are not enough. The white men knew that there must be a word of their own to put to the names, or the thing could not be real. They searched for the word.

They collected sheets of words and argued over them. They examined the words of the People, and insulted the People's professional knowledge with foolish questionings. And while they studied so earnestly Mu-ru-bul, Tu-ru-dun, Bunyip, the mysterious and unknowable, took its anger and pain into the depths of the land. Then the white men, forefathers of Happy Folk and Inlanders, knew they had been right: that if they found no word for a thing that thing did not exist. It was proved, for here was a creature they had seen and heard, but they had failed to find the word and it had vanished.

Meanwhile Tu-ru-dun came to know the deep places and secret waters. In the quiet of dawn or dusk it sometimes came to the surface to look again on land; to feel the dizzy swing of the sky and breathe deeply of forests and suns. So it had done this morning, coming out of deep places by its own ways into a pool in a gully.

It had felt the sting of ice and thought little of that, for it met ice sometimes. Then this ice had tightened suddenly into a clutching fist, and the bellow of Bunyip shivered the gully and the Ninya fled from what they had caught. And the anger of Mu-ru-bul followed them, strangers

144

who dared to trap it in its own country. So now Tu-ru-dun went silently through reeds and under banks, by swamp and river and shore, in sun and in darkness, seeking the Eldest Nargun. And the Ninya, in windy caverns from which the Nyols had fled, knew nothing of this though their leader was angry.

They huddled in a sulky group in a frosty cave while he paced at the end of the cave. They could have shouted back at his anger, but they hated his scorn. They were also shaken, for they had not meant to trap a Bunyip and had never before heard one bellow. They would not look at their leader while he lashed them with sneers.

'Come now,' he said, pretending to wheedle. 'You are not children of the People but men of the Ninya. It is certain you had reason for your act; there was thinking in it somewhere. Tell me, that I may know the thinking and see the reason. Inform my ears.'

They hunched their shoulders and said nothing.

'The task was simple: to bring me a spirit of this country, that I might make it tell where the Eldest lies. Every day we see the small weak ones, helpless against the Ninya as a lizard against the People. To keep their freedom they must talk. Yet you trap a Great One, as great as the Ninya and ancient beyond speech. Why is this?'

They shuffled their feet and looked away.

'To take the Nargun we make this long journey and lay our plans with care. A Bunyip is no less than a Nargun, yet you take it in a morning's walk. For what reason?'

Silence except for the rustle of frost under shuffling toes. The leader threw out his hands.

'I ask only your reasons and your thinking! Why do you take the Bunyip? And having taken it, why do you let it go? Once the harm was done it might have been held in ice as the Nargun may. It has been angered; it may work against us; yet you ran off and let it go. What was your thinking on this matter?'

His ice-ears caught a sullen mutter; he was pressing them too hard. They were lifting their shoulders and turning their heads; soon there would be angry shouts, excuses turned against each other, a fight or an attack on him. He changed his tone.

'Well, you have been foolish. But if you cannot tell me your reason there is one that I can tell you: your power grows strong. Now you have hope and the ice builds fast, it grows in a moment. You had caught the Bunyip before you knew it was there. That is the Ninya's part, to build the ice, and now the time has come to build a little. Let us find a high ridge looking down the shore, that the Eldest may see it from far. Let us make it a wonder of snow and ice to bring the Eldest against us. We shall see you trap a Nargun as quickly as a Bunyip.'

They did not shout or chant, as on a morning when they had not caught a Bunyip and heard it bellow, but their sullen faces lifted and they went on through the caverns looking for branches that ran towards the sea. Above them the forest's green roof enclosed a green-lit shade. Cicadas sang, a sharp vibration of sound at the edge of silence; farther away the sea hushed and dreamed; and from here and there about the inlet came the sounds of Happy Folk on holiday.

Cars laboured over bush roads, moaning to their caravans. Power boats hurtled across silent reaches and howled to their water-skiers. Happy voices twittered or lowed as climbers and swimmers called to each other. The summer day folded over these sounds and turned them into echoes, sleepy and soft. But as the morning grew a new note was heard in the voices of the Happy Folk.

It began in the village when the morning papers were delivered to the store. The storekeeper, small and wiry and brisk, snapped the fastenings on the bundles, tore them open and slapped the piles of newspapers on to the counter. Headlines leered up at her: NSW FREEZE APPROACHES BORDER! GLACIER AT TILBA-TILBA! There was a photograph, grey and unreadable.

It was hard to see in it the tribal cave of the Wa-tha-gun-darl, or the Ninya's cruel wall that had shone and glittered by moonlight.

The storekeeper bristled and reddened with shock. The last report of frost had been almost a week ago and far away safe to the north. Suddenly she was offered a great block of ice only a hundred miles or so from her counter. It was too much to believe.

'A disgrace!' she snapped fiercely. 'It ought to be stopped! Right at the beginning of the season, too! How do they expect us to make a living?'

The carrier paused in his unloading of cases and came to lean on the counter and read the headlines. He whistled. 'Looks bad.'

'It's downright wicked, that's what it is, making trouble and taking the bread out of people's mouths. And if that's supposed to be a glacier I'm Queen Elizabeth. These papers are all the same – always stirring and looking for trouble. Anything to be controversial.'

'Well . . .' said the carrier, frowning. 'They wouldn't hardly make a great block of ice and take it up there to take a picture, I don't reckon.'

'*Don't* you? I wouldn't put it past them.' She gave the pile of newspapers a ringing slap. 'Hearsay, that's all that is. And never mind what it does to the tourist trade that they're always on about. They ought to do something.'

'Still,' said the carrier, who was a peaceable and optimistic man not directly involved in the tourist trade, 'this Tilba-Tilba's well over the border. I don't reckon we'll be troubled.'

'A thing like that's bad for everyone,' said the storekeeper roundly, but she brightened a little. 'I don't know what they think they're doing in New South Wales, but they can keep it on their own side of the border. We don't want it here.'

During the day the pile of newspapers went down and

the news was carried abroad. Sunburnt people in shorts and bikinis discussed it in boats and bars, on beaches and in the bush. Since these were the Happy Folk it went without saying that they split into factions, and that each faction made fun of all the others.

One faction, mainly consisting of young people, made a holiday game of the mystery and went about in groups searching enthusiastically for ice. Not finding any, they began to map 'low temperature areas' and 'isotherms', exchanging news and theories when they met each other. Stores in all the towns and villages sold out of thermometers, and caves became very important. It was a great happiness to know and visit more caves than anyone else.

A small and gloomy faction searched their consciences instead of caves. What had they done – what had Man-Other-Than-Them done – to bring this trouble on the land? They sat in small worried groups reminding each other of all the disasters caused by Man. There were enough of these to keep them happy and make them feel better than other people.

By far the largest faction loudly refused to believe in the ice in order to make it go away. They laughed a great deal to prove that the ice was not there, and made jokes about the other factions. They quoted experts of all kinds: the Weather Bureau, physicists, psychologists, statisticians. They were not to be fooled by anything the newspapers, or the land itself, might say.

The Happy Folk who ran caravan parks and motels and stores, who hired out boats and cars and organized tours, also fell into factions. Most of them were silent, tight-lipped and disapproving. They refused to talk about ice to any of their visitors, even those who hoped to find it. They knew what they wanted of tourists, and it was not to go about excitedly looking for disaster. To go where they were supposed to go, to spend what they ought to spend, and to enjoy it without making fuss or problems: that was what tourists were for. The owner of one caravan park turned a young couple out because they claimed to have seen ice in a gully that very morning. They said they had gone for an early walk and had come upon a pool where melting ice floated, and charred wood as though someone had lit a fire.

'There's been a mistake in your booking,' said the owner of the caravan park. 'The place has been let from tomorrow. To people who won't go round spreading rumours and upsetting others.'

But some of the people in the tourist trade made the most of the ice. Tours of the Tilba-Tilba cave were arranged. Service stations selling ice kept special bags labelled 'From Tilba-Tilba', and sold them to the happy unbelievers who made a hit with them at their next parties. Some motels advertised in the papers: SWIMMING OR SKIING? EITHER WAY YOU CAN'T LOSE. It set a note that a great many Happy Folk adopted.

But no one tried to listen to the land. No one had room in his mind for a big and terrible ice, or left a quiet place there for waiting and seeing. Only, in a town not far away, an Inlander named George Morrow wondered and waited. He had brought his tractor to town for repairs, and when it was done he would load it on the back of his tabletop truck and take it home again. While the work was done he worked slowly through the list of shopping his wife had given him, and listened to the Happy Folk arguing about the ice.

Since he was an Inlander he knew the size and realities of the land. He had narrowed his eyes over the first news of the ice and had followed all the reports with care. He had read all the Happy Folk's arguments and accusations, all their angry demands or glib explanations, and thought that as usual they were missing the main point. The main point was not that the ice was possible or impossible, an insult or a joke, caused by man or flying saucers, good or bad for the tourist trade. It was something more direct and simple, something a child of

149

four could understand. The main point was the ice itself. Ice, frost, snow, cropping up again and again along a traceable route in a hot summer.

When George Morrow fixed his passive gaze on the main point, one or two other things could be seen. First, that he did not understand anything about it; second, that neither did anyone else; and third, therefore, that there was no point in any of the argument. Only two things could matter, as far as George could see. One would be a serious attempt to find out about the ice, and that might take twenty years. The second would be to find someone who did understand: someone who knew things that Happy Folk and Inlanders did not.

So George Morrow, watching and wondering, waited for those two things. And the forests and waters brooded under the sun; the small earth-creatures scurried through quiet places and the great ones went steadily on their way; the Happy Folk buzzed excitedly, and Wirrun of the People slept between the rocks. And in the hot noon, when the silence was sharp with cicada-song, he woke because he had slept enough.

Two

Wirrun woke between the rocks because he had slept enough. It was the first time since his journey by train that he had wakened for such a reason, and he was confused. He lay still for a moment, feeling for the day and the hour and the country; and when he had found them he turned his head quickly to look for the Mimi in case she had wakened him with leaves.

She was sitting on the summit of the tallest boulder dangling a dead bushrat by the tail and staring with cold dark spirit-eyes at a dog that lay beyond the boulders. It took no notice of her, whuffling in its own hair after fleas. Wirrun wondered whether it had displeased the Mimi by competing with her for the bushrat.

He asked, 'Do you want to eat that before we start? I thought we might get on a bit by daylight and eat when it's cooler, but suit yourself. We can find our way round this water after dark, there's bound to be paths.'

She blinked, for she had not expected Wirrun to postpone a meal. She examined the bushrat for a moment and lowered it to him. 'You will carry it on your back.' She watched him roll and fasten his pack, the bushrat in a paper bag in one pocket. 'I have seen many spirits,' she told him. 'Nyols from the rocks, and many small ones. They are much disturbed.'

'I s'pose they would be. It's most likely solid ice down under here.' He sighed with worry. 'We don't get ahead much, do we?'

'One greater than we two has gone ahead. We follow.'

'H'm. Hope you're right. Well, let's have a look at the way.'

In spite of what he had said to the Mimi he wanted to clear the inlet before dark. At night, even at full moon, they needed a road or track for speed; and in these forests and ridges tracks would be long and winding. By day, with only a sighting now and then from the higher ridges, he could take his own line: across ridge and gully till they passed the head of the inlet, and then directly back to the shore.

This forest journey was a delight to the Mimi. Walking by the sea where the wind waited she must stay in reach of the power, for there was no refuge in rocks where the Ninya travelled. For days she had been tied to Wirrun's belt by her loop of cord, and that was no way for an earth-spirit to walk. Here the day was still, the forests deep and sheltering. There were surface boulders, thickets, hanging vines. If wind came it must sound a warning in leaves far off: she would have time to reach shelter. She walked spring-kneed and free, keeping her distance from Wirrun and enjoying it.

Now and then she would let herself be hidden by thickets or curtains of vine. Her round eyes gleamed with a wicked red light when Wirrun stopped to look anxiously about. Seeing this at last, Wirrun hid a grin and lost sight of her as often as he could. It was not hard. Her stick-insect shape vanished easily in the forest, and he had walked too long with the Mimi at his belt not to miss her.

No hiss of leaves sent her springing for safety. The only thing that seemed to upset her was the coming and going of a dog that travelled with them. It was the black dog that scratched for fleas outside their circle of rocks. It took very little notice of them, running on its own trails through the forest nose down and tail half curled, but crossing their path every now and then. If Wirrun spoke to it it glanced at him with its mind on other things, flicked its ears and moved its tail a little, and went on with its trailing. Yet the Mimi watched it uneasily.

They were taking an easy way into a gully by following a wallaby trail when they heard human voices a little way down the slope. The Mimi stood still, watching Wirrun. He moved quietly off the track to a point where he could look down the hillside. A group of young Happy Folk were there, crouched under an overhanging rock. They were bending over something at their feet and arguing about it.

'It doesn't count,' one of the girls was saying. 'If this gets any sun it's only for half an hour or so in the evening. Of course it's cooler.'

'We're not making value judgements,' a young man retorted. 'We're plotting an isotherm. For all we know it's just the sort of place that gets iced up: a place that only gets a bit of sun in the evening. Put it in.'

The girl grumbled and made a mark on a map. The group stood up and moved off round the brow of the hill. Wirrun watched, frowning. If the Happy Folk were making a game of tracking the ice he felt sure it was going to be a nuisance. There was little enough time to spare without dodging excited groups of young explorers or rescuing them from frozen pools. When the ancient Bunyip commanded rescue, that was in the war against the Ninya, but the Happy Folk were not part of that war. He wished he could evacuate them all to good safe homes in the inland. He was about to turn back when he saw a movement under the overhanging rock.

Two small hairy earth-things stood there looking harassed. They were watching the young people out of sight and waiting for their voices to die. Wirrun had not seen their kind before: hairy little grey people with claws. He held up the power and called to them, side-stepping down the hill. They jumped, looked about in a hunted way, then fixed him with eyes like those of the Mimi's bushrat and waited. The Mimi came up with Wirrun as he reached them.

'The ice is coming,' said Wirrun, as if it were a password.

'Ice here,' they said hoarsely.

Wirrun nodded. 'But a big ice is coming, over the land. I'm looking for the Eldest Nargun, to fight the ice with fire.'

They still looked at him steadily. 'Ice here,' they said.

'Do you know where the Eldest Nargun is?'

Their eyes darkened with awe and turned away. Their hoarse voices muttered, died away, muttered again. 'That Great One . . . very big, very strong, very old. . . . That very great Nargun, that First One. . . . Not here.'

'You don't know where?'

They shook their heads and sidled off, and he let them go. From under the rock a headline was glaring at him: a fresh-looking newspaper lay where the young Happy Folk must have dropped it. He knew now why they played their game of hunting the ice. He did not pick up the newspaper, for it had nothing more to tell him. It would have no news of the fierce little fighters of Tilba-Tilba, if they recovered or whether they mourned more dead. It had not told the Happy Folk how the Wa-tha-gun-darl defended them and their land. Wirrun thought of them in silence as he and the Mimi went on down the hill. It was some time before he noticed that the Mimi seemed troubled.

'What's up?' he said then.

'The small hairy spirits,' she said, puzzled. 'Many passed while you slept. They are called Net-Net. They are not true rock-spirits: they live not in but among rocks.'

'Well? They didn't know much, did they? Just little blokes, not likely to know much.'

She cat-sneezed at him. 'When the belly is empty so is the head. You said to them that the ice is coming and they answered that it is here. Yet they do not live in the rock where the Ninya travel. Where have they seen the ice?'

'They've been talking to the Nyols. You said there were a lot about.'

'You said to them that a great ice is coming over the land, and they answered that it is here.'

Wirrun stood still and looked at her, frowning. 'Well, it isn't, is it? You can see that.'

'I cannot see over all this country from where I stand,' snapped the Mimi.

Wirrun said heavily, 'It's getting a bit much. We'll keep the Net-Net in mind. But we can't do more than we're doing, so let's get on with it.'

They walked on. The black dog came out of the forest to sniff at Wirrun's heels. The Mimi hissed and retreated into the lower branches of a lillypilly.

'Go home,' said Wirrun sternly to the dog. It gave him an absent-minded look and a half-wag of the tail and continued to mind its own business. He gave in because he had come to feel that its home (if it had one, for it wore no collar) might be very far away. How long had it been with them? Surely he remembered a dog on the road last night? 'It won't hurt you,' he called to the Mimi. 'Take no notice and it'll go away.'

She snorted crossly and swung down from the tree.

They climbed a high ridge with a patch of bare rock from which Wirrun could check their route. They must have cleared the inlet, for he could see over gullies to the shore. He chose a gully that would lead them down to the sea, and they headed for it through the forest. There were voices of more of the Happy Folk near at hand, but these they avoided. They were nearing the head of the chosen gully when Wirrun saw one girl alone, climbing the slope towards him.

The Mimi was hiding from him again, along the slope among tree-ferns. He paused, looking for a line that would avoid this girl too; but then he changed his mind and walked on. This girl was different, dark like himself, a girl of the People. She wore jeans and a sweatshirt, her feet were bare, and when she saw Wirrun watching she smiled delightfully. He thought he had never seen a more charming girl.

When they were close he said a cheerful hullo and stood aside to let her pass. In his mind was the question, Who is she? The girl smiled again and came on, turning towards him, but just then the black dog came sniffing along on one of its trails and pushed in front of her. She had to stand and wait for it to pass, and while she waited the Mimi too came out of the forest and stood beside Wirrun. The girl's eyes flicked aside to the Mimi and back to Wirrun.

Wirrun frowned. The girl still smiled delightfully and the dog still blocked her way, for only half a second had passed, but she had certainly looked at the Mimi. Quickly he put his hand on the power and felt it throbbing. And even then, though her smile had hardened a little, the girl still looked charming and real and delightful. Only her hands and feet were too small for a real girl – and then he saw that they had claws instead of fingers and toes. They were big strong claws. If the dog had not happened to come – if the creature had not glanced at the Mimi who was invisible to humans – would the power have saved him without his calling on it?

And still only a second had passed, and the question, Who is she? was still in his mind. He changed it a little.

'What are you?'

'Bagini,' said the earth-thing. It saw his eyes on its clawed hands and held them up and laughed. Its laughter was like the creaking call of cockatoos. 'I would not have eaten you, Man,' it said.

Wirrun gave his password again: 'The ice is coming.' The thing stopped its harsh laughter and looked dark and sullen, and he wondered how it could ever have made itself charming.

'The ice is here,' it snarled, 'and will grow.'

Wirrun glanced at the Mimi. Her round eyes were fixed on the Bagini's face. 'Where is the ice?' she asked.

The Bagini sneered. 'Where even a straw thing can find it. It hangs over this country.'

'It's your country,' said Wirrun. 'I'm surprised you don't get rid of this ice. There ought to be enough of you to have a go. What about the Narguns? Aren't there any left?'

The Bagini gave a shriek of cockatoo laughter. 'Watch out, Man! Keep away from caves and dark places!'

'Never you mind about me,' said Wirrun. 'The land looks after me, and the power of the People. The one I'm looking for is the Eldest Nargun. Tell me about that one.'

The Bagini shrugged; but while Wirrun held the power it was forced to answer and did so sulkily: 'All Narguns are old, but the First is old beyond knowing. A Great One mighty in size and in power. It has seen the land in the making and holds the secret of fire. It stands in the path of the sea and turns back the ocean from its country.'

'It must come out of the sea,' said Wirrun. 'It must turn back the ice from all the land. Tell me how to find it.'

The Bagini shook its head. 'I know only that you must go farther, south and west.'

Wirrun nodded wearily. 'All right. We'll go, then.'

The earth-thing turned to go into the forest, but paused a moment. 'You follow the coast?' it asked. Wirrun nodded again. 'This gully will take you quickly,' said the creature, and the Mimi looked at it sharply.

'I know. Thanks, any rate.'

It moved off into the forest, and Wirrun and the Mimi went steeply down into the gully. Shadowed in vines the Bagini stood, watching with sly hard eyes as they went down.

The gully was one of those deep folds between ridges, with a narrow rocky floor down which water trickled. They had to climb into it down rugged faces of rock, and when they reached the bottom the path between boulders was wide enough for only one at a time. The black dog came after them, leaping from boulder to ledge.

What startled Wirrun was the feeling of night in the

gully, for the sun was only halfway to the west. But the gully ran south-east, the ridges stood high and close, and he guessed that the sun shone here for no more than an hour each day. The path was rough and difficult, slippery with damp. He wondered if darkness came here before sunset, and whether they could be out by then. He must go as fast as he could without risking a broken leg.

'Stay close behind,' he said to the Mimi, 'so you can grab the cord any time. Wind might funnel up here from the sea. If I'd known this was so bad I'd have gone down the ridge instead. Might've been tough going, but it would've been daylight any rate.'

'The Bagini knew,' said the Mimi. She was troubled again for she felt that the Bagini knew something more. Some worse danger was here than damp rocks in a poor light; something to bring that sly, waiting look into the Bagini's eyes.

Three

Wirrun led the way down the gully as fast as he safely could, with the Mimi close behind. Sometimes it was rough walking, sometimes balancing from boulder to boulder, sometimes edging along damp slopes past pools or climbing over rocks and fallen trees. From time to time the dog came pushing past, to scramble over rocks and disappear. It was startling in the poor light, but even the Mimi did not hiss. The dog had done them a good turn with the Bagini.

Sometimes Wirrun would pause to look up between rock walls to the slit of sky above, to reassure himself that it was still a sunlit sky. At those times he saw that the old land held him in its fist; he felt it close its hand on him.

They edged round a bulging wall of rock and found that it opened a dark cave-mouth to the sea. The Mimi skirted wide around this, plucking at the cord on Wirrun's belt. He glanced into the cave as they went: only darkness and the shadowed shapes of rock. Beyond, the black dog sat and rested, waiting with lolling tongue. They went on past it.

Turn, said the land.

Wirrun turned with his hand on the throbbing power. He stood before the cave and looked into it. Only darkness and rock and a stealthy withdrawal of shadows. He spoke to the shadows.

'The land sent me against the ice. Where's the Eldest

Nargun, the one with fire? It's wanted out of the sea to fight the ice.'

Nothing answered or came from the cave. Only the shadows stirred. Yet the power throbbed in Wirrun's hand and he was puzzled. 'There's nothing but a great rock,' he told the Mimi.

'Nargun!' she whispered, tugging fiercely at the cord. 'Come away!' Her eyes were dark with awe, for she was a rock-spirit and to her the living rock was the deepest mystery of all. 'This too the Bagini knew. Come away.' She tugged again.

'But – hang on – if it's a Nargun it's bound to know about the Eldest! I gotta try again.'

'It may know. That is nothing to you. It is old beyond speech and will not answer.'

He gave in a little, backing away and still arguing. 'But I was *told* to turn. What for, if it's no use?'

'Stupid!' she hissed. 'Lest the Great One should crush you before it felt the power.' She hurried him on, fluttering like a twig in the wind, and the black dog followed. Fear is easily caught, and the back of Wirrun's neck prickled as they went; but when he looked back once the cave-mouth was dark and empty.

The dog now chose to behave as though Wirrun were really its master, and followed as a dog should. They rounded a bend in the gully, and suddenly it was late afternoon again, with the sun shining low over the sea ahead. The gully grew wider and shallower. Soon they came out of it onto level heathland, with the sea beyond it and the hills and ridges behind.

'There!' said Wirrun, greatly relieved. 'We got that over, and there's still time to eat before sunset. We'll be well on our way before night, and there's a good moon too.'

They lit a fire inside the lip of the gully, for privacy and for shelter from the wind. The dog lay down at a little distance to wait, and the Mimi, roasting her bush-rat, eyed it sullenly. Wirrun was surprised that she disliked the dog so much, but it was not a thing that could be helped. They ate and rested, listening to the sea.

They could not know that behind them, in the half-night of the gully, a shape had moved to the mouth of the cave; that it stood there now, humped and crooked, waiting for the sky to darken.

The young man and the rock-spirit put out their fire and found a wallaby pad through the heath. This they followed, the Mimi holding her cord again, until the track met a path that followed the line of the shore. Now they were walking south-west in the dazzle of the setting sun, with the sea on their left as it had been all along till the inlet blocked their way; with folded ridges running down on their right from the mountains farther back. The dog ran and hunted in the heath as it had in the forest, crossing their path from time to time. They met no Happy Folk on holiday, as Wirrun had feared they might. If they had been there earlier the Happy Folk must have gone back to camps and caravans and motels. There were only themselves and the dog, and back in the gully the Nargun, rocking its weight from limb to limb as it dragged its slow way from the cave.

The nearness of ridges hid the sunset, but its dazzle lay on the sea and its reflection in the south-east sky. And when the path lay across a valley's mouth Wirrun looked up the valley to mountains etched dark against crimson and gold. He had to look at them; and as the next ridge came nearer and began to intervene he had to look back, over his shoulder, to those farther mountains. It was then that something caught his eye that made him stop and turn.

'Look at that!' he said to the Mimi. 'See, back in the mountains where the sun's setting? There's a high bare face that looks south-west, about. See how it shines – it's caught the whole sunset! I never saw anything like that.'

The Mimi looked where he pointed and hissed sharply. 'You are right,' she said. 'I think you never did.' At the tone of her voice he looked again.

A fire was lit in the mountain, wonderful to see, glowing with pure red and gold. But Wirrun saw that this purity of colour was wrong, and the shadows were wrong. No other mountain shone like a mirror with such a fire, nor faded into grey and white.

'That's ice,' said Wirrun. 'And snow. Now what do I do? They've built it.' He stood helpless in the heath and stared at the far, high mountain glowing with a beauty that was wrong.

'What should you do?' said the Mimi when he had been staring for some time. 'Alone, you cannot destroy what the Ninya have built. You must bring the Eldest Nargun from the sea.'

'But no one can tell me where it is! And while I hunt it the Ninya can go on building! A whole mountain in a day – how much in a week? This Eldest Nargun better be good.'

'It has fought the ice before. Long ago it fought more than a handful of Ninya and a hillside of ice. You came for this, and did you not believe it? Have you played a children's game with the earth's old children?'

Wirrun walked a few steps, but it was no good. He had to swing round again to stand and look. 'I don't know if I did or not,' he said. 'I knew it was a big ice, and terrible; but I don't know if I knew what that meant. So fast! And what's gone wrong, any rate? They weren't going to build till they'd caught the Old Nargun. Does this mean they've caught it?'

The dog came by and nosed at his heels. The Mimi said, 'The spirits knew of the ice; they knew of the Eldest of Narguns; they did not know of its capture. But to know you must search.'

'No, no, *no*,' said Wirrun. 'I gotta think. This Nargun's not the only thing. There's the men too, the men from Mount Conner with the songs. Maybe I'm doing no good here. Maybe I should've waited and fetched the men.'

'You have fetched them. Do you not know they are coming?'

'I said I gotta think. . . . They'll come to Tilba-Tilba because that's in the papers now. Will this be in the papers? It's a lonely bit of coast, and that's one slope in the middle of a lot of others. Who's going to see it?'

The Mimi's old eyes searched the hills. 'It will be seen only from the coast, but far along that. It might have been chosen for this.'

'Far along the coast and out to sea. . . . Well, some-one's going to see it pretty soon, even if it stops where it is. Sooner if it spreads. I reckon the men'll come on here . . . only when? It takes a time for the papers to find out and print things. Any rate, I'm doing no good going on; I reckon they've caught the old Nargun. What else are they building ice for?' He dropped his pack on the heath and sat on it, frowning. The dog went by, trailing a wide circle round them.

With the dark eyes of the People, and from under the heavy brow of the People, Wirrun watched the fire on the mountain dying. The high, twisted line of the range was sharp against the gold sky. A dark drapery of forest fell over the claws of the ridges. Behind him the sea poured over and over on to the edge of the land.

Free me, for I must be free, said the land.

'I'm doing no good here either,' said Wirrun. 'I only know one thing to do.' He stood up and lifted his pack. The Mimi took the loop of cord again and walked with him.

The world darkened; only the sky still glowed. In from the sea came a flight of great white birds, screeching and wheeling over land high up in the red-gold light.

'Not hawks,' said Wirrun, his eyes drawn to them.

'They are the bird-spirits, the Yauruks who hunt whales,' said the Mimi.

The Yauruks swung towards that mountain whose fire had become a fading glow. Wirrun and the Mimi watched until a ridge had hidden them.

The path through the heath ran into others, and those into each other, and at last into a road. The heath turned into grassy slopes and thickets of trees. The dog came and went. Evening turned to night and the night was bright with moonlight. Wirrun found himself turning often to look into the moonlight. There was a sense of watchful waiting and of movement in shadows. He thought that some of the shadows had a shape: now a long-armed stooping shape that looked hairy in the moonlight, now a shape like a slender, graceful girl, once a blunt-muzzled rock-shape, squat and stealthy. These shadows watched.

'There's others here,' said Wirrun at last to the Mimi.

'They were always here,' she answered. 'We and not they are the travellers.' But Wirrun felt that the others travelled too, a company of shadows who journeyed with him.

He felt them most strongly in the scrub, for there all was shadow and the moonlight only made the shadows blacker. There he grew heavy with foreboding and in a little while found it hard to go on; step by step he walked with coldness and dread. Something pressed against his leg, warm and solid and quivering. Startled, he bent to touch it; it was the dog. It walked with him, close against his right leg.

On his left the Mimi spoke softly: 'We are one too many. A third walks with us.'

He thought for a moment that she meant the dog, but then he knew that beyond the dog something tall walked with them, close in darkness. He closed his hand on the power, but the coldness and dread stayed. He half-turned to the shape on his right, but the Mimi spoke quickly.

'Ask it no questions, only hold to the power. This one is not of the earth. It must be spoken to with care in the right way.'

'What is it, then?' whispered Wirrun.

'A Mrart. The spirit of one dead. It has evil powers, but you are protected. Walk on.'

They walked on in silence with the Mimi on Wirrun's left and the dog on his right. He kept his hand on the power, and the tall cold darkness walked with them. They reached the edge of the scrub and went forward into moonlight. A shifting of shadows followed, but the Mrart fell back into darkness.

'I didn't think much of that,' said Wirrun. The dog sat down to scratch fleas.

They all rested a little in the moonlight, listening to the one long word that the sea spoke over and over. Then they went on, close to the restless silver sea or farther back among trees as their road led them. Wirrun saw that the coast, which had been in two minds between south and west, now tended strongly west. He remembered Ko-in, far away north on another mountain and it seemed so long ago.

The coast was running almost due west and the moon reaching down to the western sea when their track ran down the bank of a river and stopped. There was no bridge or crossing in sight. For once they had been trapped, by a track that pretended to be a road. They turned north along the bank of the river in search of a crossing.

'We could waste a lot of time this way,' said Wirrun. 'If we don't find something soon we'll have to take to the water.'

The river lay wide and sleek in the moonlight, its banks shadowed by reeds and trees. The dog went nosing through long grass down the bank, and Wirrun heard it splashing at the edge.

'Better have a look,' he said to the Mimi. 'Low tide – might be shallow enough to walk across. You hang on to this tree while I go and look.'

He went down the bank, narrowing his eyes to look for the dog in the moonlight. He thought it was standing in shallow water: if that went far enough he supposed he might carry the Mimi across. He sat down by a bed of reeds to take off his shoes and try the depth. He could not see by moonlight that the water near the bank was clouded and milky.

Something heavy moved in the reeds. Red eyes glinted, strong jaws clamped and pulled. Wirrun yelled. The water rocked and gleamed as he was pulled under it.

The Bunyip had him.

Four

From habit Wirrun had clutched the power as those great jaws closed on his belt from behind. After that he did not clearly know what was happening to him: whether he was held by the power or by the Bunyip, whether he was carried under water or on the surface, whether his eyes were open or closed. Only a few things could he ever remember about that time: his own helpless stillness like a chicken in its shell; the inescapable strength that folded itself round him and bore him; the flutter of flowing water against his skin. And one other thing, a smell: of iodine and slime and decay, but mostly of age.

He did not know for how long he was carried, or how fast, or by what route. He thought it was sometimes in moonlight but mostly in black dark. It was moonlight when his senses revived for a moment and he found himself lying in shallow water near the mouth of a river. The Bunyip snortled and snuffled, sinking out of sight; then it was gone.

Wirrun raised himself on an elbow: he was lying on the shore of an inlet with his pack beside him. Across a stretch of quiet water he saw rocks and a constant leaping and dancing of waves. He dragged himself up the beach and lay dazed, but strangely warm and dry, till the Mimi found him.

When she had heard his yell and seen him dragged under the water, the Mimi had not wrung her hands or cried out in any distress. First she had felt for a wind. Finding none, she had climbed high into the tree and watched with round, cold, spirit-eyes. She saw what had taken Wirrun, and watched it up the river. She looked at once for the black dog: it was following up the bank. She looked at the clouds and the moon. Then she climbed down from the tree and considered the Ninya.

The Ninya were building ice on the mountain. Therefore the rocks on the coast would be safe. The Mimi found the nearest rock, blew on it, and disappeared into its winking dark.

The rocks easily took her to the coast and under the river's mouth. She travelled spirit-fast along the coast, sighting often from high rocks, watching always for the dog. It was certainly following Wirrun and she knew it must come to the coast, for she had no doubt of the Bunyip's purpose in carrying Wirrun off.

Her dark possum-eyes, trained in the darkness of rock, saw as only a Mimi could by moonlight. She saw the dog from time to time and tracked it for ten or twelve miles along the coast; and she saw much more than the dog.

She saw the possums themselves in their treetops; and the drifting shapes that journeyed in the shadows, still following Wirrun in their own ways and by their own paths. She saw one great lumbering shadow that rocked from limb to limb, that seemed to travel inch by inch yet travelled fast enough; and when she saw that shape the Mimi shivered. Once she saw the Yauruks fly over crying, their great wings turning from dark to silver as they banked in the moonlight and flew inland again. She watched them with questioning eyes, for she saw that they were one fewer than when they had come from the sea. Once, looking north along a ridge, she saw a mountain that gleamed as brilliant as the moon. The ice had not grown, she saw; it lay on that one mountain still.

The Yauruks that flew and cried in the moonlight

had learnt the true dread of the ice. They had feared it before as a terror from old times; but for ages now they had seen snow come and go on the mountains and remembered no ice worse than this. When, turning home from sea, they saw that mountain burn and gleam they saw only its beauty. Calling to each other in wonder they flew to the ice and circled over it, shrieking. So, full of joy, they flew into the Ninya's net of cold.

The Ninya watched with cold green eyes. A change had come over them. A few hours ago they had fumbled: they had foolishly trapped an ancient one and let it go to take revenge. But now they had built their trap for the Eldest Nargun.

They had gripped a mountain in ice and feathered it in snow, seen it glisten blue and green in the sun and turn to fire in the sunset. They had painted the delicate patterns of thaw and freeze; they were stronger and surer. They did not fumble now. At the right moment they curled a draught of cold round one of the Yauruks and drew it down.

It came falling like a spark, red in the sunset, into the cold and dying fire of the mountain. The others shrieked, hovered, and flew shrieking away. Later they flew back, calling and crying and searching, only to sweep off again in terror. And so they came and went all night, their wings black and silver by moonlight.

The fallen Yauruk plunged into a snowdrift, numbed and helpless with its wings lying limp on the snow. Now it had fallen out of the sunset and there was no fire on the mountain, only a white cold and a fading light. The cold gripped and tightened till the Yauruk gave a hoarse quark of pain. It saw green eyes above it, watching. The men of frost stood there, the Ninya. One of them spoke in creaking words.

'When will you feel the sun again?'

'Sun – ' quarked the Yauruk.

'When will you reach for the wind and fly back to your people?'

The Yauruk's wings trembled on the snow as a dog's paws tremble when it dreams of cats.

'You must speak before you fly. Tell us what we ask.'

'Can't speak,' cawed the Yauruk. 'Choking.'

The white sparkling figure moved its hand and the others drew back. The cold that gripped the Yauruk loosened a little: it breathed more easily, and after a time lifted its head and folded its wings around it in the snow. The tall white Ninya watched under heavy brows.

'Do you know the Eldest of Narguns?' it asked at last. 'The most ancient of Narguns, the one with the power of fire?'

'It calls up no fire now,' said the Yauruk, shivering. 'It crouches in the sea.'

'In the sea?' The Ninya's green eyes sharpened and narrowed. 'Where in the sea? Do you speak with knowledge or pass on the tales of others?'

The Yauruk shook its wings impatiently and jerked its head. 'Is the sea not our business? Do we not hunt and herd there? No one knows which rock is the Nargun. It has crouched among rocks from age to age till all have forgotten which is the Ancient One. But the rocks, and their place on the shore, we have always known.'

'Then,' said the frost-man, watching sharply, 'you must show us the place. Or you will never fly in the sun again but see it only through ice.'

'And if I do not fly in the sun,' said the Yauruk irritably, 'I cannot show you the place. There are those who would ask for help more politely.'

The leader of the Ninya frowned. 'And there are those who would refuse it when the ice-builders ask. You are no fighter, my friend. You love the ice?'

The Yauruk was surprised. No such question had occurred to it, and it thought little of it now. 'I know ice and snow,' it said shortly. 'Pretty stuff, but not for lying in. Unfreeze me and my people and I shall circle in the sky three times above the Eldest Nargun. You may see us and be answered.'

'That will do well. But there is no sun now. Night comes; and by moonlight one rock or one Yauruk looks very like another. You shall wait here, and the snow shall make you a warm nest for lying in. Tomorrow all questions will be answered.'

The Yauruk flounced its feathers but it did no good. That night it stayed a prisoner in the snow while its people swept over and away; and it saw them and heard them calling as the Mimi did.

The Mimi, seeing the glitter of ice and the Yauruks crying over it, noticed that one was missing; but she had no time to brood over these signs or wonder what they meant. She read no warning that the Ninya might have won their race for the Eldest Nargun; there was only a little uneasiness at the edge of her mind. The Mimi's part was to help and support Wirrun of the People. She watched for the black dog that was free to run without fear of the wind and to track Wirrun; and she followed along the shore as it directed.

The moon dropped behind the mountains, and in a grey light from the sea the Mimi looked from a headland of rock along the coast. She saw a long beach with the low tide surging in and out, and beyond it another headland above a broad shelf of rock that the sea fringed with foam and spray. She looked landward, and saw that between herself and the rocky shelf a hidden opening led into a long inlet; and on the shore of this inlet the black dog was nosing at a long dark shape. The dog had found Wirrun. While she watched he sat up as if he were waking from sleep, and half patted the dog and half pushed it away.

The Mimi travelled the last stretch in a flash. By the time Wirrun had recovered his senses and could look about with seeing eyes the dog lay at its usual distance on one side of him; the Mimi sat on a rock on the other side, staring landward.

He looked at them in the grey light with the sound of the sea in his ears, and he could hardly believe in either of them. He was still dazed with the power and speed of Bunyip; the smell of slime and age was still in his nostrils, and his skin remembered the silken plucking of water. That the dog should have followed after Tu-ru-dun – that the Mimi should have come over wind-bare country or through Ninya-haunted rocks – this made his adventure feel for the first time like a dream. Then he saw the intentness of the Mimi's stare, with something like fear in it. He put dreams aside and asked a wakeful question.

'What's up?' said Wirrun, following the Mimi's stare. There was only a rising shoreline of grass with a shadowing of trees behind.

'Close your hand on the magic,' she whispered. 'One comes from the trees.'

He held the power and felt it throbbing, but he could see nothing but shore and shadows – and movement, a stealthy stirring, in the shadows. And at last he saw that what moved was rock: a great rock, moving stealthily under the trees. As he looked he saw for a moment a beast, squat and crooked on stumpy limbs, with dark eye-shadows and a rough blunt muzzle.

'It's the one from the cave,' he whispered. 'A Nargun.' The Mimi nodded, staring.

The monster moved forward again, stiff and old and slow. It seemed not to see them, though the dog went towards it with raised hair and Wirrun held his breath. The Nargun only gazed with empty eyes beyond the inlet, out to the rocks where the sea foamed. It lifted its blunt muzzle and gave a cry: '*Nga-a-a!*' There was no other sound while that cry lay over the sea. The leaping waves stood still, there was no breathing, till the cry faded.

The Nargun waited till then. It waited till the sea sounded and a bird moved and Wirrun stirred. Then it drew secretly back into the shadow of trees. Nothing had answered it.

The Mimi watched dark-eyed and still. Wirrun waited

until she stirred, then whispered, 'What is it? What does it want?'

'Hold to the magic,' she whispered back. 'It calls to the Eldest. It cries out, one beast to another.'

Wirrun faced her. He looked stern, but the Mimi knew the eyes of the People. 'The Eldest?' he said tensely. 'Out there?'

'Did not the ancient one of the waters bring you here? Your journey ends at this place. The First of the Narguns is among those rocks.'

Wirrun turned his gaze to the tossing of foam and spray beyond the inlet. Which rock? The light warmed, and he could see them at the nearer end of the shelf. They stood humped and crouched and jaggedly erect, leaned one to another or loomed alone. There was a day's work out there to search and watch among them, and then perhaps another day's.

There was a peach-gold light in the eastern sky, and a single cloud lit up. The sun was coming. The rocks stood dark and mysterious against this light. Which rock?

'And the tide's coming in,' said Wirrun. 'It'll be pretty wild out there when it's high.'

'And look to the hills,' said the Mimi.

Wirrun looked. The massed darkness of trees and nearer ridges hid most of the hills, but there was a glimpse of farther hills with gold on their eastern slopes. One of them flashed with fire.

'The ice,' said the Mimi. 'Whatever moves on these rocks here, the Ninya may watch it.'

'I gotta think,' said Wirrun.

She nodded. It was time for thinking, and after that for eating. She moved quietly away, throwing the dog a dark look as she avoided it, and began to make a driftwood fire.

Wirrun sat gazing at the rocks. The sun rose, sending its light along the coast, and the eastern side of each rock shone so that they seemed to face that way. A flight of great white birds came down from the hills and circled above them, shrieking. He recognized them: they were Yauruks. The Mimi watched them uneasily and saw that their number was whole again, but Wirrun did not see her frown. He watched the Yauruks circle again and again, and fly off to sea. Then he gazed at the rocks.

Which rock? They stood on guard together fronting the sea, but one had movement and a hidden beast-shape; one was a First Thing, and had seen the land in the making, and was mighty in size and power and held the secret of fire. How would such a one receive Wirrun, a stranger, with his little power that it had seen in the making? Were there songs he should know? Ko-in had not said so; but Ko-in had confessed that he was no teacher and had put the power into Wirrun's hands. And what else had Ko-in said? *I have said everything, for I have said that there must be the People.*

Wirrun stood up and stretched and looked for the Mimi. She was sitting by her fire, absorbed in it as she always was since her long days without fire. He walked gratefully to the warmth and sat beside it too. He was cold – yet in spite of his journey with Mu-ru-bul he and his pack were both dry. The Mimi had nothing roasting on the fire, and the pack yielded only potatoes. He put enough for both in the coals.

'Just as well the journey ends in this place,' he said wryly. 'But we'll be all right soon. When we've eaten we've gotta go and find the People.'

'More People,' said the Mimi. 'Have you not trouble enough with People?'

'Trouble is right – I oughta be at Tilba-Tilba to bring those People here, but I gotta go to the settlement down the coast and fetch those People to the Eldest. There oughta be two of me. Only there's not.'

'The ice does not grow; the first People will be in time. And for the Eldest of Narguns, do you not have your power?'

'I'm not a man to use the power right, not for the big

things. And the Eldest is a First Thing, and there might be songs. Any rate, while I look for it in that lot down there the Ninya can watch me and make a sudden ice. These People might be able to go straight to it without bringing the Ninya.'

The Mimi cat-sneezed. It was not, as he thought, because she resented the People. It was because when he spoke of bringing the Ninya she had an uneasy feeling that they had already been brought.

Five

In his walkings about the country, meeting others of the People and talking to them, Wirrun had heard about much that he had never seen. He knew about the settlements in these parts, and his maps showed him the road to the nearest. It lay some way inland; they would have to find their way to it by rough tracks and across country. They set out westward, he and the Mimi walking together as they had for so many miles. The dog followed or led or tracked in the scrub, but was never far away.

Though he had thought about it and decided what to do, Wirrun was far from certain that he was right. Questions ran about like mice in his head. He did not know any of the men of this settlement: how would they receive him and his story? A stranger who came to them talking about Narguns . . . but at least they must know of the ice. Would they have seen the white mountain in their own country? He thought that the newspapers would not have news of it yet. That meant that the men from Mount Conner would not know either, and they could be near by now. He pictured them, in some truck or car battered by the long journey, reaching Tilba-Tilba and stopping there, baffled. There would be Happy Folk having picnics all over the hill, cars lining the road, and maybe a tourist coach or two. . . .

Beside him the Mimi was also darkly silent. She could not help her shy dislike of all people; she had to hide from them, even though they could not see her. She had grown used to Wirrun and their quiet journey among the spirits – but now there would be many strangers and a different sort of action, by the People rather than the spirits. Her part was almost over. Added to that, she had caught another glimpse of the Ninya's snow-clad mountain and it seemed to her that it was thawing. It was strange that the Ninya should have built that large ice in one place and no farther; it was even more strange that having built it they should now let it melt. Had they built for some purpose, and was it now achieved? The Yauruks came into her mind again, and she saw them circling over the rocks where the Eldest Nargun hid.

So it was that the Mimi and Wirrun, taking a short cut through forest, had their minds on other things. Neither of them saw the nets laid across their path: nets, slyly hidden under leaves, made of bark-fibre cords and meant to entangle their feet. They did not see, but the dog saw; it was its business to see.

The dog had known what to expect, for it belonged to this country. Circling about them in the forest in search of such dangers, it came back to the path ahead of the walkers and knew it could not stop them before they reached these nets. It did the only thing it could: it ran ahead on the path and was itself entangled in the wicked nets.

Wirrun stopped in his tracks. One moment the path ahead had been clear and empty – in the next it was a leaping, twisting mesh of cord that tangled and held the dog. 'Cripes!' he cried, running forward to the rescue. Then he stopped dead again. *'Cripes!'*

For there was no black dog in the nets. Only a blue-tongue lizard scuttled through the mesh, quite free. Wirrun turned a blank face to the Mimi.

'It is a spirit-dog,' she said shortly. 'Or a spirit-lizard. It has guarded you since you entered this country, not trusting me. You must have seen.'

'Seen?' Wirrun shook his head, dazed. 'No, I didn't. Too stupid. But now I see how it followed the Bunyip.'

'It came between you and the Bagini with claws; and

between you and the Mrart from the dead, and twice between you and the Nargun of the cave; and it led you to the place where Tu-ru-dun waited. But what it is you could not see, for it is a thing without shape and takes what shape it will.'

The bluetongue lizard was now a boy of the People. 'I am Yabon,' it said. 'Often my kind have helped the People of this country, and why should I not help one whom the land sends against the ice? One who carries the secret stone of earth and sky? It is true I have many shapes.'

'I'm grateful,' said Wirrun. 'It seems you've helped all right. What was it this time? What are all these nets?'

'They need not worry you,' said the Yabon, 'but you should watch. Watch always, on all sides, as the dog did. The People of this country know the paths and the spirits; they do not walk alone here as you did. The Thinan-malkia, who spread nets to trap men that they may catch and eat them, know of your journey. They have seen the power you wear and know they may not take you. Yet it is hard for them when you walk their paths alone. They would not harm you, but they could not help spreading the nets.'

Wirrun listened absently, for out of his worries an idea had come. 'Is it true you can take any shape you like?' he asked. 'Any shape at all?'

'Do you need a shape?' asked the Yabon with a smile.

'I do that,' said Wirrun. 'I need another one of me. That's if he wouldn't mind taking a message.'

The boy before him grew up at once and became Wirrun: in his own shirt and shorts soiled by the journey and with his own pack slung on his shoulder. It was like seeing his mirror-self standing on the path. At first there was something a little wrong about the chin, but as he looked it wavered as if the mirror were flawed and became his own chin, with the right amount of unshaven down upon it.

'What can Wirrun of the People do for Wirrun of the

People?' asked the Yabon in Wirrun's voice. They grinned at each other.

'Do you know Tilba-Tilba?' Wirrun asked. 'The Wa-tha-gun-darl place?'

'I can find it.'

'The Nyols might help. There's a hill, and the highway going past. There'll be People coming on that road any time now, looking for these Ninya that make the ice. They come from a long way off, to sing the Ninya back home to their own caves. No more ice if the men get here in time.'

'Then the men must have help,' said the Yabon gravely.

'They can use it. They'll go to Tilba-Tilba because they'll know the ice has been there, but they mightn't know where to come next. They'll be looking for me and there might be one that knows me. I want you to be me, and bring the men on here. Take them to the ice on the mountain.'

The Mimi stirred. 'I saw the mountain as we came,' she said, 'and it seems the ice is melting. It was more grey and not so white, a small change that a man could not see. It may be that the Ninya have gone from there.'

Wirrun stared. 'Gone? What are they playing at, then? Building a big one like that and letting it melt?'

The Mimi looked troubled. 'I do not know. But it may be that they too have found the Eldest of the Narguns. The bird-spirits, the Yauruks, circled the place at first sun. It may have been a sign.'

'The Yauruks!' cried Wirrun in disbelief. 'Helping the ice? They wouldn't even talk about it!'

She looked at him sadly, for she knew that of all the spirits they had met the Yauruks had warmed him most. She had tried to explain, but how could a man understand? 'Who knows where the wind blows?' she said. 'If you too had asked they would have told you. At sunset the Yauruks flew to the mountain and came away one fewer. All night they flew over crying, and this morning they flew again with a full number. It may be that one was trapped by the Ninya.'

Wirrun shifted his feet, frowning. Trapped by the Ninya, its great white wings stiff and frozen. . . . The Yabon waited patiently, and in a moment he turned to it. 'Bring the men to the place where we lit our fire this morning. Any rate, it's better that way. We don't know when either lot will turn up, but that's where the Eldest is. We'll meet there.'

'I go,' said the Yabon, and went very swiftly. Wirrun did not see it go. He was startled, even though he knew how fast the spirits could travel.

He and the Mimi went on, not speaking but watching more carefully as the Yabon had warned them. In the daylight they saw no shifting shadows like those that had travelled with them last night. Wherever they looked only the silent forest waited. Yet there was always a sense of hidden eyes following.

'There's others still, no doubt of that,' said Wirrun, and the Mimi's eyes turned this way and that.

They came out of the forest and found the road that the map had promised. Two cars passed them almost at once, and three more before they reached the first bend. Round the bend they came on a party of hikers who argued loudly, waving notebooks at each other. The Mimi's eyes darted about restlessly as if she were looking for a way to escape. Even to Wirrun the hikers were more disturbing than the hidden eyes in the forest, for those watched quietly and knew what they saw and were part of it. He hoped that when there was singing to be done no Happy Folk would be there to listen and argue and wave tape-recorders.

He and the Mimi skirted the edge of a village and followed a track to the settlement. The little box-cottages scattered about looked like those on other settlements. The Mimi hung back, looking obstinate and shy.

'They can't even see you,' Wirrun argued; but she

180

dropped the cord and stood back, and he had to give in. 'Oh, *all* right. Is there a rock or something where you can wait? I'll pick you up on my way out.'

The Mimi gave her sneezing snort. 'I am not your digging stick that you pick up as you go. I go my own way and meet you again when I choose.'

'But hang on! You can't walk out on me yet! These blokes might think I'm mad – they mightn't want to help! We're not finished yet. We don't know what we might have to do, you and me, and how can I get on without you?'

The Mimi stood tall and thin and proud. 'Have I not brought you safely this long way, as the spirit of the mountain said? Have I not done what the Mimi cannot do? And while you need this Mimi will I leave you to a Yabon, a thing without shape?'

'Not you,' said Wirrun, much relieved. 'You're an ice-fighter. I'll see you, then.' And he walked through the gateway to the settlement, leaving her there. When he looked back over his shoulder she was gone.

There were not many People to be seen on the settlement: three or four children playing under trees, a woman coming from a garden, another leaning in a doorway. Wirrun looked for old men and saw none. There were two of middle age, sitting in the shade with their backs against a house-wall and talking together. He walked towards them. They stopped talking and sat watching him come. Even when he was quite close they did not speak, but looked up at him and waited.

Wirrun spoke politely, telling them his name and where he came from and they nodded silently, still waiting. He opened his mouth to speak again wondering what he could say to make them sure of him: how to save the time of slow consideration and take a short cut to their belief. 'You got a thing here called a Yabon?' he found himself asking.

They looked at each other and waited. So he told them how the Yabon had seemed to be a dog, and had brought him through the country and saved him from the nets of the Thinan-malkia. He made it a joke against himself, acting his shock when the dog became a lizard and a boy. And their faces relaxed and they laughed softly.

'He's a good bloke, that Yabon,' they said.

'He is that,' said Wirrun. 'He's still helping, and I can do with it. I don't reckon he'd mostly help a stranger, would he? But he knew the land sent me. They all know that now. The word's got round.' And seeing that they looked at him differently and waited to hear, he squatted on the ground in front of them and told his tale.

It took some time, even cutting it as short as he could. He left out much of the early part but told of the spirits he had met in this country, for by these they could judge the rightness of his story. Their eyes deepened when he showed them the power, and he saw that they knew it. They grinned and looked fierce when they heard of the great rock-shape from the cave and of Mu-ru-bul, Bunyip. And at some time in the telling he saw that the two men had become ten. Several younger men and two or three older ones had come from gardens or cottages to hear.

They had not known the ice was so near and looked at each other when they heard of it; but they had known of it from farther off and wondered.

'I seen it coming,' said one wisely, and the others nodded.

They nodded again, solemnly, to hear that the men of Mount Conner were coming to sing the Ninya home; but Wirrun saw that they were uneasy when he spoke of the Eldest Nargun. At first he thought this was because he was a stranger and not a proper man, but he found that it was for another reason.

'This Eldest Nargun,' he said. 'I know which rocks but I don't know which one. And I don't know how to wake it up and make it help. It's a First Thing – are there songs for it? It's your business, this Nargun.'

They looked with shifty eyes and at last confessed that

they did not know any more than he did. They were uneasy because it was their business and yet they could not help.

'These Narguns,' they said, apologizing, 'we don't make no songs for 'em, we just keep outa their way. But that old one, now. . . .' They looked at each other, worried.

'Old Johnny Wuthergul,' said one of the older men suddenly. 'Where's he at?'

The whole group brightened at once and began to remind each other.

'He knows that old Nargun. His father told him, and his father before that. He could talk to it.'

'It was like it was their business, that family. Or they took it for theirs.'

'Up past Bairnsdale, old Johnny is, in the hills.'

'He's old, but he could talk to it.'

Now they knew what to do and were light-hearted and brisk. There was the Holden: Fred would drive it up past Bairnsdale, and Butcher would go with him to talk to old Johnny Wuthergul and bring him back. Early tomorrow, they'd be back, if someone had money for the petrol. They saw that Wirrun was worried by the loss of time and set themselves to deal with that.

There was the utility truck as well as the Holden: Percy would drive that back to the inlet with Wirrun, and the rest of the men would come too. Between them they'd keep an eye on the place, and sort of watch out for the Eldest of Narguns, till old Johnny could be brought to talk to it. They'd work out some way of looking after it. And first they'd have a good feed, and make a collection of blankets and axes and ropes and beer, and of anything else that might be useful for a night out guarding a Nargun.

They carried Wirrun off to wash and be fed while an old grey Holden, its doorsills lacy with rust, drove through the gate-way and headed for Bairnsdale.

6

The Eldest Nargun

One

The Ninya's trap, the mountain-slope of ice and snow, had stood high above the coast for a day. It had risen pure and fierce in sunlight, grey and menacing in shade; at sunrise and sunset its cold fire glittered, calling a challenge to the Eldest of Narguns. But the Eldest did not come. It lay in the sea and sometimes dreamed of fire, and never saw the fierce white stinging snow.

In these days the Eldest did not look to land for it was weary, weighted with age and power. It knew the land in every grain of its rock: the molten pouring, the long twisting and shaping, the grinding by wind and water, the hammer-strokes of sun and frost. It knew life, that warm and secret decay that crept over the land. The land was in the Nargun and of it.

Now it had set its might against the sea and the sea still rode against it. After many ages this battle was not over. It was a heavy thing to be the Eldest; to hide the secret of fire, to nurture an anemone and a coast. Sunlight lit the ripples and the shadow of a bird passed over. There came the first crash and foam of the new tide, and the Nargun spread its weight and held fast. It remembered dawn, and a cry from the shore that it answered, and this warmed it. But it did not see the mountain where the snow was turning brittle and the ice had begun to melt.

The Ninya had waited, calmer and stronger by the hour. They had waited for a great, slow power with the might and endurance of rock, to sidle from the shadows and call up red fire to destroy them. They waited to catch it in their sudden trap of ice. But the Eldest did not come.

They saw sunrise light their mountain and released the captured Yauruk. They watched a flight of Yauruks circling above a shelf of rock. Then they withdrew into twilit caverns where the wind howled again and the frost grew. They left their mountain to thaw.

Their leader was proud and boastful. 'Have I not led you well? From the far centre of the land, out to its edge and down its long coast, till we stand above the very place of the Eldest!'

'Ah,' they said. 'But why did it not come against us?'

'Who knows the ways of a First Thing? It may be that the Nargun saw the trap and would draw us down to it. No matter, for now we know where it lies. We need not wait for it to come rock-slow. We may go wind-fast and snap it in ice.'

'Ah,' they said. 'But in the sea. Perhaps we must think with another ear, for the sea is slow freezing.'

The leader frowned. 'It is slow. But the power of the Ninya has grown with freedom and use; we are few but a mighty power. Have you not learnt your strength? Let us see this place and plan with care, and in two days the land is ours.'

They nodded and thought. And while they planned, the old utility truck from the settlement rattled along the road.

Six of the men sat on the floor in the back, talking and laughing with excitement and singing snatches of songs. Wirrun sat in the cabin with Percy and Waratah, the two to whom he had first spoken. Percy drove, and all three thought in silence about guarding the Eldest Nargun until old Johnny arrived to talk to it.

The utility truck could not take the short cut through the scrub as Wirrun and the Mimi had done. It had to follow the main road through the nearest town and then find its way by secondary roads and bush tracks to the inlet. In the town they stopped to add to their mixed collection of supplies, for they had to provide for a night at the inlet with two meals and an indefinite number of snacks.

The men in the back jumped out to go in different directions: for more beer, more sausages, potatoes, butter. Waratah wound his window down and shouted after them.

'Kerosene!'

They paused to look back at him and think. The Ninya dreaded the Eldest Nargun for its power of fire; therefore fire would be a useful weapon against the Ninya. They nodded, understanding about the kerosene, and counted their money again and exchanged sums. There would have to be fewer sausages.

The three in the cabin of the utility waited for the shoppers to return and looked idly at the town. Wirrun thought it looked like an ants' nest. He found himself frowning and watching with attention: there were so many knots of people talking excitedly. Those who walked on the pavements hardly ever passed with a nod or a few words; instead they stopped and drew together like ants meeting on a trail. They were disturbed about something, he was sure. He got out of the truck and went into a newsagent's to buy the local paper.

He stood on the pavement and checked it carefully. There was no story of ice on a mountain, or any other exciting event that he could see. Yet the newsagent behind the counter was watching slyly while Wirrun read; and the nearest knot of people was silent and watching too. Something had happened: something that should have been in the paper and was not. Wirrun thought he knew what it was.

They had found the ice and snow on the nearby mountain – more of it than had been found anywhere else. They had decided not to let the news escape in case it was bad for business. It would be like the Happy Folk to keep bad news secret when they could not explain or deal with it. They would be on the watch, making trouble or playing games. Wirrun went back to his seat in the utility truck, still frowning. The eyes of the towns-people followed him. So did a pair of passive Inlander eyes.

George Morrow's tractor was repaired now. Most of his gear and his shopping was packed in the truck and now he was having the truck filled with petrol. Tonight he would load the tractor, and early tomorrow morning begin the long drive home, unless it turned out to be worth waiting for another day. News of the ice would be worth it, for when the land behaves in a wrong and mysterious way an Inlander pays attention. George Morrow was still wondering and waiting: for some serious attempt to find out about the ice, or better still for someone who already knew things that Happy Folk and Inlanders did not.

On his last day in town he saw and heard the excite-ment of the Happy Folk and only smiled tight-lipped. He saw a shabby utility truck loaded with the People and only thought they seemed in a brisk good humour. He saw Wirrun studying the newspaper and frowning at the townsfolk, and he began to watch. Was it perhaps odd that in this town only the People seemed brisk and in good humour?

He saw the shoppers come back with supplies, and with four cans of kerosene; and he listened and heard a few strange words about ice and fire. He did not dismiss the words merely because they were strange, for George had the great advantage of knowing how little he knew. 'If you don't know,' he would have said, 'there's no point in arguing.' So he simply paid for his petrol and waited again until the utility truck drove off. Then he drove after it.

In the back of the utility the men still laughed and sang. They noticed that a tabletop truck kept appearing and dropping back behind them, but they took no notice until it followed them off the main road towards the coast. Then they fell silent and watchful until it disappeared again, and laughed and sang all the louder in relief. A white man would have been badly out of place while the People looked after the business of the country, but the inlet they were looking for was a lonely one. They were pleased and not surprised that the truck was going somewhere else. They did not consider the fact that on these roads George Morrow could track them by their dust trail which hung in the air and hid his dust from them.

In the cabin, Percy and Waratah had also silently watched the truck and relaxed when it disappeared. Now they waited for Wirrun to give them a lead about the work ahead. Waratah had already made a suggestion by shouting 'Kerosene!' It was up to Wirrun to take it further. He could feel them waiting.

He said, 'Fires look like the best idea, all right. We want to get a look at this place; if we can put fires right round it we might keep the ice from getting through. There's one thing bothers me, though.'

They looked and waited.

'Well,' said Wirrun, 'it means keeping big fires going till the old man comes – keeping 'em up all night.'

'We got the utility,' said Percy, 'and nine men. And there's scrub close handy. We'll keep the wood up to 'em.'

'We'll do that all right. Only they'll show up for miles. Every man and his dog'll turn up to have a look, and there'll be some stupid thing. Fires out of season – danger to the public – trespass – something.'

'That bay, she's quiet all right,' said Waratah. 'Nobody round there. Lonely roads, and rough. Couple of ridges cutting her off most sides. Nobody to see.'

'Yes,' said Wirrun. 'Only you can see the ice from there. And the way that town looked, I reckon they've heard about the ice. They'll be up and down that mountain like bees in a bottle, trying to work out if it's there or not. They'll look down on the fires from there.'

The two older men thought about this. Percy made a half-hearted attempt to miss a washed-out section of the road; the ute bounced and banged; the men in the back roared and thumped with their hands reproachfully on the cabin roof. Percy said, 'Wait and see. Get more men and a few dogs if we need 'em.'

Wirrun was still worried but he supposed this was the best that could be said. He hoped that while his small army defended the land against the Ninya it could fight unhampered.

When they reached it the place did seem quiet and lonely enough, folded away among its ridges. Only one rough track ran east and west across the head of the inlet. Percy abandoned it and drove bumping over open ground to the mouth of the stream, near the place where Wirrun had lain before dawn while the Bunyip sank into clouded water. He showed them the place and they stood around it in silence, trying to grasp that their old and terrible monster had stood with them this time against the ice. Then they left Sam, one of the younger men, in charge of the ute while they walked down the inlet.

It ran south, long and narrow, bent in the middle like a bottle spoilt in the making, with a narrow mouth for the neck of the bottle. The eastern bank was low and scrub-covered, with a long spit of sand closing in at the bottleneck. The western bank was a grassy hill ending in a snub-nose of rock that looked across the narrow mouth to the sandspit opposite. It was beyond this headland that foam and spray always flew, where the great boulders stood jagged or humped and the Yauruks had circled and cried at sunrise. Wirrun and the men walked that way, along the green hillside of the inlet's western shore.

Soon they stood on the hill-top where it fell suddenly down. They could see, across the eastern sandspit, waves rolling in to a long white beach; and below a smashing and leaping of waves on a shelf of rock that reached out into the sea. The tide was coming in again. Skeins of water ran in channels over the shelf, eddied into rockpools, and sucked away again. At the edge of the shelf stood the company of guardian rocks. The swells broke over them, were shouldered aside, came leaping between and foamed across the shelf.

'One of 'em,' said Percy, 'is that old Nargun. Which?'

Wirrun was looking straight down, to the inmost edge of the shelf where it met the hill. 'Wonder how far up the tide comes? We'll have to go down and see.'

They looked at him. One of the younger men said, 'Can't we put the fires up here?'

'No fear,' said Wirrun. 'I hope we can do better any rate. There'll be caves through under here. Them Ninya'll just pass underneath, through the hill, and out down there to the Nargun. We won't even know they're through.'

They shrugged. There was going to be a lot of wood-carting. He saw what they were thinking.

'We don't have to come up here and then down. There'll be a way round at the bottom.'

They climbed down the hillside to the shelf. The way was almost as steep as a cliff, with sandy trails dropping between teeth of rock or past boulders draped in pigface. At the foot was a shallow crescent of sand and then the landward edge of the shelf. This sloped downward to the sea. A fringe of damp driftwood, old seaweed and shells showed the line of the high tide a yard or so out from the sand. From time to time a wash of foam came racing up the rocks towards it. The hillface, like a wall that dipped and rose again, stretched right across the shelf from side to side. The men stood looking at it, pointing and discussing.

'We can do it any rate,' said Wirrun at last. 'That's if we don't mind work. We can't go farther out or we'll lose our fires at high tide, but this oughta work. Four big fires, right across under the hill, should cut 'em off by land, and I don't reckon they'd try it from the sea. We could do with more fires if we had more men, but four's as much as we can manage. Better get going.'

'Not much time,' said Waratah, nodding.

They made their way back round the base of the hill, finding how near the utility might come and where they should build their wood-heap. At best they would have to carry firewood for some distance, and to the two farthest fires a long way; but the young men thought they might find a track to the opposite side of the hill and build a second wood-heap for those fires. They went back to the utility and explained it all to Sam over a can of beer. Then the work began.

They drove the utility slowly into the eastern scrub with men scouting alongside as it went. When someone shouted the driver stopped and the men converged; there would be a log, fallen branches, or dead standing timber. The axes barked at each other and the chips flew. It was not neat axework – as soon as the timber could be handled it was loaded into the utility. It was surprising how quickly they had their first load. Three men drove back to find or make the best track they could and un-load the timber. The other six worked on with their axes to have a second load ready when the ute came back.

When he heard it coming Wirrun leaned on his axe and waited. He was wondering when to detach two men to start the fires, but he had to stop and listen to the utility. There was something wrong: its motor muttered against a deeper roar. It came through the scrub with Percy driving and the other two sitting beside him, all three heavy-browed and sober. He walked to meet them.

'There's a bloke coming,' said Percy. 'Says he'll help.'

Wirrun's heart sank. He'd been waiting for Happy Folk bent on trouble or games. It seemed that it was to be games. The heavier motor came on: a tabletop truck. The white driver's face peered from under a felt hat. It was a cheerful face with settled eyes and a mouth that could tighten easily. Wirrun's eyes narrowed. The truck stopped and he went to it with his hand on the power.

'Day,' said the driver briefly. 'Thought you could use some help. Better truck for it. Good to see men working like that.'

Wirrun's own lips tightened, for in that last remark was the echo of old wars. He said, 'We can do with help if it's meant,' and George Morrow flicked a small smile. He had been rebuked. Wirrun went back to the men who watched in a hostile group.

'That's an Inlander,' he pointed out. 'They don't play games, and the truck's what we need, and there's nine of us. We could use him.'

The sun was already behind the western mountains. They accepted George Morrow, but silently. They loaded the ute a second time and sent it back, its three men to stay on the shelf to lay fires and stack wood at hand. The rest of them worked on with Morrow's truck, from scrub to forest.

The truck carried four times as much at each load, and the wood could be loaded with less chopping. It made short work of hills and rocks and rough ground. George Morrow drove it with flair, and took it closer to each end of the shelf than the utility could have gone. He used an axe as willingly as he drove and made no more double-edged remarks. If bitterness lay between him and the men of the People, for that afternoon they let it lie while they dealt with the realities of the land and shared a beer when it was needed. By dark they had built great wood-heaps at each end of the shelf and had their four fires well started. The men of the People nodded their silent thanks; the Inlander nodded goodnight and drove off up the inlet. Tension broke, and the young men were noisy with laughter again and forgot to listen to the departing truck. Only Wirrun, Percy and Waratah heard that George Morrow had not gone far. They lowered their brows and said nothing.

The row of bonfires reddened the dusk, and the falling tide swept hissing out of the gloom as if it would carry them away. There was wood stacked beside each fire to last until moonlight; the tired men had time to eat and rest. They dragged a small fire from the edge of a big one and sat round it to grill their sausages. Wirrun took his chance to wander off a little way, for at sunset when the fires were new and the smell of kerosene mixed with the smell of the sea he had seen the Mimi.

She had been sitting on a boulder on the hillside, gazing with wonder at the bonfires. He went that way and sat by the boulder and waited. She was there almost at once.

'Good fires?' said Wirrun smugly.

She hunched her narrow shoulders. 'Those who make them have the right. The fires will draw eyes.'

It was Wirrun's turn to shrug. He too was afraid of that. 'I've brought you a hot potato,' he said.

'I have eaten crab,' she said with dignity, and seized the potato. As she broke it open she added, 'A crab is a poor thing.'

They sat eating together, listening to the dark beyond the fires. 'Are there others about?' Wirrun asked.

'There are many. The shadows go to and fro. The wind is loud in the rocks, and the cold comes.'

'Where will you sleep then?'

'In a boulder, as you have shown me.'

Wirrun looked out to the edge of the shelf, where black shapes stood against the shine of moving water. 'And your eyes can't see, and your ears can't hear, which one out there is the Nargun?'

She looked through the leaping firelight and through the dusk beyond. 'None that my eyes can see or my ears can hear,' she told him. 'But the Eldest, the First One, is there.'

Two

The night grew dark and cool, but the four great fires kept it back. Wirrun thought that from a distance it must look like a bushfire out of control across the hill, and he worried again. The sea rumbled angrily. The stars leaned close, waiting for the moon. The fires threw their red heat from each to each, and up in great leaps of red and gold to the stars. The dark water caught and lost the firelight.

At first the men went to and fro from fire to fire without any sort of rule, wiping the sweat from their faces and thankful for the coolness of night beyond the fires. But almost at once Wirrun, for whom this day had been long and hard, fell asleep against a warmed rock. They put a folded blanket under him for softness and left him there. Soon five other men lay on blankets, sleeping or trying to sleep, so that they could take their turns at fire-watching later in the night. Three at a time would do the work.

Up near the head of the inlet George Morrow sat watching too. He was not sure what was going on down there, but whatever it was it flowed out of the land and it ought to be given a go. By good luck, whatever George needed for a long night out was stored in the cabin of the truck, ready for an early start for home. He had simply driven to a convenient point, parked the truck in a screen of trees, loaded himself with useful gear, and trudged heavily back.

George felt as Wirrun and the Mimi did: the fires would

draw eyes. There would be Happy Folk along sooner or later, importantly anxious to discover things and put them right. They would be better off minding their own magics and leaving the People to get on with theirs. George intended to do what he could.

He walked slowly back along the track, studying it and the headland and the glow of fires behind. He found the point at which, by walking off the track a few yards to the east, the first glimpse of fires and figures could be seen. Anyone who wanted to see would step aside at this point; and he would see that these were men of the People working at fires. Gratefully George put down his load and set up his own watching station.

The little folding table that Liz wanted for the tent. The big battery-lamp for outdoor work at night or breakdowns on the road. The tape-recorder for young Bill's next birthday. The exercise-book from the truck in which he kept a record of mileages, servicing, and the contract work that sometimes helped with the upkeep. He flashed the lamp and took a look at the result. It looked . . . not like anything in particular, but official. The tape-recorder was a lucky stroke. George put on a tie; it was the only disguise he had, but quite effective. Then he made himself comfortable on the grass with half a pound of a special cheese Liz had wanted, and a thermos flask.

It was not yet fully dark when the sound of a four-wheel drive warned him of the first intruder. He watched headlights pricking the dusk between trees. A little later there were heavy footsteps: only one person on the track. When the footsteps hesitated and turned his way George switched on his lamp and directed the beam. A police constable, blinking suspiciously in the light. George set the lamp on the table and walked forward into its beam.

'Evening officer.'

'Evening, sir,' said the policeman. He looked carefully at George, the well-lit table, the tape-recorder. He turned and looked at the fires and the moving men.

'Quite safe,' said George. 'No fire danger down there. It's a sea-increase ceremony, probably go on all night. I'll be recording it when they get going.'

'Yes, sir? Could I have your name please?'

'George Morrow. Anthropologist. And very lucky to have this chance. There'll be a lot of excitement all over the country if I can get these chants.'

'Is that right, sir? We should have been told about this, you know. It would have saved you answering questions and we could have kept you from being interrupted by sightseers.'

George hadn't allowed for that. He blinked. 'What? Didn't young Clark get in touch with you? That's bad, that is; I wondered when I saw you. When I left a week ago he had instructions, but he's new and a bit slow. You'll get a letter of apology, of course, but it's awkward now. This ceremony only happens when the stars are right. Once in about eighty-five years. That's why no one's recorded it yet. There'll be a howl if I lose it through a technicality.'

The policeman grew thoughtful. A howl was no good to anyone. He took out a notebook and went to the table, looking again at the tape-recorder and George's log book. 'Can I borrow your light, sir? Mr George Morrow, anthropologist. Address please?' George invented an address in Perth. 'Well, sir, I'll have to report this, of course. Can I hold you responsible for the good behaviour of these men?'

'You can that. A steady lot. You could have a word with them, but you'd need to run. Once they get started outsiders aren't allowed, or the whole thing's called off and we have to wait another eighty-five years.' George looked at his watch.

The policeman stood watching the figures at the one fire he could see. It looked like work to him: no wild dancing or waving bottles. And these scientists could raise the devil.

'I'll trust you, sir,' he said.

Gratefully George escorted him into the dusk.

The next intrusion came within half an hour and from the other way along the track. It was a single car, but loaded beyond belief with a party of young Happy Folk. They all had notebooks and thermometers, and had been out to the mountain to plot isotherms. George knew as soon as he heard their voices that a sea-increase ceremony would be right up their street. He quickly carried his table nearer the track and switched on his lamp at once.

'Evening,' he called as soon as the group had spilled from the car. 'Tickets please.'

'Eh? What's this?'

'You've got tickets, haven't you?'

'No, man. We didn't know about tickets. How much?'

George did an anxious sum. 'Six dollars each,' he said crossing his fingers. Ten of them: that would be sixty dollars. Would they – ?

'*Six dollars!* To look at some bonfires! What's going on, anyway?'

'Experimental black outdoor theatre and very expensive to put on. We can't do it cheaper. The seating alone – you've got to have a natural theatre like this, that can't be overlooked except from the seating area. Then there's the transport and – '

The young man in the lead raised his voice rudely. 'Anyone got sixty dollars on him to see the bonfires?' There were boos and groans and laughter. 'Sorry, man, you just lost ten patrons. Come on, peasants.'

'I'm sorry too,' said George severely, making sure. 'People have cash for anything these days, but if it's art they want it for nothing.'

There were cries of 'Nothing!' 'Sixty bucks to sit on a rock!' as the car doors slammed. George wiped his forehead. He had nearly blown that. They might well have had sixty dollars and an eager wish to see experimental black outdoor theatre with bonfires. He should have saved it for their elders. He went back to his cheese.

He reckoned he would soon be able to relax and get some sleep, for now he was counting on a conscientious police patrol to intercept most people on the highway and turn them back. At any rate, as it grew later few people would choose to leave that safe road and venture on the unmade tracks to the inlet. They were more likely to ring the police and report fires – that walloper had been a bit of luck after all. The main risk now should be from a few wanderers who might already have left the main roads and were finding their way amid the network of tracks.

It was nine o'clock before another car arrived, from the direction by which the young people had come. In the light of their own headlamps George observed a middle-aged couple expensively dressed. He took up his post and switched on his lamp with his mind working like a pinball machine. He could not tell whether this couple was likely to rush an increase ceremony, experimental outdoor theatre, or even a drunken brawl. He must play it safer.

'Evening,' he greeted them, and chuckled happily as they craned to look at the fires and men. 'Going down? Might as well be in it. A real experience.'

The couple hesitated. The man said, 'Well, I don't know if we have the time. What's going on?'

'Snake-bake,' said George.

'Snakes!' cried the woman. 'Down there? With those huge fires?'

'Sea-snakes,' said George, thinking fast. 'The fires bring them in, to the shallow water. Very rare, most of them, and all deadly. They're going to sell me a couple for my collection. Wish I could watch them handle them.'

'Why don't you go down, then?' she asked.

'Well, prejudice I suppose. If you go to a snake-bake you have to eat your share or it's an insult. Not that I'd mind in the ordinary way, I've eaten snake often enough. But sea-snakes are the most venomous, and if they bit each other the men mightn't notice at night. Then you've had it. But it won't happen, of course. Those blokes'll all come up alive and there's no reason why you shouldn't join in. I just know enough about snakes to be prejudiced.'

'Well,' said the man coldly, 'I don't think we feel like risking it tonight either. Do you, dear?' They nodded stiffly and returned to their car.

George watched them go with a small smile. He had never before annoyed so many of the Happy Folk in one evening.

It was his last opportunity. When another hour had gone by he rolled himself in some sacking from the truck and found a smooth place to lie. He was sure it was safe now; he would have driven back to town except for the chance of meeting that same police constable on the highway. He was sure to wake up cold and stiff in a few hours. He would drive back then.

From where he lay he could still see the fires, and a cloud of red sparks that broke upwards when a log was thrown on. They were very quiet down there. They knew what they were doing, whether it worked or not. At least he'd given them a fair go.

The moon had risen. The sea writhed like a silver-black snake, always reaching for the fires and drawing back. A great grandfather of snakes with a roar like an angry king. He had told the man and woman right: it was deadly. But the men of the People faced it with their fires, and the land faced it with the huge stillness of a First Thing. George Morrow was only an Inlander, but he felt this huge stillness even while he turned on it and slept.

Around him shadows gathered and passed. They too watched where the snake of the sea coiled, where the rocks crouched and the fires leapt; where that other First Thing, the Eldest Nargun, guarded the land. The shadows drifted and watched, a gathering and thinning of darkness under the moon. They saw how the fires in their turn guarded the Nargun, where the red light fell and where moonlight lay cold. The Thinan-malkia gathered their nets. The Yauruks flew over the writhing sea after whales. The great rock-shape from the cave inched its way up the hill. The little spirits fled to the forest. The Bagini sharpened its claws with a sweet woman-smile.

The Eldest Nargun lay under the sea and felt the tide turning. It turned its empty eyes away from the moon and watched for a wavering red light on the water. It reminded the old monster of the flaming of mountains and the golden burning of the sun and the warm secret coming of life. The Nargun spread its weight against the cold drag of the sea and cried out.

The Ninya rested together, gathering their strength. 'The sea is slow freezing,' they muttered.

Three

At about midnight Wirrun woke, aching from the hardness of rock and bewildered by the red light of fires. In a moment he knew where he was and looked for the men. Three were at work, dark shapes in the red light, one bending over a fire and two dragging wood. When Wirrun stood up stiffly they made signs to each other, and the man at the fire went off to the hill and lay down. They had let him sleep past his time.

Wirrun went to bring more wood and see what was left of the heap. The Inlander had served them well; the pile of logs and branches had sunk to only half its height. There should be enough until morning. The fires were no longer leaping bonfires but mounds of glowing red that darkened into crimson at their base. They leapt into gold and flamed upward into sparks only when a fresh log was thrown on. The rock at their edges was heat-shattered into flakes. Wirrun went to stand between two fires, where men lay asleep on folded blankets. He could feel the warmth of each fire in spite of the distance between.

The heavy wood had to be dragged a long way from each side of the shelf. The men worked slowly and steadily, exchanging a few soft words when they passed. Wirrun was working with Sam and Percy. He murmured to them that the fires at each end of the row were the two to watch, for it seemed that the Ninya might slip past an outer edge rather than between the fires. But as the moon passed over and the night drew on he found himself working oftenest at one fire only: the fire at the inner edge, where the shelf formed the mouth of the inlet. Soon Wirrun worked alone at this fire, leaving the other three to Sam and Percy. Sometimes he caught a red-lit glimpse of the Mimi, a stick-shape going from fire to fire. She had always been good with a fire.

The moon went down to the mountains and the stars swung low to the fires. The chill hours had come; Wirrun felt them in spite of the flames. The tide sent a dark wash of water to reach for the fires; it was high now and would soon be falling back. Wirrun worked harder.

The cold grew sharper. He looked to see if Sam and Percy noticed it, but their steady pace had not changed. They paused together for a moment, and above the sea's pouring he heard them chuckle. It was only here, then. Wirrun dragged logs and built his fire again into a bonfire. The Mimi came and crouched sharp-kneed in the glow to watch with round solemn eyes.

I freeze, groaned the huge still darkness behind him.

'I can't do any more,' panted Wirrun dragging another log to the fire. He worked on, and the Mimi put all her being into the blaze.

After a time he thought the cold was less sharp. The moonlight had changed too; morning was weakening it. Wirrun paused in his work and stood back from the fire. As the sweat cooled on his face and body he felt only the morning's chill. The sudden sharp cold had seeped away.

'It has passed,' said the Mimi. But still she sat and watched the fire.

Wirrun sat on a boulder to rest. He saw that Sam and Percy looked towards his fire as they kept up their steady work between the other three. Soon Percy came to the nearest fire and called a comment that Wirrun knew was a rebuke.

'Good fire, that one. Using plenty wood.'

'I know,' said Wirrun, apologizing. 'Only there was this cold snap. You never felt it?'

'Just the morning,' said Percy, going on to the wood-heap. Wirrun followed to look at the damage. The wood-heap loomed dark in the first-dawn light, and a long slow wash of the falling tide came lazily out of darkness. He had made a hole in the wood-heap on its nearer side, sure enough. He went round it to look at the farther side, and his feet slid from under him.

Ice! thought Wirrun, twisting as he fell. There was something else on the rock between the wood-heap and the water. Grimly he called to Percy while he knelt and groped in the half-dark.

The Thinan-malkia had spread their nets here. But the nets were frozen hard and lay tossed and broken.

'That ice?' said Percy's voice at his shoulder. Wirrun looked up to see him bending and feeling, and behind him Sam coming from the wood-heap.

'They've broken through,' he said in a tight voice. 'Get the men – and watch yourselves. You could break a leg here.' The cold had indeed passed, as the Mimi had said. It had passed this end of the line of fires, out to the shelf where somewhere the Eldest Nargun lay. The Ninya had won through in spite of them.

The men were coming, waking up as they ran, to look and feel. 'Who laid the nets?' someone asked.

Wirrun said, 'Others are fighting too. You ought to know which ones. Get fires started here, near as we can to the water. See you don't slip.' He was kneeling on a ridge above the water, where the sea sent long swells down the side of the shelf and through the mouth of the inlet. In the half-dark he searched with groping hands and straining eyes.

It was cold here. Channels and crevices held ice. A swell gathered ice from the rocks and floated it out to sea. He did not like the sluggish movement of the water: it should have been running out fast and strong in the ebb. And farther down where the shelf jutted into open

206

sea, there should have been a livelier leaping as the current set that way. He remembered how fast the Ninya could work, and their cold was inside him.

Men were dragging wood towards the water or running with cans of kerosene. Three, shouting 'More wood!' had gone for the utility. George Morrow, having slept on till dawn, saw and heard and ran for his truck. Wirrun suddenly saw that in all this confusion work might be wasted, and called Waratah to help him examine the shelf.

They found pools and channels filled with ice and the edge of the shelf crusting with it, but so far one edge only. The ice started within the mouth of the inlet and followed the shelf along that side to the sea.

'If they get going here,' said Wirrun grimly, 'they'll ring us from the sea and work inwards over the shelf. We'll start the fires at the sea end and work back.'

'Those big ones, they're no good now,' Waratah pointed out.

'No more they are. Might as well break 'em up – they're hot already any rate.'

They used branches to roll burning logs from the old fires closer to the sea, and those that came dry enough past rockpools and channels they heaped into new fires. Wirrun, running to and fro with the others, saw the Mimi at fire after fire nursing each. He heard the truck's heavy motor and ran to help unload. It was a small load, offcuts from yesterday hastily gathered. George Morrow unloaded with the men and Wirrun spoke to him.

'Heard you'd stayed.'

'Thought you might have visitors.'

It was not possible that there should have been no visitors. 'You got rid of 'em?'

George grinned, heaving down a branch. 'Had to tell a few tall ones.' He looked with narrowed eyes over the shelf. 'That ice? Give me three men and four axes and we'll bring another quick one. I'm off then. Good luck.'

Wirrun called to Sam while he himself went back to the ice.

He strode along the shelf, looking inward as well as outward, slipping on glassy surfaces and saving himself, and where he found most ice he called for fire. Men ran and stumbled and shouted. All along this side of the shelf were ruffles of smoke, spires of steam, and the hissing of fire as the water got to it. And soon Wirrun felt that this was no battle of ice and fire but a useless skirmish, fringe-fighting. The crust of ice along the shelf had widened; floating caps of ice had joined. He was wasting work and wood in defence when he needed to attack.

He remembered two green-eyed salt-white figures glittering in a cave. That was what he wanted: to find the ice-makers themselves, and hold them with his fires till the men of Mount Conner came – if only they would. He must look farther and better than he was looking now: he must see.

He left the fires to the men and found a high ridge to stand on, took the power of the People into his cupped hands, and waited and watched. If he did not see the Ninya he might perhaps see the Nargun. . . . Nothing in crevice or rockpool, but no ice lay there yet; the sea was drugged and heavy with ice, but men could not stand and work on it yet; among the great rocks at the edge of the shelf, was that a glitter?

'Mad! Blind!' shouted Wirrun. Of course that was the place! Only those rocks were big enough to hide a Nargun or the Ninya, and there the sea lay heaviest with ice. And the very ice that attacked those rocks made it possible for him to fight back, for it kept the sea from rushing in among them. Now he could build fires there as he could not last night – two were burning close to the rocks already. The men must cut off all that corner of the shelf with fires and then advance into it with more fires. If they could only hold that corner they could defend the old monster in it. Wirrun went quickly back and set them to work.

Now that they had a plan the men worked eagerly. The second quick load of wood arrived to feed their new line of fires. They moved inside it to build again nearer the rocks. Wirrun kept his hand on the power and his eyes on the rocks. He remembered the stirring of shadows, the secret movement, in that other Nargun's cave.

A Great One mighty in size and power: which rock? Surely his fires would not anger the Eldest who had the power of fire – but none of these men must be crushed by the monster they were all trying to save. Wirrun held the power and watched the rocks. The sun rose, and they looked at it with gold-lit faces. Beyond them the tide was at its lowest and the ice was spreading fast on the lazy sea. The men went to and fro with wood and they heard the sound of a motor.

Not the ute; not the Inlander's truck. The men from Mount Conner? For a moment Wirrun's heart leapt, but then Percy called to him.

'They've brought old Johnny. That's the Holden.'

Wirrun and Percy went back across the shelf, skirting rockpools and stepping from ridge to ridge over channels. They met the others at the base of the hill, and Fred and Butcher looked with interest at the signs of battle on the shelf and the ice in the sea. Old Johnny Wuthergul looked with interest at Wirrun.

He was old indeed, his face a powdery brown and deeply wrinkled, his hair and beard white. He had the gentle smile and seeing eyes that were common among old men of the People, but he seemed to be gently surprised by Wirrun. He said nothing until he had heard for himself what Wirrun had to ask.

'You'll see this ice,' said Wirrun. 'It's after the land. But the Ninya want this Eldest Nargun first, to freeze it so it can't call up fire against them. Can you talk to this Nargun? Tell it to call up fire and get rid of 'em?'

Old Johnny smiled. 'Where's this power they say you got, boy?' he asked.

Wirrun unfastened the power and put it into the old man's hands. He seemed to go into a dream, turning it slowly over and over. Then he handed it back.

'You want me to talk to this Old One?' he shook his head gently.

'Ice in summer,' Wirrun urged him. 'The sea's freezing down there. Fetch it out before they put a freeze on it. If they haven't already.'

'Funny thing,' said old Johnny, shaking his head.

'Can't you talk to it, then?'

The old man straightened proudly. 'My father, he showed me. And his father before. Dunno how many grandfathers talked to it first, right back to old times. . . . But you'll wait here, boy.'

'Only there's ice out there. You could fall,' said Wirrun.

'I gotta go just me.'

'You want me to bring the men back?'

Old Johnny looked carelessly at the men and fires and shook his head. 'You wait,' he said, and went slowly forward.

Wirrun waited, for he was not of these People and the others were; but he signed to Percy and Fred and Butcher to watch over the old man. It was rough walking on that rock even without ice. He himself leaned on rocks near the remains of last night's fire and watched. He found himself breathing quickly with a thudding heart. He had come a long way for this, and it seemed to be working at last. He was glad to find the Mimi waiting near him, but neither of them spoke. They watched too tensely.

The old man went on slowly but surely, turning between ridges and pools as if his feet knew a path of their own. It was a winding path, away from the rocks where the fires were and towards the centre of the shelf. Some distance out he turned to the men who followed him, and they stayed where they were. Old Johnny went on, pausing sometimes and looking into rockpools.

Beside one of these he crouched and stayed for some time; then he reached his hand into the pool and stood up again.

He turned and went slowly towards the men and fires, stood by them for a moment, then came slowly back by another path. Had he spoken while he stood and watched? Wirrun waited, tense and eager. Some of the men were leaving the fires and following old Johnny back. Words burst from Wirrun as soon as the old man was near.

'Did you talk to it?'

Johnny chuckled. 'I talked to it and I fetched it out,' he said proudly. He held out a brown-crêpe hand and opened it. On his palm lay a stone, a large pebble, the size of a teacup.

At first Wirrun did not see it at all, for it had nothing to do with the picture in his mind. When he did see it he felt as if something had kicked him hard in the middle. He could only gasp, '*What's that?*'

Old Johnny spoke warningly. 'Watch your words, boy. That's very old. That's a First Thing.'

'That's not – you sure it's the right one? *Eldest* Nargun? Greatest one ever?'

'That's right. Biggest and strongest. Been in the sea a very long time. Used itself up fighting the sea.'

The men had come up full of triumph to hear what old Johnny had done. The triumph went out of them. There was bewilderment, shame – and suddenly all the tiredness of the long hard hours. They stood in silence and looked at the pebble to avoid meeting each other's eyes. No one turned to the fires.

And the Eldest Nargun, heavy with age and power, felt again the warmth of the sun. Little wet weeds still clung to it, but the fish had darted out of them when Johnny's hand appeared. The tiny crab had burrowed under sand in the rockpool; at ebb tide the whelk and the limpet had made their long journeys to feed in the pool, and Johnny had carefully lifted the anemone from the Nargun. When the tide poured into the pool again

these must all look for other shelter; they would find no
Great One crouched in the pool to hide them from the
sea. But the Eldest Nargun felt the warm tide of blood
hidden in veins: it spread its weight on Johnny's palm
and stirred a little. For a moment Wirrun saw it: blunt
muzzle, empty eyes and stumpy limbs. The First of
Narguns, for dread of which the Ninya had journeyed
far and frozen a mountain in ice.

Yet he tried once more to prove this was the wrong
stone. 'Can it call up fire?'

'Can if it wants to, boy, it's got the power.' The old
man gathered a little dried seaweed, bunched it on a
rock, and carefully set the pebble on it. He bent over it
with a crooning sound and stood up proudly.

A drift of smoke rose from the seaweed. It smouldered
for a moment and went out.

'Well,' said Wirrun carefully, 'thank you, Johnny.
We saved it from the Ninya, far as that goes. Hope they
didn't see it.' He floundered into silence while the old
man smiled gently. What now, he wondered? He knew
he should try to get the men back to the fires.

If the Ninya had seen the Eldest they would know they
need not battle for it. They would slip away through caves
to the mountains, leaving the men with their useless fires.
Then, when the men from Mount Conner came, the
Ninya would be gone and building their ice somewhere
far away. But perhaps they had not seen the Eldest.
Then they would lock those rocks down there in ice and
believe they had caught it, and build on from there;
if the men let them. He should get the men back to the
fires.

But they were all tired; they ached with tiredness.
Worse still, they felt foolish and betrayed, and no longer
believed in the battle. Wirrun too. He had worked
harder and longer than any of them for that useless
pebble, and felt more foolish. And he was empty: empty
with shock, and weary days and nights, and wasted
work.

He had done all he could. It was up to the men from Mount Conner, as he had told Ko-in in the first place. There was only one thing left – to find some way to satisfy old Johnny, who had travelled all night to help.

And then Wirrun noticed the Mimi.

Four

None of the men could see the Mimi or guess that she was there. Only Wirrun saw her, standing like a tall stick-insect by the rock where the Eldest Nargun lay. She had drawn back a little, fearfully. Her eyes were round and solemn, full of awe. She looked on the stone and saw it whole, as she had seen the Nargun of the cave. For her this journey had not failed.

Wirrun in his weariness saw this with surprise, and then with wonder. He put his hand on the power again and saw more. Though the men stood silent avoiding each other's eyes, yet behind them the fires were tended and fed. Those strong little wrestlers from the rocks, the Nyols, scurried to and fro dragging wood from the forest. Down the shelf where the rocks stood the Nyols swarmed like grey ants and the fires burnt bright.

Among those rocks he saw that something moved: a squat and hairy figure, long-armed, creeping. The nets of the Thinan-malkia had failed but the Dulugar had come. And on this side, peering slyly between the rocks, a woman of the People smiled and sharpened her claws: the Bagini was there.

These see me true, for they are me, said the land crouching over the sea. *But where are the eyes of men?*

'Come on!' shouted Wirrun. 'We got these Ninya worried – do we want 'em to get away? The ice is here!'

The men looked up quickly, glad to hear. They were weary but they hated this failure. They wanted to be lifted out of it. They grinned to each other and strode to the wood-heap – and now the Nyols fed that instead of the fires.

Wirrun turned to Johnny Wuthergul. 'Can I hold this Old One, or does it have to be you?'

The old man gave him a straight look. 'You got the power. Go ahead.'

So Wirrun took up the First of the Narguns, the Eldest, the Great One with the power of fire, and carried it into battle with the Ninya. And his palm tingled as he held it, still damp from its rockpool.

As he went down the shelf in the early sunlight he looked over the battle. The outer ring of fires was dying and useless now, for the inner ring, closer to the standing rocks, was burning well. Yet among the rocks was the gleam of ice building fast, and fastest near the sea. The Ninya were fighting with all their strength. He saw a salt-white sparkle – a frost-man crouched between the rocks and the sea. A long hairy arm swung and the Dulugar hurled a stone; there was a grating cry, a splintering of ice, and white blood flowing on the rock. Wirrun smiled grimly and hurried on, but he was worried by the look of the sea.

It was deep at the edge of the shelf, even at low tide. It should have ruffled the shelf with waves and spray, but since first light it had lain sluggish with cold. Now it was still. The Ninya had used the low tide well to crust it with ice, and the ice extended along the shelf into the mouth of the inlet. They would need many more men to build fires all along that line; yet if the Ninya were allowed to build a base in the sea they could outflank any line of fires.

There was no time to send for more men. They must somehow attack the freezing sea with those they had. They could not build fires on it – when the sea-ice was thick enough for men to stand and work on it the Ninya would have won. Could they hurl rocks and burning logs on to the ice? It should easily crack, but the Ninya were powerful builders. They could mend the ice, crack by crack, as fast as the men could break it. If it could be broken all over – if they had dynamite, for instance – then the pull of the sea would be released and might carry the broken ice out fast enough. The sea is slow freezing; the Ninya could hardly repair in a few minutes what it had taken them hours to build.

But there was no time to send to town for dynamite.

Even as Wirrun thought this he heard cries that he knew. He looked to the sky: the Yauruks were coming. At first he could not see them but their shrieking was near. He looked lower.

They were coming on their great white wings low over the sea. Something broke the surface of the sea, something dark and shining that swam ahead. A fountain of water broke upwards. There were several shining backs and the Yauruks herded them, swooping and shrieking. The Yauruks were bringing the whales.

Wirrun stood still, full of delight. Were there three whales or four? No matter. The Yauruks shrieked and drove them on. The men stood at their fires and watched. The whales drove in, veered at the mouth of the inlet, swung aside into deep water and away. They had escaped, and the Yauruks flew in pursuit screaming of failure. But they had not failed.

The thin ice was shattered. The water, lifting sluggishly again, began to tip broken ice over its shoulder and out to sea. The men shouted and jumped about and threw more wood on the fires. Wirrun shouted too and began to run, but stopped again, still watching.

On the edge of the shelf two frosty figures crouched. They were looking with angry green eyes at the broken ice drifting out of reach . . . but near the edge of the shelf the water clouded . . . something drifted there, large and slow. A wetness of scales or feathers or fur – an arm or flipper reaching – one of the Ninya went into the sea, the other scuttled back. Wirrun caught a drifting smell of slime and age, but Mu-ru-bul, Tu-ru-dun, Bunyip, had taken his revenge and gone.

216

Wirrun leapt the last few yards over the rocks shouting for more fires nearer the inlet. He set the Eldest Nargun high on a boulder where men and spirits could see it and seized freshly caught branches from old fires and carried them to new. Men came and went with wood, and Nyols came and went among them. The Bagini prowled; today she was looking only for frosty men. Her cockatoo-laugh screeched – she had gouged one with her claws. The fires caught and leapt, but the ice between the rocks grew a little. The cold in there was menacing. It held the men back, as the jagged rocks held the fires back. Wirrun could not take his fires closer, for now that the sea was released it washed in and out again and would have carried fires away as it had carried the ice.

Wirrun was enraged. He seized burning branches and hurled them between rocks at the ice. The younger men shouted and hurled more. The flames sizzled and died as the branches flew: they were white with frost before they fell. The ice grew, and again Wirrun felt the cold of the Ninya inside him. They were a fearful power. Only here by the sea could they have been held for this little while.

'Behind you!' screamed the Mimi suddenly at his side. 'Up on the hill! Look back!'

He looked and saw nothing: only the clean line of the hill against the sky, and the dark outline of one great rock. His puzzled eyes came back to that rock even as the Mimi screamed again.

'The Nargun of the cave! It comes!'

'Back!' shouted Wirrun. 'Percy, get them back! Sam – Waratah – over this way!' He leapt backward away from the fires and had the men staring after him when the monster plunged. Then they leapt quickly enough.

The Nargun from the cave laid its terrible cry over the sea, '*Nga-a-a!*' No one heard the Eldest on its boulder scream in reply like a tide-drawn pebble on a beach. The other plunged from the hill to the path and rolled and tumbled down, scrambling and pushing with squat invisible limbs. It passed above old Johnny crouching back against the hill, and thundered on scattering a wreckage of dead fires. From there they could not see how it went between rocks and pools and channels, only that it came on fast rumbling and grinding down the shelf. But they saw a darkness of empty eyes and a glimpse of snarling muzzle, and they watched, not breathing.

It did not turn towards the men but rumbled down the edge of the shelf beyond the fires; in among rocks, knocking some aside and smashing ice; out through the fires, scattering them; to rest at last between its most ancient brother and the sea. There was a long stillness on the shelf. The world itself hung still. At last the sea spoke one long peaceful word.

Even then the men did not speak; but they looked at each other, knowing what they had seen. No one moved towards the broken fires. They would go no closer; they did not even see that the broken ice was melting or that the rocks were stained white with the blood of Ninya.

The Ninya who were left were huddled in deep cracks at the edge of the shelf. 'We have lost six men,' said their leader bleakly. 'We must find another plan. We have not the strength for this one.'

The Nyols had crept away to the forest to see if the rocks were yet safe. The Dulugar had flown when the Nargun plunged; the Bagini's cockatoo-laugh came from inshore. They had left the mighty and ancient one, the First of Narguns, to the care of its brother. The men, finding they could breathe again, went up the shelf to see that old Johnny Wuthergul was safe. They found him unhurt, standing straight and gazing down the shelf.

'It'll be all right now,' said Johnny.

In the thunder of the Nargun's attack they had not heard the rattle-bang of an old car approaching. It was only when Wirrun saw himself coming from the wood-heap with three or four men and was shaking off the

218

shock of this that he realized the men of Mount Conner had come. Relief and gladness rushed into him and he ran to meet them. The Yabon, taken by surprise but always helpful, slipped away behind the wood-heap and came back as a dog.

'Am I glad to see you!' cried Wirrun, holding out his hand.

They were surprised, for they thought he had been seeing them since he stopped them on the road last night; but they were glad to be greeted so warmly and shook hands again all round. Wirrun introduced them to the People of the settlement and told them quickly what had been happening and where he believed the Ninya were.

'They won't cause no more trouble,' said the oldest of the Mount Conner men comfortably. 'We come to sing them home.'

'Sooner you than me,' said Wirrun. 'It's a long way to sing.'

The men laughed, and the oldest explained kindly. 'We don't sing 'em the whole way. We sing 'em a little bit and wait along the way and sing a bit more. They'll go. There's others waiting up north'll sing 'em along. We split, see, account of cutting the road in half. We come south and they went north.' Wirrun admired the wisdom of this pincer movement, and the man shifted his eyes and spoke again with apology. 'When we get 'em home we won't let 'em out again.'

'Only I reckon you better hurry,' said Wirrun. 'The way they are, they might scatter again and we won't know where to find 'em. You want us to go?'

The men of Mount Conner shook their heads, for the song was not very big business. They were shown where the Narguns lay and went off down the shelf. The men of the settlement, their own part done, stayed under the hill to light one more fire and cook what breakfast they could for everyone.

Wirrun sat wearily down and patted the dog. He lay

back on the warm sandy rock and listened to the sea. Above, where rock jutted from the hillside, he could see the Mimi; she was watching the Mount Conner men with brooding eyes. He wondered with a pang how she would enjoy travelling with them. Under the sound of the sea came the deep drone of chanting: a low strong song, rising gradually, breaking off and starting again. Someone handed Wirrun a sausage folded in toast, and he ate it while he listened to the men of Mount Conner singing the Ninya home. And suddenly he slept.

He woke several hours later in the shade of the hill, with his pack beside him and a folded blanket under his head. There was no one else on the shelf; he was alone. Only the dog lay near, and over his head the Mimi perched. She was eating a root that she had roasted in dying coals, and a handful of ripe pigfaces lay beside her.

Wirrun sat up. 'Where have they gone?' he asked, bewildered.

The Mimi answered. 'Those of this country have left in their cars and would not let the others wake you. They have called you their brother and placed a gift under your head.'

Wirrun lowered his brows and gazed down the shelf. The tide had risen and was falling again, leaving a dark line of charcoal and charred wood. The Nargun of the cave lay sea-washed where it had rested, but Wirrun could not see its ancient brother. Back under the hill lay the four great mounds of ash that they had fed last night; the rock was grey and flaked around them, and Wirrun knew there would still be red coals deep inside. He fingered the blanket that the men had left. How they had worked; and he was too tired and drained to go after them. But he would come back. . . .

'Have the others gone too?' he asked, suddenly anxious for the Mimi.

'They have gone to their car near the stream; they have food there. They wait to take you home.'

'So we'll be travelling together a while longer yet,' said Wirrun, pleased; and then he saw that the Mimi was wearing her obstinate look.

'I go my own way,' she said.

'Come off it, Mimi, none of that. I'm too tired. The Ninya are going home through the rocks. They'll have their wind and their freezing, like before.'

'They go through caverns and I through rock. I will find a way.'

'You said you couldn't. You said that in strange rocks there were other spirits and they'd fight you.'

'Have I not ridden the winds and done all things that a Mimi cannot do? And should I ride home with men in a car like – '

'Like a can of peaches on wheels? No.' He never had managed to move the Mimi when she wore her obstinate look. He unfastened the power and held it up to her. 'You'll take this to watch out for you.' When she drew back he added, exasperated, 'You've used it before, and if anyone's earned the right you have. You could go on the wind.'

She would not touch the power. 'That is magic for the People,' she said, 'not for an earth-spirit. I will find my own way to my far dear land.'

Wirrun frowned in thought. Time was passing, the men might soon come, and he could not let the Mimi make that long journey without help. He put his hand on the black dog and said, 'Yabon. Do you want to help?'

If a man hears a dog talk he will turn into stone. The Yabon became a boy of the People.

'There is no spirit in this land,' said the boy, 'who would not help Wirrun the fighter of ice.'

'Right,' said Wirrun. '*Right!* Can you pass a message to all the rock-spirits? Get it sent along all the way through the land?'

'This message, I can,' said the Yabon. 'There are evil spirits as well as good, and countries that are hard to pass, but this message will fly through the land like a bird. For I will add whatever threats are needed and others will bear me out.'

'Good. Tell 'em a Mimi comes through to the north and all roads are open to her. Say that this Mimi's a Great One, she fought the ice all through the land.' He saw the Mimi's look of astonished pride and began to enlarge; she had earned whatever he or the spirits could give. 'Tell 'em to light her way with fires and see she has roots and lizards and rats. Wherever she goes she's free, whatever she wants they give, because she's the one that saved 'em from the ice. Tell 'em that.'

The Yabon rose, bowed to the delighted Mimi, walked a few steps up the path, and disappeared.

'Give him a bit of time,' said Wirrun to the Mimi, for he did not want to part from her too quickly. 'He won't be much past Tilba-Tilba yet.' The thought of Tilba-Tilba was a sadness added to the sadness of parting; for there lay the small frozen fighters, the only victims of the Ninya.

The Mimi was sitting very erect on her rock. 'You have shamed me,' she said proudly, 'for only you are the fighter. I am no fighter but – '

'A poor frail hider,' said Wirrun. 'I know. . . . I saw you looking at that Eldest Nargun. Tell me what you saw.'

'The Ancient One, the First, that we had come far to find.'

'Yeah. The mighty Eldest Nargun. Big as my hand.'

She hissed at him. 'A man! What does a man know of size? Greater than you is great, smaller than you is small; you know no more. There lies the Nargun from the cave: is it great? I tell you it lies among the stars smaller than a grain of sand.'

'H'm,' said Wirrun. 'Maybe. Only it wouldn't lie in a rockpool, would it?'

'And is not the rockpool a world among the stars? Life and death are in it, and darkness and light; there are journeys and home-coming there. Is a starfish smaller than a star?'

Wirrun was silent, hearing his own voice speaking to Ko-in: *There's a dung-beetle by that log. I care for that. There's a rotten toadstool with a worm in it: I care for both of 'em,* and Ko-in had answered: *You are of the People.* He must be tired if it took a Mimi to tell him what the People knew.

'Sometimes,' he said, teasing, 'I think I'd like you better if you weren't always right.' He stood up. 'But I want to remember you saying that, so don't say any more. I want it to be the last word. Till next time we meet any rate.' He knew the bit about next time was a lie, but the lie was spoken to cushion the truth that must come. 'Goodbye, Mimi. I won't forget you. And thanks.'

He bowed as the Yabon had done, and she bowed back with dark sad eyes like a possum's, and he took up his pack once more and walked away.

Nothing plucked at the loop of fur-cord that hung from his belt. He walked up the inlet to a shabby waiting car and the men from Mount Conner.

MIMI
COUNTRY

track

High

The Dark Bright Water

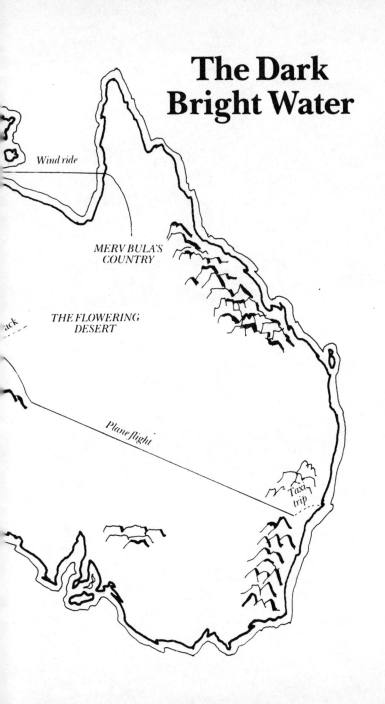

Wind ride

MERV BULA'S
COUNTRY

THE FLOWERING
DESERT

ack

Plane flight

Taxi
trip

The Dark Bright Water

Author's Note

Twice lately I have explained that, in stories of my own making, fairy and monster characters were drawn from the folklore of the Australian Aborigines. I have to refer to it again this time in order to make a confession.

All the spirits of this story come from the same source — except for one species that I have invented. These are the nameless, shapeless shadows I have placed in the deepest underground. It seemed right that at those depths and in that dark something should move that was quite unknown to man.

ONE

Journeys and Homecomings

I

The old south land lay across the world like an open hand, with the weight of summer heavy in its palm. The wind washed over it, polishing its gibber-plains; the sea leapt and worried at its endless coast; but the land lay flat and still, full of summer and secrets. And in one far corner, north and west across mirage-shrouded lakes and polished plains and beyond the haze-hung monoliths of the Centre, the first cyclone of the year was building.

It began as a tropical wind over the ocean, building grey-green hillocks of water that hurried before it until they were rolled and broken into foam. As the wind neared the land it found an area of low pressure and soared upward into it, curling its tail. Now it was trapped, and it screamed in mounting fury - a wind-dragon howling after its own tail as it still swept on towards land. Clouds were caught in its whirling; it darkened the sky and hurled rain senselessly. Small and big ships fled from it where it lashed at the funnelled, flying sea. It let them go and howled on towards land, breaking over the coast at its north-west corner.

To the old south land lying broad and still under the weight of summer this fury of wind was no more than a swarm of bees; but to all who lived in that one country under the cyclone it was more. There were no towns there; only a few grim-faced Inlanders, a handful or so of the dark People, and the unknown earth-spirits of the land itself. To them the cyclone was a fury.

It hurled the sea high over rocks and inland over beaches. It pummelled the country with fists of rain and wind, tore down buildings, tossed cars and boats about, uprooted trees or stripped them of leaves. It gathered up rivers, flung them down again, rained new rivers into them and spilt them over the country. And all the time, while men cowered, the cyclone shrieked and howled and the earth-spirits howled back. Some of them fought it, some hid from it, some mounted it and rode the circling wind.

The water-spirits rode the floods, out of the fierce river-currents into quieter water. All but the Yunggamurra. They could be as wild as any wind. Their fierce eyes flashed, they dug their long sharp nails into root and bank and fought the current with joy. They joined hands, a chain of sisters reaching from bank to bank of their flooded river, their grey-slimed bodies knifing through the water. Their dark hair netted flood-wash and bound it to rocks, and they sang a wild-dog chorus to the storm. One of them stopped to listen and laugh, loosening her hold for a moment - and in that moment she was torn from her sisters and blown and tumbled away down the river. That startled her, for she had never been alone before, and while she howled for help she was rolled and tumbled out to sea.

She hardly knew when she had reached it, all the land was so wild and wet and the muddy floodwaters reached so far into the grey sea. She went on calling for her sisters into the noise of the storm until the storm itself paused to listen. The wind quietened. There was only the roar and crash of water, and the Yunggamurra quivered with fear. She knew the storm had not passed but was looking down at her through its great central eye, and it was terrible to be alone. She knew the wind would start again, and there were no banks to dig into and no chain of clinging hands. From land to sky, only the waves drove and smashed; they seized her and dragged her out, out, and their salt burnt her body. In terror the Yunggamurra dived and flicked away with the speed of a spirit. It was some time before she was calmer and began to look for the shore. By then she had left the storm behind.

She could see no shore. She had come a long way in her panic and thought of going back through the sea; but by now her soft slimy body was badly burnt from the salt. She needed a river - a flood - a storm - even dry land. Here there was only a wide and shallow sea, quite calm, but grey under cloud that the cyclone had pushed ahead of it. She saw a rain-squall coming, and lay on the water and waited for it until the rain gave her some relief from the burning. Then she dived again in search of an upward-sloping sea-floor. Her dark eyes were hard again; there was no panic in them.

She met fish and shark, strangers to her. They gaped and slid quickly away and she barely noticed. The sea-floor was rising to the south and she knew she was coming near land. The sea tugged at her in pulls and currents, but she slid through those as easily as the fish did. Then, like a feather spiralling up from below, she felt the lightest touch of another current. Fresh water! She hung where she was, sensing and testing. The swell lifted her dark hair like weed, and that feather-touch of fresh water rose through the swell. There must be some current or pressure to make it flow upward like that.

She followed it down to the ooze, and the flow strengthened a little as she went. She dug down with her sharp nails, working in a swirl of grey-brown ooze that hung in the sea as she stirred it up. She found a basin of sandstone filled with sand and ooze, and cleared it until she had found a fist-sized hole. The water gushed through more strongly. Being a water-spirit, and slimy, she was able to slide into the hole.

After the strong salt sea, this water was as gentle as a summer evening; but the sandstone was rough and scraped the soft slime from her body. The hole widened as she went, working her way in darkness on and up, sure that she was leaving the sea for land, waiting for the moment when her tunnel would lead into some sunny pool. When she had found it, and rested and recovered, she would find the river-roads back to her sisters. Until then she would not think of them, for she needed them too badly. She would think only of the water.

Yet she would rather not think too much about the water

for it had begun to worry her. It was a strange sort of water, with no smell or taste or feel of river or pool.

'It is old water,' said the Yunggamurra, and turned her thoughts away from it. Whatever it was, it was life to her for she could not stand the sea. Pressed in the narrow darkness and longing for space she fought her way on, driving her own sore body with the ferocity of her kind. The tunnel went on and up, on and up. 'It will surface somewhere,' hissed the Yunggamurra.

Suddenly she slid forward into freedom and wider water. She could feel it all around, and above and below. She took two quick turns for the joy of free movement, then lay for a long time and rested. She had reached the pool. She felt like a man who has run a long way through fire.

After some time she raised herself unwillingly, for she had to take notice of something. It was the darkness: it was still there. Not as close, but just as thick and solid. With an eel's wriggle she rose through the water feeling for the surface. There was no surface, only more rock, above as below and on all sides. The water, the old water, was imprisoned in rock. Yet she could feel its sly and secret flowing.

She knew then what the water was and where it had led her: into deep and hidden secrets of the land. These were the waters the thirsty land had locked away in store, drop by drop and age by age, far down under rock and desert. They were rains and floods and melted ice that had seen younger suns, when men were small and hairy and beasts were giants. They were the old land's private thoughts, its youth remembered. The Yunggamurra shuddered and clenched her sharp nails into her palms. She felt the might of the land locking her in. She must go back through the tunnel and back through the sea.

But she could not go back. Could a man run a second time through fire? She thrashed to and fro in the pool, and its waters stirred as they had not for an age. It frightened her; she cowered at the bottom. There was a gentle touch of slime on the rock: that was comforting, for it was life, even here. She scraped some off with her nails and ate it. After that she was able to still her terror, and even her longing for light and company. She could wait, and listen for the old slow thought of the land. And as the water stilled and settled she heard it.

It was in that sly and secret flowing, the tendril of movement that curled through the quiet water.

'It flows in as well as out,' whispered the Yunggamurra. 'It will surface somewhere.'

She crept along the thread of current till the stirring of water hid it. Then she waited, ate more slime, allowed her body to heal and rebuild its own soft cover. In this way, little by little, she tracked the water to its entrance and found a second, larger, tunnel. She went into it and on into the depths of the land.

Darkness, even First Darkness, is not the same to an earth-thing as to a man; an earth-thing has more seeing. Loneness is not so heavy, nor silence so deep; there are rhythms and pulses to feel. Harmonies and discords that vibrate from other spirits; the strong, deep singing of stone and the soft consent of water. And there is life making its tiny response in the growth of a fungus, the groping of a cricket, the scurry of a spider. All this is intelligence to the old things.

But this was an old thing of running waters and open sky, not of waters quiet under the weight of a land. She had lost her own country, which is darkness and loss to her kind as it is to the People. She was used to wild laughter and singing, savage play and the joining of hands - all her life, wherever she looked, she had seen herself everywhere in her sisters. Alone she had no self. Most bitterly she missed her sisters.

But she went on, from tunnel to pool and from passage to cave, not knowing night from day and choosing only one direction: up. Even that was not always possible. Often the water was hot, and she fled in fear. The current led nowhere and often disappeared: there was no pattern in it. Yet in time she did reach levels so high that the dark and bitter water lay only in the floor of cave or passage, and others where she felt it only in the shale under her feet. She was glad to be free of it at first, for it was a powerful and stinging water, but soon she was forced to seek it again. By degrees she grew used to it and it ceased to sting.

She grew used to many strange things. Sometimes there were heavy, choking airs that she had to escape by diving under water. The first time she knocked a stone into a cave-pool she thought she was hunted by spirits, and ran and hid - for the water sang a clear note like a magpie's, and the rocks picked it up and sent it back and forth till caves and passages rang with magpie-calls. Afterwards she knew the voices of water and rock calling each other, and sometimes roused them for company. Her eyes grew wide and sharp; she saw a grinning shape and ran in terror before she felt what it was - the skull of some ancient monster, dead an age ago. Later she saw stone with the sparkle of rain and shaped like the flowing or dripping of water; but it was stone, hard and still and brittle.

Once she heard a sound that was the strangest thing of all in this deep place: the distant shrieking and howling of wind. The air in her cave sucked out and breathed a cold breath in, yet she knew it was too deep for wind or cold. She stood listening, quivering, all her wildness frozen still. This was no wind for a Yunggamurra to howl at. It was a spirit-wind. She slipped into a pool and lay still.

It was some time after this that she strayed into a cave of ice. She had never seen ice and thought at first that it was hot and burnt her. But she found it was a burning cold and remembered, from the talk of earth-things she had met in past times, that this was ice.

She longed for other spirits but dared not meet them, for here she was a stranger and an intruder. Sometimes there was a brooding heaviness that hung in niches or blocked a passage, and she knew that some spirit of the place was near and she hid in water. Once or twice she saw a moving glow and crept after it, not daring to come near, until she lost it. Then she sat in a pool and wept angry, lonely tears, since she must not howl.

There came a time when she followed such a glow and found it growing stronger as it went. She grew afraid and turned away into a passage that ran beside the cave where the light travelled. But the passage turned back suddenly into the cave, and the light was there before her eyes, and she saw earth-things. It was so long since she had seen any of her own kind that she could not slip away. She stayed and watched.

She was lucky. It was a gathering of earth-things of several kinds, aware of each other's strange vibrations and so not aware of hers. She was able to climb high up in the darkness of rocks and look down at them. Their faint glow seemed a strong light after her long time in the dark, but soon there was added another stronger light: the leaping red and yellow of fire. That worried her, for she hated fire, but now it was too dangerous to climb down again. And she wanted to stay, to watch.

It excited her to see these other spirits; she shook with the wild Yunggamurra laughter that she had to hold back. There were shapes like men and women of the People, except that they were tailed like dogs. There were more fearful shadows, shapeless at the edge of the light, flowing a little forward and a little back as the firelight wavered. There were women without heads, groping in spite of the firelight - the Yunggamurra held her laughter all the tighter. Most of the spirits were a starry-eyed Little People with voices that rumbled together like stones. They were as small as young children, but the Yunggamurra looked at them with respect. She knew that the races of Little People have a wonderful strength.

They seemed to be waiting as if there were more to come, and she wondered if this were some corroboree. The smoke of the fire rose straight up in the stillness of the cave and drove her back. What had they found to burn? She took another look: dried grass and sticks brought, surely, from far away; handfuls of rubbish that might have been scraped from the sides of pools; ancient bones such as she had seen here sometimes. And - strange! - laid out beside the fire there was food. Not food for all of them, but a meal for one: a limp sooty bat, a pale lizard, three or four strange grubs. It was not a corroboree, then. They were waiting for some important being. The Yunggamurra waited too, and looked where they looked.

She felt them stir. Another spirit had come out of the shadows into the cave. This one was tall and stick-thin, with dark round eyes and a wisp of hair that floated as she walked spring-kneed. She drooped a little as she walked, a shy and timid creature; but when she saw the fire and the waiting crowd she straightened and lifted her head. She looked proud then, but the Yunggamurra failed to see it.

The Yunggamurra had crushed her hands to her mouth and bitten them to hold back a wild, fierce cry, for this spirit was a kind she knew. It was a Mimi, a rock-spirit from a country near her own - a frail and gentle type, in constant fear of the wind and of breaking; and a stranger here, as the Yunggamurra was. Of all the earth-things she might have chosen to help her home, none could have been better than this.

'She shall help me,' whispered the Yunggamurra savagely into her fingers, 'or I will break her into tiny straws. Let her only see me and she will know and tremble.'

2

The Yunggamurra was so filled with wicked triumph that she quivered like a string. The creatures below must have felt her presence if they had not been welcoming another stranger. A rock-spirit! What else could travel so surely through these roads of rock? And where should she travel but to her own country, so near the Yunggamurra's? The river-spirit crouched in the darkness above, ready to spring. A Mimi - what was a Mimi to a Yunggamurra?

But she did not spring; just in time she remembered the

others below. The bright-eyed Little People were many and strong; the tailed creatures had a free, fierce manner that matched her own. For the headless women she felt only scorn, but she dreaded the shapeless shadows. They most of all seemed to belong to the dark, imprisoning heart of the land. They would not tolerate an intruder here.

It was clear that they had expected the Mimi and welcomed her. She had paused, lank and frail, at the edge of the shadows while her large round eyes took in the scene. Now she turned away with shy ceremony, folded her wispy length down, and sat on the rock with her back to the fire. At once the others surged forward with a murmur and rumble of voices, inviting her, bowing their heads and speaking with respect. The dark formless shapes flowed towards her. The Yunggamurra watched sharply, frowning. She had never seen so much respect shown to a stranger and a Mimi.

'We have fire, we have food,' the Little People coaxed.

'We have heard the word,' said those with tails, 'and we have heard the wind and felt the ice. Our roads are open to the Fighter of Ice.'

At these words the Yunggamurra quivered again, with curiosity and angry disbelief. She and her sisters had heard no word of ice, but she had seen it here in a cave. No Mimi had fought it; she could not believe in a Mimi fighting anything at all. She watched while the Mimi rose and turned, standing very straight with her dark eyes glowing green, yet looking more defiant than proud as she walked to the fire.

'See her!' The Yuggamurra whispered, scratching her own arms with her nails as she hugged herself in scorn. 'Too timid even for a proper pride! Wau! When I have her alone! I will make the fighter wilt like a broken fern!' But she listened sharply, and grinned when the Mimi's first words confirmed her disbelief.

'You shame me, for I am no fighter. My part was only to help the fighter on his way. The word that came to you was his word, for he is both good and brave.'

'Who are we to know these things?' said one of the tailed

women. 'We know only that the Ninya came this way with their cold wind, building ice, and now they have gone back. You have the knowledge, Great One. Inform our ears.'

The Little People had been busy laying bat and lizard and grubs in the ashes of the fire. Now they looked up with their star-like eyes fixed on the Mimi. 'You tell,' they begged in a soft rumble, and made room beside the fire.

The Mimi folded herself down again like one who has travelled a long and weary way. Smoke rose in the heavy stillness, the smoke of burning bones and rubbish, of singed fur and scales. The Yunggamurra cowered between her rocks, but the Mimi sniffed gratefully and gazed at the fire as if she saw her story in it.

'The Men of Ice,' she murmured, and all the earth-creatures were still and listened. She knew they had heard the story for all the roads were buzzing with it, but they needed to hear it again from her. And had they not met to bring her fire and food?

'They came from their home under the red sand,' she said, 'for they planned to lock the land in ice as in the old days when they were strong. But first they would find the Eldest Nargun, the one with the power of fire, lest it should defeat them with fire before they were strong again. And so they came, through your country and many more, east to the sea and down to the far end of the land in search of the Eldest. And we followed, to warn the Nargun and rouse it.'

Still the listeners were silent, for to the name of the Ninya was added the name of the Nargun, and that name was known in the deep rocks. The Mimi gazed at the fire seeing what she had seen; and at last another of the tailed creatures spoke.

'It was a terrible ice. It cracked rocks. You have seen them? Great rocks that never saw the light, a dreaming of mountains whose time is not yet come. And the ice, swelling like a frog, has burst them apart.' He spoke solemnly, but a quick red spark in his black eyes made the Yunggamurra grin.

The Mimi saw it too. 'The land will shape the unborn

mountains, child of Kooleen,' she said sternly, and the spirit shifted its eyes. 'The ice was our affair.'

'You tell,' urged the Little People, bringing singed food set out on stones.

'We tracked it to the beach where the Eldest lay, but the Eldest was beyond its time. We fought the ice with the fires of Men. There never were such fires. They too cracked rocks, child of Kooleen.'

'The fires of Men . . . .' A crowd of eyes, bright and dark, stared at her. Even the Yunggamurra was caught up in the tale.

'Men and spirits fought together under one leader.' The Mimi's twiglike fingers grasped the bat by the leg but she had forgotten it. 'That was a fight. The Ninya crawled back into their holes, and the People of their country came to sing them home.'

'And the leader? Who was that?'

'A man. Wirrun of the People.'

Voices rumbled, half believing. 'A man of the People!' 'Are the old times come again?' 'Was this an Old One beyond his time?'

'A young man of this time, one who lives in the towns of the white men. But he hears the voice of the land and carries an old power. Wirrun of the People, the Fighter of Ice . . . .' Her head drooped and she stared unseeing at the singed and broken bat. 'I grieve to lose him,' whispered the Mimi, who had nagged and scolded Wirrun down half the length of the land. The headless, groping women swayed towards her, the Yunggamurra sniggered, the Little People were respectfully silent, the shadow-shapes fluttered and were still, and one of the tailed women gave her tail an insolent flick.

'And what was your part, Great One? How came a Mimi from the far north to cross the land and fight the ice with this great leader?'

The Mimi lifted her head in sudden pride that made the Yunggamurra frown. 'I rode the winds, wife of Kooleen, as the Mimi cannot do. I was carried off from my home and rode the winds from sea to sea and was not broken. This was my part: to help the Fighter ride the winds. And to use my eyes and ears for him, and acquaint him with strange spirits.' Her eyes fell to the fire again, brooding. 'The land ordered it; but I am weary for my country. Weary with wanting.'

'Soon now,' the Little People comforted her. 'You eat. You rest.' They offered her the grubs, which were their own secret kind and a great restorer of strength.

The Mimi ate politely but absently, drooping beside the fire. She had played her part as an honoured guest; she had sat by their fire, eaten their food, spoken what they needed to hear. She hoped there would be no corroboree. The journey home, through so many countries and with so much honour, was wearier than ever the journey with Wirrun had been, and the nearer she came to her own country the sharper was the pain of her need.

The Yunggamurra watched narrow-eyed from above, avoiding the smoke as well as she could. She had never before had to endure smoke - at home she and her sisters would have dived deep into the sweet water - and it filled her with a shuddering unease. She dreaded that the smoke would bring her drifting down like a withered leaf on the crowd below. Besides, she needed clear eyes and ears to see, to hear, and to think.

She had heard the Mimi's story with some awe, for even a lost Yunggamurra knows how the land must be served. But this serving was over, and the ice had never reached her country. She had seen only the remains of it in a cave. Her own need for her country was as sharp a pain as any, and she knew fiercely that this Mimi must take her home. But while the Mimi rested there beside the fire in the care of so many, there was nothing to be done but to wait and think.

It would not be as easy as the Yunggamurra had hoped. The Mimi was no fighter, that was confirmed, but her story showed that she had courage and pride. And if she should refuse to help - what use was a broken Mimi to the Yunggamurra? Yet she thought that the Mimi would not refuse, for there had been that moment when they two might have been sisters: when the Mimi had spoken of the weariness of waiting, and the river-spirit had felt the weight of loneliness and despair.

'Let me only come to her alone,' whispered the Yunggamurra, clenching her nails into her palms. Yet even that would not be easy, for all the spirits of the land had a duty to watch for and welcome and help this Mimi.

On the rocks below the fire was dying. The tailed creatures and the headless ones stood apart in groups. The Mimi, watched over by shadow-shapes and Little People, lay sleeping by the fire - or was she sleeping? The Yunggamurra, peering, thought she caught a green glint of eyes and drew quickly back. She waited and listened. It seemed a long time before she heard a stirring and crept forward again.

The Mimi had roused and the tailed figures were scattering the fire. There was only the dim glow of the spirits themselves as they prepared to set the Mimi on her way. No light came from those shapeless shadows, the most dreaded. They were only a movement of dark at the edge of the glow, and the Yunggamurra bit her lip. She must go carefully. She watched the group trail away into a passage at the far end of the cave and their glow fade. She waited for a moment longer, then, swift and silent, climbed down and followed.

The next cave held a pool of the secret water. She had to wait behind a rock while the Mimi stooped and drank; all the others drank with her. When the water's clear call had been answered by the rocks and was silent, the Yunggamurra slipped without a splash into the pool. She was glad of it, for it restored her slimy skin and rid her of smoke.

She knew the water-ways better than those of rock and for some time could follow the travellers by those ways, winding through tunnels and cutting back through flooded caves that they must go round or under or over. The sense of their nearness guided her, and the murmur and rumble of voices; echoes in a cavern; sometimes a reflected glow. It was good travelling, swift and safe.

But a moment came when the dark threads and pools of water would not lead her to the voices she could hear. The Yunggamurra, refreshed again, had to leave the water and climb over rock. She crawled into a cleft and saw the spirit-light at its other end. She went through quickly, pausing in the dark mouth of the cleft to look into the cave beyond.

It was one of those caves where sparkling stone had grown into the flowing and dripping shapes of water. At first she though it was ice, but it glittered with colours and had no burning cold. Lit by the spirit-light it shone against the darker rock behind, a dreaming of water in stone. At the centre of the cave a pool caught this sparkle and colour, so that all the cave shone doubled in the water. The Yunggamurra caught her breath and came forward almost into the light. She had not known that any stone could live like this in light. It was another of the land's private thoughts, kept in darkness.

Just in time she clutched at rock to hold herself back from the earth-things in the cave. They were clustered beyond the pool, far too close for safety, but by good fortune turned away from the pool and towards the Mimi. She faced them alone, speaking her farewells. The Yunggamurra, looking out across the pool from her dark cleft, saw this with a curling back of lips from sharp white teeth, a dog's snarl. The moment was near; she stood ready.

'You have brought me far on my way,' the Mimi was saying. 'I thank you for your kindness and will trouble you no more. From here my own road is fastest.'

A spirit's speed is fast indeed, and the Yunggamurra tensed. She must not lose the Mimi in the moment of parting, while she waited for the others to go. She leaned forward, poised.

'We come, we watch,' the Little People were begging. 'We go your road.'

The Mimi stood tall and frail, looking not at the Little People but over their heads.

'I would take you if I could,' she said, 'but the road is dangerous to strangers, and there are evil spirits as well as good. And I must go by my own road, fast and straight and alone, for my country is near and I hunger. You know that hunger.'

She lifted a hand in farewell, and turned to the dark rock and blew on it. A great blackness opened for a moment in the rock, and the Mimi stepped into it and was gone. The rock closed again.

The Yunggamurra slumped back into her crevice. She did not know how long ago the Mimi had seen her and read her purpose. She did not care that the Mimi had kept her secret and saved her from the earth-things of this place. She felt only bitter fury that she had forgotten what she should have known of the ways of the Mimi and their camps and roads within rock.

She lay in her fury until long after the Little People and the tailed people, the headless women and the hovering shadows, had gone. She was alone in the dark, and blind again after the light. She stumbled into the cave that was a wonder of beauty if only it could have been seen, and found her way into the water. There she lay, feeling the emptiness of the cave, the closeness of the dark, and the hugeness of the land that had caught her in its secret heart. After a time she forgot danger in the pain of her loneliness and longing, and she lifted her head from the water and howled.

That wild-dog howl went crying and wailing down caverns and tunnels in the dark, and was caught and answered and built into a pack of howling as though all the Yunggamurra howled with this one. The spirits of the place heard it and cowered; they thought the land itself was howling in its heart. And when the sound had come and gone and died away, when the dark places were silent, the Yunggamurra crawled on her weary way into the depths of the land.

3

Of the men who live in the old south land the brown-skinned People are the eldest race. The two white races, Happy Folk and Inlanders, are two branches from the stem of the first white settlers, and very recent comers. They are so new to the land that the Inlanders still struggle to manage it while they slowly adapt to it; and the Happy Folk, engrossed in the serious business of happiness, do their best to forget the land altogether. The coming of the People was long before, and by now the land has made them its own and flows in their veins. Yet there is an older race still: the old things that the land itself has bred, of whom only the People are aware. The earth-creatures, of spirit kind.

They are scarcely seen even by the People, but they are many, for their time is not yet past. As the land bred them so they live by it: by rock, sand, forest, river, and the quiet breadth of night. Any tree, any whirlwind may harbour its spirit; the surface caves and deep caverns are full of them. They are fearful or charming, cruel or kind, by no law but their own or the will of the land. Yet though they are many and everywhere, few of the spirits themselves know the camps and roads of the Mimi. These lie within solid rock, in the First Dark. The Yunggamurra would have remembered this if it had not seemed to her, a spirit of the open rivers, that she herself was enclosed in solid rock.

When the rock closed round the Mimi in answer to her blowing, its dark stillness wrapped her in peace and the certainty of home. She was sorry for the river-spirit trapped in so strange a country, but she had told that spirit the truth: she could not travel by slow water-paths, or with so wild and fierce a companion. She remembered the day when she herself had been taken by the wind up into the dizzy sky: how she had dreaded that she would never see her home again! How helpless she had been, and how afraid. She had not known herself then. A hundred ages had not taught her

27

what she had learnt in the last few weeks. So she set off fast and true on her own road home, knowing what she would meet when she reached it and how she must face it. And on a day when the Wet was beginning - when the swamps lay open to the clouds that came down, and only within rock was there peace and a fire - she came back to her kind.

'Wa!' they said. 'You are here.' They said no more just then, for they knew no more and needed time to adjust. No word from the south had reached them, and in their warm wet country they knew nothing of the ice. On the day the wind had carried one of them off they had found her bark dish and her digging stick where she had dropped them, and had guessed what had happened and hidden it decently.

The Mimi are too light to resist the wind, and so frail that it breaks them easily. For this reason they gather their food only in still weather and every Mimi obeys the tabu of the wind. So to be caught by the wind has become improper, and if possible some other reason must be found to explain such accidents. They had preferred to believe that this Mimi and been carried off by a more evil spirit; they had mourned her suitably, revenged her by magic, and given her up. Now here she stood and the truth would have to come out.

All this the Mimi knew. 'The wind took me,' she confessed with drooping head, 'and the land saved me. It had work for a Mimi.' And she told them the story as briefly as possible with no pride. Pride was her secret from now on, for she knew what was right in her country. She would be no Great One here; it was only right.

Her kind listened, tall and wispy and embarrassed, avoiding each other's eyes. They still had no knowledge of the ice, for words are only words, but they did not know how to punish or reject one who had been called to do the work of the land. Yet it was wrong that one Mimi should come down safe from the wind and perhaps lead into it many others who would not be saved to do the land's work. They needed more time to see what grew out of this. Silently they went away.

The Mimi made her fire where she was and sat by it alone.

She was not depressed by the coldness of the others for she had known how it must be. She was back in her dear north country with the swamps filling outside, and her stick-like body was silently singing for joy. She wanted to dance with the slender flying grace of the Mimi, but she must not for her people's sake. She stayed demure, downcast, and alone.

In the next few days she spent much time alone, hearing the voices of her kind and hiding a smile of content. She followed out all her adventure, needing this time to make it a secret part of her. She felt again her parting from Wirrun, and opened her wispy fingers and let it go. She thought of the wild water-woman trapped inside the land, and pitied her but not too much: if she did not find her home again, at any rate she would find herself. She sat alone and thought of these things while the others watched her secretly for any sign of a swollen head. They watched her gathering wood and food in the shelter of rocks, making a digging stick or spinning string, eating alone by her fire, always decently timid and drooping.

They began to come in twos and threes, late when the fires were low, to whisper to her. It was always the same question, morbidly eager: 'Is it terrible on the wind?'

She answered soberly with a shiver: 'It is terrible . . . . It is rising and falling and twisting, with the limbs cracking . . . . The land and the sky change places and roll about. The stars are sharp, and the wind-spirits cry . . . . You are nothing. There is no fire and no home.'

The inquisitive ones would creep away in silence, burdened. By day they turned to look at her and whisper, and she knew they spoke of it. In a little while they spoke of it aloud, pointing her out with pity and at last with kindly scorn. 'See, here is the one that the wind caught. It took her ears away, but she thinks with a better ear now.'

Then the Mimi knew she had won back a place among her people; a lowly place, but it would do. She never told them anything but the terror of the wind. She never spoke of battle or the young man of the People, but she thought of him often and wondered if he too had come home.

And Wirrun of the People was as near home as he could be. He was in that eastern country by the sea that was his own country, even weighed down as it was by concrete and bitumen. He was in the town from which he had set out, and in which not long ago he had gone to school with the children of the Happy Folk. He had not yet found a job, for the world of spirits and moonlit seas still hung about him and he could not cast it off; but he had borrowed money from his friend Ularra to pay his rent and restock the noisy old refrigerator in his room. He told himself restlessly that he would find a job next week. Next week would be better and more real, or he tried to think so.

He was sitting now in a dimly lit milkbar, sprawling in a high-backed bench with Ularra sprawling in another across the narrow table. These two had each another name among the Happy Folk, but when they were together they used the names known to the People. Wirrun's eyes were shadowed, for he had been telling the story that Ularra had a right to hear. Ularra was grinning with delight and disbelief, and sometimes laughing loudly and throwing his long arms and legs about as he went back over the impossible story.

'And that old bunyip, eh?' he said again, boisterously because he was not much older than Wirrun. 'I bet *he's* scared a lot of little kids.' Wirrun stirred restlessly, and Ularra saw and looked subdued. He was concerned for his friend without knowing how to say so or what to do. The adventure sounded like a crazy game to him, and young Wirrun had won it and done all right for himself. He ought to be wagging his tail a bit. But there was something different about him, and Ularra couldn't pick it.

The broad east-country face, so different from Ularra's longer northern one, was the same yet not the same. That hair, always tangled into curls like a kid's, that was Wirrun all right. The quietness, with the wide white grin coming through ... it still came through, but it wasn't the same grin. He'd always been quiet, but not ... stern. Stern? Ularra heaved around on his bench, knocking over a cup. Not stern ... tired, maybe. It had been a rough time. What was it? About two weeks? Not enough, you'd think, to turn a boy into a man. In the old days it took longer.

'It was good seeing the mob from Conner,' he said; for the men from Mount Conner who had brought Wirrun home belonged to the country near Ularra's own, and his eyes had lit up and his laugh had been loud while he talked to them. 'They think a lot of you.'

'They're good men,' said Wirrun, smiling; but then he sighed.

Ularra tried again. 'I heard the pub down the street's looking for a yard man. Not bad, a job in a pub - I wouldn't mind it. But look, you don't want to worry about it. I got cash, and if I run short there's others. It's only right.'

Wirrun knew it was only right, for the Ninya - the Ice-Men - had been the People's concern and not just his; but he also knew he must get a job as soon as he could. It was the only way to live in the Happy Folk's town - and the only way to get out into the country as he needed to do, and walk on the land and feel it flowing into him through his feet.

'I'll see them Monday,' he said, and hesitated. 'Only there's something I gotta do first. If you can spare the cash.'

Ularra's hand was in his pocket. 'How much?'

'Five should do. Gotta go north to that mountain and put the power back where I found it.'

Ularra pushed a note across the table, waited till Wirrun had pocketed it, and said, 'You're crazy. You'd do better to stay home and get some sleep - looks as if you need it. What's the point? It's yours, that stone. Who else is around to look after it? Keep it, man.'

'Can't,' said Wirrun, not trying to explain because Ularra knew the reasons. He knew the age and power of the great quartz crystal in its wrapping of possum-fur string; that it was a power for a man and Wirrun had never been made a man; that he had been led to it only by the old spirit of the mountain - by Ko-in, who was Hero, and whose stern, strong voice Wirrun heard so often in his mind .... *I will speak to no more men till the ice comes again.*

'Crazy,' said Ularra uneasily, because he could see that for some reason Wirrun had to go back to the mountain.

So Wirrun bought a train ticket that same night, and made the short journey north and slept by a stream. And the next morning, with his travel-stained pack on his back, he walked to the mountain.

4

This mountain that Wirrun sought was the one on which his adventure with the ice had properly begun. He walked to it with his long, loose stride away from the highway, along dusty roads that he remembered; and the power, the magic stone hidden so deep in its fur-string wrapping, hung in its bag from his belt. He knew that Ularra was partly right: he need not have made this short journey so soon just to put the power back in its place. They had done the land's work together, and he was used now to having it in trust; he and the power did each other no harm. He could have waited until he had a job and money of his own for the trip, without borrowing Ularra's. And he did need rest. That was partly what he came for; that, and to be alone.

They'd always said he was a loner, and he knew they were right - but in his wanderings round the country he had always liked to meet and talk to the People. He had felt at home with them. He'd been glad of the People's help in fighting the ice. Good men, all of them. So why had he needed to get away from them to be alone? He had spent weeks talking only to spirits, and it had felt easy and right; he had travelled a long way with a Mimi and parted from her sadly. He missed her more than the People and it worried him. He was real, and life in the town was real, and he couldn't get it started. He was tired and empty and spirit-haunted and he couldn't believe in a job on Monday. He needed . . . rest . . . .

But how could he come from that shadowy company and rest with a motorbike revving outside a broken window? How could he come from a moonlit, calling sea to Ularra's laughter in a murky milkbar? He knew he was running away to the mountain, to something that was unreal and yet more than real. He needed to be alone.

He saw the heads of mountains looking at him over a wooded ridge, and sat down for a while and looked back. And he knew he was partly fooling himself: he didn't come here only to be alone, but to be alone with his mountain. That mountain had shown him old terrors and old evils as well as old powers; he had walked on it at night and heard its voice. He wanted to walk on it again with everything put right, and perhaps the mountain would know. Perhaps it would feel like home again.

I will speak to no more men until the ice comes again. But that had been Ko-in, not the mountain.

At midday he came to a village on a ridge with the scrub-draped, forest-hung mountains standing over it. He did not go to the village shop to buy supplies; he had carried a heavier pack all this way in order to avoid it. It was only a couple of weeks since the Inlanders of this place had watched him with hard suspicion, and he had known they thought of bushfires and careless shots meant for rabbits and the noisy nuisance of a silly young drunk, and other realities of their lives. He did not want to be seen again so soon. He skirted the village and took his old path to the one mountain, the nearest one.

He knew the way up through the lower forest, between the boulders of the steepening slope, to the sheer heights of rock and scrub. He went straight to the sheltering ledge where he had camped before, and began to build his fire in the old place where the shoulder of the mountain hid it from the village. Often he paused to stare at a hollow tree or an outline of rock, remembering. It seemed so long ago . . . .

He did not light the fire but sat beside it in the shade of the ledge and ate a cold lunch, looking from the mountain across the ridge to blue-hazed valleys in the summer heat, and farther mountains, and the dark tree-lined course of a river, to a distant misty blue that might be the sea. It felt like home, but the mountain did not speak.

After a time he took his canvas water-bag and climbed around to the steep rocky gully where the stream trickled, and down into the gully. It was deeply shadowed, for the sun was already behind the high wall of rock that closed the head of the gully. Wirrun sat for some time by a little pool between rocks. The moss was still black from that impossible summer frost, but new curled fronds were showing among the blackened ferns. He touched one gently, saying that everything was all right again. His fingers strayed from the fern to the net bag hanging at his belt.

Now he was here, in the very place. In three minutes he could return the power to that dark hole where a dying man had hidden it long ago. He might as well climb up there now, to the hole in the cliff at the head of the gully; but he only sank his canvas bag into the pool, wetting and filling it, holding it carefully to draw in clean water. He would sleep another night here on the mountain with the power. Tomorrow was time enough.

He climbed back to his camp as the day's heat was ebbing, hung the water-bag in its place on a root that curled over the ledge, and lit his fire. Then he sat feeding it, waiting for the good red coals that would grill his steak, watching the sunset reflected in the eastern sky from behind the mountain. He saw the gold drain away, and pinpoint stars shine in the clear green of evening; sitting with his hand on the power, feeling the soft ball of cord and the hardness of the stone within, and the roundness that swelled to the roundness of the world inside his hand. He felt again the lift and swell of the mountain under him, but it did not speak.

When the coals were right he cooked his steak, then built the fire into a blaze and ate by its light. The dark breathed in and out as the flames rose and fell, but there was no thickening of fearful shapes in it. He could just see, farther along the ledge, the tree that he knew had a hole in the trunk from which Ko-in had dragged forth the Mimi. How spindly and cantankerous and staunch she had been, and how much he missed her. What a lot of sadness there was mixed up in the joy of restoration . . . and as he thought this the hard sadness softened and began to flow.

He put his head down to rub the wetness off his chocolate-brown cheek on to his knee; and when he lifted it again he saw that a shape did stand at the edge of the firelight, watching him. The red-yellow light washed over it: a man of the People, tall and strong, painted with white markings and carrying a firestick.

'Welcome to my country, Hero,' said Ko-in.

Wirrun goggled at him as he came forward into the firelight. 'I never hoped -' he stammered. 'You said no more - I brought the power back.'

'The power is yours and in your keeping. Hero must honour hero, and you were in need.'

'I was that,' Wirrun confessed. 'I'm in a lot better shape for seeing you. You know it's turned out all right?'

'I know and I honour you.'

'It was others, mainly - the Mimi most of all. Did she get home safe? Do you know that?'

'All is well,' said Ko-in on a note of exasperation. 'I never met a man so hard to honour. Again: I salute you, Hero.'

'You needn't. I'm no hero. You know well enough what I am.'

Ko-in bowed his head in agreement. 'Better than you know. And there are words to be spoken.' He crossed the firelight and sat himself formally, cross-legged, by Wirrun's side. 'We will speak at your fire, for the time is past when I might carry you through the wind to mine.'

'I know that,' said Wirrun a bit roughly. He was no little kid looking for favours. The time had passed with the need.

'Hear me,' said Ko-in, 'for you know only what you will

not know, and what you will know is all greenness. You have come to this country as a tired man comes home, and I welcome you. But you must know the truth. This country is my home. Yours is wider.'

Wirrun gazed at him under lowered brows, and the firelight hid his eyes in shadow.

'Hold back your anger and hear me. You came here first as a boy with down on your chin, knowing nothing, only listening to the land. I gave you knowledge and power, and sent you forth with help beside you. I could do no less, for the land called you and the men are gone and there was no help at hand but mine.'

'And I'm thankful,' muttered Wirrun angrily. He burst out, 'I remember every word you said, always! You said your love would follow me, and I rested on that. Is it any wonder if this place feels like home? Was it wrong to come back and say what's done?'

'It is no wonder and it was right. Have I not welcomed you? But tonight I have stood by your fire and watched, and I see more than a young hero returned. I see a man, a man whose country has found him. I came to salute you and welcome you to my country. I stay to show you yours.'

To be called hero was a thing that washed over Wirrun like firelight, but to be called a man touched him like a finger. He smiled wryly, rubbing his chin. 'Still a bit fuzzy,' he said. 'Can't change much in a couple of weeks.'

'No?' Ko-in smiled gravely. 'The men would have taken a little longer, but you have been made a man by other means. You have not learnt the lore of this country, but there are lores for all countries. Which of the youths of your People has journeyed to manhood in the arms of Tu-ru-dun? Has made his man's journey with a Mimi for companion? Has been taught spirits by the spirits themselves? Has fought beside and against them, and led them to victory? I could say more.'

'Don't bother. I don't feel no different, any rate.'

'Only because you will not know. By shoulders, mouth

and eyes a man reveals himself and not by the hair on his chin. Such a man-making cannot be denied; you must accept it. Come, Hero. I will show you your country.'

Wirrun rose with him unwillingly and followed beyond the firelight to the dark edge of the mountain. Grey starlight lay over ridge and forest, outlining the lift of hills and the long arms of spurs. The old south land, released from the day's heat, stretched and expanded in the breadth of night. Wirrun laid his hand on the power and found it was throbbing. The land reached for him, night-murmuring and hung with stars. Ko-in spoke beside him.

'From sea to sea, there lies your country.'

'It's a lonely country,' said Wirrun, 'too big for me. I'd sooner have just this bit.'

'You cannot take back your name from the places where it is known. There are makings that cannot be denied, Hero, and names that must be accepted. You have said that you remember the words of Ko-in: remember these, for in time you must believe them.'

'Eh?' said Wirrun. 'Of course I - you know I -' He saw Ko-in's grave smile and pulled himself together. 'It's all a bit big for me, that's all, like the country. All I know is, you're chucking me out of the place I thought I had . . . .'

'If the name is too big you must grow. And do not envy me my country, for it too is yours. When your fire burns where it burns tonight I will come to you. Now rest well,' said Ko-in as he had said once before, 'and wake well, and journey well out of my country.' And he sprang up into the wind and rose between the trees and was gone.

Wirrun went back to his fire confused, like a man between sleeping and waking. He could not seize on and remember the words of Ko-in; they slid away as he reached for them, and would not hold together. He gave up trying at last, and sat and stared at the fire while it died; and then one sentence did come back clearly in the strong voice of Ko-in.

When your fire burns where it burns tonight I will come to you: he could never have hoped for such comfort as that.

He climbed into his sleeping-bag, taking the power with him as he always had, and fell deeply asleep.

If the scrub stood closer about his ledge while he slept, he did not know it. If the darkness gathered in fantastic shapes and whispered, 'Hero, the ice is gone,' he heard nothing. He had been given rest. Tiredness and haunting drained away; partings were made and finished; all the realities merged into one and grew whole. Even the words of Ko-in sank through his sleep into deep places in his mind, to be remembered in time. Only when grey starlight thinned to the first grey of dawn did his sleep thin a little, and then he was hushed by the sound of water. There was a rushing of water rising and falling through his sleep, sometimes with words singing in it. It held him and charmed him till the sun probed under his ledge and he woke. He turned his head to look for the water, saw where he was, and forgot it.

He felt good. Even the spiderweb tangled on his dark face and hair felt good. Beyond the shelter of his ledge there was dew that the sunlight struck into sparks. He looked at it for a while, then sat up and looked farther: out from the mountain and down to the ridge where the village lay under a thin streak of mist .... He had been given a land for a country. To a man of the People it was a stern gift, as Ko-in had known. But he had been given manhood to accept it, and the mountain was part of it too. He got up and went to the water-bag to splash his face with cold water.

He ate breakfast, tidied the camp, buried the fire, and left his pack rolled under the ledge. Then, with the power hanging at his belt for the last time, he set off for the gully. *The power is yours and in your keeping*: well, he was putting it back in its place. His time with the earth-spirits had finished while he slept - a man had to go back to town and find a job.

The gully was full of morning sunlight as he climbed down into it and up its narrow bed to the cliff. The rock had warmed already. The frost-blackened mosses would not be green again before autumn, he thought. He climbed a little way up the cliff by a narrow ledge, towards that hole in the rock where a man of the old People had hidden the power. Balanced and leaning against the rock, he unfastened his belt and slipped off the net bag. But he held the bag for a little while, and put one hand into it to hold the soft roundness of fur. He had held it like that often . . . but only once, at Ko-in's bidding, had he unwound the fur cord and looked at the pointed, hexagonal crystal of quartz, glinting and veined with pink. He held it - and felt it throb - and suddenly there was the sound of water, and a daylight dreaming.

He thought a waterfall poured over the cliff above him and into the gully. He saw the swirl of water and the whiteness of foam and heard its roar. It wavered, the water dwindled to a silver curtain, and the song of water softened; and again it broke forth, and leapt and tumbled and foamed. It wavered, and rushed and roared again, and he heard words singing in the sound of the water.

Are you not coming?
sings the bright water,
are you not coming?

Wirrun snatched his hand away from the power, holding only the net bag. The waterfall vanished: but still the sound of it was in his ears, and the words singing from low to high and drifting down again like a wind-dropped leaf. He thrust the power into its hole and pushed it back into darkness as far as he could reach.

He had just woken to the ordinary things that a man had to live with. He would not be caught again by a dreaming.

TWO

The Name of Hero

I

On Monday Wirrun went to the pub down the street and got
the job as a yardman and cleaner. It was not as good a job as
his last one at the service station, but he could have all his
meals in the hotel kitchen and that would make the money
go further; and there was a clean, dull room across the yard
near the garages, where he could live and save the rent of his
old flat.

'You'll clean it yourself,' said the stout white woman who
ran the hotel, 'and get a change of linen from the house-
keeper once a week. You'll stay out of the house unless
you're sent for. The room's your own but there'll be no
rowdyism. That clear?'

Wirrun nodded. His thick-lipped, broad-nosed People's
face was heavily serious. The woman noticed it.

'We've got no prejudices here,' she said roundly as if he
had accused her. 'The same rules for everyone.'

Wirrun nodded again. He was not resentful; the Happy
Folk had rested in his hands along with the beetle and the
starfish and would never again be large enough for anger.
He was simply holding on to the ordinary things that a man
had to live with.

Ularra approved of the job, partly because of the free
meals and cheap beer that went with it but chiefly because it
seemed to have ended Wirrun's restless unhappiness. On
Monday night, when he helped Wirrun to move his belong-
ings from the flat to the room behind the hotel, he was noisy
with pleasure. Standing tall and loose-limbed under the
light, he looked at Wirrun's new home and nodded.

'More room and cheap beer. You'll be all right here, man.'

'No rowdyism, mind,' said Wirrun with the wide grin that lightened all his face. He had taken a bottle from the small refrigerator and was pouring beer. Ularra took his chipped glass with noises of approval, and his eyes gleamed against the darkness of his skin.

'That's the stuff,' he said, and dropped untidily into the one armchair with his feet on Wirrun's bed. 'What's it like any rate?'

Wirrun had taken his own glass over to the old wardrobe; it had a deep bottom drawer in which he was storing the things he wouldn't be needing for a while. His sleeping-bag and camping gear; his collection of maps; clippings from newspapers, pasted on to sheets of paper. He glanced at those as he laid them away: SUMMER FREEZE ON TABLELANDS. But suddenly it was the rushing music of water that filled his mind, and a haunting drift of song ... *are you not coming*? He shut his mind to it quickly.

'I said, what's it like?' shouted Ularra.

'Eh? Oh ... all right. Good tucker. Funny eating in the kitchen with them watching, but I'll get used to it.'

'You can bring home some of that take-away stuff for a change. What about time off?'

'About usual. Finish at four-thirty. Couple of weeks' leave a year, maybe - I'm not sure. Makes no difference.'

'Go on - that's not you. You'll be off somewhere for a few days sooner than that.'

Wirrun shut the drawer with a bang and began to unpack clothes into smaller drawers. 'No money,' he said firmly. 'Got to keep my head down till I pay what I owe.'

Ularra sat up and reached for the beer. 'You know better than that, man.' He sounded hurt. 'Never's soon enough - you paid it back before I lent it.' The beer had already made him earnest. 'I got rights too, you know. Maybe I missed out on these Ninya and Mimi and those, but any rate I can put a bit of cash in. They're nearer my business than yours.'

'I know that,' said Wirrun quickly, for Ularra's home was near Mount Conner and the country of the Ninya. Into the

silence came the distant roar of the hotel's bar, where the
Happy Folk were avoiding rowdyism in their own way
under the eye of the stout lady. 'If that's how you want it.
Only I still gotta keep my head down. Time I settled down a
bit. A man's not a kid all his life.'

Ularra threw himself back in the chair, hurled his legs on
to Wirrun's bed, spilt a little beer, and laughed for some
time. 'Listen to him! Couple of weeks and he's got grey hairs
coming! Man, you'll have that gear out and be off for a
weekend before you're a month older.'

> *Are you not coming?*
> *sings the bright water*

'Not me,' said Wirrun. 'It's a year till I get any leave. Then
we'll see.'

'I've got a fiver says it'll be in a month,' declared Ularra.

He would have lost his money. Wirrun settled into his
room and his job, worked silently by day and read the
newspaper at night. He grew used to the roar of the bar,
began to exchange grave smiles with the staff and to like
some of them. He often spent an evening with Ularra, in a
milkbar or in his own room; and Ularra's easy chatter began
to dry up, and he sometimes looked at Wirrun with puzzled
respect.

Wirrun looked at concrete and smog and painted metal;
he watched the Happy Folk eagerly chasing happiness or
sternly marketing it; sometimes he saw the People lost and
searching. He would not look at far-off moonlit seas. He
closed his mind to the haunting sound of water. That water-
dream still haunted him, but he held on to the ordinary
things that a man had to live with and grew older and
sterner; and more than one month went by.

One evening Ularra brought two strangers to the
milkbar: men of the People, visitors from an inland
country. They were shabbily dressed, with stubble on their
chins, and they sat silently at the table gazing at Wirrun. He
asked them about their country and they answered with
short, blunt shyness. He could see that someone had told

them stories about him and he looked reproachfully at
Ularra. But Ularra only stared intently at the waitress, for
this was his latest game. He called it 'eyeing off a chick'.
Wirrun was glad when the evening was over and the
strangers went away, still silent and respectful.

'You got no right cheating men like that,' he said roundly
to Ularra, and got only a look of puzzled surprise.

A few weeks later, on an evening when Wirrun was at
home reading the newspaper, Ularra brought another
stranger of the People. This one too was shy and silent and
only looked with shadowed eyes at Wirrun while Ularra, a
little nervous and therefore showing off, shouted for beer.

Wirrun produced it. He had noticed lately that an
evening at home with Ularra used up more bottles than it
would have used once. Ularra talked a lot, Wirrun a little,
and the stranger not at all until the third bottle was empty.
Then he leaned forward suddenly and laid a hand on
Wirrun's sleeve.

'Had to see the hero,' he said very earnestly. 'Couldn't - go
home and not - tell 'em.' He lifted his glass unsteadily. 'All
the men - thanks.'

'You want to forget that,' said Wirrun shortly.

It was a terrible evening. Even Ularra seemed to realise it,
and rose and stretched and took the visitor away. When they
had gone and Wirrun had closed the yard gate behind them
he went quickly into his room and opened a fourth bottle of
beer.

He reproached Ularra when he came alone the next
evening. Ularra looked dogged.

'What's the harm, letting 'em come and look? It means a
lot to them and it don't cost you a cent. How can you turn
'em down, man? What else can I do?'

'You can stop filling 'em up with yarns, and then it won't
happen,' said Wirrun.

Ularra stood under the light and gazed down at him. 'You
been telling me lies, then?' Wirrun frowned with anger. 'If it
happened,' said Ularra, 'it happened. No good pretending
it didn't.'

'What's done's over and best forgotten,' snapped Wirrun. 'I'm just a bloke like them - I got nothing to give 'em but a bit of free beer. You ought to grow up, man, it's time.'

Ularra lowered his brows. 'You could do a bit of that yourself, for a man that grew up quick. I tell 'em nothing they don't ask. They come looking - what do you expect? There's been near a dozen, I reckon, but you never saw 'em. Only the few that need it.'

'Need it!' Wirrun was shaken, even shocked. He had seen the People as lost and searching; he would not have them cheated with false hopes. For a little time he had been an instrument used by the land and guided by its spirits, nothing more. 'They need to get out and stand on their own feet, that's what they need. And you and me too.'

Ularra dropped into the armchair and grinned. They had been close to a quarrel, but he would not quarrel with Wirrun. '*You* need it. Me, I'm getting out soon as my leave's due, only you won't come. Where's this beer? And won't that heater do any better? I can't wait to get out of this and away to the sun. You oughta come, man. You need a break.'

'My turn'll come,' said Wirrun, kicking the heater closer. He knew he would not dare to leave the town while the water-music haunted him; and lately it seemed to be growing worse. He listened while Ularra talked of his own leave, due in only a month, and of the trip he would make to his People in the centre of the land. The thought of it shone in Ularra's eyes and boomed in his voice. It led him into fantasies about a dark-eyed girl of the People, one he remembered from his last visit; maybe he might bring her back as a wife.

'You couldn't do better,' said Wirrun firmly, and he meant it.

It was a long journey that Ularra planned for his leave: more than a thousand miles across the old south land. It never occurred to him to travel as Wirrun had once or twice, by the speedy and expensive routes of the Happy Folk. There would need to be a strong reason for such extravagance. Ularra would go by the slower routes of the

People, from country to country, seeing as many friends as he could on the way and spending only a few days with his own People. The journey had to be thought out, planned and discussed; a month was only time enough. For a month Wirrun listened and nodded and approved, and forced himself to speak warmly while the grooves on his face deepened. He could scarcely sleep for the haunting of water-music. He was glad when at last the evening came to see Ularra off on the first stage of his journey by train.

'Have a good time, man. I'll miss you.'

'Serves you right, too. You oughta be coming.'

. . . sings the bright water. . . .

Wirrun went home with relief. It was true that he would miss Ularra, yet a strain had crept into their friendship. He told himself that he needed time alone - that he had to sort himself out. He went home to quietness.

For a few days the quietness helped. He worked hard all day and retreated to his room after work. The noise of the streets sounded far away, shut off by the brick wall of the hotel yard. He was used to the background roar of the bar and occasional footsteps stumbling across the yard. There was nothing that needed to be heard, nothing to distract him from his newspaper . . . or his thoughts . . . or the water-haunting . . . .

Try as he would he could not shake it off, and neither could he understand it. In his mind he went over all his adventure with the ice and remembered no singing of bright water. If it had been wind, now: one who had ridden the wind might well be haunted by a song of wind. But this haunting came from nothing but a dream that had soothed him on the mountain, and then had leapt at him out of the power he had carried for weeks - or out of the rocks of the mountain itself. And the mountain had only a trickling stream that would dry up in a hard summer. There was no waterfall rushing and fading, no bright stream . . . *alight with the glancing of glimmer-bright eyes* . . . Wirrun twisted and groaned. He had never even heard that phrase before, not even in a dream on the mountain. Where had it come from, into his mind in a voice like wild honey, its notes drifting down a scale like falling leaves? He wondered if he was going mad, and was glad when Ularra came home.

Ularra brought no dark-eyed bride but came back enlarged by his journey. He talked of sun-gold days and frosty nights round fires, and gave news of the People whom Wirrun had once visited. The journey lasted weeks in the telling, and for a time Ularra drank less beer than usual; but now and then his flow of talk would falter, and he would look doubtfully at Wirrun from under his brows as if there was something more to say for which he could not find the words.

At last, one night, he found them and they startled Wirrun. 'There's bores stopped flowing,' said Ularra. 'They want you to go and see.'

'Eh?' said Wirrun. 'What bores?'

'Bores, man, you know the bores they get water from. There's some stopped flowing.'

'Bad luck for the Inlanders,' said Wirrun lightly. 'Didn't know they had bores in your country.'

'Not bores, they don't,' said Ularra. He was clearly finding it hard to explain. 'They got a spring - same thing. They got word about the bores. They're worried. Want you to go and see.'

'But a lot of those bores don't flow no more without they pump 'em.'

'They know that, man. These do. And there's the spring. It's drying up.'

'You said it was a bad year, no rain. Bound to dry up.'

Ularra had stopped looking embarrassed and began to look irritated. 'There's been other bad years. You think they don't know that spring? Never dried up before. You've got leave. You could go.'

'What for? I don't know bores.'

'You think they're stupid?' shouted Ularra. 'There'll be more, won't there? I dont know what - they're not saying. Only they want you to go. They think a lot of you, like you used to think a lot of them.' He flung himself into the armchair. 'Never thought I'd see you hiding in a pub yard turning your back on your own People.'

'What are you talking about?' roared Wirrun in rage. 'I'd sooner turn my back on 'em than cheat 'em any rate.'

For a long, angry minute they stared at each other in silence. Then Ularra got up and went away.

Are you not coming? No, said Wirrun angrily getting into bed; he was not. If the People wanted to make some sort of hero of him, maybe he couldn't help that. But he wasn't going half across the land on a white man's business like bores.

For weeks after that he did not see Ularra at all. The winter grew restless and blew cold and warm; spring was on the way. Paper bags and drink cartons scuttled furtively along pavements and lay still when Wirrun looked at them; then, as he passed, they rustled again and were flung into spirit-dances. Bits of paper that had been trees, thought Wirrun. Square-cut stones that had been rocks on a hillside. Bricks and concrete and bitumen out of the dark earth. All of them crumbling and wearing away; creeping secretly back into the earth, too slow for a man to see. Sometimes he was frightened and did not know why.

The winds died and the days brightened. It was still strongly daylight when Wirrun sat in his room after work. The doorway darkened, and when he looked up Ularra was standing there. Wirrun hoped this was good.

'There you are, then,' he said in greeting.

Ularra smiled widely and nodded. 'I brought someone,' he said. Wirrun had turned like a good host to the refrigerator, but he turned back at that. 'This is Tommy. Tommy Hunter. From out west, near my country. He's come a long way to see you.'

'Glad to see him,' said Wirrun cautiously.

Tommy smiled and put out a hand. Wirrun took it and felt healed. Tommy Hunter was an older man, straight-looking and firm, a man who lived outside the tightening circles of the Happy Folk and their cities. He wore frayed corduroy trousers, a checked shirt and an old waistcoat, and he waited with dignity to be shown where to sit. Wirrun turned the armchair towards him and Ularra sat on the bed. Tommy said nothing at all until the business of pouring drinks was over and Wirrun sat by him at the table. Then he took a slow sip, put his glass down and wiped his lips with his hand.

'I come to fetch you,' he said.

2

Wirrun lowered his brows and gazed steadily at old Tom Hunter: not a curious traveller come to look at a young man of whom he had heard strange tales, but a steady and mature man who had journeyed more than a thousand miles with a purpose. Here it was, then: the battle he had to fight with his own People for the sake of the truth as he saw it. He was glad it should be fought with a man like Tom Hunter, one who would understand what the battle was about and that Wirrun fought for his People and not against them. He thought maybe Tom understood already, for his gaze was as steady as Wirrun's. And though he must have journeyed to see a man, he would know that manhood itself is a long journey and that Wirrun had only begun it. He would understand that the wise men of the People should not depend on one as young as Wirrun, or put the name of hero on him because for a little while he had been guided by spirits. The name was too big.

And at that, though he gazed at Tommy Hunter, the figure of Ko-in filled his eyes. *You cannot take back your name from the places where it is known . . . . If the name is too big you must grow.* And maybe I will, thought Wirrun; if they give me time.

'You're needed in my country,' said Tommy Hunter, watching him. 'They sent me to fetch you.'

'I'm no good to 'em,' said Wirrun. 'Any man there knows more than what I do.'

Tommy smiled gently, an old man's smile to a young one. But he went on relentlessly. 'We heard there's bores stopped flowing, and we got this spring drying up.'

'Ularra told me,' said Wirrun. 'I don't know bores.'

Ularra poured himself another drink and said nothing. He sat back on the bed and watched both men as closely as they watched each other.

'No harm looking,' said Tom. His voice was deep, rumbling on its low notes. 'A young feller that's been where you been, seen what you seen, he might see something we missed.'

'I've never been down where the bores go. I can't see deep under, more than you can. You know your own spring better.' Wirrun spoke firmly, and hardly knew that part of his mind was asking questions. Why? - why send for him to look at bores and a spring? What other mystery was there that the men were not telling?

Tom chuckled deeply. 'Know Ninya better too, but we never saw what you saw. Lucky you came that time, eh? You're one that's got the eyes for it, a man born Clever.'

'I'm a man,' said Wirrun wearily, 'and I don't know what else. I did what I was sent for. I had help. I can't go under where the bores go.'

'These Ninya can,' said Tommy. 'What about that, eh? You think maybe they're up to something with this spring?'

Could that be it - the reason why they had sent for him? Because they suspected the Ninya again? Wirrun thought for a moment. 'I've been told that all's well,' he said, 'and you don't tell me nothing else.' And he said it as a challenge.

Tommy was silent for a while, staring into his beer. He might have been listening for some word. At last he looked up again and spoke.

'There's this ridge,' he said, 'and under it this stretch where the white gums grow. Like it was a river, only there's no river, wet or dry. But this bit's greener. There's a river down underneath, see. Deep down, and the trees know it. Always been there. My old grandfather told me about that river deep under. He reckoned it came from under the ridge.' Wirrun listened and waited. 'No rain for a long time now,' the older man went on. 'Trees dropping their leaves in the river-beds, everything drying up, just red sand all round ... but that green stretch, she's greener. She's flowering.' He held Wirrun's eyes and saw in them shadows of doubt and wonder. 'That old river's flooding down under there, coming higher, making it greener. But there's been no rain. And the spring's drying that never dried up before.'

The glimmer-bright water alight with the glancing .... No, said Wirrun to his water-haunted mind; that'd be dark water down there.

'Better you come and look,' said old Tom. They drank in silence. Ularra sat on the bed watching their faces.

Tom glanced up almost shyly and spoke again. 'There's these old Pungalunga, or there was. Like men only big, tall as a hill. Did a lot of damage in the old times, ate a lot of People. You can see their bones lying around still, only they're rocks now. A long time back, it was. None of them been about since white men came. Only now there's new tracks. One of 'em's left his prints on the ridges.'

Wirrun heard Ularra's sharply drawn breath; evidently the Pungalunga were new to him too. 'Tracks?' asked Wirrun with a keenness he could not hide. 'Where from? Where to?'

'Can't tell,' said Tom. 'Too big.' In reply to Wirrun's incredulous stare he tried to explain. 'Those sand-ridges, they're bare on top. A man walks up one, he sees a, like a big dish, pressed in the sand. Sixty feet long, might be, and no reason for it. He's got to see it three or four times before he sees the shape right. A month or so, maybe another man goes up another ridge, finds another one. It takes time.'

'Must do,' said Wirrun. 'I don't know how you'd be sure.'

'We know,' said the old man. 'Five or six ridges now, all with a dent on top. A Pungalunga's walked over there, one ridge to the next.'

Wirrun sounded doubtful. 'Maybe. What's it mean any rate? A Pungalunga's a long way from a dried-up spring, isn't it?'

'Can't be sure. We think it's all of a piece. Better you come and see.'

Ularra leaned forward, grasped the bottle, and spoke for the first time. 'You got time off coming, man. Might as well go somewhere.'

Wirrun swung towards him. 'How many times - ' he began, and stopped.

'That's right,' said old Tom. 'You come. We'll look after you all right. If you don't see nothing - you can't help it, that's all. No harm trying.'

Wirrun sat gazing at Ularra, who was filling his glass again. Ularra felt the gaze, looked up, shifted a little, and leaned back trying to get out of range. Wirrun's frowning gaze followed him.

'Easy for you to talk,' he said at last. 'Maybe you think a man just walks out and calls up a few spirits when he wants 'em. I dunno what you do think and that's a fact. Well, last time I gave up my job; this time you can give up yours. Maybe I will go and have a look, only if I do you're coming too.'

Ularra splashed beer over the edge of the bed and brushed it off with his hand, staring at Wirrun. 'Me? What good'll I be? I'm not Clever.'

'It's your country. Well? Are we going?'

On Ularra's long dark face a wondering grin was dawning. 'If that's all you want. Sure we're going.' He sat rocking to and fro on the bed and grinning.

Wirrun ran his hands through his hair, startling it into curls. Why had he said that, when he had never meant to go? A glimpse of Ularra caught in the circles of the Happy Folk, sitting on a bed with his third glass of beer and believing too easily in Wirrun's powers. A story of the desert flowering in the dry, a tale of the Pungalunga stepping from ridge to ridge. Was that all it took to make a man give in when he knew he was right? He couldn't get out of it now, any rate; not with Ularra grinning in pure delight and old Tom nodding with some inner certainty of his own.

'It'll do no good,' he warned them - and felt his conviction loosening its grip as he spoke. When old Tom answered it was as if his words came from somewhere deep in Wirrun's mind.

'Maybe. Can't say. A man can't turn his back on his own country.'

From sea to sea, there lies your country. Ko-in had said it, but the men of the Centre could not know that.

'I'll give a week's notice tomorrow,' said Ularra, still grinning.

They began to talk about the journey. Tommy had taken two weeks to come by the devious routes of the People, sent forward by one group to the next: from the huge quiet Centre northward to the coast, east across the cape, and southward stage by stage as the People of each country arranged; in little boats and in trucks, on foot and on horseback, even once or twice by taxi. He expected to take Wirrun and Ularra back by the same routes, and to Ularra it seemed a reasonabale plan. But Wirrun, after thinking in silence, shook his head.

'Best if we fly and save time.'

Ularra stared at him. 'Three of us? Man - that'll take a lot of money!'

'Trains cost near as much and take longer. Use up all my leave to get there. Best if we can keep one job between us - that's more money than flying.'

Ularra threw himself back on the bed and laughed with excitement, for he had never flown and had envied Wirrun his one trip. 'Me up there in a little tin plane? I'll be broke twice over - going up and falling down!'

Wirrun grinned broadly. It was good to be at one with Ularra again, good to see his eagerness and his willing sacrifice of job and money. He found himself wishing that one

day before he died Ularra might ride the wind and find a real
adventure.

As for Tommy Hunter, at this talk of planes he sat very
straight and unmoved, staring ahead. He had never
travelled the wind's way or wished to do so, but he had been
sent with a call for help to the new young hero and he must
travel as the hero did. It was his fate.

He slept in Wirrun's bed that night, accepting it with
dignity and no argument as an older man and a guest, while
Wirrun unrolled his sleeping-bag on the floor. Wirrun lay
awake for a long time, listening to old Tom's grunting
snores and wondering how much more of the story Tom
knew and had not told. He knew the ways of his People
when they were troubled and unsure. First the message
about bores and a spring, then the tale of the flowering
desert and the Pungalunga's tracks; Tom had told him just
enough to bring him and only what could be shown. As
Ularra had said months ago, there would be more: something that they wanted him to see or feel for himself. It
saddened him to know that they had put too big a name on
him and there was little chance that he could help. But at
least he was taking that chance and not turning his back.

He remembered his last visit and the wonder it had
wakened. The tired red country and its delicate hazes; the
early morning when the Ninya had walked and the country
hung upside down. His cramped spirit uncurled and
expanded - maybe it wasn't right to go, but it was good. He
fell asleep to the rushing of water and the singing of words:
Are you not coming? ... coming? ... coming?

It took the whole week of Ularra's notice to arrange the
journey. Wirrun had to ask for his leave, to which the strout
lady agreed after a little fuss. A leathery old man called
Charlie, who was to do Wirrun's work while he was away,
came once or twice to chew his moustache and watch what
had to be done. There were two or three visits to the airlines
office, where Wirrun or Ularra asked shy, curt questions
and took the answers home to be discussed. It was as well
that Wirrun had been saving up for a year and that Ularra

had severance pay to collect: the fares for three travellers, one way only, cost a frightening sum. When Ularra finally bought the tickets he handed the three bright folders to Wirrun with awe.

'That pretty little book, that cost all I've got. We'll have to get a job in Alice when we need more.'

'I got a bit more,' Wirrun reminded him, but Tom Hunter looked at them proudly.

'You won't need no more,' he said.

They knew what he meant: they were travelling on the People's business and of course the People would take care of them. But it would be a long way home, and travel cost money, and few of the People had much of that to spare.

Meanwhile the weekend had arrived and Wirrun had something to do alone. He took his camping gear, caught the train again, and spent another night on Ko-in's mountain. To have even a slender chance of seeing whatever it was the People wanted him to see he must take the power with him.

He did not light his fire in the old place but made a new camp farther along the ledge. He did not want to summon Ko-in - partly for fear that the summons might fail and prove that all he remembered was a dream; partly because, in answering the People's call, he was groping towards some knowledge of himself and he could not yet face the largeness and certainty of Ko-in; and partly because he was still too young and shy to call up the ancient hero except at need.

Haunted as he had been all these months since he laid the power away within the rock, he dreaded the moment of drawing it out again. He went as soon as he had made camp. It was late afternoon, the sun behind the mountain and the gully already filled with shadow. Though the days were lengthening these walls of rock held a chill, but Wirrun saw that the moss was green again. He climbed to the ledge he knew, thrust his arm into the rock-hole and closed his hand on the power, his fingers remembering its roundness and the harshness of twine and the softness of fur . . . .

The rush and roar of water was all around him, with the high, bird-sweet voices singing through it. It dwindled, died, and broke forth again, and the song soared high and drifted down. Then all the singing voices were silent except one, and that one soft as moonlight and sharply sweet as wild honey, singing the words he had heard or had not heard but remembered. He was frightened and enchanted, gripping the power and sternly drawing it forth. He climbed down from the ledge not knowing the moment when the music stopped and the singing was only in his mind; but when the power hung in its place on his belt and he climbed up from the gully into the gold and perfume of wattles the dreaming had gone.

It did not come again, though he sat late by his fire gazing at the village under the stars and holding the power with fear and longing. The power was still, and the song only haunted his mind as it had done for months.

'It's in the mountain, then,' muttered Wirrun, daring at last to climb into his sleeping-bag with the power. The song must be in the rocks and not in the power; he would be journeying away from it and not towards it. He was deeply relieved and shaken with loss. Yet he slept as he always did on the mountain, deeply and in peace.

In the morning he left as early as he could, and was back in his room before sunset. Ularra's eyes and old Tom's passed over the bark-fibre bag at his belt but neither of them spoke of it.

And now, with only two more days to wait, Wirrun was as eager as Ularra for the journey to begin. All the decisions that could be taken were taken; there were only questions left, and the answers lay far away. He felt the long miles of the old south land stretching westward. They plucked at him. The city, feverish with Happy Folk, tightened round him and he fretted to break free. He felt like a schoolboy waiting for the holidays, and told himself that this *was* his holiday and he needed the break. And at last the morning came when, long before daylight, he closed the door of his room behind himself and old Tom.

The streets were very quiet. The lights stretched away one behind the other into loneliness. Wirrun, passing under them beside Tom, looked as he had a year ago when he followed the ice: wearing old shorts and strong boots for walking, with a sweater for the dark cool of morning; his camping gear on his shoulders hiding their extra width, the net bag at his belt. The lights threw shadows on his strong dark face. It could have been a boy's.

The city was a dark bulk behind the lights, holding the Happy Folk caged and contained. Ularra was waiting at the corner, a tall shape bulging at the shoulders with a pack like Wirrun's but newer. The dark city strung with lights and the sense of the journey to come had quietened him; he only said, 'Here we are, then,' and fell into step beside the other two. They walked on in search of a taxi.

3

At the airport Tom and Ularra fell in behind Wirrun and followed him doggedly through the confusion of glass doors, flashing signs and giant voices, a tunnel that suddenly entered a plane, a girl dressed up like a doll who smiled as she robbed them of their packs. Wirrun, remembering, had curtly asked for three window seats and was given them: one behind the other, with Tom in the middle and Wirrun behind. The plane shook with a fearful power restrained - Ularra's eyes were fixed and Tom's were closed. The city and the sea fell away; hills flattened, crouching like cats; roads revealed themselves. The journey became theirs and they the travellers.

The land lay under them, grey-brown and immense, draped with the purple shadows of clouds. With majestic authority it set forth its cratered hills and looping rivers, its endless plains relentlessly fenced into squares, the patched fur of its forests. The dark eyes watching from little round windows darkened again with awe. Each man travelled alone.

A children's game of trays and tea brought them together for a moment. They twisted around in their seats to exchange embarrassed looks, but they were glad of the tea. When the trays were emptied they were alone again, each to himself. ·

The grey-brown land became red misted over with slate and stranded into channels. The dunes lay folded, the hills bared fangs of rock, a purple haze dissolved land into sky. The land opened its fearful and beautiful heart; they saw it as the wind sees it and felt it as only the earth-things or the People can.

Old Tom leaned hard against the glass of his window, looking down. He turned to Wirrun and made signs, jabbing at the glass with his thumb, then leaned against it to look again. Wirrun leaned against his own window, peering down at the dunes to see what Tom had seen.

'Tracks,' said Tom's voice in his ear over the back of the seat. 'Them Pungalunga prints.'

Wirrun searched. Just as the dunes were falling away he saw them: a line of craters, shallow and elongated, one depression in the red and sandy top of each dune as though something big had gone leaping from ridge to ridge.

The plane swam down like a shark towards jagged hills. Tom was looking a question: had Wirrun seen the prints? He nodded and pointed to the sign about fastening seat-belts. The men had been right. From the ground those craters would be too large, too far apart, for easy reading; only from the air would they show as a line of prints. What had startled Wirrun was the singing of his own blood in his ears when he saw them.

He had spent a year in banishing the earth's old spirits to the darkness where they belonged, in holding on to the ordinary things that were real. Now his blood sang in his ears that the old things were real and the city a dream, and perhaps he had chosen wrongly and lost the spirits. From the air anyone could see the Pungalunga's tracks. Wirrun longed with a fierce terror to see the Pungalunga.

When Wirrun had seen the Centre before it had been in a spring that promised a hard summer. Now he saw it in a year when the rains had not come. In the blue-china bowl of the sky the air shimmered with heat; mulga, ironwood and ghost gums folded their leaves and endured it; the red earth, sparsely covered here and there, received it and submitted. Only the jagged, tip-tilted ranges proudly breasted the heat. Only in the town had gardeners with hoses kept the green alive.

In the streets he saw only Inlanders and People. There were no Happy Folk hung with cameras; they had taken offence at the season and withdrawn to places where happiness was better understood. Wirrun and Ularra visited stores and bought supplies while old Tom hovered uneasily.

'You don't want no more now,' he objected. 'There's time.'

'What about water?' said Wirrun.

'Time for that too.'

Since it was now too hot to find a camp outside the town, they bought cold cans of beer and settled in the shade in a park to wait for evening. Passing Inlanders glanced at them and looked away frowning. Tom politely emptied one can and rose to leave. 'Back later,' he said, and slouched off down the street.

'Gone to spread the word,' said Ularra.

Wirrun nodded, watching the old man with affection. 'He's grown since we got off the plane.'

Ularra smiled, then frowned. 'It's no good, man. I see what you meant.'

Wirrun turned away on his elbow. 'What did I mean?'

Ularra growled a little and pulled up a grass-stem. Wirrun stared through leaves at the sky and waited. Ularra jerked his legs and spoke.

'Well - now we're *here*, man. We spent all that money and lost my job, and what can you do?'

'I dunno what,' said Wirrun, gazing at leaves. 'It was worth it, just coming.'

'You never wanted to come. And now they're expecting something. And here we are like a couple of ants on a billiard table, don't even know what we're looking for. It's no good.'

'You won't make a hero that way,' said Wirrun. 'We've come, that's all. We don't know what we're looking for, but maybe ... if it's here, if it wants us, it'll find us don't you worry.'

Ularra glanced at him sideways and glanced away again.

'Can't stop 'em expecting,' Wirrun told him. 'Can't live their lives for 'em. All we can do is watch and listen, and do what comes up if it wants doing.'

They lay in silence under the heat for a long five minutes. Then Wirrun spoke to the leaves, telling Ularra about the Pungalunga's footprints on the ridges. 'It was - like there was more to it. I dunno what but I'm waiting.'

After more moments of quiet Ularra said, 'You gotta see it from a plane before you know. I never thought of it like that, all spread out.'

Then, because of the heat and the beer and because it had already been a long day, they slept on the grass.

They woke to find that the park, which had been sunlit splotched with shadows, was now shadow lit with sun. They could feel the heat rising into the sky like a monster leaving its nest. Tommy Hunter stood there with a man more grizzled than himself, both of them holding white-wrapped parcels. Tommy had grown again and was looking at them with a smile pink and white in his dark face.

'Don't you want no tucker? Me and Jump-up thought you might.'

Jump-up greeted Ularra with goodwill and Wirrun with a respect that made that young man sigh. They took up their packs and went through the streets, out of the town; and dark eyes watched under heavy brows as they went. In twos and threes, from benches and bars and side streets, little knots of men and women and children collected and trailed after them towards the river. The People were gathering.

Tom and Jump-up took Wirrun and Ularra over sunburnt flats and the dry sandy bed of the river towards the rock wall of the range. 'Good cool camp over here,' said Tom. 'You'll want water.' He bent and lifted an iron lid that lay on the sandy river-bed. Under the lid was a hole roughly lined and half full of water. 'Good water,' said Tom.

Wirrun and Ularra knelt and filled their waterbags with the sweet, secret water that flowed under the dry sand. *The glimmer-bright water* ... secretly guarded in the land's indomitable heart.

Near a gap in the range by which road and river passed through, they reached a clump of ironwood trees that clung near the base of the rocks. Behind the trees was a shaded cranny where the older men waited with expectant grins.

'Couldn't be better,' said Wirrun, admiring the camp they had found for him. 'Cool all day and handy to water. You ever had a better camp, Ularra?'

'Put your fire safe under the rocks,' said Jump-up, chuckling. 'Quiet here, no one round.'

'Just what we want, man' said Ularra.

Gratefully the travellers dropped their packs on the rocks and hung waterbags and some of their supplies safely from branches. They all went back across the river, where the People had gathered on the bank and were collecting wood and making a few small fires.

The sun had gone leaving only a red-gold shining in the west. The land expanded and breathed in the cool of evening. Food was spread on paper wrappings on the grass; children played, young people laughed, women called to each other from fire to fire, older men sat watching and smoking. The good smell of singed fat was already beginning. Tom and Jump-up handed their parcels to the women and took Wirrun from fire to fire.

It became clear that Tom really had grown larger in the eyes of his People: not only had he travelled far and brought the hero back, but he had brought him back by plane. He had seen the land as the wind sees it. He told them in short phrases and wide movements about the plane and the tea-trays and his terror, and they roared with laughter. He told them in words and in silence about the breadth and wonder of the land, and they too were silent. There was no need for Wirrun to talk, nothing that he needed to explain.

Ularra had found friends among the young People and sat with them on the grass near one of the fires. The dusk came down and the air chilled. Trees stood dark against the luminous sky; behind them the town hung out its lights, and in front the range rose dark against the stars. And Wirrun noticed that the People, the noisy laughing groups, stayed closer and closer by the fires. He saw that they looked often over their shoulders, and that if a child wandered to the outskirts of a group its mother sharply called it back. He saw that the People were afraid. He watched and listened.

When the meal was over the talking grew quieter and fell away. The firelight showed faces turning often to Wirrun. They were waiting for him to speak.

'You been having trouble,' said Wirrun.

Silence and a turning to the fires. Older men coughed. Tommy Hunter began to speak, telling again about the spring that had never dried before and the flowering desert. 'Better you look,' he said. 'We take you tomorrow.'

'Dunno what I can do,' said Wirrun. 'I wouldn't want to fool you. Last time I was helped. All I know is to look and listen - maybe something'll come, I dunno.'

Voices murmured to each other round the fires. They weren't fooled, they said; look and listen and wait; couldn't do more.

'You know more than what I do,' said Wirrun. 'It's your country and your trouble.'

But this they would not have. The murmurs round the fires dissented. Jump-up coughed and spoke.

'It's bigger. There's men here from three - four countries, come on purpose. Plenty fights sometimes, but not now. None of us knows the whole of it, had to get you here. It's bigger.'

That was something to know; and perhaps it explained why they would not talk but insisted that he should look for himself. Wirrun began to fish a little.

'I seen those prints on the ridges. From the plane you can see them clear.'

The silence thickened. There were movements towards the fires and a flaring of fresh fuel. They would not speak of the Pungalunga while the dark moved round the fires; or of any spirit, Wirrun guessed. Behind him Tommy Hunter said, 'Tomorrow. We fetch you in the car before light.' He saw that this meeting had not been held to inform him but to welcome him and show the People he was here.

'We best get to bed, then,' he answered. 'A long day today and another one tomorrow. Right, Ularra?'

Ularra's long form rose from one of the fires. Jump-up and Tom moved too, but Wirrun, remembering the spirits, waved them back. 'No sense walking two ways for nothing. We know the way.' He and Ularra shouted goodnights. The People called back and sat close to the fires and watched them go.

'Must be a terrible feller, this Pungalunga,' muttered Wirrun as he and Ularra crossed the dry river by starlight.

'They're worried all right,' said Ularra, sounding puzzled. 'Too worried. It's not enough, this Pungalunga's not.'

'Big as a hill? Eats People? Gone a long time and coming back?'

'Yeah, but they *know* it, man. They'd stay by the fires but they wouldn't be scared to talk. That's something they don't know, something else.'

Wirrun agreed. 'Something we gotta see for ourselves.'

At the camp by the Gap they unrolled their sleeping-bags, finding what flatness they could between the rocks. They were so tired that Wirrun said the men would have to stone him awake in the morning. He was asleep almost before he had finished saying it.

He woke some time later to a prickling awareness - of what? Beyond the shade of the ironwoods moonlight

flooded the flats and the dark winding snake of the highway, turning the tawny-gold rocks of the range to dull
brown. He lay still and alert, searching the shadows near at
hand. There was a throbbing at his shoulder: it was the
power. Under his eyelids he searched the camp.

Ularra stirred in his sleeping-bag and settled again. On a
moonlit rock above his head Wirrun saw the intruders. Two
of them, perching together and watching Ularra with evil
little faces. They looked like wicked little men of the People,
perhaps three or four feet tall, hairy all over and with long
dark beards. One of the pair was stick-thin, the other stout
and round-bellied. There they crouched, side by side,
watching Ularra.

Wirrun sat up suddenly, holding the power and speaking
sternly. 'Clear off, you. Get back where you belong.'

Their heads swung round at him, startled, but they
sneered and answered mockingly. 'Too far,' they said,
pulling faces and jerking their hands insultingly. 'Too far
for you, earless.' They slid off the rock and vanished into
shadows.

Cheeky rubbish, thought Wirrun. What did they mean,
too far? But he was warm with strength and pleasure. He
hadn't lost them, any rate. He had seen and dealt with these
earth-things as easily as if the Mimi had been with him, and
they too had known the power as Ko-in had once promised.
He chuckled at the thought that Ularra might have
wakened to see them perched above his head, and fell asleep
wondering if Ularra could have seen them at all.

It seemed still to be night when he woke again; but the air
had the chill of morning, the moonlight had paled a little, a
small fire crackled under the rocks, and Ularra stood over
him with a little icy water in a can. He stepped back
grinning when Wirrun rolled over and yawned. Wirrun
heaved himself up, fastening the power to his belt.

'What woke you, then? You were sound asleep when
those two old hairy things were looking at you in the night.'

Ularra scoffed. 'What are you talking about, man?'

'I'm telling you. Two of 'em, sitting on that rock.

Keeping an eye on you, they were, only they cleared off when I showed 'em the power.'

'Pull the other leg,' said Ularra uneasily.

'Nasty-looking little pair, one of 'em half-starved and the other fat as a pig. You ought to know 'em.'

'Never heard of anything like that in these parts,' said Ularra firmly. 'You were dreaming.'

'No fear. The power woke me and I sent 'em off.'

'Next time you wake me up first, man. I want to see 'em myself.'

'Next time I will,' said Wirrun, rolling his sleeping-bag. 'You ever see an earth-thing? Any time?'

Ularra was silent, thinking back. 'I might've,' he said shortly, and left it at that.

They ate breakfast quickly and stowed things away among rocks. In the chill quiet morning they heard the chatter and grumble of a motor long before it was near and saw headlights, one bright and one dull, coming from the town. When the car drew up with a rattle Wirrun and Ularra were waiting by the road.

The driver was a young man named Harry. Ularra squeezed in beside him and a middle-aged man named Duke. Wirrun sat in the back seat with Tom Hunter and Jump-up. The car headed north.

Harry drove fast along the highway, between rough hills and across high plains curving with the curve of the earth. Watery moonlight turned to watery dawn. The sky was a pale and polished blue flushed with gold when they turned off the highway to the east. For a while the track was good and Harry still drove fast in a race with the sun. Later they bounced and rattled over salt-crusted clay and red sand, between spinifex and mulga, with a dust-cloud rolling behind them and blue-hazed hills in the distance to left and right. The sun climbed higher, the heat closed down, and for hours they rattled on. The men spoke little and drank often from bottles of water.

The land called up its heat-magic, it shimmered and wavered. Mulga branches writhed and twisted, mocking and beckoning. Remembered lakes and seas spread over the sands, magical water that lay invitingly ahead: *Are you not coming?* I've come, thought Wirrun, I'm here; show me.

When the heat pressed down like a great flat hand Harry turned the car towards mulga on the shady side of a scooped-out ridge of rock. Tom went ahead on foot into the mulga, to look for broken-off stumps that might spike a tyre. The car followed and drew up in shade flickered with sunlight. The men climbed out and stretched. Harry loosened the radiator-cap, flicking his fingers, and steam rose from the radiator. Duke brought a battered old cooler from the boot of the car. The men sat or lay in the shade to rest, eat, and wait out the heat. They were silent, not looking at each other. Wirrun noticed it.

Ularra too was looking puzzled. 'Man, I'm too soft for it . . . . Is this the best shade you got? What's wrong with the ridge?' The shade of the ridge was deeper and he knew its rocks would be cooler.

Something like an electric shock passed through the men. No one spoke; no one moved. Wirrun looked at them and frowned.

'Come on, Ularra,' he said. He waited while Ularra slowly stood up, and they two walked back towards the ridge. The men did not speak or watch them go.

Broken and stony ground led them upward to a patch of boulders. They went with care, Ularra looking sharply among the boulders and now and then glancing at Wirrun's face. Wirrun's eyes went from the boulders at his feet to the shaded cliffs ahead. There was a deep cleft in the rocks, black with shadow, a place where the cool of night might linger. He aimed for that, dropping his hand to the power and feeling its throb.

They climbed upward, sweat drying on their faces. A little below the cleft they stopped and looked, trying to penetrate the darkness in it. It gathered and moved. Wirrun stepped forward. The darkness snarled, savage and menacing, with a glint of red eyes.

'*Man!*' breathed Ularra in horror.

4

The darkness was a dog, huge and red-eyed. It stood hunched to spring and its snarl rattled between the rocks. Wirrun fumbled the power out of its bag and held it like a shield. He stepped forward, and the snarl rattled viciously. He took another step. The angry dark slunk back and hung for a moment. At his next step it drew off into the cleft.

'Man,' whispered Ularra again.

Wirrun kept the power in his hand as he turned away, stumbling a little. 'I told you, didn't I? I said if there was something it'd find us.'

They went back down the rocks, stopping now and then to remind themselves where they were.

'They knew,' said Ularra angrily. 'They never said a word, just let us go.'

'They had to let us see for ourselves,' Wirrun reminded him. 'It's no use bellyaching, that's the way it is. There might be more yet.' His face softened into half a grin. 'One thing any rate - we know you've got eyes for the old things. You saw that one all right.' Ularra muttered darkly. 'Well, you said you wanted to see.'

They returned to the men who sat or lay where they were and did not speak.

'Not so cool back there,' said Wirrun. 'I reckon you blokes knew better. What do you call that brute any rate?'

At last the men looked at each other. 'Don't call him nothing,' said Jump-up strongly. 'None of us knows him. He don't come from no country round here.'

Wirrun frowned heavily. 'Must belong somewhere near.'

They all stared obstinately at the ground or the sky. After a moment Tom Hunter spoke. 'Old Ngunta, he's a very old man, he says they got these dogs on the Darling somewhere. Jugi, they call 'em there.'

'The *Darling*? Why'd he come here, then?' Silence. 'How long ago?' They all looked at Duke.

'Near three months ago I seen him,' mumbled Duke. 'Only they never believed me.'

That was it, then. What they knew and could show they had told him. What was foreign and wrong, what rested on the evidence of one man, to that they would not commit themselves. He must see and judge for himself.

'Mm,' said Wirrun. 'So you don't know the songs to send him off.'

'Don't know nothing,' said Jump-up firmly.

The sun had moved a little. Old Tom dragged himself into deeper shade. 'That rock where he is, that belongs underground. Land used to be all up there till the wind took it. That rock goes deep under.'

It was another thing that they knew and Tom must have thought it had meaning. 'This Pungalunga,' said Wirrun. 'Where does he come from?'

They knew the Pungalunga and could talk of them by daylight without fear of strange and ancient ears that listened in the dark.

'Used to be in the ranges,' said Tom. 'There's bones out there near the Olgas, I seen 'em, only they're stone now. It was that long ago.'

'I seen 'em too,' said Harry.

'One killed hisself,' added Tom, 'stepping across a gorge on a cloudy day. Missed his step in the clouds, crashed down and got smashed. Bones everywhere. That was old times. Dunno where they been hiding since.'

'Underground,' said Jump-up. 'Only place.' He spoke with a certainty that Wirrun did not like to question; for now that the men had begun to talk he did not want to dam the flow by reminding them that he was a stranger. Ularra, watching his face, rolled over to argue.

'I dunno - some of these ranges are pretty wild. A lot of room for a Pungalunga. More than underground.'

Jump-up scoffed at the idea. 'All these cattle and mines, Inlanders everywhere and now these airy-planes. Someone'd see a monstrous great thing like that. Like a hill walking. They're all gone or they're underground - and this one ain't gone if it's walking. Eh?'

'Underground's a big place,' said Tom severely. 'You know that.'

Still watching Wirrun's face, Ularra gave in.

'He's a bit upset,' said Wirrun, excusing him. 'Couple of old things sitting over his head last night, and he slept like a baby and never saw 'em. Nasty-looking pair, kid-sized, all hairy with long beards. One fat and one skinny. What do you call those?'

The men were troubled; they refused to look at each other or at him. 'Don't call 'em nothing', grunted Jump-up. 'Never heard of 'em.' And the others agreed, when Wirrun pressed them, that no such old creatures as those belonged in any of their countries.

It was a strange picture that had emerged while the men talked. Wirrun brooded over it with tingling nerves. 'Any more like that?' he asked at last. 'Any more stories of old things out of their places?'

The older men stared at ground or sky and said nothing, but Harry stirred.

'Danny,' he said.

The others frowned and looked away, but Harry went doggedly on.

'Camped two - three miles out and let the fire go down. Woke up with hands pulling at him, some woman dragging him off. He said she had no head.'

Ularra's eyes flared. 'No *head*?'

'Moonlight night,' said Harry. 'He says he saw her clear. Came driving back like she was still after him and wouldn't go outside for three days.'

'And none of the men know about this woman?'

None of them did. None of these would speak again about spirits strange or familiar. Harry, out of his impetuous youth, had broken the agreed pattern of telling only what they knew and leaving the hero to see the rest for himself. They waited for the sun to pass over, repacked the car and topped up the water in its radiator, and at four o'clock drove on to show him the spring that was drying up.

To Wirrun the heat seemed unbearably worse than ever and the baking country seemed to reject all life. He hung grimly to a door-handle to steady himself in the bouncing car and thought about what he had heard. The sun beat through the rear window on to the back of his neck; the distant hills were a tingling, living blue. By the time they reached the ancient spring even Wirrun could feel that the heat was not so fierce.

The spring lay on another of those low rocky hills that the wind had quarried out of the land. They had to scramble up to it on foot and found a wide pool deeply cupped in the hill's flat top. Through ages of evaporation it had built itself a rim of sediment overlaid with red sand, wind-plastered. The water lay eight feet below the rim, walled by dried mud that was cracked and scabby. Jump-up pointed to a rock, black with old slime, that lay only two or three feet under the rim.

'Oughta be under water,' he told Wirrun. 'Always under water, that old rock. Always.'

To Wirrun the spring was not a sight worth travelling over a thousand miles to see. It told him nothing, but the men brooded over it, measuring its fall with their eyes. 'Any more drying up like this?' he asked.

'No more,' said Jump-up. 'There's more down south, don't know if they're drying. We only got the one. That's the old water, that is. From underground.' He looked sideways at Wirrun.

'It's her own water, that is,' added Tom, 'that she keeps deep down. All these things wanting water - sun, people, trees, snakes - she's gotta keep some hid away for herself. Eh?'

... sings the dark water. ...

Bright, thought Wirrun correcting his wayward mind. It's bright water. That's different.

... of dark-floating hair, sang his mind. More words that he had never heard.

They went down the hill again, and back to the car. As they bounced and rattled eastward the mountains to the south curved to meet them. At sunset the range shone ahead, red and gold, with one dark ridge lying nearer than the others. Along the base of this ridge lay the flowering desert.

There was no depression where water might flow in the wet, yet the large old gums with their ghostly white trunks showed that water lay below. Wirrun knew that there were such places, yet now when even the river-beds were baked it was a strange sight. There was green grass under the trees, and the gold of flowering acacia and the pink-white of hakea. Wirrun and Ularra walked through it with Tom and Jump-up while Harry and Duke made camp for the night, unloading supplies from the car.

'And it's not always like this?' said Wirrun.

Tom shook his head. 'Not in the dry. Just the trees. You can dig down and you won't find water; she don't lay near, she just soaks up. From deep down. Only now she's soaking more . . . . Where's she getting it from?'

'From the spring,' Wirrun suggested. 'The old water finding a new way.'

'And what's it want to do that for? What's going on down there?'

'Them Ninya, might be,' said Jump-up, and they both looked at Wirrun. He shook his head, frowning.

'Don't see how they'd do nothing with the water. Except freeze it, and they're not doing that. Any rate there's all these old things, strangers coming in that don't belong. All the ones that I met, they didn't like the ice. I reckon they'd keep away if it was Ninya.'

Tom glanced quickly over his shoulder in the fading light.

They went back to the camp before dusk and found that Duke and Harry had lit three fires. It was too many, but Wirrun understood when he saw how the men kept between the fires. They ate stew and drank strong black tea and watched the stars looming close from the clear chill sky. Leaping flames lit up small green stars on the ground: the eyes of the big huntsman spiders crouching by their burrows. When the men had eaten they went early to bed, for the homeward race against the sun would begin before daylight. They kept the fires burning.

Wirrun lay for a while and felt the land wide around him, felt it stirring with silent life under the burning stars. Tell me, he begged it; show me. But only the old haunting sang in his mind: *the dark-flowing water like washes and ripples* . . . . He thought of the old water, her own that she kept deep down, and of the Inlanders' bores that drilled into it and stole it. Well, he and his People could not deal with that; they must wait for the land to deal with it in her own inescapable time . . . . Duke got up softly to feed the fires, and Wirrun slept.

He woke to a sky that glowed like a black pearl and to a chorus of singing. They were women's voices, free and wild, unlike the sweetness of his haunting. He felt the throbbing of the power, and the stiffness of the men lying awake and listening with him. The singing came near and swept by, shadowy women dancing by in the moonlight and singing as they went. He saw shields and spear-throwers lifted, and a flowing of limbs and breasts and hair, then the shapes and the singing were gone. The men lay unspeaking until Tom got up and fed the fires. One by one they stirred.

'Were those some of yours?' asked Wirrun at breakfast. 'Or were they out of their place?'

'Eh?' said Tom. 'Them. That's them Unthippa, them women.' He went back to his breakfast. 'A long time,' he said at last. 'A long time since we seen them around. We got unused to 'em.'

'Restless,' said Jump-up, frowning. 'All restless, them old things. There's something's up.'

'Better move before the sun,' said Tom. 'Got to get back. Tomorrow you'll see them prints.'

'No need,' Wirrun told him. 'I seen 'em. Tomorrow I want to go north. If I can. There's someone might help.'

'Where north?'

'Right north. Mimi country - it's a Mimi.'

All the People had heard that story. The men considered.

'Harry'll take you,' said Jump-up.

THREE

A Trouble in the East

I

By evening of that day the old car came back along the highway to the town. Wirrun knew the People would expect him to spend another evening by the fires on the riverbank, but this he could not do for he needed a lonelier fire and the night at his shoulder. He sent messages instead.

'Tell 'em we've seen and heard and now we gotta find our road. Maybe Harry'll bring word down from the north if we find it. And we'll see 'em again later when things are back in their places.'

The men accepted this soberly and drove off, Harry promising to come again before daylight; and Wirrun and Ularra spent another night in their camp by the Gap.

'We need to chew things over,' said Wirrun; and Ularra looked pleased, for he had thought his part was to fetch and carry and maybe to stand with the hero if he was needed. But at first there was no chewing over. Wirrun only sat on a rock with his arms draped over his knees, weary and silent, frowning at nothing.

Ularra checked the water supply, unrolled sleeping-bags on rocks, laid the small fierce fire of the dry country, and looked over cans of food consideringly.

'These women, these Unthippa,' said Wirrun at last. 'They big business?'

Ularra paused. 'N-no. They got mixed up in it a bit, got 'emselves in a dance or two. But they're not real big, just weird.'

'They're that. Where do they live?'

'Underground. In these caves where it's always sunny with rivers running. We got a lot live there.'

'Underground again,' muttered Wirrun.

Ularra chose a can of stew and ventured to ask a question. 'This Mimi friend of yours. Can you find her? There's a lot of rock up there.'

'If I'm lucky I reckon she might find me.'

'She's a long way off. Will she know what's going on here?'

'She knows most things - and why not, the way things are shifting round out of their places?' Wirrun kicked suddenly at a rock. 'That's got me, that's what I can't understand. All these things out of their places - why? What are they after? What's bringing 'em?'

Ularra restored the tin opener to his pack. 'Some of 'em aren't,' he pointed out. 'The Pungalunga and these Unthippa. And they're restless too.'

'They would be, wouldn't they, with all these strangers coming in. No wonder they're restless. I want to know what brought the strangers.'

Ularra placed a couple of flat stones near the fire and set the stew in place. He said carefully, 'Last time you said you were told; the land told you. Maybe she will again.'

Wirrun swore. After a moment he confessed, speaking harshly and in jerks. 'There's just this haunting. Months now - ever since I got home. Waterfalls and singing. I can't hear nothing else.' He pressed his hands against his eyes. 'I can't get rid of it .... And if I did,' he muttered, 'maybe that'd drive me mad too.'

Silently Ularra stirred the stew. A haunting; months of it; all that silent time in town. There was more than you'd think in being a hero.

While they were eating he pointed with his fork at the power hanging in its bag. 'Reckon this haunting might come from that thing?'

Wirrun shook his head. 'It came out of the mountain; out of the rocks. But maybe the stone might've brought it.'

'Well ... can't be helped, you gotta trust the stone. And

you've gotta get some rest. Between haunting and bouncing round in the heat all day, you look about done in, and we're off again before daylight. Get yourself off while I clean up.'

'Cleaning up's my turn. You did the cooking.'

Ularra tossed his limbs about. 'Listen to him, he's crazy. What else am I for? Have *I* got a power? Or a Mimi friend? Nothing talks to me, man, you're the one we count on. Turn in and get some rest.' He had Wirren in his sleeping-bag a little after dark and himself half an hour after that.

They were so tired that they slept without stirring while the night moved and whispered around them. They woke in time for a quick breakfast and a hasty packing up and were waiting with their packs by the road when Harry's lopsided lights came creeping from town.

'We'll get on a bit in the cool,' said Harry, 'and doss down somewhere till night. Travel better at night.'

Wirrun agreed, remembering the last time he had travelled by night: on foot, with the Mimi holding to the cord of the power lest some wandering wind should catch her. That was when the land had spoken to him, through his feet or through its old spirits as he met them. Perhaps if he walked again .... But he could walk in this country, two hundred miles from one water to the next and a thousand miles in a few precious days.

Even in the car it took a morning and two nights, though Harry drove fast up the long highway north. The car probed ahead with its lopsided lights like an old camel with one good eye. Harry, removed from the stern gaze of the older men, sometimes talked of restless spirits and sometimes drove in silence for long hours. Twice he stopped to fill the tank from drums of petrol that he carried in the boot; twice he filled it from lonely outpost pumps and wordlessly failed to see the money that Wirrun offered. When it was time to sleep he turned the car aside into some waiting and expected shade.

The first morning they crossed mulga flats between low hills and slept out the day at the edge of a worn, stony tableland, heading north again in the sunset. All night they saw only the yellow-lit road, and sometimes a shine of green eyes beside it; but they felt the ridges that the car nosed through and dark bluffs that cut off the stars. Towards morning the moon rose and they saw plains stretching ahead, and broken hills on either side misted by moonlight. They saw the sunrise drape these hills in silken hazes of lavender and apricot; and in a little while they camped in a tumbledown shed on a marshy sand-plain.

On the second night's driving the road seemed to go on forever with nothing to mark it but a hotel or two for tourists; but just as the moon had risen the highway began to swing farther west. They had been climbing imperceptibly; the moonlight showed rolling grasslands and the silvered trunks of gums. Harry found a track that Wirrun might not have seen and turned east off the highway, driving more slowly as the track grew rougher. A darkness of trees received them; Harry stopped the car.

'Need daylight for the next bit. Sleep a couple of hours and start early.'

They climbed out gratefully to stretch and stamp about. Wirrun felt the watching of owls and possums and other soft small things. Beyond the trees lay a stretch of grassland and a city of low, rough towers dark in the moonlight: termite mounds, some as tall as Ularra, pointing their jagged fingers at the stars. The men gathered sticks to light a small fire and ate, sitting with their backs warmly to the fire and resting their tired eyes on the moonlight beyond. The pointing fingers of the termite mounds uttered some silent message that they could not read. Ularra stopped chewing for a moment, leaning forward to look.

'What's moving?'

'Where?' said Wirrun, trying to follow his gaze into the moonlight.

'By that mound, the near one . . . . It's gone - no, to the right - there's something - ' He stopped with a strangled grunt.

Shadows moved between the mounds, shadows that swayed and beckoned in the silver light. They heard soft laughter and the voices of young girls calling. They were like girls of the People; their slender forms drew near and drew away.

'Get in the car,' said Harry wrenching the door open.

'But - hang on, man - ' Ularra was staring. 'I know that one, she's from up near Darwin!'

'What's she doing here, then?' said Wirrun sternly. 'Get back, man.'

Ularra gave a short, excited laugh and stepped forward instead. Wirrun grabbed his arm and pushed in front, holding the throbbing power. The girl-shapes laughed uneasily and began to drift away, swinging their hips in the moonlight. He followed a little way; in the moment before they disappeared, each one into a termite mound, he saw the nearest closely. He had seen a girl like these before, but not from a termite mound.

He went back to the car where Harry was thrusting an angry Ularra into a seat. 'They won't give no more trouble,' he assured him.

'Get in,' said Harry. 'We're shifting all the same.' Wirrun climbed in beside Ularra and Harry started the motor. 'Out of their place,' he muttered. 'Can't trust the country any more.'

'What are they?' Wirrun asked.

'Mungga-mungga,' said Harry shortly.

Ularra stirred and laughed his short laugh. 'Them. Always reckoned I wouldn't mind meeting one. Only for you two I'd give it a go.'

'You'd change your mind when you saw their big sharp claws,' Wirrun retorted. 'Only then it'd be too late.'

Ularra laughed again.

Harry drove carefully for a mile or so along the rough track and over the feet of ridges. He stopped again on level ground clear of termite mounds. They rested in the car, eyes closed but not sleeping. When the moonlight began to pale they did sleep a little.

Wirrun and Ularra were wakened by the movement of the car to find the sun well up and Harry driving carefully over the bumps. When he saw that they were awake he said, 'Not far now. Sleep a bit more when we get there - safer by daylight.'

By now there was hardly a track to be seen. They travelled along the spines of ridges above gullies that Harry said would be rivers in a week or so if the wet was on time. The old car bucked over rocks hidden in the grass and kept gallantly on. Wirrun had begun to watch for the faces of sandstone that he glimpsed from time to time; that seemed to hang in the sky beyond the reach of any car. They crawled steeply up another long ridge - and suddenly the cliffs were in front to the north: red-gold, sheer and shadowed, pencilled with the darker lines of clefts and gorges, and reaching away to east and west. The blood sang in Wirrun's ears at the sight of them.

Harry drove into the shade of trees and stopped the car. 'Close as I can come,' he said pointing to the cliffs. 'You'll have to walk the rest. After a bit of tucker and a doss down.'

Ularra climbed out and stretched with his eyes on those brooding faces of stone, immense and endless. 'Mimi country, eh?' he said and stole a doubtful look at Wirrun. It seemed impossible to find one Mimi in that.

Harry confirmed his doubts. 'If this ain't right we'll have to try again.'

Wirrun was not troubled; as far as he had thought at all he was counting on his Mimi to find him. He sat on a log, eating whatever Harry or Ularra passed to him, and looked at the cliffs reaching away against the sky. He could climb to them in half an hour, once he had slept. He let his mind go to them now, not exploring but only feeling the age of the stone and the depth of its shadows. He was not aware of the heat or the sting of an ant; but he heard the grass whisper and the birds call, and under those the surging of the land. When Harry passed him a blanket he spread it in the shade and lay watching the cliffs till he slept.

He woke in the late afternoon. Harry and Ularra were still asleep and he was alone. He got up and began to walk. His feet found their own way - stepping around the lizard and

over the log, waiting before the rocks for the snake to pass -
and his mind lay ahead of him brooding in the shadow of
the cliffs. They drew him.

He reached them when the sun slanted low along their
faces; he wandered along beneath them, clambering over the
lower crags, laying a hand on the rock and feeling it like a
note of deep music. He looked out as the rocks did, over
folded grass and forest, down where the waters ran in the
wet; and he smiled a little and waited for the Mimi.

She did not come; and yet he was sure she was near and
knew he was there.

He found a shadowed gorge and wandered in seeking her.
It was only a shallow cleft between soaring walls of rock; he
laid a hand on them, calling her out, but she did not come.
He left that cleft and found a deeper one and sat down there.
He was so still that a spider scuttled over his leg.

After a time he went on, entering clefts or climbing
outcrops, certain and waiting. He opened his mouth to call
her and instead began to sing; the song soared high and
dropped in falling phrases.

> *Are you not coming?*
> *sings the bright water;*
> *are you not coming?*
>
> *The glimmer-bright water*
> *alight with the glancing*
> *of glimmer-bright eyes.*

Nothing answered. The silence deepened suddenly, but
he did not hear it.

> *Are you not coming?*
> *sings the dark water;*
> *are you not coming?*
>
> *The dark-flowing water*
> *Like washes and ripples*
> *of dark-floating hair.*

She was there. She stood by him in the shadows of a cleft. She was outraged, rigid and quivering, her stick-like body towering over him, her large dark eyes glinting green. When she could, she hissed at him furiously.

'Sst, Man! Be silent!' hissed the Mimi.

2

Wirrun was so full of joy at seeing the Mimi that at first he saw only herself and his face broadened in contentment.

'I knew you'd find me,' he said. 'I need you bad.'

The Mimi gave her snort that was like the sneezing of a cat, and suddenly folded herself down on a rock as if her spindly legs had given way.

'What's up?' said Wirrun. 'Shouldn't I come? But there's trouble.' She was still rigid and silent, so he tried coaxing. 'I'm no good on my own, you know that.'

'You do me great wrong,' hissed the Mimi, and now he saw how angry she was. He had never seen her so angry, even when he dropped her roughly off the wind and endangered her fragile body. He stood up, hurt and disappointed.

'I never meant any wrong. I came looking for a friend.'

'Is it friendly, then,' hissed the Mimi, 'to shame me among my kind? To sing me for all to hear with an evil love-singing?'

He could only stare.

'Is a man's friendship in itself no shame to a Mimi? Yet friendship is sacred, and for yours I have earned the sneers of my kind. I have been called earless, the wind's plaything, and this I have endured and remembered you with friendship by my fire. Earless indeed! For now you seek me with a love-singing as if the Mimi could be trapped like an earless girl of the People!'

'A love-singing!' He stammered, walked away, came back; then Wirrun too sank down on a rock.

The Mimi's dark eyes followed smouldering; but when she spoke again there was a note of resignation in her anger. 'You did not know. I had forgotten how little a man knows. Yet I see you have still your power: you will give me the cord as before, and we will go farther off where the rocks do not listen.' Then, as Wirrun still sat and gazed dumbly, 'Stiffen your spine, Man. The cord.'

He unwound a length and passed it to her through the mesh of the bag. Protected so from the winds she walked with him, spring-kneed like a mantis, away from the cliffs and down the ridge. They sat on a log.

'You have spoken truly,' said the Mimi, 'for I think you do need help. Where did you find that singing?' She watched him sternly.

He was still too bewildered to answer clearly. 'Ko-in's mountain . . . out of the rocks . . . .'

She looked away. 'So far east? And from rock?'

'I . . . can't get rid of it. It haunts me.'

She hissed. 'And will. It was made for that.'

'Just now . . . it came of itself. I never knew - I never even heard it all before.' He saw that she was frowning. 'Oh, Mimi! Would I come this far and call you up on a trouble of my own? I came for something bigger!'

She was still frowning and he could not read her dark possum-eyes, but when she spoke he knew he was forgiven. 'What is bigger than the friendship of heroes?' said the Mimi grandly. He could have smiled except that her anger and distress still troubled him and her greeting rang in his ears.

'Why do you have to be ashamed here? Don't they know you're an Ice Fighter, a Great One?'

'In my country Great Ones are not taken by the wind.'

'That's rubbish,' he said hotly. 'I better go up there and tell 'em the story. Put 'em right.'

She cat-sneezed at him. 'Have I worked and waited for a place among my kind and the right to live in my own dear country, and will you take it from me out of friendship? Tell me your trouble. And speak softly. And sit low in the grass like a lizard and be still.'

Wirrun looked obstinate; but he slid from the log down among the tall browned grass and endured the ants. 'I came on a trouble of the land and I reckon you know what it is. You must do.' And he told her, speaking softly, how a rest-lessness had seized the earth's old creatures; how some of them were driven out of their places to countries far apart; how the spring fell and the desert flowered as if the old water had found a new way; how it seemed that the trouble might come from under the ground.

'You'd know about that, wouldn't you, living inside the rocks like you do? Ever hear the Ninya's wind in there these days? Ever feel a chill?'

'The Ninya are quiet in their own ice-caves and few in number. There is no trouble under the ground in my coun-try, Man.' Yet she was frowning again. 'There is ill hum-our,' she admitted, 'and wandering, and spirits out of their places. Not many but a few, from east and west and south. This is your trouble, Man, and not the Ninya who keep at home; it is this that makes us restless and ill-humoured. For when strangers come in, may we not need to fight for our places? And how can the countries feed many where there should be few?'

Wirrun broke off a grass-stem. 'I know. But why are they coming in? What brings 'em?'

'They come because strangers have driven them forth in their turn, and so the evil spreads. When a stone falls into a pool, does not the troubled water widen around it? You may see the trouble spread.'

'Where does it spread from? Where did the stone fall?'

'There are strangers from east and from west but more from the east.' She gazed down where the tree-tops spread be-low. 'Some quarrel, perhaps . . . some war . . . it may be even that the Ninya in their travels have left some footprint of trouble . . . .'

'Mimi . . . . When they called me Hero I thought it was like Fighter of Ice: something over and done. But they've put the name on me for good and called me to stop this trouble, and I can't go down under there the way you can. The land doesn't speak to me and I need help. Come with me again.'

For a moment the Mimi looked fierce and eager, but then she shook her head. 'Can I leave my kind when strangers wander near? You are the hero, it is you who are called; if the land does not speak to you yet it will hold and support you. I am an earth-thing, I have only one place. I must stay with my kind.'

His face was heavy with disappointment but he knew she must be right. She always had been. The Mimi looked at him kindly.

'Yet I would come if I could, and not only to ride the wind again. I would come to help you in your own trouble, this love-singing of which you do not speak.'

Wirrun's hand moved among the grass-stems. He was used to bearing his own trouble but not yet used to the new name she had given it. 'Forget it,' he muttered.

'You cannot. You have said so and I know. Yet how can I speak? For it may be that the land has need of your trouble and how can I know what your own need may be? I cannot think for a man or a hero. Only remember . . . .' she hesitated. 'Remember the kunai grass.'

He was puzzled. 'The kunai grass?'

'It grows in the west: tall, as tall as a young tree, and slender-leaved. When it burns its smoke has a power. If a day comes when you need to fight your trouble, fight it with the smoke of a tall grass.' She rose, stooping to keep hold of the cord from the power. 'Come, Man. I must return to my one place.'

He stood up and walked with her back to where the crannied cliffs brooded over the land. 'I'm glad I've seen your place. I'm glad I've seen you. I've missed you, Mimi, worse than wind-riding.'

She let go the cord and stepped close to the rock. 'And I you, Man. But the friendship of heroes will not break for a little parting.' She blew on the rock and stepped into its darkness quickly lest a wind should come.

Wirrun too walked away quickly and softly in case the rock should watch as well as listen. The thought of the Mimi went with him down the ridge; and first he thought of her returned from her great adventure, enduring shame and sneers as proudly and staunchly as ever to win back a lowly place among her kind. It seemed a bitter wrong to him, and yet it was somehow right for the Mimi. Then he thought of her sending him off to walk alone as a hero; and after that of journeying east in search of a place where trouble had dropped like a stone among the spirits; and so at last he approached his own trouble that gnawed and worried at his mind.

How it had angered her: a love-singing, and evil. Why should it leap at him out of a mountain and never let him go? Why should it come from his lips when he opened them to call the Mimi - come whole, as he had never yet heard it? And now, whole, it went over and over in his mind until he clenched his teeth and thought of the smoke of a tall grass. Maybe a man could fight a love-singing if he knew the singer - but how could he fight the love-singing of a mountain?

'Oh, Mimi!' whispered Wirrun striding fast down the ridge in the sunset. But there was only Ularra to travel with him: Ularra now just ahead by Harry's car, cooking something over a couple of burning sticks as he watched Wirrun coming down the ridge.

And Ularra too watched him with the eyes of a friend.

'Just in time, man!' shouted Ularra pouring baked beans on to a plate. 'Half an hour and we'd have gone off and left you. Come and get outside this - Harry wants to shift.'

Harry stared doggedly at the baked beans. He was not at all sure that he did want to drive over an invisible track through rough country after dark; he merely hoped that it might be safer than camping at night a stranger among restless and unreliable spirits. Wirrun knew his problem and hurried on to the fire. Ularra passed him a plate and asked anxiously, 'Didn't find her, did you?' At Wirrun's nod he gave a whistle of delighted surprise.

'Wish I knew this country like you do,' said Wirrun to Harry by way of thanks, and Harry looked even more dogged with satisfaction.

They ate quickly, bundled things back into the car, and true to Ularra's threat were retreating down the ridge within half an hour. Harry drove as fast as he could to make the most of the evening light, Wirrun and Ularra hung on and no one had time or breath for talking. Only Wirrun kept twisting his head to catch glimpses of the haze-hung cliffs of the Mimi's country.

It grew dusk, and then dark; Harry picked his way with care, but he kept on till they reached their last camp which now had the safety of a familiar place. Here, at last, he stopped the car with some relief. 'We want the moon,' he said, putting his head out of the window to stare at the sky.

'Not due for hours yet,' Ularra pointed out rubbing an elbow that had caught a door-handle at the last bump; but Harry was not looking for the moon. He had caught the sound of wind in the trees.

'Westerly,' he grunted. 'No cloud. Wouldn't want to be caught too far out in rain. Got to watch it from now on.'

They got out of the car to feel the wind; it swept down on them in gusts and lifted eastward over ridges. Harry built a bark shelter for a small fire, for safety and companionship rather than for warmth, and he and Ularra sat by it to wait for sleep or hunger or a moon. Wirrun was too restless; he wandered close to the fire and away again, stared at the stars, leaned against the car feeling the wind. Ularra watched him.

'Where to after this, man?'

Wirrun tangled his hair with a hand. 'What's the best way east?'

'East?' said Harry. 'There's bad country that way. How far east?'

'Right across, say.'

'Couldn't do it in the car - too far for me. Take you north to the coast, that's not far, and pick up a boat or a truck. One to another the men'll get you across.'

'Mm,' said Wirrun swaying to a gust of wind. 'That'll take time.'

Ularra tugged at the lobe of one ear. 'Back where we came from? Is that what your friend said?'

'She didn't know too much,' said Wirrun. He added gruffly, 'She couldn't come .... I just gotta try my own way ....' and gazed up at the stars. They hung low, beckoning. The wind's tide swept over him again and poured away through the treetops. Harry placed another sheet of bark to shelter the fire.

'Hum,' said Ularra. 'Better start thinking, then. You got any money left?'

Wirrun shook his head, one hand going from habit to his pocket and finding the power instead. It was thrumming; the wind pounced and tugged, lifting him a little. Wirrun gave a shout.

'Ularra, get your pack on - ' he wrenched open the car door and reached inside - 'here, quick! Harry - ' he paused, struggling into his own pack, for how could he leave Harry alone with the spirits? Yet was he not Hero, and travelling on the land's business? 'Harry, I hate leaving you like this after all you've done but it's a right wind. There'll be power enough left after we're gone to keep you safe till morning. Ularra, hang on to this cord and don't drop it -*don't let go* - and run when I run. Thanks, Harry! *Now*, Ularra - run!'

Stumbling on stones in the dark, they ran together into the wind and were lifted and tumbled in its tide. There was a glimpse of Harry's firelit face, eyes staring up and mouth gaping. Wirrun, gripping the power and breasting the wind like a surfer, felt its wild tumbling ease and knew that now it carried them with it. He shouted at Ularra to stop threshing about and wind that cord round his hand.

A ridge fell away below as the dark and windy sky gathered them up. Wirrun remembered a night that seemed long ago, when he had wished that Ularra too might ride the wind before he died.

3

When the wind at last gave its message to Wirrun it gave him too some of its own rushing freedom. He had been called hero by Ko-in and the Mimi, but the laws of their kind were strange to him: he had been called on as a hero by the People and had groped his way with worry and doubt. But when the wind itself had called on him to mount and ride then Wirrun of the People knew himself. It was all the knowledge he had but it was enough, for now he could travel wherever he was led and do whatever he must. He was released.

And at first he needed all his power to cope with Ularra, for Ularra gaped and gasped and threshed and struggled. He tugged on the cord of the power like a drowning man, he tangled Wirrun in it as he sank low and shot high with a flailing of arms and legs. He even grabbed desperately at Wirrun's head for support. It reminded Wirrun of his own struggles when Ko-in had carried him over the treetops. He managed at last to seize Ularra's free hand in his and place it firmly on his own shoulder, which steadied Ularra and allowed Wirrun to shout reassurances into his ear.

'Don't fight it, man! Let go and ride it like a wave. Here - wind that thing round your wrist before you lose it!'

'Man!' gasped Ularra at last on a windy breath. 'You shoulda warned me!'

'I know that. Sorry, mate. Only you gotta grab the right wind when it comes. Right now?'

Ularra looked down into depths of darkness that were gullies and on to forested ridges touched with starlight. He looked up into depths of sky at the coldly burning stars. He gave a sudden shout of joy and laughed like a giant.

'Riding the wind, eh?' he said. 'Poor old Harry!'

'He'll have a story to tell when he gets back home any rate, and that should suit him.' Harry would shut himself into the car until morning; he and Ularra were flying to meet it. He could see a far-off lightening in the sky where a pale slice of moon was now hanging.

Ularra was trying to settle the pack he had shouldered so quickly. Suddenly he gaped in fresh dismay. 'Hey, man - I hope you know what you're doing! Wherever we're going we've left most of the tucker behind!'

For a moment Wirrun gaped too. Except for a few things tucked into pockets of their packs their supplies and water-bags had been left behind in the car; and he did not know where the wind might set them down or how long the journey might take. Then he laughed in his new freedom as Ularra had.

'She's putting us on our way, man. She won't let us starve!'

'Hum,' said Ularra. 'She mighta thought we'd take all our stuff.'

The wind had been drawing them higher: up into dawn while the land was still shadowed below. Hanging between the shadows and the pearly sky Ularra's worry could not last. His face shone.

'I'm dreaming, man, only I never did it so good before. It's like . . . what? Lying on a big pillow that keeps pushing at you . . . only that's too soft. You gotta keep your balance or you lose it.'

'It's like nothing,' said Wirrun, 'only riding the wind. There's nothing the same.' Ularra's delight doubled his own.

They blew on into morning: one moment banners of colour and light in the sky and the next a dazzle of sun in their eyes. They were crossing a broken, sandy coast still grey in the dawn; they watched sunlight come sweeping towards it over the sea. To their left the broken coastline swept north and vanished. To their right it turned south-east with a sweep of sandhills; for a while they travelled along it over the islanded sea.

'Is it the Gulf?'

'I reckon - what else?'

'Harry was right, then. It wasn't far.'

'A bit longer going up and down ridges,' Wirrun pointed out.

Gulls swung and wheeled below. The shallow sea lay broad and quiet, shaded blue and green in the contours that lay beneath. The coast turned more southerly and threaded away into haze. There was only sea under them, and Ularra looked sideways at Wirrun.

'You reckon you can find land?'

Wirrun grinned. 'No, mate. It'll have to find me. But we gotta hit the Cape sooner or later unless the wind changes.'

'Man, that's a long way,' said Ularra, but he said no more.

Hours went by with only sea below and deep blue sky above. Wirrun, his left hand aching on the power, managed to use the pocket of his shorts as a sling. Ularra had tied the possum-fur cord round his hand for safety. Between them, bobbing and tumbling out of control for some moments, they succeeded in drawing from a pocket in Wirrun's pack a cake of chocolate and a carton of orange-juice. The sea was painted with lines of movement that never seemed to move. The push of wind at their backs became something solid and permanent. They were caught in a great stillness, it seemed, under a dome of glass.

Into this stillness Wirrun began to speak. About the sad staunch pride of the Mimi keeping her lowly place among her kind, hugging the secret of her fame among spirits. About the trouble that had fallen like a stone, perhaps in the east and perhaps made by the Ninya on their travels. And at last, haltingly, about his own deep trouble: how the mountain had caught him with a love-singing, and if it should be fought it must be with the smoke of a tall grass.

Ularra knew the kunai grass. In the glassy stillness of sky he listened and frowned and asked a question or two.

'Ever seem to you that this mountain's . . . got you?'

'Not that way,' said Wirrun. 'It makes no sense. The mountain's sort of a home. It's the singing's got me.'

'Been hearing it up here?'

Wirrun turned and looked at him. 'No. I've thought about it but that's me worrying at it. Not it worrying at me.'

'Hum,' said Ularra. 'Well, you're *coming* any rate, straight as you can. Can't do more, only wait and remember the smoke. I'll be there keeping an eye - just as well you told me.'

And Wirrun knew that Ularra was in his own way as staunch a companion as even the gallant Mimi.

The afternoon found them weary and silent, still blowing eastward before the wind with the shallow sea below; but now Wirrun watched a mistiness ahead and thought it might be land. He saw that Ularra watched it too, but before either of them could be sure enough to mention it the wind dropped them into its pocket, caught them out again at a lower level, buffeted and tossed them and tore their breath away, and swung them farther south.

'Man!' gasped Ularra when he could speak. 'You never told me about that. Where to now?'

'Dunno, but I hope we get there soon. I reckon this wind's getting ready to drop, and I'm not keen on coming down blind into strange country at night.'

'Me either, man.'

The sun was now low in the west. They watched a mistiness grow into a coastline, and a little after sunset saw it clearly. 'I never saw anything like that!' cried Wirrun. 'Bush coming out to meet us! Mangroves, they must be.'

The sea washed in gently between spreading trees; they passed over a forest that stood in the water.

Ularra had crossed the Gulf by boat and knew and welcomed the mangroves but they did not tell him, as Wirrun hoped, what part of the coast they were crossing.

'The Gulf - you know that, man. There's mangrove forests walking out to sea all along here.'

Behind the mangroves the sunset shone on low, rolling sandhills that held between them the wet glint of marshes. It looked a desolate country, with low flat-topped hills to trap flyers in the dark. As dusk rose towards him like the filling of a well Wirrun peered anxiously down.

'Had it yet, mate?' he asked Ularra.

'A bit of chocolate and a drink of orange don't keep up a man's strength too good,' Ularra confessed. 'But I reckon I can keep going while you can. I don't like the look of that down there much, do you?'

'Not much - but now you can see it any rate. It'll be dark in a minute or so. Still . . . I reckon we'll trust it a bit longer if it'll take us . . . .'

They kept on south while the stars brightened over them. Below there were no lights: no string of bright beads to show a township, not even the lonely yellow light of an Inlander's home. But Wirrun had forgotten the starlight which his eyes were learning to use again. He could see at least the flat-topped hills that grew more frequent as they went; he would feel them looming as one feels a presence in the dark, and by looking could pick out their shapes.

When he caught Ularra yawning once he thought of coming down on one of these hills. He even loosened his stiff fingers on the power and experimented, bringing them down a few feet. But to sleep dry and hungry on a bare hill and wake lost among marshes was not what he wanted. The right wind might not come again, and the Ninya's known route was still far to the south and east. Hilly country with streams, if he could find it, would lead them across.

By the time he had found it it was all he could do to keep his hand closed on the power and his eyes open. Beside him Ularra would doze, droop, begin to fall; wake with a start and peer ahead and down for a while; doze and droop again. Like a sleepy driver who suddenly sees another car, Wirrun was roused into panic: he had felt two changes in one moment. One was a looming of strength and power in the darkness - the land rising to meet him. The other was a change in the wind - it fumbled, dropped him six feet, roused itself and swept him higher. Wirrun grabbed Ularra's shoulder and shook it roughly.

'Wake up, man, wake up! There's hills ahead and we're going into 'em! Watch out - try not to break a leg!' His eyes found the shape of the ridge, grey-edged with starlight, reaching away left and right.

'Eh?' muttered Ularra, and woke up. 'Glory be,' he said and peered helplessly down at the dark.

Wirrun, loosening and tightening his fingers on the power to bring them down by degrees, had no choices. They were falling off the wind; they might overshoot into some deep gorge or smash into rocks. He must take the first slope as he met it. He felt it near.

Leaves struck at them, sweet and keen with the smell of eucalyptus. A tree - he caught at it and with one foot shoved Ularra hard into its branches. Clinging with one hand he forced the other, stiff and numb, to release the power at last.

'Eh?' said Ularra scrambling among leaves. He was suddenly too heavy to support himself and slid and crashed to the ground with Wirrun on top of him.

It was darker under the tree. Wirrun rolled aside and they sat peering at each other, both unhurt. The possum-fur cord that linked them was still unbroken. Ularra untied it from his hand.

'Man, I'm starving,' he mumbled, and fell back on his pack and slept. Wirrun dragged off his own pack, pushed it under his head on the stony ground, and slept too. The dark crept around them and murmured with wonder. It had been a great riding of the wind.

They woke in the shade of stringybarks with strong sunlight beyond, on a slope looking westward over the marshes and broken hills they had crossed. They wasted no time in admiring this view but tore at their packs to see what food they had.

'Chicken and mushroom!' breathed Wirrun producing a can.

'Meatballs here - and I got the tin opener - wow!'

They ripped the cans open and ate with their knives, wriggling their backs uncomfortably from time to time because they felt bare without the push of the wind. Ularra licked the blade of his knife with care.

'That's breakfast any rate. I'm not too sure about lunch.'

'Rabbit,' Wirrun suggested without much confidence. 'Or maybe wallaby.'

'Lizards,' said Ularra. 'Witchetty grubs - they don't run fast. With all that hunting we won't get too far in a day.'

'Water first,' said Wirrun, draining the gravy from his can. 'And when we find it we'll light up and brew - I got the tea here.'

'Brew, what in?'

Wirrun thought quickly. 'In these two cans . . . . Lucky we both got knives.'

They flattened the hacked edges of the empty cans by hammering them with stones, rolled back the partly removed lids to make handles, and stowed them carefully in their packs. Then they climbed the steep ridge in search of a gully and water.

The flat-topped ridge showed them a wide wild country stretching east and south into sharp blue sunlit hazes and purple shadow. A sandstone country, not high at its edges but deeply chasmed and ravined, a country to know and revere. The gorges, filled with purple, were cut sharp and narrow at the top but widened under overhanging walls as they plunged down. Wirrun gazed at it in sober silence and Ularra whistled.

'Thanks, man.'

'What for?' said Wirrun, gazing. There'd be water down there all right if they could reach it; and the ridges melted away so far to the east that they must lead him to the Divide and so to the coast.

'Thanks for not dropping me in one of those in the dark.'

Wirrun's face grooved into a grin but he was still thinking. 'I bet there was ice in here somewhere. The first we knew was at Toowoomba, but that's only the one the papers told about. If we're tracking the Ninya we could start here, only we don't know where to look . . . . Well, better try for some easier water.'

They turned west along the ridge looking for some younger gully opening to the plains. They found one cutting deep into the sandstone and followed its course down the ridge to a point where they could climb in. Its floor was only damp; they turned upward looking for hollowed pools where water might lie. The rock walls of the gully rose higher as they went, and closed in towards each other overhanging at the top. Above them the scrub rose higher still, deepening the coolness and shade.

They found small potholes with a little water and a great activity of wrigglers. They were thirsty enough to drink this water if it had not promised better near at hand. Higher up, among umbrella fern and forest mint and spreading crowsnests cool under overhanging rock, they found their pool and drank. A magpie's call rang as cool and clear as the water.

'Man!' sighed Ularra, and lay back in a hollow of rock to let the water settle inside him. 'I could drink her dry only she mightn't fill up again. You reckon it's a shame to make this stuff into tea?' Wirrun didn't answer; he too sat in a hollow of rock, but his face was deeply grooved and strained. Ularra glanced at him and repeated the question.

'Eh?' said Wirrun, his face relaxing. 'I reckon I'll have tea next, and after that more water.'

'That's sense. Better wash those tins out while I see if there's any dry wood in here.'

The wood was mostly damp and rotting, but he found a half dead branch fallen in from above and laid a fire on flat rock.

Wirrun had washed the two cans and filled them. Ularra set them in place and lit his fire. Smoke billowed up from the green and rotten fuel.

'Bit of a change from our last camp - now there's a country where you can light a fire. This one'll want watching.' He glanced at Wirrun. 'Wish we had something to cook on it.' Wirrun was silent and strained again, with a look of tight-lipped eagerness. Ularra looked at him closely. 'I said, what are we going to cook on this fire besides tea?'

Wirrun jumped almost guiltily and smoothed the strain out of his face. 'Don't get in a twist, man. Fetch a rabbit.'

'It's that singing again, eh? Worrying at you.' Wirrun looked away, moody and resentful. Ularra broke a branch with great energy. 'Shoulda had more sense, making a fire in all these rocks. You just watch this water boil and keep your mind on rabbits.'

High overhead there was a rustle of leaves. Something whooshed through the air and thudded down two yards from the fire. It was a rabbit, freshly killed. It lay on the rock and stared up from one glazed eye.

4

Wirrun and Ularra sprang to their feet; they stared at the rabbit, and at each other, and then upward. A face hung over the edge of the gully, a dark face slashed by a white grin and topped by an old felt hat. An arm in a rolled-up shirt-sleeve waved over the head.

Ularra shouted between anger and delight and jabbed one hand at the rabbit. The dark man above grinned again and held up a hessian bag: he had many rabbits. As he lowered the bag the felt hat toppled from his head and floated down into the gully. It landed almost on the fire and Wirrun pounced on it.

The man above stopped grinning and held out an arm. 'Throw her up,' he called; but Wirrun held on to the hat.

'She won't travel - too light. You come down.'

'I'll take her up,' Ularra offered. 'We owe him for a rabbit.'

'Let him come. We need him more than his rabbit. This country's not for strangers.'

The man had disappeared. They could hear him grumbling, and the clumping of his boots along the gully. He did not go far before the boots rang on rock: he was taking some track of his own down the steep walls that Wirrun and Ularra would not have dared. In a few minutes he came up the gully into view.

'Saw your smoke,' he greeted them, and his eyes went deliberately over their packs and the two small cans of water on the fire. The look was the kind by which the People said much, a silent criticism easy to read: 'Strangers with empty packs and empty bellies and no sense; maybe they'll know what to do with a rabbit.'

Ularra was driven to defence. 'Man, we're glad of that rabbit if you can spare it. Left in a hurry yesterday, and our tucker's back in Alice.'

The man gave him another measuring look and answered with only one word. 'Yesterday.' Ularra was flustered.

Wirrun held out the old hat. The measuring eyes ran over him too - and went back to the bag on his belt. 'Yesterday,' said the man, and took back his hat with a slight bend of the head. 'Merv Bula. Glad you've come. You're needed.'

'You're needed too,' Wirrun told him. 'You heard we were coming?'

Merv Bula dumped his hessian bag at his feet and took out a billy; used his hat to lift the cans from the fire and empty them into the billy; set it carefully to boil; took a knife from a sheath on his belt and began to skin and gut the rabbit. Ularra moved to take this job from him, was ignored, and retreated to make the tea.

'Hoped you might,' Merv grunted, answering Wirrun as he worked. 'Saw Tom Hunter going through back east .... Yesterday, eh?'

It would be known in any case since Harry had seen it.

Wirrun said, 'We came on the wind, Ularra and me. It was sudden.'

'Ah,' said Merv, tugging at the rabbit skin.

'We needed water first, and this was nearest - and then we couldn't leave it right away. But we wanted someone like you that knows the country. You and your rabbit turned up like a storm in a bad year.'

'Or a man for an Ice-Fighter, maybe,' said Merv. He rolled the rabbit skin neatly, thrust it into his bag, drew out a pannikin and began to cut up the rabbit.

'You got trouble here too, then?'

'Trouble all over. You can't move of a night.'

'Strangers out of their places?'

'Never been anything like it.' Merv took out an ancient enamel mug and placed it by the two cans for Ularra to fill with tea. Ularra had also searched the packs and found salt and an onion, and now offered these small finds to Merv. 'Ah,' said Merv. 'That's handy.'

'From the look of it,' said Wirrun, 'I'd say you might've had trouble last time too. High rocks on the road east: a likely place for ice. The papers never said, but they wouldn't.'

'Ah,' said Merv pausing in his work to sip tea. 'They wouldn't know. No one to see it but me, and all I told was the right men.'

'There was ice, then? How near?'

'Can't see from here.' Merv sat back on his heels to finish his tea. When the mug was empty he rinsed it out, measured water into the pannikin and set it on the fire that Ularra had been nursing. He picked leaves from a small creeping plant and tossed them in with the rabbit. 'Give her a while to boil down a bit,' he advised. Ularra looked resentful, being familiar with the cooking of rabbit stew. Merv stood up and heaved his bag to his shoulder. 'I'll put me rabbit skins to dry and be back. Show you that place.' He pushed the old hat hard on to his head and strode off down the gully. They heard the scrape of his boots climbing rock and saw him peer down again from above with a grin of farewell. They

waited and listened for a little longer feeling that the ears of
Merv Bula could hear farther than other men's ears. Then
Ularra huffed a little and moved the pannikin two inches.

'I been cooking rabbit stew since I was *that* high. What
were those leaves he put in?'

'There you are, then,' said Wirrun with a grin. 'You know
rabbit stew but you don't know the leaves of the country.
That's a sizeable man. We've been lucky. Helped, more
like.'

Ularra had to agree. 'The only one seeing that ice, too.
You reckon it'll do any good going to look? What are you
looking for?'

'Told you before - I'm not looking, just waiting. If it's
there it'll find us.'

They rested in silence till the fire needed more wood and
Ularra went off up the gully to find it. When he came back
he saw that Wirrun's face had darkened again into a hungry
listening. Ularra dropped his wood noisily and began to
feed the fire, calling on Wirrun to smell that stew, rubbing
his own stomach and sniffing loudly. Wirrun roused
himself to agree that he could handle the lot without
Ularra's help, and lapsed back into his own darkness.
Ularra squatted by the fire and watched him with helpless
anxiety.

'Wish I could take it from you, man.'

Wirrun only hunched a little. When he spoke it was only
to himself and like a fretful child. 'Will I ever get free?'

Ularra broke a branch savagely. 'When I find this tall
grass I'm gonna smoke you black.' He was startled to see a
flash of anger in the hero's frowning eyes. If it was like that
it was going to be tough; could you cure a man of a love-
singing if he was so bad that he didn't want to be cured?

After midday when the sun filtered green light into the
gully they used knives and fingers to eat stewed rabbit and
drank the gravy from their useful cans. The darkness had
drained out of Wirrun leaving him only tired, and they were
both so hungry that the meal was a feast. Afterwards they
made more tea, cleaned up the camp and let the fire go out.

'Been trying to long enough - it won't need no help,' declared Ularra, but he emptied the billy over it for safety.

They were bored with resting and anxiously watching the angle of the sunlight when the boots of Merv Bula rang on the rocks and he came clumping up the gully. Though he had dealt with his morning's catch he still carried his bag, rolled and roped and slung from his shoulder. He glanced at the dead fire and the packs strapped ready and nodded.

'Best stew I ever ate,' Wirrun told him gratefully as he and Ularra shouldered their packs.

Merv smiled widely. 'Hungriest you ever were,' he suggested.

His way out of the gully proved to be an easy climb, under an overhang of rock weathered into holds that could only be seen from below. After the coolness of the gully the ridge seemed heavy with heat even in the scrub.

'Watch out for warrens,' said Merv. 'I got traps.' He pointed now and then to a rabbit warren as he took them east along the ridge.

'Wouldn't like to step in one of those traps,' Ularra agreed keeping clear. But Merv had not been considering Ularra's feet.

'Do you no harm only maybe waste a rabbit. I got me own make of traps. A rabbit's got rights like anyone else.'

They nodded, for they both remembered with what agony the shriek of a rabbit in an Inlander's trap came whistling through the night.

They came out of the scrub on the edge of a gorge cutting sharp-edged across the ridge. The frowning cliffs of its opposite shore led their eyes down, past hanging rock and clinging scrub, down through blue distance to a far-away canopy of forest. The blue filled it like some magically translucent sea into which they might dive or over which they might sail.

'Take an hour to get down,' said Merv with a glance at the sky. 'We'll be there for the night.'

'An hour?' Ularra gripped his pack-straps. 'Couple of steps and I'd be down a lot faster.'

Merv grinned widely and turned along the gorge, following its course until the ridge began to dip. 'Lucky it's dry - we'll go in the way the water goes.' He led them into the dip.

It was hardly a watercourse but it had nibbled a little at the sheer cliffs of the gorge. They could see how it would run in the wet, channelling a way down the cliffs; Wirrun pictured a long fluttering plume of water free-falling past the undercut lower walls into the hazy depth. He wished for a wind but none came. He and Ularra, avoiding each other's eyes, had no choice but to follow Merv Bula over the edge of that terrifying gap.

They never really knew how they made the climb. They used no rope though Merv had one. They simply followed Merv through the tunnellings of weather, over pavements quarried by roots, behind the balusters of stunted trees. They were slow and cautious even where the path was wide, for that blue distance sang always into one ear. They watched where Merv placed a foot, where he sat and slid, where he hung on and dropped. Wind-holes led them from one hanging cave into a lower one; narrow water-courses threaded behind domes. The only moment that stayed clear in Wirrun's mind was that of leaving the cliffs for the deeper-cut shale below; and though he knew the descent had been made by way of a cave and a tree he remembered only the thought that if they fell now any rate they could roll.

It took more than an hour to reach the bottom, and there they sat resting and looking; for the far-bottomed blue of the gorge had become a wide place of grass and scrub with a creek winding through it and a complex geography of hillsides and ridges, and high above, blue and distant, a soaring of impregnable cliffs.

'Coulda gone round,' said Merv, 'if we'd had three days.'

'I wish you'd said,' retorted Ularra, and Wirrun grinned.

'What about this ice place?' he asked.

'Up the creek,' said Merv. 'When you're ready.'

The creek was no more than a trickle between small pools until they reached its head, in a gully cut deep into hills of shale. Here under hanging sandstone cliffs lay a wide deep pool with river oaks standing over it and an outflow into the creek. It reminded Ularra of mysterious waters in his own red country, and it pulled at Wirrun like a magnet. He could only stand and stare.

'How long since we had a bath?' he asked with his eyes on the water. 'Nothing but little dishes for a week.'

'You don't want a bath now, man. Sun's gone and it's getting cool. Merv's showing you where the ice was.'

'Here,' said Merv.

Wirrun dragged his eyes from the pool. 'You mean up there on the cliff?'

'Down here,' said Merv. 'Water iced over.'

Wirrun was puzzled. 'You'd have thought up there, with all that high rock to look out of.'

'Down here,' said Merv stolidly. He added, 'They mighta come down through the cave.'

'Cave?'

Merv took them through the river oaks to the farther end of the pool and they saw that the gully's head cut deep under the sandstone, making a cave with a wide, low entrance that ran back into darkness under the mass of the cliffs.

'Might have a look in there,' said Wirrun.

'You do. I'll set a few traps for morning.' Merve un-hitched his swaglike roll and began to untie it. Ularra followed Wirrun into the cave.

Though the sky was still sunlit the cliffs shouldered the sunlight aside and a long evening had begun in the gorge. Four yards in from the entrance of the cave the light was failing; but they could see that the cave narrowed sharply and went steeply up in height. There was a fine soft dust under their feet, and a sense of soft, continuing darkness above and beyond. The darkness drew them on.

Just at its edge something moved and the two young men were suddenly still. Something laughed, soft and teasing; a shape moved into the twilight.

She was charming: broad cheeks, small round chin, dark eyes bright with mischief, dark hair soft over her forehead.

She held out the small fine hands of the People in welcome and even Wirrun, clutching the power and feeling it throb, could see no sign of claws. She looked at him knowingly but it was at Ularra she smiled, turning her firm young body towards him, preening. Ularra's eyes shone and he laughed shortly. She laughed back.

'Come, then, Big One,' she said cheekily.

Ularra stumbled forward, Wirrun grabbed his arm - and they stopped as they were, transfixed, for the darkness came alive and screamed in chorus. The girl cringed, then swung round to face it. There were glimpses of dark women struggling round her, fierce dark women with lashing tails.

'Out!' screamed the voices. 'Catch her!' 'Tear her!' 'Send her out!' 'Have we not trouble enough with things of her kind?' 'Go, you! Take your smiles and your teasing and kissing away!' Their fury was a darkness in itself and Wirrun felt it swirling like a black tide out of the cave. He was shaken.

They reached for the girl with their nails. For a moment she fought back as fiercely, but the tailed women were too many. She sprang away and fled past the two young men and out of the cave. Wirrun would have followed the tailed women into the dark, but Ularra growled and swung after the girl. Wirrun had to run after him and try to hold him. Ularra fought him off.

'Let go, man, I'm not a kid! Up on the cliff - in that hole - Get off! I know what I'm doing.' He was an angry stranger and too strong for Wirrun to hold. Wirrun hung on and shouted for Merv Bula.

Merv came running, looking as he ran from Ularra's straining face to the cave that Ularra stared at on the cliffs. Merv seized Ularra's other arm, and between them he and Wirrun got him away. At the pool Merv tore off his hat, slooshed it full of water and jammed it hard on Ularra's head. Ularra growled and shuddered and at last gave in, and Merv and Wirrun led him quietly down the creek.

'They were after her,' he said once in a dazed way.

'Not our business, mate,' said Wirrun soothingly. 'Let 'em fight their own battles.'

'They had tails .... She never had a chance ....'

'They're none of 'em any good to you, mate. Let 'em go.'

Farther down the creek they found another waterhole under river oaks, and Wirrun sat by Ularra while Merv made camp, lit a fire and fried sausages in his pannikin. Ularra was quiet and dogged. 'Fool,' he muttered once avoiding Wirrun's eye.

'You get Merv's sausages into you and forget it, man. I near made the same mistake once, only I had the power and the Mimi.'

'Ah,' said Merv. 'Wouldn't want to make it with that one. That one's no good to a man.'

Wirrun looked at him sharply. 'You know it, then?'

'Knew she was there,' said Merv. 'Should be further north by rights. That's that Abuba.' He seemed unwilling to say more, and Wirrun let the question drop. Tomorrow when Ularra was his cocky self again he would ask more about the Abuba; and about the tailed women from whom trouble seemed to flow in a dark tide. Now he only sat watching Merv at work by the fire: steady and solid, aware of restless spirits and yet not seeming afraid. Wirrun was again glad that the land had sent him such a man.

'Time to roll in,' said Merv when the dark came down; and Wirrun agreed, remembering how they had slept on the stones last night. His body ached from the flight, the rough sleeping, and the climb down from the cliffs. Yet when Merv had rolled himself into a blanket near the fire and Ularra had climbed doggedly into his sleeping-bag Wirrun, lying in his own bag a yard away, was at first too tired to sleep.

He lay watching the channel of stars between the darkness of cliffs and thought of Ularra: Ularra walking steadily with him to meet the Jugi, laughing with delight on the wind, frowning anxiously over Wirrun's own trouble, following him into the cave of the tailed women. He should have watched out for Ularra ... he'd take more care after this ....

He fell asleep with no haunting of water-music and only the wind singing in the needles of the river-oaks.

He woke startled and confused with his hand on the power: it was still and gave no sign. There was deep dark under the trees and the dimness of starlight beyond. The fire gleamed red under ash, with the rolled-up shape of Merv nearby. The camp was quiet. Too quiet. He put out a hand and felt Ularra's sleeping-bag.

It was empty. Ularra was gone.

5

Wirrun fought his way out of his sleeping-bag looking for the stars and feeling for the time. It was hard to tell under the black shoreline of the cliffs but he knew it was between midnight and morning. He hoped fiercely, he demanded, that Ularra should be wandering near the camp dazed with sleep. He stumbled into the darkness to look for an angular, loose-limbed blackness moving somewhere. He could not find it.

He crossed the creek below the waterhole and ran along the opposite bank. Still nothing. Ularra must have fallen, sleepy and stupid, and gone back to sleep where he lay. Wirrun began to call.

'Ularra! Wake up, man! Ularra, where are you?'

He waited and listened. No sleepy grunt or stumbling footstep. He called again; and again.

A figure loomed out of the dark and he bounded towards it. But it was Merv Bula. Merv grasped him by the shoulder and tried to draw him back towards the creek. Wirrun shook him off.

'It's Ularra - he's gone - we gotta find him. Wandering round half asleep -'

Merv held him firmly by both shoulders. 'No good, Ice-Fighter. Back to the fire till daylight.'

'Not me!' shouted Wirrun. 'Ularra! Where are you, man?'

Merv's grip and his voice were both iron. 'Back to the fire and we'll see.'

Still Wirrun would not hear, for had he not brought Ularra out of his safe job and the milkbar into this danger? Had he not, thinking only of spirits, failed to protect his friend though the power lay in his hand? He struggled again. '*You* go and sit over your fire till morning. I don't need it.'

'Ah,' said Merv, 'but you do. Fire's sense and work and no shivering. You need this one. And you need your head. And you need mine. We got work to do.'

Then Wirrun knew that he was indeed shivering, and that he did need his own head and Merv's. He let Merv lead him back over the creek to the camp.

The fire was already blazing with fresh wood. Merv added more and set a billy in place. 'Tea,' he said.

Wirrun answered sternly. 'All right. No more. Tell me.'

'That Abuba,' said Merv. 'He's gone looking.'

'I know that.'

'Sure you do. That cliff-hole, that cave. He's there.'

'Not yet, maybe. He's gotta find it in the dark.'

'Look up at the cliffs, Ice-Fighter. You'll see her fire. She's lit it for him.'

Wirrun remembered a red point of fire that he had refused to see.

'His bed's cold,' Merv added. 'He's gone long enough.'

'To climb up there in the dark? He can't.'

'Ah,' said Merv. 'That's it. Eh? She'll help him but she won't help you. He can do it. You need daylight.' He made the tea. 'And you need a lot more.'

The cold that lay inside Wirrun was for grasping and using. He was hero and Ice-Fighter: for his People, for his country, and for his friend Ularra. He watched frowning while the tea was poured and took his mug in a firm hand. 'This Abuba. What sort is it?'

'That's right,' said Merv. 'Use the head.' But he seemed to
have trouble answering the question and stared at the fire.
'She's a cheeky one,' he said at last. 'She'll coax a man to
marry her, see, and then she'll . . . turn him.'

'Turn him how?'

'Change him. Make him something else, not a man. You
gotta catch him and turn him back.'

'How?' said Wirrun again sternly.

'Takes time and work - no use rushing off in the dark . . . .
You gotta make him again. Make him a man like he was.'

Wirrun closed his hand on the power. If he had to do
impossible things he must do them. 'How does a man make
a man?'

Merv stoked the fire and seemed to think. 'Bit by bit,' he
said at last. 'I don't know all I'd like, I just heard the story.
It's old stuff, this, and we'll take it bit by bit. Catch him first
and then we'll know more. Now we want ironwood.'

'Ironwood?'

'It's got a power we want. We'll need a load or two.'

'Can we find it in the dark?'

'I know where.' Merv banked the fire, drawing ash and
charcoal over it to hold it. Then he took a cloth bundle from
his pack and unwrapped a small, short-handled axe. He
stood up with the axe in his hand and waited for Wirrun.

There was a glow in the darkness of the sky and the stars
had paled, but the gully itself was as dark as ever. Yet
Wirrun could see well enough, for by now he had lost the
night-blindness that is a habit of city eyes. Merv paused now
and then to choose his path, but he chose it with certainty
and walked like a man without fear. Only a man like this
could have brought Wirrun back from the cliffs and forced
him to listen by the fire; only from Merv could he have
accepted the rule of 'bit by bit'.

They climbed the first slopes of the hill to a darkness of
trees. Merv's hands moved over bark, identifying.

'This one and those two, all ironwood. Small, but they'll
do.'

He took Wirrun's hand and placed it on smooth, thin bark shedding here and there in twisted flakes, and among blunt-pointed leaves on which he could feel the gloss. Merv's own hands moved among branches, feeling and exploring. At last he took up the axe and used it like an adze, hacking off one branch and drawing it long and slender from the tree. Then he passed the axe to Wirrun.

'Fetch all you can cut - the whole tree if she's not too much for the little axe. You'll find her as tough as her name. Me, I got things to do.' He went away down the slope into darkness trailing his slender branch.

Wirrun set to work, starting on the outer branches that he could best see. His first fumbling blow only set the branch springing and jarred his hand. He learnt to cut lightly through bark till the pale gleam of wood gave him a target, and then to use the spring of the axe. It was hard work and he did not know why he must do it, but he did it with fierce satisfaction: unleashing all the haste and fear he had kept back, hacking into his dread of the things he must find and do by daylight. He tossed aside branch after branch until he could begin to see a greenness of bark patched with brown and the pale silvery wood that his axe chewed out of it; and then he began on the trunks. When the first small tree creaked and was pushed into breaking he took three branches in one hand, the trunk in the other, and dragged them behind him down the slope to the camp under the oaks.

Merv was working at the fire. A rabbit was cooking in a pannikin to one side of it, but Merv had drawn out red coals from the other side and sat there at work with his knife. He set it down and held his work over the coals, turning it slowly, drawing it back and forth; laid it over his knees again and rubbed at it with a hard rough bark; took up his knife again. As Wirrun watched the coldness came back inside him. Merv was making something like a spear. Slender and about six feet long; hardened in the fire and rubbed smooth; flattened and sharpened at one end; a rough and hurried job that looked primitive and dangerous. Merv said nothing to Wirrun who stood and watched; he only reached into his pack and tossed over a coil of light rope.

Wirrun dropped his load, took up the rope, turned on his heel and went off. He would not speak about the spear. He would do as Merv had said - take the impossible bit by bit and deal with each bit in its own time.

He had chopped down the second ironwood, roped the whole pile together, and dragged it bouncing back to camp when the first sunlight edged the tops of the cliffs. He had to turn and stare in the direction of the Abuba's cave.

'Eat first,' said Merv.

Wirrun swung on him. 'Man -'

'Eat,' said Merv with authority. 'No good on a cliff with an empty belly.' He put chunks of rabbit on a tin plate and Wirrun tore at them savagely. The spear's slender length rested against an oak, its silvery wood darkened by fire. It was strengthened below the point by a binding of string and had a handgrip of string on the shaft because Merv had not had time or skill to make it well. Wirrun watched it while he ate, but Merv rubbed up his knife and sheathed it, coiled the rope and laid it at hand, set beside it a short staff of ironwood, banked the fire again.

When they were ready he took up the spear, balanced it for a moment and handed it to Wirrun. 'Ever used one?'

Wirrun took the spear. 'Tried it, that's all.'

'Me either,' said Merv. 'I'd have made something shorter only you might need the length. She's not much but she's the right wood. You remember that. What we find in that cave, no matter what, if you want your friend back you take to it with ironwood. Understand?'

Wirrun gazed at him from under lowered brows. Merv gazed steadily back.

'No pity, mind. It won't be true pity. Your mate wants to be a man again. You think of that, Ice-Fighter. Best go.' He took up the rope and the ironwood staff.

They started up the creek. The highest western cliffs were painted with sunlight, but the Abuba's cave was low in the southern wall and always shadowed. They would climb towards it as the Abuba had done, by the eastern wall of the gully above the pool, and where the hillside cut in under the cliffs Wirrun knew Merv would find a way up. He had brought them down that giddy climb from the top without using the rope he carried now. Wirrun carried only the ironwood spear, at first awkwardly and with distrust; but as they went on his hand got to know it and carried it as if it belonged there. Merv's all-seeing eyes saw this too but he said nothing. His face was as dark with strain as Wirrun's own.

They went in silence. Once they stopped to look up at the cliffs, picking out ledge and channel and wind-weathered cave - and the one cave, rounder and deeper and darker, that was the Abuba's. Wirrun felt a tremor like a touch on a tightened string. Once he spoke.

'What kind of thing not a man?'

'Eh?' said Merv. 'Some kind of beast, maybe.'

They went on east, past the dark cave-mouth where pity would not be true pity.

Under overhanging cliffs Merv found a tree, and fallen sandstone blocks, and then a ledge running west, and from that a channel. The rope stayed coiled on his shoulder. It would have taken Wirrun half a day to find the path . . . but Ularra had found it in the dark . . . spirit-helped. . . .

Merv had stopped and was waiting ahead. When Wirrun came up he spoke softly.

'The way's easy - she'd have it easy. But the next bit wants to be quick and quiet so take a look. This that we're on opens up in a little cave - see, just up there. That's got a hole that goes straight into hers. Take it quick, in a jump - spear handy, mind, and don't get bit. I'll be back of you.'

He stood aside and Wirrun went on ahead. He laid a hand on the power: it had been quiet all these fearful hours but it was throbbing now. His right hand held the spear as if it belonged there, and he followed the channel up under arching rock that went back into a cave. He saw the hole, an elongated opening fretted by wind and blowing sand through a thinness of rock into a darkness beyond. A sound came through it. Wirrun listened for a grim moment and his blood turned to angry fire. It was a snuffling, whining sound, an animal noise. With his anger throbbing Wirrun gripped the spear, trod softly to the opening and leapt through.

A deeper, darker cave opened round him. He heard laughter in the shadows and his eyes found the Abuba. She stood against the farther wall, charming and cheeky, her dark eyes eagerly alight. She rolled her hips in derision and slipped away into darkness.

Something crouched against the wall where she had stood, something monstrous and shaggy that crouched like a beaten dog. A harsh growl rattled in its throat and it rose and stood on four limbs as man might in stooping, but the limbs too were covered in coarse hair and the hands and feet bore the talons of an eagle. It growled again and faced Wirrun, lips drawn back from long white fangs, he saw its eyes. They were a man's eyes, Ularra's eyes, and dark with misery. They begged for pity. Wirrun's anger sang in his ears and the point of his spear fell.

Coarse hair rose on the beast's neck and back. The growl rose to a savage attacking snarl. Baring its fangs and pleading with its eyes the monstrous thing that was Ularra launched itself at Wirrun.

FOUR

The Remaking of Ularra

I

As the great beast flew at him Wirrun acted by instinct. One hand dropped to the power, the other raised the ironwood spear, and he stood poised, ready to leap. Yet the spear-point wavered and dipped for the eyes of the beast still pleaded, and they were the eyes of his friend. And the beast, launched in its spring, seemed to hang there snarling - hair erect, talons striking, fangs bared, yet holding back like a dog that turns in fury on its master and cannot bite.

'Ularra, man!' cried Wirrun in pain and in power.

The beast launched itself again with rattling snarls and met the point of the spear. Wirrun felt its weight as the spear dragged at the hairy hide of its shoulder. It gave a roaring growl, twisted in fury with snapping jaws and striking talons, and its eyes wept.

'Hold steady!'

From behind Wirrun came Merv, grim-faced with his rope and staff, his eyes fixed on the struggling beast. In a moment he leapt forward, thrust the staff of ironwood into the snapping jaws and leapt back. The jaws clamped on the wood and opened roaring. The staff rolled free; there were broken fangs bedded in it and the monster snapped with broken stumps.

Merv threw a loop of rope round the beast as it fought on the end of the spear. He gave one end of the rope to Wirrun, pulled tight and threw again. Leaping in and away he tossed loop after loop and pulled them tight till the beast lay jerking on the rock snapping its broken teeth, baring its rope-tangled claws and weeping with Ularra's eyes. Wirrun tore free the spear with which he had held it and flung it clattering on the rock. He and Merv held the rope between them, each of them one free end; by pulling against each other they held and controlled the beast. They propped themselves against the cave wall to rest, looking only at the monster. It lay on the rock, struggling and bleeding and weeping.

'Shoulda brought poles,' muttered Merv. There were poles for the cutting on the hillside below, but Wirrun knew he meant poles of ironwood. He answered shortly for he was breathless and choked by pity.

'Two men can't do it. There's this hole. Gotta get through.'

He gave his rope-end to Merv to hold, unwound a length of cord from the power and went slowly forward to the beast that struggled and jerked.

'Ularra, man,' said Wirrun, 'we're taking you home.'

He stooped, extending his hands; the beast writhed and snapped its jaws but not at him. He passed the cord round the hairy neck and tied it; the beast snarled and snapped as his hand neared its wounded shoulder. Wirrun forced himself to work at the rope, freeing the hairy limbs for walking. One of them struck at him, he saw the wicked claws curve near his face and draw away. Merv watched with lowered brows.

'Your mate's not rightly turned. Lucky you woke, Ice-Fighter - maybe she never had time.'

Wirrun unwound more cord as he stepped back. Then he and Merv pulled on their ends of rope. The beast snarled and fought, dug at the rock with its claws, came forward a little, pulled back and came on again. At the cave opening it drew strongly back twisting its head away from the light, fighting to keep to the dimness. Merv climbed out of the cave and pulled with all his weight; Wirrun stayed talking and coaxing and even, shuddering, put his hands on the rough hair and pushed. The beast snarled and roared; it struck with its claws and snapped with its broken fangs; but in the end it fought its way into the outer cave. Wirrun climbed after it. He thought an echo of girlish laughter followed him out of the shadows.

That was the worst part of a bad journey. Once in daylight the creature's mood changed. It snarled and fought, struck and snapped, hung back on the rope with the hair stiffened along its spine and the ragged growl rattling in its throat, but it did not fight only in resistance. It fought to gain the shelter of rock, to hide in a hollow, to reach the shadow of trees, and the men could often make use of this. Once when Merv was slow to jump aside its talons gashed his boot and drew blood from his instep. Those talons never reached Wirrun though he came near them again and again; the beast snapped and struck but never quite attacked. Some field of force held it back: the force of the power or of pity or friendship.

It took an immeasurable time to reach the camp. For the men it was time suspended as in dreams. For the beast there was no time, only the eternity of now. But when at last they struggled into camp and tied the ends of the rope to two oaks with the beast crouched sullen and despairing between them, the men were exhausted. Yet even then they could not rest.

'Fires,' panted Merv. 'Here and here. Ironwood.'

Sweating in the heat they dug coals from the banked campfire, laid another two fires and burnt ironwood on all three. However the wind might shift it would carry the smoke of ironwood to the beast. They put water in a pannikin near it with a rabbit from Merv's last catch, but the creature only snarled and drew back. It would not eat or drink.

The men sank down in the shade beyond the fires and drank water. Time was still suspended, but as they rested it began again. They ate a little of the remains of the stew. They even turned and looked at each other. What the look said could not be spoken or written, but they understood.

Wirrun rewound the fur cord of the power. 'Bit by bit,' he

said heavily. 'How does a man make a man?' The beast's eyes were on him; the blood welled a little from its wounded shoulder and he was too tired to try to wash it.

Merv shifted and spoke. 'We broke his teeth on ironwood. That's first . . . . Burn off his pointy ears with the leaves . . . cut off his claws and make hands and feet . . . skin him . . . give him a new skin and insides.'

Wirrun laughed harshly. 'That all? That's what. I said how.' He had never heard of this impossible magic but he counted on Merv who was of the country. Merv shifted again.

'That's all I know, Ice-Fighter. How is for you.'

In his rage and despair Wirrun stood up and walked out of the camp, leaving Merv alone to watch over the beast.

'Bit by bit,' muttered Merv watching him go. He had done what he knew, but he was no hero or holder of a power. The next bit would come from the Ice-Fighter. Merv stayed in camp and kept up the fires and saw that they made the beast drowsy. He drew water and rummaged in his pack for the makings of a meal. As evening came on the beast grew restless and savage and he tightened the rope that held it. And while he did this Wirrun lay sleeping under trees.

They were ironwood trees; he had walked along the hill until he found them. He lay down under them, battered and weary, gazing upward through leaves at the distant soaring of cliffs; and he thought of Ularra and the making of a man. It would be by no mere cutting with knives. It would be done by Clever Men of the People and by the powers of the country. And though he was hero and Ice-Fighter he did not know the country or its powers. He laid his hand on his own power that was known in all countries as Ko-in had said; and he knew he must journey to the country of his fathers and seek the help of spirits. He did not think how he must make this journey but only that he must make it. And he lay with his hands closed about the power and slept.

And while he slept his spirit slid out of his body as the spirits of his People had done for a thousand ages when they must journey fast and far. He hovered above his weary body and left it sleeping and took only the spirit of the power that lay in its hands. It was like taking the shadow and leaving the stone.

His spirit felt the powers of that country: they brooded in the stern cliffs that loomed against the sky, they watched from the shadows and lay along the winds, and they did not know him but waited to know. He thought of the camp where Merv was alone with the beast amid these powers - and he was there. He laid a power on the beast to quieten it and on Merv for rest and renewal, and he did this by the welling up of power within himself and by willing it. Then he thought of the mountain that was like home to him and lay far down the land to the south; and in a flowing of hills and washing seas, of sunny plain and shadowed forest and a blown-away screeching of Happy Folk, he was there. The quiet of the mountain received him, the township dreamed in the sun on the ridge below.

He stood in his old camp under the wall of rock, and out of the rock flowed the love-singing of his haunting. But his spirit knew that it came through rocks from deep places far off and had laid hold only of the ears and mind that were sleeping in the north.

He laid his fire in the old place, the first place.

'Welcome, Hero,' said Ko-in. His tone was grave, for this was Wirrun's first spirit-journey and the dream-travel of the spirit is a grave matter and dangerous. So Ko-in wasted no time in asking or listening but answered at once the question Wirrun had brought.

'A man does not make a man. That is for greater powers. A man makes the Clever Business that calls up the power. If you cannot know the old business you must call on your strength to make a new one.'

'You gave me a power known in all countries,' Wirrun reminded him. 'Can't you give me a business that's clever in all countries?'

'I know none,' said Ko-in. 'It must be your business and you must make it. Yet I may feed your ears with a thought or two. Before the man can be made the beast must be unmade as you were told: its ears, its skin, its insides. How does a man do this to a beast? How does he unmake the wallaby and turn it into a meal?'

Wirrun let the words of Ko-in feed his ears. 'He cooks the wallaby in the earth.'

'And how do we drive the evil out of a sick and aching man?'

There were many ways; but Wirrun's spirit reached out to Ko-in and took the one he meant. 'We cook the sick and aching man gently in the earth with water and leaves.'

Ko-in bowed his head. 'Is not the cooking-pit a grave to the wallaby and the steaming-pit a grave to the evil? Has the earth no power for its creatures? Tell me, is a grave an end or a beginning?'

This at least Wirrun knew well from the People. 'It's the end of one thing and the beginning of another.' He too bowed his head. 'I thank you, Ko-in.'

Ko-in smiled gravely. 'Only you can make a business from my words, Clever One. When you have used your strength for your friend use it again for your People. Travel well and safely. I may send the night to carry news if you leave an ear awake.'

He sprang up among leaves and was gone. Wirrun heaped earth on his fire and travelled through a flowing of mountains and slow rivers back to the north where his body slept below cliffs. It was safe. He slid into it and felt it pressing the ground again, and the air pumping cool in its lungs, and the power soft and hard in its hands. He slept until evening and woke and went back to the camp.

The beast snarled and grunted struggling on a tightened rope; but it quieted as Wirrun came out of the dusk.

'Been away,' said Merv, heating a can at the fire.

'Far and fast,' said Wirrun. 'I'm hungry.' He laid one hand on the older man's shoulder - very lightly, for his spirit still tingled and he did not know if Merv might feel it prick. 'Time you turned in, mate. I'll watch the night. I got thinking to do.' The beast turned its eyes on him, old with despair. He could not speak to it.

He must sit through the night with the beast and make a business, a magic, his first. It must come not from his mind but from his spirit, and reach out to the powers of this country that he did not know. He must let the beast Ularra fill him with horror and with love.

He did so, keeping up the fires while Merv slept exhausted. When the beast grew wild with night and snarled at the sly-moving dark or the far-off stars he spoke to it quietly and shivered. For the first time since the night Ko-in gave it to him he unwound the cord of the power and held it bare, frost-sparkling in the firelight for the dark to see. The night stilled; he felt its awe. His spirit called to the powers in it that Wirrun, Ice-Fighter and holder of the great quartz crystal, sought to remake his friend Ularra from the beast; that all the land was his country and his business was for all its powers. He claimed their help.

At dawn Merv woke to see Wirrun rifling his pack in search of breakfast.

'Nothing much but sardines and toast,' he called when he saw Merv watching. 'Better come and have it. We gotta dig an oven.'

Merv crawled out of his blanket and went to the creek to splash his face. The next bit was coming sure enough.

2

It was a hard remaking as it had to be; hard for all of them. The gully, its hours of sunlight shortened by the cliffs, was cooler than the ridges above yet hot enough. The fires of ironwood had to be kept up and the men sweated as they worked. Meals were not easy, for Merv's astonishing pack was at last running low in supplies.

They dug their oven in the sandy soil by the creek.

'No spades,' muttered Merv in displeasure for he did not like to be caught poorly equipped.

'The old People never had 'em,' Wirrun retorted. He was tense with worry about the beast.

It lay in its rope cowed by daylight and the ironwood smoke. It had not eaten or drunk or slept and perhaps had no need. But it watched them with brooding eyes and Wirrun thought the eyes had darkened, and that Ularra no longer looked out of them. They no longer begged for pity. Wirrun toiled at the digging in dread that he might remake the body of his friend and fail to remake his mind.

'He's taming,' said Merv trying to comfort him. 'They gotta tame, even when they're turned back. Can't be quicker.'

They dug with sharp-ended branches of ironwood and lifted out the loosened sand with pannikins. The trench was long and wide enough for Ularra to lie in and nearly three feet deep. The sand they dug was heaped beside it, ready to be filled in again.

'More like a grave than an oven,' said Merv, surprised at the depth of the trench.

'It's that too,' said Wirrun. 'An oven's a grave for a wallaby.'

When the trench was dug they collected fallen sandstone from under the cliffs to lay in it. They paved with flat stones the whole of its floor, and on the stone they laid a fire of ironwood. Wirrun took the small axe up the hillside and brought back more ironwood while Merv, after inspecting his pack, dug yams to roast and filled a billy with yabbies caught in the creek so that they might eat. It gave Wirrun courage that at this time they should eat the old food taken in the old way. The crayfish should have been roasted on stones instead of boiled in a billy, and there should have been no crayfish-flavoured tea to follow, but the meal was the land's gift as it should have been and it gave him strength.

'That's lunch,' said Merv. 'Better think about tonight - a man's no good without his tucker. There'll be duck on the swamp down the creek. If you're all right here I'll see what I can do. Set a trap or two on the way for tomorrer.'

'I'd be in a mess without you,' said Wirrun in thanks. Merv knew it. He went off down the creek with his knife on his belt, a ball of string in his pocket and a few wire snares in his hand.

Wirrun lit the fire in his oven which was also a grave, and sat feeding the fire and wiping the sweat from his face. The beast watched and brooded, and sometimes snarled and fought in sudden anger till the smoking fires quietened it again. The heat of the oven forced Wirrun farther back as the great fire roared and laid down its bed of coals. All the earth about it was warm and the stones beneath cracked with heat. Wirrun fed it and watched the sun pass over and thought with dread of the next bit. When the sun had passed he left the fire to die and went with the axe to bring back leafy outer branches of ironwood. To drive out sickness and aching the leaves would have been eucalypt, but he was treating another evil. As he dumped the last of his load beside the trench Merv came back through the river-oaks. He carried a duck by the legs, its head hanging limply down.

'Just in time,' said Wirrun tightly.

Merv hung the duck from a branch and came silently, watching under his brows. What Wirrun did he did.

They took their digging-sticks and raked over the coals in the trench to hurry their dying. They filled billy and tin cans and pannikins with water and stood them ready. When the coals were black they laid on top armfulls of leafy branches, a deep and springy bed. Then Wirrun took a spray of green leaves to the fire nearest the beast; what he knew of the old business he would carry out. Merv followed.

Wirrun held his small branch in the fire till the leaves smoked and crackled. He strode quickly behind the beast, and it roused as he came and lunged against the rope snarling. Its eyes lit red and Merv stood by the rope. With the power in his hand and dodging as the beast twisted and snarled, Wirrun beat it lightly about the head and ears with his crackling branch. It fought in the rope, snarling viciously, snapping broken fangs, striking with talons, and the smell of singed hair mingled with the smell of burning leaves, but Wirrun knew the beast was not hurt. It fought against healing and against man and perhaps against fear, but not against pain. This light singeing was all that Wirrun's pity could stand of the business of burning off its ears.

Perhaps a power reached it, for it slumped on the rope as Wirrun threw his dead torch into the fire. He and Merv untied the rope and dragged the beast between them to the oven, sweating and grunting. Sometimes it roused and lumbered a few paces and sometimes it pulled back. When it smelt the heat and the leaves it grew wild and snarled and snapped and fought again, and they prodded and levered it over the edge with their digging-sticks till it crashed down on the bed of branches.

'Take the evil out of this man!' shouted Wirrun. He did not know if his lips shouted, but his spirit did. It shouted to cliffs and hills, to watching shadows and the remoteness of trees. 'Give him back his skin and his insides and his brain! Take the beast out of him and make him Ularra again!'

The beast struggled and roared. Wirrun grabbed the billy and poured water into the pit till a cloud of steam rolled out of it. He poured in all the water and passed each container to Merv who filled it again. When the steam thinned and the beast lay still and grunting they pushed earth back into the pit and covered it all but its head. Then they left it.

They had not spoken one word to each other during this business and they did not now. They sat wearily in camp with their backs to the pit and their faces to the fire. Now and then the beast whined as Wirrun had heard it whine inside the cave. Sometimes it grunted as if it struggled in its rope under the sand. Mostly it was silent. Wirrun sat slumped and heavy; his eyes were open but his spirit was not in them.

The sky above the gully was still lit with sun and the tops of the western cliffs glowed. Merv roused himself to fetch the duck and set about preparing a meal. Wirrun stirred, and in a little while rose and left the camp to wander listlessly up the creek.

He went like a feather in a breeze, moving some way and resting, carried on by a thought, stopping again to look at a stone; and as he went his spirit came back to him. He felt like a man who has been through a long illness or a long sorrow: all that could go out of him was gone, all that could be used had been used. What was left must start again. He thought of Ularra and the horror of the beast, and called up strength to wait. He thought of the Abuba and knew she was not wicked but an earth-thing as the land had made her. He remembered the Mimi - she too was an earth-thing as the land had made her. He thought of the tailed women from whom a darkness seemed to flow, and they reminded him of the trouble of his People and the People's trust in him. He even remembered, with a wry smile for so small a thing and a hand ruffling his hair, that his leave was over and his job in the city probably lost with Ularra's.

In this wandering and thinking he came at last through a hush of river-oaks to the wide silent water under the cliffs, and here he stopped in a sort of astonishment. The water pulled at him like a magnet; it drew and charmed him; he longed to strip off his clothes and jump in. He would have done it except for the burnt-out weariness that held him. As it was he stood looking for a long time, telling himself that he would come back in the warmth of the day and never mind the camp's drinking-water . . . . And it was here that the Ninya had come; here deep in the gorge and not high on the lookout of the cliffs. That was strange . . . but they might have come through the cave . . . . He wandered on into that, but not much farther than the entrance, for he was no more ready for the Abuba or the tailed women than he was for the pool. He went only to the edge of the twilight and leaned against the rock wall to look and remember and think.

He felt the howling through the rock before his mind caught it. He shivered and jerked, thinking at first that it was the beast; but the beast had never howled. This was the wild and heart-stopping howl of a dingo. It came faintly with distance from deep within the cave, and was caught and answered and built into a pack of howling, and died away at last.

Wirrun's face was set, for the blood was cold in his veins. There could be dingoes deep inside the cave but he knew there were not. This was a spirit-howling, and it brought him a deeper chill than the trouble that flowed from the tailed women. Well, he was not ready for it. He went out of the cave and back down the creek to the camp.

The first stars were out when he reached it, and Merv was waiting to serve the roasted duck. They looked at each other and nodded, two tired drained men ready to eat. They would have spoken then, but some struggle broke out in the pit; the beast struggling against its rope, snarling and grunting. It held them silent.

When they had eaten and cleaned the camp and built up the wood-heap and banked the fire, always with their backs to the pit, Wirrun did speak at last. He put his hand again on Merv's shoulder for a moment and said, 'You turn in, mate. I'll be - around.' For he knew that in the night, when the beast was wild and darkness flowed about, he must stay awake with the power, near but not too near. Merv nodded and rolled himself into his blanket near the fire. Wirrun pulled on a sweater and sat leaning against a tree with his legs in his sleeping-bag for warmth. He did not unwind the power again for the business was done. He only sat with the ball of possum-fur cord between his hands feeling it thrum; feeling in its roundness the curve of the sky and the turning of the world; seeing in his mind the crystal coloured like a pink-tinged cloud and magic with the sparkle of rain, the power that was known in all countries of this land.

For a long time he sat awake and listening but the pit was mostly as silent as the camp and now and then he dozed. But sometimes there were sounds, of struggling and snarling or of whimpering and fear. Then Wirrun sat tense and his spirit sought help for the beast in the pit. In the first hour of morning he leapt out of a doze and sat gripping the power:

for the first time there was a howl from the pit and it was the howl of a man. He did not go. He sat rigid and listening for another hour. Then he came out of his sleeping-bag running.

'Oh man - oh man - let me out - ' howled Ularra's voice in fear and fury.

Wirrun was by the pit, peering in the starlight, seeing Ularra's face and almost weeping for its wild and angry despair. He was groping through sandy soil feeling for hands and feet free of claws - groping to loosen rope and scoop away sand - bringing water to wash the sandy face and wet the heat-dried lips. 'You're all right, mate, you're all right,' he gabbled as Ularra began to heave out of the earth - and suddenly he laughed a little and dropped down by the pit and slept.

Merv reached the pit only a few minutes later. He found Wirrun sleeping beside the pit and Ularra crouched on it, head down over the billy which was tilted between his jaws while he sucked noisily at the water. Merv frowned and thought. Then he took up one of the ironwood digging-sticks and with careful judgement brought it down on Ularra's head.

3

In the new daylight Wirrun woke astonished. He was in his sleeping-bag a little way from the pit where Merv had rolled him. Ularra too was in his sleeping-bag; roped in. His head was raised on a pile of branches and Merv was trying to feed him with roasted yam and the remains of the duck. Ularra shouted curses, butted the yam away with his head but snapped viciously at the duck.

'You're driving him mad!' yelled Wirrun struggling out of his bag.

Merv looked up, backing away from the snapping jaws. He answered firmly.

'Gotta tame him first. I told you. He's still a little bit beast.'

Then Wirrun looked and saw that Ularra's eyes, which had once begged for pity from the head of the beast, now held the red light of the beast's anger of yesterday. His joy was dimmed and he came slowly to the pit.

'How long?'

'Ah,' said Merv. 'A day or two, that's all. We'll have him out of the bag with the two of us, and just his hands tied. He'll be thankful when he knows. That was a good quick turning, Ice-Fighter, and none of the old ones to help. I'm proud I saw it.'

'Let me out let me out let me out - ' roared Ularra.

'I'm proud you're proud,' said Wirrun to Merv. 'Well, it was my turning sure enough and not the old one, and I don't keep a little bit back for later. This man stood the turning and if it wasn't good enough that's not his fault. I won't have him roped like a dog. He's my friend Ularra. He can suit himself when he remembers it.' He laid the power against Ularra's tossing head and loosened the rope and stood back.

Merv dropped the duck and leapt back too.

Ularra writhed and heaved and sat up. His hands erupted from the bag and seized the fallen duck; he held it hard against his chest with one arm while the other reached for the billy. He tried to put his head into the billy, found that he could not, tipped it up and drank as the water ran down his face. Then he heaved himself free of the bag and stood, half crouching, unbalanced, weak from his turning and from hunger and thirst. Only fear and fury had given him the strength to struggle. Merv saw it and relaxed.

Wirrun spoke to him softly. 'Come on, Ularra man. Back to camp for a proper feed.'

Ularra looked at him with brooding eyes, turned and

slouched away stumbling up the hill. Sometimes he went stooped, helping himself with hands as well as feet; sometimes he toppled over and sat and rested; but he did not, as Wirrun dreaded, turn towards the cave of the Abuba. He crawled away out of sight among trees.

'Sorry,' said Wirrun to Merv. 'I had to.'

'Can't be helped then,' said Merv. 'We'll just stick together for a bit.' He took up the billy and one of the sleeping-bags while Wirrun coiled the rope.

They went silently back to camp. The business was over, the turning had worked, but there was no joy in it yet. There was only a new sense of strain. For Merv it lay in the danger of the untamed man wandering free and unseen. For Wirrun it came from the beast-look in Ularra's eyes and in his clumsy shambling movements. Wirrun had slept only a few hours in two nights and days. Merv had been up and busy since he found the hero sleeping by the pit where the beast-man grovelled. Most of his work had been undone when Wirrun untied the rope, but at least there remained a damper cooked in the ashes for breakfast.

They boiled the billy and ate and drank. Wirrun put Ularra's sleeping-bag in its old place and set beside it a pannikin of water, with roasted yam and a part of the damper wrapped in Ularra's spare shirt.

'Man's food,' said Merv, watching. He was alert to every sound and movement, watching for a shadow, listening for a stumbling rush. Wirrun saw it and tried to argue.

'He can't do much, poor bloke.'

Merv was not reassured. 'He'll get his strength back quick when he eats and drinks.' He went on watching and listening for two days more, insisting that he and Wirrun should stick together and that one of them should always be awake.

Wirrun too watched and waited; he watched for his friend and waited to see the turning complete. It was an anxious waiting, but now that his part was done another waiting mingled with the first and troubled him too: he was aware of the cave that waited in the gully. There lay the business that

was not yet done, the business of the land and the People;
the screeching of the tailed women came often into his ears,
or the wild and lonely howling of a dingo. Yet he could not
go into the cave leaving Ularra roaming wild and Merv
watching shadows; he could not go with a mind half free
and unrested. Sometimes his mind caught a falling phrase
of music, of dark or bright water and flowing hair; he would
have been tense and irritable, an easy prey to the love-
singing, if Merv had not kept him busy.

For Merv too had another care: since now they must live
off the country he would make the Ice-Fighter free of it as he
himself was free of it. He showed Wirrun his own rabbit-
traps: snares of wire carefully triggered, set and cocked with
a stone or stick or tree-limb on the site. 'Don't take so many
but you take 'em like a man should.' He taught Wirrun to
set the snares, for rabbit and for other small game. He took
Wirrun foraging for berries and roots, and showed him
which could be eaten at once and which needed to lie in the
creek till the poison was washed out of them. He showed
him which creek-holes were rich in yabbies and where to
look for fish. He took Wirrun downstream to the swamp
and showed him how to snare a duck among the reeds.

When Wirrun first saw the swamp he halted, frowning
and wary. Merv waited, following his gaze. 'Grass,' he
explained. 'Biggest you ever saw. More like that cane they
grow, eh? Or that bamboo. They never grew this, though.
Just swamp-grass.'

Wirrun relaxed, remembering that Merv knew nothing of
his haunting or the Mimi's advice. Merv had brought him to
take a duck, and not because a tall grass grew on the farther
margin of the swamp.

Once or twice as they went about the gorge they heard
stones rattle under a foot or saw branches wave as something
pushed a way through. Once as they walked up a ridge a
figure went at a shambling run over its crest and away. Once
something splashed in a hole in the creek, and when they
reached it the water was heaving and tossing. Wirrun
thought painfully of Ularra lying in the water to soak away

two days of fires and smoking. He and Merv never spoke of it but only waited till the sounds had gone.

Towards evening of the first day they came back to camp and stood under the oaks looking and frowning. The camp had been visited. The campfire, which had been banked, was black and steaming with the strong smell of wet ash and charcoal; the billy lay beside it. The dead remains of the other two fires were beaten and scattered about the camp. Packs had been torn open and emptied on the ground. Merv strode to Ularra's sleeping-bag and looked up smiling.

'He's took it - man's food! Wouldn't touch it this morning.'

Wirrun grinned back and ran quickly round the camp looking and calling, but there was no one.

'Give him another day,' said Merv.

They put the camp in order again and lit a new fire. That night they slept and watched in turn. During one of Wirrun's watches there was a scuffling in the darkness near at hand. He spoke to it softly.

'Come and have a feed of stew, mate.'

When there was no answer he took a pannikin of stew into the night and left it a little way from the camp. In the morning he found it empty, but there was no sign of what had eaten the stew.

On the second day, still weary after their broken sleep, he and Merv came early back to the camp and rested by turn during the afternoon. Their foraging had by now restocked the camp for several days and taught Wirrun enough of this country. A duck and a rabbit, wrapped in cloth, hung from branches of an oak; a pile of yams lay between stones in the creek. Merv, satisfied, slept in the shade. Wirrun used his turn of watching to build up the woodheap with fresh wood.

He was bringing back his second load when a movement along the hill caught his eye: a loose-limbed figure ambling towards the southern cliffs. It was Ularra, headed towards the Abuba's cave. Wirrun dropped his wood and went quickly into the cover of trees along the creek. He would not interfere unless he must, but he could not let Ularra go back into the cave. He ran up the creek among its trees, pausing now and then to sight the Abuba's cave in the cliff. If Ularra began to climb . . . .

Ularra did not climb. He stood under the cliffs and shouted. Wirrun heard his voice ragged with anger and despair, and the cliffs mocking him as they threw it back, and was chilled as he listened.

'Girl, girl!' shouted Ularra. 'Why did you call me, then?' Nothing answered but the cliffs.

'What sort of thing are you, then?' shouted Ularra. 'Did you want a beast to tear you? Call me now, girl! Call me again. I'll tear you.'

Wirrun listening was torn himself and crept away up the creek. This was a painful and private shouting, not meant to be heard even by a friend; but it was the shouting of a man. Ularra must be left alone to work out his pain and protest, and Merv could safely sleep alone in the camp. Wirrun crept on till the gully wall hid him and he found himself beside the pool. He sat beside it to rest in the cool and to wait. He could not by any power take away what Ularra must suffer, but he was full of relief and thanks that is was Ularra himself who suffered.

After a while through his relief he felt the water tugging at him as before. The afternoon was still warm and almost unknowing he tugged off his clothes, folded the power into them, and slid into the pool. At once all his senses were lost in it.

The water wrapped him, icy and silken, and drew him under. The singing drowned him, cool like moonlight and sweet like honey. He gave himself to the water knowing that he would drown. The singing swirled down with him note by note and word by word.

I sing in the sunlight
with dark eyes aglimmer:
are you not coming?

I sing in the shadows
with dark hair down-flowing:
are you not here?

His feet sank through a softness of mud among stones and moved a little of themselves, seeking to stand. This instinctive movement was enough to set him rising through the still water. He broke the surface and breathed, and the singing stopped. The bank was at his shoulder; like a sleeper struggling to wake he threw up an arm and drew himself inch by inch out of the pool. Fear did not come till he lay on the bank prickled by oak-needles. Anger and loss came with it, but fear moved his hand to reach for and grasp the power.

After a moment he sat up shaken and rested his head on his knees and let the warm day breathe over him, healing and soothing. He listened: there was only silence under the cliffs. Slowly and tiredly he put on his clothes and went back down the creek. As he went a thought came unquestioning into his mind.

'That was the old water, her own that she keeps for herself.'

He did question it a moment later for he could not recall the flat mineral taste of the old water, and the creek that ran from the pool was as sweet and soft as any creek. Yet he dismissed the question; however the water came filtered and sweet to the sunlight he knew it was the old water. His lips tightened eagerly at the thought that he might go back into the pool and search for the way the water entered, filled with the love-singing. He gave up that idea when the fear stirred again, and he thought of dark water-filled tunnels that might run for miles.

The sun was high on the cliffs when he reached the camp, and evening was beginning. Merv was awake and cutting up a rabbit; he looked under his brows at Wirrun but made no remark about having been left alone. Perhaps the shouting from the cliffs had wakened him. Wirrun brought in the load of wood he had dropped and then, for pure weariness of body and spirit, lay on his sleeping-bag and slept.

He woke in the cool of dusk, with the stars pricking out and the smell of stew in the camp.

'Can't live on rabbit,' said Merv serving it up. 'We'll have fish for a change tomorrer.' He had dished a third portion into a pannikin, and Wirrun carried it to the place he had left it last night.

'Give him another day,' said Merv with certainty.

They ate their own stew in quiet by the fire and Merv spoke again thoughtfully. 'That Abuba. Not its fault. You can't blame a snake when you get bit.'

'I know that,' Wirrun agreed.

'That Abuba's itself: what it is. Your friend made it into something else: what he wanted.'

'That's right,' said Wirrun. He knew now that Merv had heard the painful shouting at the cliff, and that Merv too knew it should not have been heard even by a friend.

'Heard a man once,' said Merv sucking a bone. 'One of them Happy Folk. In a pub, it was. He said a man makes his own god the way he wants. Ah. Might be. Dunno how you'd know. He'd better have said a man makes his own woman the way he wants. And gets mad when she stays what she is, same as him.'

'Um,' said Wirrun. He knew that Ularra had made the Abuba into what he wanted, but he felt that the Abuba had had some hand in this.

'Ah,' said Merv. 'You're young. Tired too, by the look of you - that bit of a nap wasn't much. I'll take first watch. See you when the Cross turns over.'

'You won't see it,' said Wirrun, for the Southern Cross in the sky would have sunk below the cliffs before it turned in the old bushman's sign. He went to sleep knowing that Merv would wake him by some other star-sign.

It was past midnight when he did wake, and Merv had not called him. He was wakened by a grunting and scuffling near at hand. He lay alert and still, searching the camp from under his eyelids. Merv was sitting by the fire and only his stillness showed that he too was alert.

The scuffling came again. It was very near.

'See you, Ularra,' murmured Wirrun drowsily.

'See you, man,' muttered Ularra sliding down into his sleeping-bag.

4

When Wirrun woke again sunlight streamed into the gorge yet the camp was still. He sat up quietly. Merv grunted in his sleep by the fire: he had given up, then, and abandoned his watch without waking Wirrun. And there lay Ularra in his own place. Even in sleep his face looked worn but he lay free-limbed and himself. Worn! They were all worn, and only sun and a sense of waiting had roused Wirrun. He got up quietly and went down to the creek to splash his face.

The water felt cold and alive. Strange that it flowed out of the pool in the gully and yet felt so alive. There was no singing in it, or any fear or loss. He stayed looking at it while it ran down his face; and perhaps there was some power in it for he saw clearly the mud-caked spring out west where the heatwaves shimmered with a memory of old seas. He saw the Jugi in its cave, and the tall wispy Mimi sending him forth alone, and the tailed women struggling. He felt again the trouble looming over him while he waited for Ularra. He would wait as long as was needed, but the trouble reached for him. And through it he felt someone else come beside him at the creek. He spoke with his eyes on the water.

'It's the old water, this. Sweetens up somehow.'

He thought he spoke to Merv, but when he looked he

found Ularra kneeling beside him. Ularra's face, worn and twisted, was turned up to the cliffs.

'She's old all through,' he said thickly. 'Old and bitter.'

'But she sweetens.' Wirrun let the water dry on his face while he spoke to his friend. 'It was my first time, mate. Sorry I didn't do it better. I was - scared.'

Ularra's gaze came back to him from the cliffs. 'All the time,' he said, 'when I couldn't - when I was - *that*, I counted on you. There was a little bit left somewhere. It counted on you.'

'I know that. It made it worse. I was - scared and bleeding.'

Ularra nodded. 'I saw, man. I saw you bleeding.'

They said no more. They never spoke of the turning again. But Wirrun was thankful, that day and later, for that one moment of direct speaking.

He was glad of it at breakfast, another damper made from the last of Merv's flour. Wirrun saw that Ularra would not eat near the fire in the old way but took his mug of tea and went farther off. He held himself with care like a man who fears he has drunk too much, keeping a distrustful watch on himself and all around him. Merv broke the damper into three equal parts, but Ularra's part he broke again and offered him half.

'The rest soon. You're starved, boy.'

Ularra's eyes flared red and his lips drew back. In a moment he made an effort, relaxed, took the first piece quietly, and waited a while before he ate the second.

Merv did not seem to have noticed. He looked placidly at the two young men and breathed on his tea to cool it. 'Ah. A good day. Feels like a holiday. Only we gotta get some fish before we turn into rabbits.' He drank his tea, put down the empty mug, stood up and stretched. 'Coming fishing?' he invited Ularra.

Ularra looked at him sideways, looked to Wirrun and seemed uncertain. Wirrun crushed a pang of uneasiness.

'You go,' he suggested. 'He'll show you the country. I gotta think what next.'

Like a dog at a word from its master Ularra got up and followed Merv. Wirrun watched frowning. He had never, like Merv, feared danger from Ularra and he would not fear it now. He had done all he could; the rest was for time and for Ularra himself. For Wirrun trouble was waiting and reaching out. He could feel it in the heat and silence and in the shadowed cliffs. They hung against the sky like a great stone beehive angrily humming, and he knew he must soon go into the cave. He knew it with eagerness and dread.

He got up to wander restlessly, and his feet took him again up the creek and into the gully. The pool beckoned, sweet and dangerous, and he passed it with an angry shrug. He would not know what the pool had told him. He went into the cave as far back as the twilight and leaned against the rock with his hands pressed to it. The cliffs stood over him mounting to the sky; the gorge itself lay between the bones of the land. He could feel the twilight leading away deeper and deeper into dark. A First Dark, never broken by sun or moon; an utter dark that would clot here and there into the land's oldest creatures. Could a man, even one with a power, go into such a dark and still be? Would he not cease to exist?

He remembered with panic that he had no torch. It was a senseless thought but he had to fight to crush it. In such a dark as that First Dark a torch was a tiny irrelevance; he would take the power that was all his strength, and maybe a firestick in the old way, and wait for what came. If he must go there must be a way, and it was not by means of a torch. He thought of spirit-travel, sleep-travel - and shuddered. A frail human spirit drifting in that dark among such creatures . . . .

He was about to turn away to the light when the rocks vibrated to the sound he had felt before: the weird wild crying of a dingo that was answered and grew. He went away shivering, full of a dread that he would not face though it sank deep into him and stayed. The dingo crying in the dark . . . .

When he reached the camp Ularra was there skinning catfish. The billy was boiling on the fire. Wirrun looked sharply round the camp.

'Where's Merv?'

'Gone,' said Ularra. He watched Wirrun sullenly from under his brows. Wirrun's uneasiness tightened into a knot but he forced himself to sit quietly down on oak-needles. Ularra's face twisted into a bitter smile.

'Can't ever be sure, can we?' he said.

'Dunno,' said Wirrun, for he would not at this time pretend to misunderstand anything Ularra said. 'That's your problem; you'll have to sort it out. Where's Merv gone?'

'Home. Left a message.'

'Go on, then. What?'

Ularra's hands were still while he thought. 'Said he was proud to help when needed but he never meant to stay so long and he's got skins to see to. He'll keep an eye, and a fire in a dead tree'll fetch him if he's wanted. He said ... something like ... maybe a man can make a god or a woman but a friend's got to come bit by bit.' Ularra frowned, checking his memory. 'That's all, I reckon.'

The knot inside Wirrun loosened for that was certainly a farewell message from Merv. After this he would stick to what he knew and leave doubts of Ularra to Ularra.

'Uh,' said Ularra remembering. 'He said he won't forget.'

'Not easy, he won't,' Wirrun agreed. 'He showed you the country?'

'And fed me all the way. Little bits. Left us some gear too.' He nodded towards their packs and went to the creek to wash the fish. Wirrun strolled over to inspect the gear. He had already noted the billy on the fire and two pannikins near it with their own tin-can mugs. On his pack he found two of Merv's wire snares, a fishing-line wound on a bottle, and a tobacco tin with spare hooks and sinkers.

'He's thorough any rate.'

Ularra coming back with the fish grinned a normal grin. 'He's that. There's even bush lemons for the fish.'

'Yeah? I hope there's salt.'

They laughed like ordinary young men. It was so good that they went on doing it after the small joke was worn out. Wirrun watched with pleasure while Ularra, seeming to have conquered his dislike of the fire, laid the fish on hot stones to grill.

'We won't meet a better man than Merv,' he said firmly.

Ularra's lips tightened for a moment. Then he nodded.

They talked of fishing and hunting and living off the land. Wirrun pointed out that the catfish should have been grilled in their skins; Ularra looked startled and disgusted and they laughed again. They managed to scrape the fish into pannikins and ate them with salt and lemon.

'Man, that's *good*,' said Ularra cleaning every bone. His eyes darted sideways suspiciously as he ate, and Wirrun remembered how the beast and the wild man had starved.

Afterwards they lay on the brown needles of oaks and rested, and after a time Wirrun talked. He spoke of the cave and the anger of the tailed women; of the pool where the water was filled with his haunting and drew him down like a leaf; of the First Dark and the crying of the dingo. As he spoke the trouble reached out to him again so that he forgot Ularra and talked to himself. 'I gotta go in there and talk to those women . . . a torch is no good anyhow, I'd sooner have a firestick . . . and sleep-travel's worse . . . .'

'NO!' roared Ularra. He was on his feet and standing over Wirrun. There was red anger in his eyes.

Wirrun sat up startled. 'Eh? What else can I do? I gotta talk to the ones with the tails; that's where the trouble starts. I know that, knew it when I first laid eyes on 'em.'

Words rattled in Ularra's throat but he couldn't speak them. He snarled and grinned, baring his teeth. He made a new effort and roared, 'NO!'

'Look,' Wirrun argued, 'what else am I here for?'

Ularra paced back and forth half-crouching. His mouth worked. Wirrun, fully awake at last, saw that this was unreasonable rage and spoke soothingly.

'Come on, mate, untwist now. I got the power, haven't I?

What's going to hurt me while I've got that? Sit down, now. Come on. Sit down and talk it over.'

He talked on until Ularra quietened, looked confused and bewildered, and at last sat down.

'I said I won't sleep-travel,' Wirrun promised. 'I know that's risky. I'll go like I am with the power. You've seen 'em all taking notice of that. Nothing can hurt me.'

'It won't want to,' growled Ularra looking dark and confused. 'I'll tear it.'

Here was a new dilemma, for Wirrun had never for a moment thought of taking Ularra into the cave. That was a dark into which no man should go spirit-troubled - into which no man should go at all unless he must.

He tried a little teasing. 'Now where's your power, then? Been hiding it, have you? How many powers have we got any rate? And who'll be on the outside watching out for us? Who'll put a fire in a tree to fetch Merv if we want him?'

Ularra listened puzzled, but as soon as he understood he broke into a worse rage than before. He leapt up, striding half-crouched in a circle round Wirrun, choked words rattling in his throat. He stooped and picked up a stone, looked at it bewildered, dropped it and struggled for words. There was more than rage in the struggle, there was some deep pain and perhaps despair. He made a great effort like a stammerer and found words: 'That power - the haunting - never stopped! It's near!' He fought with himself. 'That grass - I know - swamp - tall grass -' He took a deep breath and grew suddenly clear. 'You get smoked or you don't go!'

And now Wirrun's face darkened. The haunting was his trouble, his own. He had carried it half across the land and back to its source; he would not be robbed of it now, he would not hear. He growled at Ularra.

'Give up, will you? It's my job and I'll do it. I never asked you to wipe my nose for me.'

'Never asked you!' roared Ularra twisting in pain. He fought for control. 'Not without smoking!' He picked up the stone.

Wirrun sat tight with rejection. His ears might be

wearied, his spirit burdened, his body drawn down under water like a leaf, but the haunting was in him. He would not hear. Ularra stood over him, the red light in his eyes, threatening with the stone; and Wirrun, who had not feared the anger of the beast, saw at last that he needed to fear its protection. The shock of it opened his mind to fear itself, the fear of sweet drowning and the dingo in the First Dark.

'All right,' he mumbled. 'I said *all right!*' he yelled. And then, fighting like Ularra to control himself, 'If I get smoked will you stay on the outside and let me get on with it?'

Ularra dropped the stone. He stood confused and lost, holding on to himself. Breathing hard he went down to the creek and splashed his face and stood covering it with his hands. He came slowly back, shoulders hunched, so bitter and defeated that Wirrun felt a stab of hope. But with the defeat still on his face Ularra said, 'Now?'

And there was no other way to keep him out of the cave. Wirrun stood up, sullen and defeated himself. He grunted, 'Mind, you gotta do your bit too.'

Ularra nodded. He looked despairing.

They went down the creek to the swamp, Ularra slouching ahead and Wirrun after him. Wirrun's mind cried out for the sweet burning coolness of the singing, and when another voice rose through it he pushed it down. But the voice rose again: *I think you do need help . . . fight it with the smoke of a tall grass.* In the core of himself he knew that the Mimi's day had come, that Ularra was right, that he would be mad to go into that cave without protection.

They left the creek as the swamp began and worked their way along its margin till the tall grass stood over them. They broke green branches for fire-fighting and chose a stand of grass that stood out into the swamp and beat through it to warn furred and feathered things. Then Ularra put a match to the dead lower leaves of the grass.

They were both smoked. Where the fire met the swamp it hissed and spat and died easily; but flames leapt high in the narrow leaves over their heads and threatened to spring on

142

heated air or gases to other stands. They fought with sweat and tears running down their faces and their lungs aching with smoke, and Wirrun had no time to mourn for lost magic in his fear that Merv might see the smoke and come. When only dainty ruffles of smoke rose from the blackened stalks and they knew the swamp would take care of the rest, the two young men threw down their branches and staggered to the creek to drink.

They went silently back to the camp to prepare the next meal. Wirrun ached inside; yet he saw how Ularra's eyes followed him, brooding and questioning, and that Ularra was still locked in his strange and bitter defeat. He could not leave Ularra there. He roused himself to speak warmly and joke a little and to talk of the next day; and when he spoke of going into the cave he discovered a secret, wicked glee.

That was when he knew, with anger for his own secret triumph, that the smoking had not cured him.

FIVE

The First Dark

I

That evening Ko-in sent the night to Wirrun with news.

He had taken his secret glee and his self-anger away from the camp and Ularra's brooding eyes. Self-anger became self-disgust and laid a slimy slug-track of failure over all he had done or tried to do. The plight of Ularra, torn from the safety of the city; his own enchantment, that he clung to while it crippled him; his shivering dread of the dingo in the dark; all these grew into the certainty of worse failures to come. He needed the strength of the hills leading up to the looming cliffs, and the sharp clean remoteness of early stars pricking a green sky. He went to them, leaving Ularra under the sighing oaks.

He set his sick spirit free and called for power. Power for his friend Ularra who was a man again but whose spirit remembered the beast. Power for himself: if not the power to be free then at least the power to wish to be free. And from somewhere a power came but it was neither of those. It was the power to do what he must in spite of failure: to go limping, if he must limp, with strength and courage. So Wirrun's spirit sought the indifferent stars and came back to him. And the night came, and the darkness thickened round him, and he saw that it waited for him.

'What are you?' he asked the darkness.

It answered him like a woman of the People. 'You know me for you have run from me. I bring one you do not know.'

The night gathered into the shape of a woman with a great sharp horn rising from each shoulder. Wirrun did know it: the horned woman from Ko-in's mountain that had run at him with its horns while he waited for the ice.

'Why are you here so far from your place?' he asked it, and it grinned slyly.

'What is one shadow when all the night wanders? Only the hero stays at home in these times. Ko-in stays to watch for strangers. He sends me to bring his wife with news.'

Wirrun was astonished for he had never known of Ko-in's wife. He had heard no tale of a spirit-woman as great and good as the hero, or gentle enough to need the protection of the horned one on a journey in troubled times. He waited to greet her with respect.

It came from behind the other. It was a hag, cruel and cunning. It carried a spear and a large net bag, and Wirrun's angry blood knew what they were for. It was wise of Ko-in to send with it a familiar shadow; without that Wirrun would not have believed that the hero could have taken a monster for a wife.

The shadows watched and grinned. The horned one spoke. 'Truly a wife for a hero, Bimpo-in who feeds on the People. She brings news.'

Wirrun held in his anger. It was not for these two old shadows bred by the land, and he had no right to be angry with Ko-in whom he loved. He only said, 'What news?'

Bimpo-in answered. Her voice was as cunning and cruel as her shape. 'Ko-in greets you. The trouble you seek is in his country too, but Ko-in is strong. From those that come and go he has found out the beginnings of the trouble.'

Wirrun could believe it. He remembered Ko-in's questioning of the Mimi when she wandered a stranger in his country. He nodded. 'Go on.'

'Small beginnings,' said Bimpo-in, and the two shadows nodded and grinned. 'There is one stranger lost in the deep places and that one angers the wives of Kooleen. For Kooleen and all his wives and children are tailed; they mock at the People and all who wear no tails. Now Kooleen would make this stranger one of his wives, a slimy thing without a tail!' The two hags hugged themselves and cackled. 'The wives are shamed and angry. They keep the stranger fast in a cavern and will not let Kooleen come.'

The shadows stood grinning. Wirrun knew well the darkness of trouble that flowed from the tailed women, yet he did not fully understand. He questioned the one with the spear. 'Are others angry too, then? Why does the trouble spread? Why do they leave their places and send others out of theirs?'

Bimpo-in shook her bag. 'Have you not ears? Are not the wives and children of Kooleen many, and their place far to the south? The angry wives divide, they and their children. Some hold their own place and some the caverns of the north, and so they drive others from their places and leave them nowhere to go. Are you a fool and earless?'

Wirrun frowned but stood thinking. 'Why does the old water flow in new ways? Is that from Kooleen and his wives? Or from the Ninya, maybe?'

Bimpo-in sneered. 'You have sent the Ninya home, Hero. Leave the land to care for its water.'

'That's my business,' said Wirrun sternly, 'and while I hold this stone you'll give me an answer.'

The bag shook impatiently. 'What answer? The Ninya's ice cracked some rock. The stranger is a water-spirit. One or the other may have opened new ways for the water. It is nothing to me. I have told what I know.'

The water-spirit trapped in the rocks where the dingo cried . . . the pool that sang and drew him under like a leaf. He would not know - but he was shaken. It was all he could do to send the shadows off with thanks to Ko-in. They flowed back into the night.

Wirrun wandered for a long time under the stars. He thought of two troubles, his own and the land's, and of the deep places where the stars were shut out. And Ularra lay under the oaks awake and despairing.

In the morning they went together to the cave. Wirrun carried a firestick with a smouldering point and Ularra looked at it with flashes of anger. He himself carried some remains of cold duck tied up in a spare shirt, and Wirrun frowned at that. He had said over and over that this first trip was no more than an exploration, that he would be out again soon; holding down his own foreboding and fear he had done and said all he could to lighten Ularra's. But Ularra came prepared to wait and kept his dark watch on himself, and his eyes still held defeat and sometimes fear.

It was the first time Ularra had entered the cave since he had seen the Abuba driven out of it. He gave it one flaring look, stood rigid, and fixed his eyes on Wirrun.

'You'll be cooler waiting under the trees,' said Wirrun tightly. 'I won't be that long.' Ularra nodded. Wirrun wanted to tear himself roughly away for he could not much longer hold down his secret knowledge that the smoking had failed or hide eagerness and dread. He nerved himself to make one more effort, to leave Ularra in the old light-hearted way. 'Untwist, mate. Nothing to worry about. *You're* all right.' He patted the net bag at his belt. '*I'm* all right. See you.' He turned and strode into the twilight.

He looked back once. Ularra's tall and gangling shape was sharp against the light; he stood there as though he would not turn away until Wirrun came back from the cave. It was hard to leave him there so lost, but Wirrun waved the firestick and strode on. The night led away in front. He went into it.

As he went he wondered if perhaps after all it was only a small night, a single cave leading nowhere; if the tailed women had come into it through some spirit-path he could not follow. If that were so he could only wait in the cave itself and hope they would come again, and the dread could die away and the quivering hunger go unsatisfied; he could release this tightness. For a moment, reaching a hollowed wall of rock, he thought it must be so. He stood in the cave-night looking for darker shapes and saw at last a blackness to the right. He felt his way to it: it was a slit opening into deeper night. He stepped through.

Now the firestick became a red eye with a few inches of

sight. He held it close to walls and floor peering with his one red eye. If he went with great care the dim red glow might just save him from potholes and ledges; it was not enough by which to find a way. He groped forward round a boulder and over a hollow but he could not tell where.

He turned back. The dark slit through which he had come was now a grey slit into the outer cave. He would have to work along walls to keep some idea of where he was. He found the wall and groped along it with his firestick. Something stirred behind him: a breath of air from outside, or a bat's wing or a fall of dust. His hand was on the power, questioning, but it did not throb. He went on.

Staring eyes - he stood rigid - the power was still - he raised the firestick. They were painted on the wall: eyes of charcoal and pipeclay, round and solemn and sad. As he moved the firestick over the wall the painted figure raised arms and spread its fingers in the red glow; it adjured him. He had not yet reached the First Dark. The fires of his People had lit this cave and their voices had sung here. If he lit a fire now he would see their hands spread like those of the figure, outlined in ochre, reaching out to him from the past and from forgetting. He felt those hands above him as he groped on along the wall.

His stick's glow vanished into a darkness it could not light, an opening deeper into the land. Wirrun hesitated, tightening his grip on that dread that would send him back and the hunger that would draw him on into any danger. In this second cave he could find himself even when his firestick burnt out: he need only crawl along walls and feel his way till he found the grey opening to the outer cave. But from here? Should he go on? Or should he wait under the painted hands of his People until something came to him? The power gave him no sign. He thought that if he could he must go deeper into the land before he waited.

He groped about for a loose stone, freed the end of the power's fur cord and drew it from the bag, unwound a length and tied it to the stone. That he wedged into the worn base of a boulder. Then, unwinding the cord, he entered the blackness. He could go at least some distance before the cord ran out.

He stood still and extended his arms: each found a wall. He was in a rock passage. He went on slowly, an elbow against one wall, the dark pressing close to his firestick and his uneasiness growing. There should be old things in this thick dark, yet as he fed out its cord the power lay inert, a stone without life. Then why did the air stir? He stopped to listen. Did something breathe? Had a stone moved under the rustle of a blind cave-snake? Was that the slither of dust or the scuttle of a spider? And why did the cord vibrate in his hand? Caught on a roughness of rock, maybe, and the air and the dust stirred by his passing. Yet there should be old things.

He went on.

Space widened and gaped, but only his skin felt it. He had reached the First Dark. He felt it like a massive monster, ancient and aware, waiting without warmth or cold or movement for his next most dangerous step. He did not take the step.

He set down the firestick with care: it was useless now but at least it remembered the light. He unwound more cord in the hope that he might crawl a little - and the dark thinned and light was glowing in his hand. The power under its wrapping shone in the First Dark. He pulled off the last of the cord and had light, dim and magical like starlight. He saw that from the broad ledge where he stood the dark vaulted up and down. With the light in his hand he dared to shout 'Hoo!' and heard the cry ring wide and come ringing back many times over. But for all his daring he knew he could not find a way down into the vault by the starlight of the stone. And while he thought this the power gave one throb in his hand and was still again.

He shouted, 'Come back here! What are you?' but the thing had gone. It had come and gone in a flash, spirit-fast, and he frowned and was uneasy again. There should be old things here in such a dark. Could they have felt his coming, felt the power, and fled to avoid it? He had not allowed for that, but the Mimi had once warned him that the need to obey was not always the wish. Well, he could not move without their help. He must keep still, play their game, and try to catch the next that came to peep. He sat down.

It was as well, for the moment he had dreaded and wished for was on him and his limbs and brain were weak and if he had been standing he might have run. The rock vibrated and hummed like a great bell humming into silence and the singing was under and over and all around. *Are you not coming . . . coming . . . coming . . . sings the bright water . . . sings . . . sings. . . .* He shook and sweated as he gripped the rock and fought it. When it hummed into silence he wiped his face with his sleeve and sat fighting for resistance and strength.

So he was not ready when the power throbbed once more and was still, and that angered him and gave him back his wits.

'Come, whatever you are!' he roared, and the vault gave back the roar over and over but the power was still. There was only a clink of stone that his shouting might have disturbed, and a scuttle of tiny legs over his hand.

Wirrun swore. His frustrated mind remembered another spirit-telling: *There is no spirit in this land that would not help Wirrun the Fighter of Ice.* That had been the Yabon after the battle on the shelf, and he thought morosely that the Yabon had been wrong. To prove it he shouted again into the First Dark:

'Come on, then, all you that'll help the Ice-Fighter! I'm waiting, me that sent the ice back. I need help. What's coming?'

Silence. The stone was still. He swore again.

The power began to throb and its light to pulse.

He waited, rigid.

They came: darkness billowing like smoke. They had no shape firm enough for speech or seeing. Ancient and formless things of the First Dark, they only rolled about him like smoke and thinned away from the light in his hand. Wirrun was awed. They might be the land's First Thoughts, stored and remembered with the waters of its youth. He bent his head and covered the power and let them come.

He felt the dark thicken till he struggled to breathe. It supported him and bore him along the ledge and down, far down, by some long and twisting slope. The fur cord hanging loose from its net trailed behind him and reached its full length and was gone. Stones never disturbed slid behind him, ancient dust slithered. He stood on level rock; his foot touched water and the shadows drew him back. Without them he was nothing, he had ceased to be; no more than a passing thought in the unimagined dark.

But the First Dark had its own lights. He saw them, small cold lights that thinned the dark as they came and glimmered high and low. Others were coming. The shapeless shadows drew away from them into hiding and Wirrun uncovered the power. It flared and sank and flared, pulsing as the power throbbed. It and the tiny points of light were reflected in a dark pool at his feet, he could not tell for how far, which lights were reflected and which moved over rock.

When the little moving lights were near he saw that they were eyes and he knew them: the old bright eyes of the Nyols, the little grey people. He was glad to see them.

'You call,' they said in the soft rumbling voices he remembered. 'We come.'

They were clustered at his feet and on rocks over his head watching him with their old bright eyes. Behind them he could see other shapes, most of them strange and some of them fearful, a crowd of shapes gathering in answer to his call. There were small hairy man-shapes, and bouncing shapes, and groping shapes like women without heads. He wished the Yabon might be among them but its place was on the surface of the land. These were all dwellers in the dark. He searched among them for the angry tailed women but none of those had come.

He spoke to the Nyols. 'Where are these tailed women, Kooleen's wives? I want to talk to them.'

They rumbled softly together exchanging glances like glow-worms and flickering the black pool with lights. They answered him in several voices. 'They not come.' 'They run, they hide.' 'They angry. They not come near.'

'They won't, won't they? Well, I'll have to go to them. Can you take me?'

Little grey heads were bent. 'We take you. Other one too?'

Wirrun was puzzled. 'Other one? What other?'

'Other man behind. One that follows.'

Wirrun's brows drew down. He swung round to the dark where the dust slithered, where a snake had rustled and a stone had fallen; behind him where, since he left the first cave, something had moved and breathed.

'Ularra!' he roared. 'Come out of that!'

Nothing stirred but the air. He turned back to the Nyols, those strong little wrestlers who watched bright-eyed. 'You fetch this other and we'll see,' he said.

They flowed past him in a tide of little grey bodies and scrambling limbs. They came back bearing Ularra struggling in their midst, and set him before Wirrun with his parcel of cold duck in his hand.

2

Wirrun and Ularra faced each other in the First Dark in the dim light of the Nyols' eyes and the pulsing power. The tightness vibrating between them sent the old things wavering back. Wirrun glowered from under jutting brows. Ularra's face was set and determined, holding back fear. Wirrun drew breath to speak but Ularra got in first.

'It's no good, man. I got no choice. That smoking never took - it's like you never had it.'

So he had seen. Wirrun flinched and dropped his eyes. He growled, 'How did you get here any rate?'

'Same way you did.' Ularra opened his large hand and up sprang a released bundle of fur. The cord of the power had brought him silently following Wirrun. 'I was right behind.' His eyes widened and narrowed. 'Them old ones took me down after you.'

Wirrun swore. He waved the cord away. 'Shove it in your pocket, it might do you some good. Old ones! Look at 'em, then. Go on, look around. The ones without the heads, see? And the bouncing ones. A man's not meant to be here, mate.'

Ularra gave a small tight smile. 'A man's not, maybe. I'll do all right. If you can do it I can.'

'Do what?' roared Wirrun. 'What do you think you can do?' Ularra muttered something. 'Anxious! A pity, that is! Anxious! What about me, then?'

'I never said anxious,' Ularra flared. 'I said anchor.' But Wirrun, being launched, never noticed.

'Haven't I got enough on my hands and now you down here before you're ready? And getting you into the trouble - what about that? - standing there with the power and doing nothing? Anxious! What about dragging you out of your job in the first place? What about that?'

Ularra's eyes were sombre. His head was bent as if he listened to something other than Wirrun's raging. 'What about living, man?' he said gently. 'What about the wind?'

Wirrun turned abruptly away. The old things murmured in the silence. Now that the men had stopped quarrelling they drifted near again.

'Well - ' said Wirrun at last. He looked for the Nyols. They clustered round him, waiting. 'Can you find these women of Kooleen's? Give 'em a message and bring me the answer?'

They nodded.

'All right. Tell 'em I know they're holding a stranger here and I know why. It's doing no good to anyone, just making trouble all round. Say - say I've come to take this stranger -

back to its own place. Then they can stop worrying and go home. Tell 'em to bring the stranger to me here.'

'They not come,' said the Nyols, but some of them scurried off into the dark and some of them stayed.

'Well - ' grunted Wirrun again. Ularra watched him with grim satisfaction; he knew that this change of plan was made on his account but he approved of it all the same. Wirrun ruffled a hand through his hair. 'Well . . . might as well have some lunch while we're waiting.'

Ularra nodded and began to untie his bundle.

They sat on the rock by the dark water, the rivers and rains of her youth hoarded and remembered. They ate cold duck while the First Dark flowed with ancient shapes watching curiously. They were two men in the eye of a cyclone, not speaking but clinging to peace.

And the love-singing struck again: a tingle in rock that Ularra could barely feel but that Wirrun heard like a bell humming into silence. The shadows stilled and listened. Wirrun sat tight and racked. Ularra watched him with brooding eyes that held fear. It died at last.

The Nyols nodded wisely at Wirrun, seeing that he heard what they did. 'That one sings,' they said, telling him aloud what till then he would not hear. 'That one Kooleen wants.'

He tried to reject it - but he had known since the pool drew him under and since Ko-in sent the night with news. That his trouble and the land's were one; that to heal the land's trouble he must meet and resolve his own; that here in the immense and waiting dark Kooleen's women would bring him his own haunting. While he still trembled the rocks hummed again, chilling him with the lone, wild howling of the dingo.

'And that,' he whispered. 'What's that?'

They nodded again. 'That one cries. That water-spirit.'

And that too he had known: that the singing and the howling, the hunger and the dread, were the same. Wirrun stared into one dark and Ularra into another; they would not look at each other for there was fear in the eyes of both.

The shadows were listening again, this time to something Wirrun could not hear. The Nyols grew restless and rumbled together, all their heads turned to the curtain of blackness beyond the pool. Soon Wirrun saw a star-flicker in it: the search party was coming back. The waiting Nyols scurried to meet it rumbling excitedly.

The tide of bodies flowed back carrying with it a taller and angrier shape with a lashing tail. The Nyols had caught one of Kooleen's women. They brought her to Wirrun as a flood might bring a struggling wallaby. He and Ularra stood up.

'No use fighting now,' Wirrun told her holding the power. 'You're here.'

She faced him sullenly. 'I got no business with you, Man.'

'I say you have.' Wirrun spoke harshly because of the care he must take now that his haunting was named. 'This water-spirit. You don't want it. You only want it away. Bring it here and I'll take it away, back to its own place. And you can go back to yours and stop making trouble.'

She sneered. 'What am I, Man? I am one. The wives of Kooleen are many and fierce with anger. All these little no-tails could not hold them. Can this one take the stranger from them and bring it to you? Earless words.'

Ularra growled. He was shaking, for the tailed woman brought his own haunting near. Wirrun put a hand on his arm but it had been a man's growl.

'Those were your words,' Wirrun told the woman. 'These are mine.' He held up the power pulsing with light. 'Tell Kooleen's women what I say. Bring 'em here with the water-spirit. And make it fast.'

The woman flounced off and went tail-swinging back into darkness between banks of Nyols that parted to let her go. Ularra shook himself fiercely.

'Untwist,' Wirrun told him. He was angry with Ularra: angry that, still troubled, he had forced his way into the spirit-troubled dark; angry that he would not wait in safety but must tangle Wirrun's feet with his fierce protection. But

Ularra was his friend; he was angry because of his care. He said firmly, 'They're only earth-things. You're a man.'

Ularra sat down and laid his head on his knees.

Wirrun sat with him. They waited again . . . . *The dark-flowing water . . . like dark-floating hair . . .* the rock hummed sweetly. Wirrun sat tormented and at last laid his own head wearily on his knees. He must not part with his senses now - he had almost leapt up and rushed into the dark leaving Ularra alone.

'Is it bad?' whispered Ularra.

Wirrun's mouth twisted. 'I wish you'd stayed where you were told,' he muttered harshly.

The old things wavered and murmured and drew into shelter. Something had disturbed them. Nyols scrambled higher and hung watching. The black curtain of the dark was disturbed and wavered too: shadows were moving in it. They slipped along walls, slid behind boulders: the tailed women, creeping and hiding. When Wirrun was sure of it he stood up quickly with the stone.

'Come on, you women! Come out and talk.'

They had to obey. Out of the dark, out of niches and hollows and round the shoulders of rock, they gathered into a crowd and came forward with sly grins to see how the others hung back. The smiles became titters and grew into shrill laughter. They pointed at Wirrun and Ularra, rolled their eyes, nodded to each other and laughed. The vault gathered their laughter and threw it back and forth. The First Dark shrieked with mirth.

'No-tails!' the women screamed, holding each other as they laughed. 'Unfinished! See how they cover their ends - even they are ashamed! No tails, no tails!' They cackled and shrilled and held their shadowy sides.

Wirrun waited with a hard smile and a hand on Ularra's shoulder. He could feel its stiffness. He feared that the beast would rise again and leap among the women red-eyed and raving.

'No more!' he roared. 'That's enough!'

They tittered and sniggered into silence; the laughter died among the rocks.

'We got no time for games,' said Wirrun. 'You know me or you wouldn't have hid. And you've had my message or you wouldn't have come. Where's this water-spirit?' But he knew they had not brought it.

They looked at each other with secret smiles. 'If the power says bring the water-spirit we must bring it. But it will never reach you, Man.' They nodded and grinned and twirled their tails.

Wirrun frowned and said nothing, only waiting. They nodded and grinned a little more and then had to explain.

'Slimy as weed, slippery as a fish, that water-spirit,' they told him. 'If we take it from its place, in a flash it slips into the water and away to Kooleen. It will never reach you.' They smiled in triumph.

'There's enough of you and I've seen you fighting. You can keep it from the water.'

They shook their heads and tittered. 'Who are we, Ice-Fighter? Only poor wives of Kooleen. We cannot live in water or grip slime.' They nodded to each other sideways. 'We have no great power like yours to make the stranger obey.' They glanced secretly at each other. 'Lend us your stone, Great One, and we will bring the no-tail fish.' They hid smiles behind their hands.

Wirrun gave only one bark of laughter and shook his head as mockingly as the tailed women themselves. Their eyes flashed and their tails began to twitch. 'Wait,' he ordered them, and turned to Ularra.

'You'll have to tie me up,' said Ularra at once; and even if he had Merv's rope again that was more than Wirrun could have done. There was no help for it. He glowered at Ularra and turned back to the women.

'You'll take me and my friend to this spirit and I'll fetch it out.' Their eyes were sullen and their tails lashed. 'There's more,' said Wirrun. 'I'm doing you a favour and I'm not doing it for nothing. When I've got this stranger out of the way you'll go back to your own place and stay there. Right?'

They muttered and twitched, for they had enjoyed the excitement of battles with Kooleen and their power over the water-spirit. 'I lay it on you,' said Wirrun with the stone pulsing in his hand. 'First you take us there and back and give us what help we need. After you go to your own place.'

They flounced and sulked but they were ordered. 'If the slimy one goes we go. What should we stay for?'

'Good. And one more thing. The old water's finding new ways. Springs are drying and deserts are green. What made the new ways?'

They shrugged. 'Who are we to know the ways of the water? Ask the old ones that hide.' They remembered something, giving each other glances and a grin or two. 'The slippery one has long nails. It scraped and scratched to open a way but it could not slip through. We heard it howling.'

Wirrun thought for a moment. The Ninya or the water-spirit: what difference? The old and formless ones would know, for the land's dark heart was their own being. He would not bring them out of shelter into the faint light. He called to them where they hid.

'Eldest Ones, I lay it on you. When the stranger's gone you'll find the new ways of the water and close them up.' He was not sure of his power to command these ancient things that might be her own First Thoughts; but they had come first to his call and he was sure of their help.

He turned back to the tailed women. Now the ordering was done and the doing had to be faced, the dread and the hunger resolved. He, knowing, must go where Ularra had gone unknowing and fight for the power to command himself; for if he were lost there was no hero at hand, no Clever Man with a power, to bring him back. He could not keep the hoarseness out of his voice.

'All right. Take us to this place.'

The long months of waiting and seeking were like a river that carried him on into the monstrous waiting dark, aware, without cold or warmth. He was burning to go and cold with fear: fear of the cold fish-spirit, the slimy thing that sang like wild honey and howled like a dingo. He would not look at Ularra. But Ularra looked darkly and forebodingly at him.

3

The old south land lay under the sun like an open hand, but its secrets were hidden in its heart. There in that unknowable dark it held them all alike: its old remembered waters and the bones of forgotten creatures; its secret dreams of fretted, fragile beauty and the drifting shapes of old lost fears. And now it held with those, as deeply hidden and unknown, a lost love-singing and the torment of Wirrun and the pain of Ularra. It hid them, and knew, and was silent.

They fumbled their way deeper in as the old things flowed with them and led them on. The faint little lights of the Nyols' eyes flickered and the power pulsed on Wirrun's belt. So they travelled in a small moving starlight, and in this immensity of dark it was no more than a half-thought never uttered. Sometimes it lit a hidden spark, sometimes only the looming rock and flowing shadows. Kooleen's women shrilled and tittered ahead or watched at hand with slitted eyes and their tails curved like cats. The others that came with them Wirrun did not see. He was poised always on the twin points of hunger and dread, of longing for the singing and fear of the singer and himself. He fought for power.

They waded deep through water and crawled through sand and dust. They climbed up and again climbed down. They walked upright through echoing vaults, edged along narrow twisting places, squeezed themselves through slits. Once the inert dark warmed and breathed; there was a gushing of hot water and the curl of steam. Once Wirrun rested on a thing that crumbled: a skull, long and narrow and strange.

The first time the singing struck at him Wirrun was picking his way down a rough passage. He stood frozen, fighting it with teeth and hands clenched, while Ularra watched frowning and the spirits looked on curiously and listened to the song. The second time he and Ularra were jammed together in a slit, scraping a way through. Wirrun drew a sharp breath that jammed him tighter and gripped the rock and closed his eyes - but he heard Ularra's indrawn breath and opened them again. They were close together with the light of the power pulsing on their faces. He saw the shock on Ularra's face and knew that he heard with his ears what had haunted Wirrun's own mind all this time. Jealousy flared through him like a fire in grass.

> *Are you not coming?*
> *sings the bright water,*
> *are you not coming?*

The phrases dropped like falling leaves, the voice was as clear as a bird's and as sweet and sharp as wild honey. Ularra was dazed and his hands too gripped the rock.

'Man!' he whispered, and Wirrun snarled.

> *The glimmer-bright water*
> *alight with the glances*
> *of glimmer-bright eyes.*

Ularra shivered. 'It's a fish, man,' he whispered hoarsely. 'It's a bit of slime.' But Wirrun saw that the brooding had gone from his eyes; they were hard and afraid like Wirrun's own. He bared his teeth at Ularra like a dog.

'My business, mate. You keep out.'

The rocks sang into silence. The eyes, angry and afraid, fell away from each other. The Nyols waited indifferent but respectful. The two men stirred and went on. But Wirrun was always aware now of Ularra near and watching, grimly watching.

They skirted a pool, crawled through a low passage, and

stood upright again in a vaulting dark where the eyes of the Nyols twinkled from near to far and the darker shadows flowed between. The singing struck them again. Here it rang soft and free and an echo picked it up.

> *Are you not coming?*
> *sings the dark water,*
> *are you not coming?*

Ularra groaned. 'A man can't - a man can't - ' He stood rigid as Wirrun did, fighting with himself.

'Mine,' panted Wirrun. 'Mine.'

> *The dark-flowing water*
> *like washes and ripples*
> *of dark-floating hair.*

It was cool as moonlight. Wirrun broke into a stumbling run. In one leap Ularra was on him, gripping him in a vice. 'That's cold stuff,' he said harshly, 'that dark water. Old and bitter all through.'

Wirrun fought him. 'Keep out - keep off! I been all this time - Mine. Mine. You just got here.'

Ularra fought to hold him. 'I'm here. I'm staying.'

'And who brought you?'

'You did, man, you did.'

The spirits watched and listened, drawing a little farther off. The singing died. The knowing dark waited immense and unmoving. Ularra's grip loosened, Wirrun threw it off and the two stood panting.

'A man can't - ' muttered Ularra again, and Wirrun laughed hard and bitter; but Ularra looked dark with despair.

'You not come?' said the Nyols.

Another passage. A cleft through which Wirrun fought his way possessed. The singing again: sweet and cool, echoing into a chorus.

> *I sing in the sunlight*
> *with dark eyes aglimmer:*
> *are you not coming?*

'No good to a man,' said Ularra and his voice cracked. Wirrun, rounding on him, saw that he had picked up a stone. Wirrun ranted.

'Haven't you had enough, eh? Haven't you had enough? Come here on my power - my power - dogging me like a beast - like a beast - '

> *I sing in the shadows*
> *with dark hair downflowing:*
> *are you not here?*

Ularra stood shaking and shaking. He threw the stone into a clattering dark. 'Can't ever be sure . . . can't ever be sure . . . . But I'll tell you something, man . . . there's all kinds of beast.' He pulled the possum-fur cord from his pocket and thrust it at Wirrun; it fell between them and merged into the dark. 'You keep it,' gasped Ularra, his eyes flaring with fear. 'You need it.'

And through the pain of the haunting another pain struck Wirrun. He hardly knew what he had said or done but it should not have been said or done. He could only look pleading at Ularra as the beast had looked pleading at him. And Ularra's eyes were still hard and afraid.

There was shouting ahead, and the tailed women running in a crowd. The haunting gripped Wirrun and dragged him after them.

'Wa!' they were shouting. 'Slimy weed! Slippery fish! Fireless fool with no place! Take yourself out of our place, no-tail! Go back where you came from, slime-weed!' Tails lashing they worked at the stone of a rock-face. In a moment they had pulled away three large stones and were screaming insults through a cleft where the old water trickled. Wirrun rushed in among them and forced himself into the cleft. He was cold with horror and burning with need.

The water slipped over a ledge and clinked into a pool. The singing echoed and rang and he shuddered with longing. The power flared into brightness and he crawled along the ledge above the magical, cooling, enchanted water that his burning body craved. Something moved in it, flowing and lovely, and came out of the water on the farther side. He saw her at last and knew her from her singing, and the knowing held him while he looked.

She was silver like moonlight and lovely and dew-wet like a flower. Her dark hair flowed over slender shoulders to the rock where she sat, and she combed it back with delicate fingers. Her dark eyes were truly lit with moonlight, soft and shining, and she smiled with the sweetness of honey. She was dark and silver like moonlit water, lovely and remote like a dream. She longed for him, the singer in the dark, and his longing flowed back and he began to slide over the ledge.

But something scraped in the entrance. Something breathed hard. Ularra shot from the cleft and halfway across the pool in a dive, and cut the water so that it rang and echoed like the singing.

Wirrun shouted and dived too, fumbling with the power, but Ularra was already near. The water-spirit watched and quivered. As he came close she leaned towards him and held out two slender fingers.

4

When the Mimi had vanished into rock and those who came to honour her had gone, when the Yunggamurra had howled in despair and the howling had died in the dark, she had done all that was left to her. She had crawled on through the First Dark not knowing where but aimlessly seeking.

Her brown had paled to gold under its silver slime and her moonlit eyes had widened. She could see those fretted shapes of stone that glittered like ice: she was used to the dark. She had lost sunrise and sunset, north and south and the wheeling of the stars: she abandoned them and thought only of up and down and the secret flowing of water. She grew used to the weight of the land lying on its rocks. Only the pain of loneliness never softened or passed; that and her fear of the others in the dark, in whose place she was a stranger.

There came a time when she slipped on a trickle of water into a cavern with a different feel. A pool was cupped in it, wide and deep with ledges of rock above; a good pool, but she had found many of those. She lay quiet to sense the difference of this pool and found it with relief that was almost joy. Nothing old had lived here or came here. The rock and water were old as the land but the cleft that led in was new. She might rest here safely.

She did not choose to stay. She only stayed.

Rest and safety were healing. Her delicate slime was renewed, her dark hair grew sleek again. Sometimes she even played alone like a dolphin. She made one expedition to stock the water with blind fish and the cavern with pale spiders. It became her place.

But there was still the pain of loneliness. When she sang it was not to draw Wirrun of the People or Kooleen the tailed one but for memory. She sang for her river where the waterfall roared and faded and roared again. She sang for her sisters: for the glowing eyes and wild-honey smiles and slender shapes that showed her to herself; for the laughter and clinging hands, the water-tangling of dark hair and limbs, the sweet bad mischief of the games. When she sang the cavern caught and answered her singing till her voice was one of a chorus. Her sisters were there when she sang - but they never spoke or played or showed themselves. Sometimes she howled for this. The rock caught both the howling and the singing and carried them far.

And others heard. They lay quiet and listened. In a hundred years or so they might have come to whisper in the dark, perhaps to play a little. Only Kooleen the bold one with the tail came at once from the south to see.

When he saw he laughed, as he always laughed at those

who were shaped like the people and wore no tails. The Yunggamurra laughed back. She was filled with wild excitement by his visit. She slid into her pool and played like a dolphin to amuse him more. Kooleen narrowed his eyes.

'You will be one of my wives,' he said.

'Yes,' said the Yunggamurra for the sake of the company of spirits. Her sisters would have howled in fury.

The rock carried the words as it had carried the singing. The wives of Kooleen heard them and came eagerly to see. Her cavern filled with dark tailed women, new sisters. The Yunggamurra climbed from her pool to greet them with joy.

The joy was lost in a shrieking fury of women lashing their tails. Before she understood it Kooleen was gone, the cavern closed with stones, and she a scratched and beaten prisoner.

First she struggled to remove the stones. Then she pleaded. Later she searched for another way out, working at a fault in the rock below the water. It was useless; only the water, which before had trickled in to fill the pool, now began to flow a little. The Yunggamurra was defeated.

Sometimes Kooleen came to tease his wives, and laughed to her through the stones and called her his little fish. There would be another shrieking battle, and after it the Yunggamurra howling alone. Sometimes the wives would shriek taunts and insults through the stones. That was all she ever heard, but it was better than before.

When she sang it was not to draw Kooleen for he was her own kind and not to be charmed. She did not hear what others whispered, that the Ice-Fighter was at hand. She still did not know it when she felt the old sweet wickedness working in her and the game beginning. She only guessed that somehow, here in the deeps of the land, men of the People were near.

And the game was beginning! Her singing vibrated with magic and echoed into her sisters' chorus. Her moonlit eyes glimmered, her dark flowing hair shone. Her lovely silvered body quivered with the old fierce waiting, sharpened by long loneliness in the dark. She sang with the echoes and measured the pauses to build up doubt and wonder. She spread her fingers delicately like a dancer and smiled at them and listened and waited.

She heard as the others did the Ice-Fighter calling for help. She would not have gone if she could; to her he was a man of the People whose name she had heard in the dark. The game should bring him to her. She did remember that they had called him hero, and that lit her to fiercer excitement.

An uneasy stirring beyond her cavern, a pressure of Kooleen's wives who whispered and muttered: they lay close and hid, and she smiled her wild-honey smile. Did they think a crowd of tailed shadows could spoil her game? What did they know of the hunger of a love-sung man? She sang again, sending into the rock and the dark her sweetness, her remoteness, her waiting.

The pressure of uneasy wives had thinned: most were gone and only a few waited. Now, if a water-spirit had power with rocks, she might move the stones and slip away to freedom. But she would not if she could - not now - not when by some wonder a man was close - after so long - She sang of tenderness and loveliness and longing.

When she felt the nearness of many spirits she hugged herself and laughed. They should know her now. They should see what they kept closed up among them lonely in rocks and dark. They should see the game played, the man not stolen in sleep but coming free and eager. Let them see.

When next she paused in her singing and heard the voices of men she trembled. Two! There were two of them! And one a hero, and only one Yunggamurra. No sisters to help if help were needed - her fierce waiting was pricked with fear. She had forgotten the fear for every game holds a point of fear and in the old days it had been small. But now! She nerved herself. This game, played alone in the deepest dark, should ring for ages to come in the laughter of her sisters - if only she could play it - and they could know -

She heard the men near and slipped into the pool to wait

for the moment of love: that strange sad moment that belonged in some way to the fear and sweetened every game .... The stones were moved amid shrieking ... it was coming .... Now! They had found her! Soften the smile, light the eyes to a dewy shine, and watch, watch, watch ....

There he was, the man, creeping above on the ledge, as burning and eager as herself. And after him in the entrance the second. She placed herself quickly on rock and leaned forward with longing and sang. Her shining eyes watched and waited spirit-old; and what they saw sharpened the needle of fear. For these were charmed men as they should be, and filled with torment as they should be; but each of them knew his torment as he should not. And where she had looked for only one hero there were two, each holding tight to his purpose. For both the purpose was strong and desperate, but for one the purpose was not hers -

That one leapt from the entrance into the water as the Yunggamurra summoned all her power. She saw him coming and was pierced with fear because she could not read his purpose. The man on the ledge shouted, at first with jealous rage as was right and then desperately as he plunged into the pool. The other was close, and yet she did not know - But she put out two fingers in the old way, like a crab's claw, and easily held him under the water.

Now the second was near. He had a strong power - he ordered and she had to obey - sullen with fear and defeat she drew back her crab-claw. The man under water bobbed to the surface and was still. The other stayed by him; he did not come on though his power had defeated her. Fear ebbed; now she was curious and a little sad. She watched with moonlit eyes.

It was sad that he lay so still so soon, the man who had come to her singing and played her lovely game - the man she had loved for a moment and failed to read. He had not struggled at all.

5

When Wirrun saw the water-spirit shining in the starlit dark he knew her for his own: his strength and purpose and power, his dream and his haunting, all that he needed. This was what had called to him from the mountain, whispered in the desert, carried him on the wind. It was for this that the land was troubled and the spirits restless: that Wirrun of the People might find and claim his own. The certainty held him and Ularra shot past into the pool.

He shouted with rage - but the power burnt his hand and the water-spirit moved and he saw Ularra's face as it went under water. Dread seized him, he shouted again in desperate warning and fumbled for the power as he leapt.

The delicate silvery shape drew back, watching with old and fearful eyes. Ularra bobbed up and Wirrun grabbed him. The old water lapped his face: a man's face, stern and calm. Wirrun had seen the sternness already as Ularra sank; but the other thing, the weary dread, was changed now into this deep, accepting calm.

'No,' grunted Wirrun panting and fighting to drag Ularra from the water. 'No . . . a man can't drown so quick.'

It was true; but even as he rolled Ularra over, the ancient air of the cavern stirred and sweetened. Something passed through it, something warm and strong and gentle that stayed by him for a moment and was gone. And he knew it: it was Ularra's spirit.

His own spirit called after it, a cry for forgiveness and restoration while he worked to revive Ularra's body. Useless work, only that he could not believe it. A man can't drown so soon . . . .

He worked on, pumping steadily at Ularra's lungs. Nyols and small hairy things crept into the cavern and looked. They looked longest at the water-spirit for they had seen dead men before. 'Drowned like a lizard,' they told each other nodding wisely.

At last Wirrun's aching body gave in; his mind was locked away somewhere behind glass. Gently he turned Ularra over again. The face was so deeply, so strongly, at peace. 'Mate,' whispered Wirrun, pleading, but Ularra's peace was not to be broken by a word.

He stood up stiff and aching and his eyes fell on the water-spirit. It watched as old as moonlight, knowing and yearning and uncaring all at once. *Old all through, man. Old and bitter* . . . . His eyes narrowed and hardened. The thing had done its work. Now it should show like a hag and not as remotely lovely as before.

He said, 'What are you?'

She had drowned one man too easily and the other would not drown. She answered sullenly. 'Yunggamurra.'

He repeated it. 'Yunggamurra.' *A fish, man. A bit of slime.* 'You'll stay here, Yunggamurra, and wait.'

She glanced indifferently at the open cleft. The tailed women were there smirking and staring but it had not mattered for some time now. She was already ordered.

He saw that the cavern was full of old things that drifted and stared. He spoke to them harshly. 'This was a hero.'

They looked at the face so sternly and strongly at peace, and shifted and murmured.

'Take him to a hero's place,' ordered Wirrun.

They only looked again, and those that had faces turned them away. They did not know a hero's place. But the form-less ones, the land's First Thoughts, flowed even into the light and thickened around Ularra and bore him out of the cavern. Wirrun found that this, the thickness of dark bearing Ularra away, was more than his mind could now accept. He retreated behind his wall of glass, bewildered. The Nyols closed about him and he went with them like a child, following the shadows. Kooleen's women closed up the cavern behind them and stayed by it. Other shapes went with the Nyols deeper into the land.

Behind rose a crying wild and chill and lonely that rang away down corridors of rock and was caught and answered and came back from all sides till the dark was shaken.

Wirrun shuddered and waited thinking that this crying came from him; but the Nyols looked behind and hurried on, and he knew that it was the Yunggamurra's howling. The rock pulsed with it, crying for Wirrun who must not yet feel pain or cry.

He could not see what went ahead through the dark where a man may cease to be. He saw only the little eyes of the Nyols and the shapes that flittered near. Peering close in the dim light he gave careful attention to broken rock, to dust and sand and water, for these things he could comprehend; and he went obediently where the Nyols led. When they held him back he waited obedient.

Those ahead were busy, darting like glow worms about some wide dark place. Light blossomed, the red and gold light of fire, and he frowned over that: what fuel had they found? The flames rose; he saw the cavern, and the journey through dark had meaning again.

The fire lit the cavern to frost-sparkle and rainbow-shine. Its flames leaping and playing flung back curtains of dark and let them fall again. Now here, now there in the moving light stone glistened and flowered and soared. Glistening folds of stone swept down from an upper darkness, glittering columns and spires rose into it. In its old dark heart the land had dreamed of beauty and its oldest shadows had found the dream.

To the right a pool caught and doubled the frost-sparkled fretted shapes. Above it jutted a shelf of rock over which flowstone had laid a drapery that hung fringed to the water. On this drapery of gleaming stone the shadows had laid Ularra with spires glistening round him. Wirrun could not come near, but he climbed a boulder on that side and looked down.

'Pretty,' crooned the Nyols clustering near. They stole glances at Wirrun, and he saw and answered them.

'It's a place for a hero.'

'It grows,' they told him, and he nodded and looked quickly away. He understood what they said but he could not yet think of Ularra wrapped close in the gleaming stone.

Ularra's loose-jointed legs lay neatly, his long arms rested at his sides. The dark swept its curtains over his face and away as the firelight played; sometimes it showed sternly and calmly at peace and at others it moved and darkened. Clearly Wirrun heard Ularra's voice in its pain: *Can't ever be sure, can we?*

He rubbed a hand over his face. Yes, Mate. We're sure. I'll never need to be so sure.

It did not seem possible to climb down, to go away from the cavern and leave him. But it was made possible. When the busy Nyols could find no more fuel the fire died. The dark drew its curtains close again, and only the power and the glow-worm lights of the Nyols drew a secret glint from stone. Not Wirrun but Ularra had gone.

Wirrun came down from the boulder and carefully thanked the shadows. They took him back through the weary dark to the cavern where the Yunggamurra now lay silent and the tailed women waited. The women confronted him.

'The slime-weed. The no-tail fish. You take it now?'

His face twisted and he tried to pass but they flounced ahead of him.

'A bargain! It was a bargain!' They hugged themselves in anger and jerked their tails.

Wirrun drove his fist into his palm. 'No more!' he shouted, and they were silent and sullen. He knew it had been a bargain, but he wanted with a sudden fierce disgust never again to see that silver shape or hear the falling phrases of the song. 'Maybe I'll be back,' he said more quietly. 'Now I have to think of my friend.'

'Friend,' rumbled the Nyols. They had known the word for a long time but still did not understand it as men did.

They took Wirrun on. The tailed women stayed by the cavern and stared after him insolently until the next passage hid him from them.

In the passage some of the Nyols stooped, rumbling to each other and gathering something between them. Wirrun found it pressed into his hands, a soft and growing bundle:

the cord from the power. Loosely bundled it was too big for its bag; he struggled to force it in. It had gone more easily into Ularra's large pocket - and if it had stayed there Ularra might be here now - something large and dull inside him sharpened and tore and he groaned.

They took him on through the huge aware dark: through slits and caverns and passages, through water and dust and sand. Sometimes he forgot what he should do and they herded him gently like a mob of small grey sheep herding the dog. They took him past a pool that reflected their glow-worm eyes in a vaulting dark, and there he saw Ularra's spare shirt and stood gazing at it uncertainly for a time and turned and left it. They led him up a mounting slope to a higher level and through a passage to a lesser dark.

'You call,' they said. 'We come.'

And they left him. The power had ceased to glow.

He stood alone and bewildered turning here and there to look at the dark, not knowing what to do. He could not escape from behind his wall of glass. After a time he found a greyness away in the dark and looked at that; and while he looked his mind suddenly saw, as clearly as if his eyes had seen, the hands of his ancestors outlined in ochre on the walls above. The hands of his ancestors reaching from the past, spread over him in pity; the eyes of charcoal and pipe-clay knowing and sadly forgiving.

They knew he had faced his haunting and found no power over himself; that to save him had cost the making and losing of a hero. He felt a choking hardness that would not break into sobs; and he dropped to his knees beneath those pitying hands and crawled to the grey light.

So Wirrun came alone out of the First Dark to mourn for his friend Ularra. Behind him, though he did not hear, the rock vibrated again to the howling of the dingo. The Yunggamurra mourned too. She howled for dark and loneliness, and for men who would not play her game but lived or died too easily.

SIX

Singer in the Sunlight

I

The mourning of Wirrun for Ularra was such as could be born by only one man: the man who climbs the rugged track to hero. It was mourning embittered by every step that led to it. Not softened by friendship for friendship sharpened Wirrun's failure into a spear. Not relieved by hatred of the killer, for hatred and enchantment were still horribly one and he could not untangle them. Not sweetened by discovery of Ularra the Hero for a friend's greatness should be seen while he lives. Not warmed by gratitude, for when a hero dies for a friend who has failed gratitude is a mean and cowardly thing. There was no help for Wirrun.

For three days and nights he roamed the gorge not knowing where he was. Flashes of vision came and went -

He was sitting in the creek with a cut on his leg. It bled and he watched -

He was rewinding the cord on the power. He threw it down and wearily took it up again -

Are you not coming? - he writhed, hating himself for hearing and for the stab of hunger -

He sat eating fish that someone gave him in pieces. He looked and saw it was Merv Bula and said, 'Get out.'

Merv knew the curtness was inability to speak. He put the fish at hand and went. Not smoke but the lack of it had brought him: there was no campfire. He had found Wirrun wandering alone, his spirit gone, and had made his own camp under the cliffs and watched and followed. Twice more he put into Wirrun's hands food that the hero ate blindly.

Wirrun's spirit had gone out of him to plead with the powers of that country. 'Bring him back. Bring him out of there. I'll live haunted and never listen.' The powers withdrew into cliffs and shadows and far blue hazes; they could undo a magic and reshape a form but they could not remake life. That river flowed from another source.

Wirrun thought they refused him because he could not, even while he promised and pleaded, live haunted and never listen. *Sings the dark water . . .* he cursed and beat at rock.

Pleading broke into anger. He raged at the unmoved powers. He raged at the singer, the slimy evil howler. He raged at himself for a weak fool and a coward; and at last he raged at the land itself, the cruellest monster of all.

'Old hag - old beast - you called didn't you? We came - you took us - dropped us both into hell. What for? What for?'

I did not call, said the land. *You were mine and I aided you. No more.*

He had not heard that voice when he listened for it but it reached him now in his crazy anger: remote and near, stern and gentle. It was the beginning of sanity. Anger broke into purest pain and he threw himself down on that arrested strength. He lay at the still centre of pain till the land drew its darkness over him and itself sent him help.

The air stirred and sweetened. Leaves moved and whispered.

What about living, man? What about the wind?

'Oh mate!' cried Wirrun's agonised spirit. 'Ularra, where are you?'

A man's place . . . a man's place . . . .

'Nothing surer. Never was. Wish I was with you.'

Hush, man. Listen, man. Listen . . . .

He lay at the still centre of pain while Ularra's spirit drifted near, in the wind, in the grass, in the slipping of the creek. He let Ularra speak to him, in words he had heard or spoken and in new words.

A man can't drown so quick . . . unless he wants to . . . a beast's too much for a man . . . .

The air stirred and the trees murmured.

Had to take it from you ... my own way ....

The night trilled with insects and softened into young moonlight.

Dreaming only I never did it so good ... the wind and a man's place ... thanks, man ....

And as the sweetness passed and the grass whispered into silence:

Can't drown so quick ... unless he wants to ....

Pain broke at last into weeping, and Wirrun could lie weeping on the earth until he slept. At dawn he woke and went down to the creek and washed. Merv Bula saw it from under the cliffs and came down to light a fire and bake a damper.

Wirrun accepted him with a look and ate and drank in silence. Merv asked nothing. Over a second mug of tea Wirrun found his voice, rough with disuse and hunger and thirst.

'He's in there ... deep down ... under the cave ....'

'A man?' said Merv quietly.

Wirrun raised bloodshot eyes with a spark in them. 'None better. Died saving me.'

'Ah. He had no choice, then.'

... unless he wants to .... Wirrun said roughly, 'There's always a choice.'

Merv nodded. 'A man's choice,' he amended. 'He'll be glad of that.' He took a rabbit from his pack and began to cut it up for a stew. Since he asked nothing but was only there Wirrun was able to tell more.

'The beast. It was too much for him. He couldn't trust - '

'That'd be bad, then,' said Merv with deep sadness. 'He'd need to find out. Poor boys. Poor boys.'

Pain rushed over Wirrun again and he laid his head on his knees. And still he had not told the worst.

Merv could not know how much was untold. He only watched and stayed: stocking the new camp he had made, bringing Wirrun's pack from the old one, quietly taking Ularra's things away to the cliffs. He was not waiting to hear more but for the right time to go. He did not like to see the Ice-Fighter listen wincing to something unheard, or the darkness that came over him then.

Wirrun was finding how to use his pain to defeat the singing. It struck at him often, and the hunger it roused filled him with shame and horror for Ularra's sake. He could harden it now into hatred but he could not yet speak of it to Merv. Yet he wanted to speak for he wished the People might understand his failure - and while he wished it he found himself rejecting failure, rejecting it for Ularra as well as for himself. Shielded by hatred from the silvery singer with the moonlit eyes he thought again of his bargain with the tailed women. Yet nothing shielded him from the chill of the First Dark.

To go back to the darkness where Ularra was, where forever stifled today; to be led again by shadows where he and Ularra had fought; to see that shirt again; he could not. He fought his dread all day and at night while Merv slept. Near morning he knew that for him as for Ularra there was no other way.

Only he and the power could bring out the Yunggamurra. If he did not go hate-shielded into the First Dark and bring it out then the trouble of spirits and People would go unhealed. That would make Ularra's death a mockery indeed, a useless failure, a slaughtering by Wirrun of his friend. He had to go.

Merv woke early to find him filling a billy with yabbies for breakfast. It should have been a healthy sight but the darkness was still on the Ice-Fighter. They ate in silence; and afterwards when Wirrun spoke Merv's face darkened too.

'I never said what he saved me from. I'm sung.'

Merv's glance went quickly over him: not bone-pointed or sung with the stones or string. In his body at least the hero was not sickening but recovering. Merv waited.

'A long time now,' muttered Wirrun. 'Turns out it's all of a piece with this other trouble. It's a - love-singing - an old thing down there - got *him* a bit, too. That's why - ' He stopped, out of words.

Merv's voice shook a little. 'You went knowing? Both?'

Wirrun nodded. 'We fought,' he whispered. 'I called him - I don't know what - '

'Poor boys. Poor boys.'

At least it was told now. Wirrun coughed to get his voice back. 'Trouble is, I gotta go down again. No good without. Gotta bring this - thing - out, send it home.'

Merv's eyes shifted. 'You want help.'

'No!' shouted Wirrun spilling his tea. He got hold of himself. 'Not another one. No fear. You keep well out where you can't hear no singing. Stay up on the cliffs.' He ran a hand through his hair. 'I just want you to know, that's all. Know and keep off.'

There was silence for a moment. Almost in despair Merv asked, 'What *can* I do?'

'If I don't come out don't try. Just leave it. Only tell Tom Hunter, that's all. They got a right to know. And he - Ularra - he came from that country. He's got a right. Tell Tom.'

'And what about your country, Ice-Fighter?'

Wirrun smiled tightly. 'From sea to sea it's all my country.'

'That's all, then? That's everything to do?'

'Look,' said Wirrun, 'you don't want to get in a twist. It's safe - beaten - that's what he did for me. Long as I can handle myself I can handle the rest. If I can't - well, just tell old Tom. And don't let no one in there after us. Right?'

'Right.' Merve stood up and turned his back to look at the cliffs. 'Two of you . . . young blokes. You cut a man down to size, Ice-Fighter.'

'Not you. No one cuts you down.' Wirrun hesitated, not wanting to say the next part badly. 'Only I want you safe out of this. Thanks, mate, but I'm right now. You get going. I can't fetch this - water-thing out till you do.'

'Today?'

'I'd feel safer.'

Merv began to roll his pack.

'And don't hang around on top,' said Wirrun urgently. 'Don't watch for fire. It travels, this singing.'

Merv finished rolling his pack and shouldered it. Wirrun walked beside him up the hill. A little way up Merv stopped.

'No more. You gotta get your strength back.'

Wirrun struggled for words to say good-bye. 'There's this old spirit-bloke,' he said. 'Ko-in, sort of a grandfather. There's my friend Ularra, he's gone now. After them there's you.' He held out a hand.

Merv said nothing. In a gesture that was strange yet old, dignified and right, he folded Wirrun's hand between his older hands and pressed it to his chest. Then he turned away and went on up the hill.

Wirrun watched for a moment and went back down the hill to the new camp. He poured more tea and thought of going into the cave. But not today. Not yet.

It was hate that sent him. He was wakened next dawn by the singing and the eager leaping of his blood, and his spirit rebelled. It was not enough to reject the cool sweet magic; it still struck. There was still that piercing moment and afterwards the shame and horror. The singer must go to its own place and he must put distance between or he would go mad. He must go now, before pain softened and his shield of hatred softened with it.

He ate a little cold baked yam and made tea. He took no firestick but unrolled the cord from the power and left it safe in his sleeping-bag. The crystal lay in his palm: grey-white stranded with pink, the colour of the dawn sky. He held it for a while for strength before he laid it carefully in its netted bag. Then he went up the creek again to the cave.

He did not notice that he trembled and his knees were weak. He had enough to do to keep his mind narrowed to its purpose, to walk tight-lipped and frowning through the twilight of the cave and on into its night; to find again the darker slit and climb into the second cave; to feel his way along the painted walls. Without a firestick he found the entrance to the passage only by groping. He went a foot or so in and shouted.

'Hoo, there! Come on, you Nyols! It's the Ice-Fighter needs you.'

Then he leaned against the rock and waited.

It was bad waiting. The First Dark probed along the passage knowing he was there. Ularra would have stood here fingering the fur cord, waiting to follow .... He narrowed his mind to its purpose again and watched for the first points of light, wondered only if they would come, thought nothing of the last journey or the end of this one.

Pinpoints of light flickered and came, soft voices rumbled. The Nyols peered with their bright lizard-eyes in the faces of small grey children. 'We come,' they pointed out.

'Take me back to Kooleen's women,' he asked and let himself be led as he had before. The power began to glow and pulse, strengthening as they went.

The way seemed long. Wirrun looked only at the nearest rocks and the pinpoints of light. It was not as hard as he had feared for now he knew where the journey led and there were no stranger shadows drifting with them; this journey alone with the Nyols was a different one and less fearful. But sometimes the other stabbed at him out of the dark: in a shoulder of rock remembered, the crumbling of a skull, a slit through which he knew the way. He trod on Ularra's shirt and could not leave it again but had to push it away inside his own. He stood trembling where he had ranted at Ularra and was helped by Merv Bula's thickened voice saying, 'Poor boys. Poor boys.' After that he could hear the shrill squabbling of Kooleen's women; it was easier to hold to his purpose but harder not to think ahead.

Kooleen's women felt his coming and began to shriek in welcome. 'He is here, the one with the power!' 'The Ice-Fighter keeps his bargain!' 'He comes for the slippery thing! Out! Send it out!' A little farther and he saw them: shadows clustered in the starlight, flashing grins and jerking tails. Already they were working at the stones that blocked the cavern.

'Here, then, Ice-Fighter! The singer is waiting and wishing for you!' They stood grinning round the open slit. His mind leapt ahead in panic and found a solution: he would order the Nyols to take the Yunggamurra home. Five minutes to find out its place - then be rid of it - try not to see - Shaking he crawled through the entrance. The power flared.

It was there, a silver glimmer in the dark watching with old moonlit eyes. He longed and sickened and called up hatred: Ularra's face stern and calm in the water. He spoke hoarsely.

'Yunggamurra. Where's your right place? Where did you come from?'

It said, 'Up.'

He frowned. 'I'm taking you out of this, sending you home. But I gotta know where.' He held up the stone and the spirit watched it like a child watching a candle. 'Tell me where.'

She did not believe what he told her for that was not how the game was played; but she was ordered and had already answered. She tried harder. The moonlit eyes dreamed.

'My sisters are there. The sun shines and the river flows. The water leaps far over rocks.'

He had heard the leaping water . . . . He saw that anger was useless for the creature had tried to obey. But his mind, held tight to its purpose, met this new problem slowly and struggled to think. He asked, 'How did you come here?'

The shining dark eyes widened and aged. 'Through rocks. In the dark. Many ways.' She thought again. 'With the water and against it. This way and that.'

He watched intent, grappling with the problem. 'A long time?'

'Alone in the dark, a long time.' The bird-sweet voice was cool and indifferent but he had seen the spirit quiver. He felt a quick unexpected pang. Lovely and loathsome, delicate and enduring, gallant and terrible. He frowned again and thought.

'Does the river come out of the rocks? How did you get in?'

'There was a storm. The water spread wide. I was carried into the sea. In the sea I found the old water trickling.'

The sea. 'What sea?'

It frowned, was puzzled, folded itself in indifference again. 'There is only one sea. That sea.'

'What if I took you back to the sea? Could you find your way home?'

It shook its head quickly and was wrapped in its own flowing hair. 'The sea is a cold wet fire. It burns. I cannot live in it.'

Wirrun brooded in silence. The Nyols listened and peeped like inquisitive children. The tailed women whispered and sniggered. The Yunggamurra saw and heard and gave no sign.

In this place where Ularra had died Wirrun faced his own shame and dread: there was no easy way out. The water-spirit, a creature of sunlight and rivers, had been in the dark a long and twisting time; it was lost. If he sent it away with the Nyols they might wander and search for years and the trouble go with them. He himself would never know when he might meet it again, when its singing might pierce him from some creek or pool. He must take it with him into daylight, give it time to recover and find itself, treat it like any earth-creature.

He said, 'You'll come with me. No slipping off in the water to Kooleen, mind. No singing. No howling. Just come.'

He did not see the fear in its eyes. Like a diver filling his lungs with air it slipped into the pool to wet itself and came.

2

'Wa!' cried the tailed women waggling their fingers and jerking their tails. 'It is going, the slippery thing, the no-tail!' They leaned towards the Yunggamurra grinning and shaking their heads. 'Ko-ki! The slime-weed is going! You will never see Kooleen, fish-thing! Go, now, go!'

Gleaming wet and silver the Yunggamura passed through them following Wirrun. These were the sisters she would have welcomed in spite of their tails; even now, jeering and mocking, they were company of her own kind. But she gave no sign that she saw or heard, yearned or resented. Slender as a strand of weed in the water and cool and remote as moonlight she walked between them after the man with the power. She had played and lost. That was a rare and terrible thing; what came next she partly knew and did not understand. But she was a Yunggamurra.

'Go, no-tail! Go, slime-weed!'

'That's enough!' roared Wirrun in disgust. 'You go too; trouble-makers. Back to your own place and leave others to theirs. That was the bargain.'

They laughed and swung their hips and curled their tails. The power would not hold them forever but he knew the bargain would.

The Nyols gathered round and the journey began. The water-spirit came behind all the way and never spoke. It slipped easily through narrow slits that he climbed through with care, but once or twice it was scraped by rock and he heard its quivering indrawn breath. Once it paused, holding up dainty fingers and wiggling them like a child. He paused too thinking it was hurt, but he saw that its eyes smiled a little. He frowned, wondering, and felt again that strange unexpected pang. It was looking at the glow of light on its silver fingers; after so long in the dark this twilight was bright to it.

When they reached the long pool it slipped in and he jerked with quick suspicion. But he saw that it followed still, a ripple in a cloud of hair. At the beginning of the long climb up he called it from the water. It came dripping and delicate out on the rock, its old bright eyes showing nothing; not eager, not reluctant, only ordered. Wirrun grunted a little and muttered a word to Ularra, yet he did not know why. The water-spirit made no claim, its wild-honey voice was silent, his shield of pain and disgust was not lowered. There was only that small odd pang that passed before he felt it.

He did not see how the Yunggamurra mounted the slope for the Nyols were all about him. Climbing or carried it came with them and was there, a remote glimmer, on the ledge. It followed down the passage and into the cave where the power ceased to glow, where the Nyols rumbled a soft farewell and went away. He feared that in the dark the spirit might slip away with them, but when he turned suspiciously he found he could still see its glimmer. The gorge must be in full sunlight; there was more light in here than before. He could easily see the slit to the outer cave. The spirit's eyes were fixed on it too but they showed no feeling.

He must still grope his way to the slit with care. The spirit watched curiously and followed at a pace slowed to his. At the slit it hung back.

'Go through,' ordered Wirrun sternly. It laid its silver fingers on the rock and groped through. He followed.

The Yunggamurra was cringing against the wall of the cave, eyes closed, an arm shielding its face. He frowned in surprise and looked for the cause. There was only the long twilit tunnel of the cave and a dazzle of sunlight at its mouth. He thought of the Nyols that came and went underground and above, of the Mimi coming from the blackness of rock into light. He had not thought that a daylight spirit long underground might be hurt by the sun.

'We'll wait,' he said gruffly and sat down.

In a short time the Yunggamurra lowered its arm; a minute later it stood upright and faced the cave. Still looking only at the floor it waited, ready. He felt that peculiar pang again.

'We'll go nearer and wait again.'

It followed him down the cave from twilight to morning and when he stopped, watching under his brows, it turned its shoulder to the cave-mouth and hid against the wall. The day's heat came in like the breath of a monster. Even for him, coming from so short a time in the huge First Dark, the heat and light were sharp.

'You gotta get used to it if you want to go home,' he muttered.

It was the first time he had seen the spirit in daylight. He looked warily. Its silvery colour came from a covering of silver-grey slime. Where the slime had been scraped by rocks it showed a golden colour underneath; he wondered if that was the dark and if sunlight would brown it. Over its shoulders the dark hair tumbled and shone, moving lightly with the air because it was now dry. The creature was smaller than he had thought and its face was hidden in its long-nailed hands, but nothing could hide its slender curving beauty. In shape as in movement it flowed.

It raised its head and looked at him with those lovely dew-shining eyes that held only waiting and age. He turned roughly away and led it farther, to the edge of the sun. Here again it cringed and hid and quivered, and in a moment cried out its first words since the journey began.

'There must be water!' it cried in agony.

'There's a pool,' he said quickly. 'Down the hill a bit.'

'But I cannot see to go!'

He did not mean to torture it, only to be rid of it. He said, 'Shut your eyes and give me your hand.' It did as it was ordered and he took the small silvery hand and led it to the pool.

There was no magic in its touch. He felt a quick disgust that had nothing to do with Ularra. The hand was inert with none of the response or telling of a human hand. It was cool and moist like a frog without firmness or the frog's tense life. It felt like twigs in mud and slime. The spirit sensed the pool when they neared. Its hand slipped free. It sprang with no splash into the water and sank out of sight.

Wirrun gathered oak-needles and wiped the slime from his hand scrubbing it clean. The creek was shallow where it ran from the pool; the spirit could not slip away without his seeing it. He sat on the bank to wait.

The Yunggamurra went deep, down into the soft mud below. The water pressed her down as if it would hold her till the man with the power had gone. She curled and straightened, feeling its softness and sweetness - the sweetest she had felt since the storm. It soothed the bare burnt places where the slime was scraped off and softened the slime that was left. She looked up at the surface through water-light to the shadows of trees; and she did what she had not known a Yunggamurra could do. She wept.

She had not thought for a long time of daylight filtered through soft brown water and patterned with the shadows of trees. To see it again was sweet; and perhaps soon she could look at the trees, and beyond them to those widths of world she had forgotten. She could look but she could not stay. The man had her.

She wept only a little while. When her eyes found the light soft and dim she floated up into stronger light and looked again. She thought wistfully that she might sink to the bottom and stay a little while till the earth whirled once or twice around the sun; and the man would be gone. The pool could be hers, for nothing lived here. But that was not the way the game was played. She was a Yunggamurra; the man had come called by her singing and defeated her. When her eyes were stronger she floated higher.

Now she could see through the water to a blueness of sky and the wavering shapes of trees. For a year she had been in blackness, but to a spirit that in itself was a little time. In the sudden joy of trees she forgot it and looked for her sisters: where were the silver limbs and the dark clouds of hair? She shot up through the lid of the water to look and in the strangeness of looking remembered. She put back her head and gave a soft wild howl.

'Stop that!' shouted Wirrun, at once rigid.

She looked at him remembering that too, and cut off the howl.

Wirrun had waited by the pool for a long time suspecting some trick. There was nothing he could do about it for the thing had needed water, but he watched darkly. When he saw the silvery shape through the brown water he breathed hard in relief. To lose it, let it loose among men who knew nothing of it, would be the worst failure of all. He grew patient in his relief and watched it float higher, understanding that it treated its own light-blindness in the best way. Emerging it took him by surprise and he shouted his order - he could not become chilled or enchanted, he must stay in charge. But when the old yearning moonlit eyes looked at him half seeing and the howl broke off, that unrecognised pang needled him again. Why should it howl? All he wanted was to send it home.

'What did you howl for?' he asked it gruffly.

'For my sisters,' it said with the same indifference as before, and waited to be ordered further. When no order came it floated in its own spreading hair and looked and looked: not at Wirrun but above and far off, at trees and sky and cliffs and perhaps birds.

When sunlight had left the gorge and Wirrun was hungry he called. 'Can you come out now? There's another pool lower down.'

It came out of the pool into the creek. He walked down the bank to his new camp and it followed, sliding or swimming or sometimes walking in the creek. When they reached the small pool at his camp he spoke very sternly.

'I could tie you into a bag like a fish. I won't if you behave. You're ordered not to leave this pool till I say and to come when I call.'

It nodded and sank in a swirl of dark hair.

Wirrun lit his fire and cooked a meal and ate. Then he lay in the grass and watched the fire die while evening turned to night. He was deeply tired, deeply sad; he understood that. But he was also guilty and ashamed, and that he did not understand. He had made the hard journey into the dark and kept off horror with the business in hand. He had sent the tailed women home so that quiet would spread through the land; he had ordered that the old water should return to its old ways. He had taken charge of the water-spirit and kept off dread and enchantment. The thing was beside him now in the pool, Ularra's killer; but it was there because it must be and he could do nothing else. Why shame and guilt? How had he failed this time?

There was a bulk that he had grown used to and now felt: Ularra's shirt inside his own. He took it out and lay with it in his hands and was shaken again by pain and hate. Hate: that was it. He had forgotten for many hours to hate.

Was it then only the singing he hated? Only the howling he dreaded? Only his own danger and not Ularra's fate? What sort of thing was Wirrun of the People? He had betrayed his friend again.

The air sweetened and stirred, the grass whispered, but he did not hear it for a long time. He was weary to death and sick. The grass whispered on.

There's all kinds of beast, man ... all kinds of beast ... there's gotta be pity ... pity ....

He heard it at last and knew what that odd recurring pang had been. Pity ... for Ularra's killer ... how strange men were.

3

That night Wirrun slept where he lay and did not feel the deep cold before dawn or the chill of dew or the eyes of the Yunggamurra watching from the pool. He woke aching. He ached all through with the weariness of this bitter time in the gorge. His muscles ached with cold, his belly with hunger, and his mind with the sadness of a hate collapsed under the weight of pity.

He lit his fire quickly and while it warmed him made a damper with flour from a bag that Merv had left hanging on a branch. Merv would see his smoke and know he had come back safe; he hoped the old man would stick to instructions and keep away. He had forbidden the singing, but while the singer lay in the gorge no man should be put at risk ... And even while he thought this he heard the singing, clear and sweet and cool as before: *are you not coming?*

The longing struck - he sprang up in fury but could not find the spirit. While he glared at the pool the silvery face rose from the water amid its hair, looked with wide fixed eyes at his fire, and quickly sank.

It had not sung. The singing was in his mind. The spirit itself might be to him no more than a handful of slime, but the singing was barbed deep into his mind.

He ate, tidied the camp, banked down the fire, folded Ularra's shirt away in his own pack, prepared his gear for fishing. Then he went to search under fallen branches for bait. He would be eating fish again today: doing his hunting in the creek. When he had a few crickets and worms he came back to the pool and called to the water-spirit while he baited his hook.

'Yunggamurra! Up you come.'

It rose without a ripple on the far side of the pool, its back pressed into the opposite bank like an animal at bay, only its head above water. It stared past him at the camp and then at him with something like dread. Wirrun cast his line on his own side of the pool.

'It's all right,' he told it but he was puzzled. The spirit was held by the power, yet the power had done it no harm. It had suffered at first in heat and sunlight but he had allowed it time to recover. He had forbidden only its singing, its howling, and its freedom in a country that was not its own. What should it dread?

'Do you want to go back to the dark?' he asked.

It shook its head, tangling and untangling its hair.

'Just as well. You can't do that. Do you want to go home to your sisters?'

It nodded.

'Well then,' he retorted in exasperation, 'you better try and help me. Instead of staring as if I was going to eat you. What are you scared of any rate?'

It looked at him with darkened eyes and beyond him at the camp. He glanced over his shoulder: his pack; a branch from which two hessian bags swung keeping Merv's provisions from the ants; a small heap of yams; a curl of smoke from the banked fire. He considered.

'Are you scared of fire?' It quivered. 'That one's only smoke.' Its eyes darkened. 'I won't let it hurt you any rate. I'll look after it.'

The spirit said nothing but eyed him with reserve. He frowned and gave some attention to his line. It was natural that a water-spirit should dread fire but this one would have to trust him if he was to get it home. How it watched: as if it knew something dreadful that he did not. He could not meet its darkened shining eyes. He spoke to his line.

'You've had a bit of time out here now. Could you find your own place yet?'

The spirit shook its head.

'Tell me about it, then. Go on. Talk about your country. I might know it.'

It answered in its cool sweet voice almost exactly as it had before. 'The river flows and leaps over rock, a long leap. The sun shines. My sisters are there.'

'Yeah. Well that could be a lot of places. You'll have to do better than that. What else is in your country?' It only looked at him. 'Come on - you lived there a long time. You must know your own country.'

Its eyes yearned. 'I know it well. The river is my country.'

'But didn't you ever leave the river and go about the land? You've got legs.' The loveliest legs, slender and silver with curving thighs. 'What are your legs for?'

It gazed dreaming. 'We walked in the shallows. And there were rocks; we often came on to the rocks to play. The fish hid in the shadows . . . .'

Wirrun waited hoping, but though the Yunggamurra dreamed on it said nothing more. He was distracted by a bite at his hook and in a moment pulled in a catfish. He unhooked it taking care of the spines and laid it in safety on the bank. The water-spirit had stopped dreaming. It watched with the sharp interest of a hunter of fish. He rebaited and cast out again.

'Which way did your river flow?' he called.

'Many ways, a gathering of many rivers. We travelled

wide. East and west, north and south,' it said proudly having remembered them, 'and never left the river.'

One of the big systems, then. He thought of the nearest and most likely. 'Was there always water? Were the rivers dry, some of 'em? Only run when it rained?'

'There were such rivers,' said the spirit indifferently, and he saw that indifference hid a passionate pride. 'We did not trouble with them. Our rivers had much water, a great water.'

The pride belonged to the yearning perhaps, but probably the river was permanent. There were few of those to the west entering the Gulf - and surely none with falls? East of the Cape, then? One of the big Queensland systems?

The Yunggamurra sank without permission. No matter; he needed time to think. He was getting nowhere on this line. How could he have guessed that the creature would know its own river and nothing beyond? He'd have to find some other approach, look at some of his maps maybe . . . .

The Yunggamurra rose suddenly on his side of the pool and fixed him with a new look - was it mischief? It leapt upward and swung its arm: a catfish came swim-jerking through the air and thudded on the bank. The spirit sank with a gurgle that must be laughter.

Wirren sat frowning at the fish until its jerking took it almost over the bank. Then he put it safely with the other, wound in his line and gathered his gear. No point fishing any more; two big catfish were enough. But why had it thrown him a fish?

He gutted and washed both fish and wondered uneasily if it were safe to eat them from a Yunggamurra's pool. That was the danger of things out of their place: only the People of their own country knew the rules of safety. He decided that a whole river-system infected with love-sung fish would have earned a reputation wide enough for him to have heard, wrapped his catch in a wet cloth and took it back to camp. There he went through the pockets of his pack to find the maps he kept there but had not needed.

The water-spirit disturbed his thinking. He needed to be

free of it without losing sight of its pool. He took his maps a little way up the hill and sat behind a rock from which he could watch concealed. He would study the river-systems in search of new questions, staying in charge without letting the creature confuse him.

The Yunggamurra too was confused. She lay watching shafts of sunlight filter through brown water while she puzzled about the man. He had a power . . . had used it twice . . . and now he left her alone again and free. He questioned and questioned about her river . . . as though he would truly send her home. It was strange. In the stillness of light and the fluttering current came the thought that perhaps the man did not know.

She rose to look at him again. He was not even in sight! It was too much to believe, that he did not know - yet if he did it was almost as strange. To be alone and out of the dark; a night of stars, a day of sun and sweet water, of fish that were truly alive, of weed and moving shadows and a bank fringed with grass. It hardly mattered that she could not leave this one small pool . . . unless the man did not know?

She sank again. Free in this small water-world she needed only her sisters and their play. It was a pity that the man would not play - not the old game again but water-play. She knew he would not; he was too stern. He frowned even when she threw him a fish. Yet he left her alone in the sweet sunny water . . . she forgot him and played.

She chased fish and played with shadows, danced with weeds and rode tumbling in the current. She played dolphin-games, rippling silver in the shadow of her hair. Where the creek flowed in over waterworn rock she curled herself and dammed it till it trickled past her shoulders - then, laughing like bubbles or the trill of a bird, she let herself be washed like foam over the rock's edge and down into the pool.

And Wirrun watched. Hearing the laughter and looking from behind his rock he watched the water-spirit play: sharply sweet as wild honey, magic as sunlight on water, lovely and merry as a girl. He watched with his maps neglected on his knee, half a smile grooving his face and his eyes shadowed in sadness. And he saw the spirit, as the stream tumbled it over the rocks for the third time, suddenly stop its laughing and turn a face full of loneliness and longing to the sky. He had forbidden it to howl but he knew it howled in its heart. It howled for its sisters.

He bundled his maps together and stood up and strode down to the pool. 'The flood washed you into the sea!' he shouted to the spirit. 'Which way? East?'

It looked at him with old eyes that had forgotten him for a while and now remembered. 'The river flows south and west. It turns north to the sea.'

He scrabbled with his maps on the bank. That could be anywhere ... anywhere ... on the southern shore of an eastern inlet, even a small stream on a southern promontory ... memory and longing would make a big system of a creek. He swore and began to smooth and fold the maps. He had to do better than this; there had to be a way. He went heavily back to his camp and built up the fire to grill one of his fish. At once the Yunggamurra went under the water and stayed there.

In the afternoon he went over his maps again looking at rivers and creeks one by one, trying to probe the uncertainties of scale. How many that seemed from the map to enter the sea flowing east might in fact turn north for half a mile or so? How many looping between coastal hills might be said to flow south and west? A new question occurred to him and he turned his eyes, absent and thoughtful, to the pool. The sun had gone out of the gorge and the Yunggamurra had come out of the water to the rocks above the pool. It sat watching him, its eyes as absent and thoughtful as his own.

He was wrung with sudden pain - how pity could hurt! If only it felt warm and alive, and not a thing of mud and slime .... He put the idea angrily away and went to ask his question.

'You went north to the sea but how did you get back into the rocks? From the east?'

It gazed at him absently and answered with its thoughts still on other things. 'From the sea. The sea is not east.'

Under his brows his eyes narrowed. 'Show me the east,' he ordered.

It waved one arm in a careless graceful gesture. 'Into the sun's path. That is not to the sea.'

'How, then? Which way? Where was the sea?'

'It was north. I was blown in the storm. I came south to where the old water trickled off a northern coast.'

The Gulf? Had it after all come in from the Gulf? Then where was the waterfall? He needed more maps - there must be a river with falls - he was about to turn back to camp when the spirit spoke again.

'Your friend is between us,' it said like a seeker who has found a truth.

Wirrun was suddenly rigid, a staring stone. He could not speak. The old moonlit eyes watched him, knowing more than he did.

'It was the game and he sought it but he did not play. He sought peace and found that. Should his peace lie between us?'

Wirrun's voice shook with anger that the creature should dare to speak to him of Ularra. 'My friend was a hero. He died for me.'

'And for peace. For love and peace. Which lies between us?'

'He's not between us,' snapped Wirrun, for Ularra had made it true. '*You're* between us.'

'Is that why you seek my country and leave me free?'

He laughed harshly and touched the stone on his belt. 'I don't leave you free.'

At that the Yunggamurra laughed too, a magpie's note, and slipped down into the water. In a moment it rose again and threw him another fish. Wirrun left the fish flapping and jerking on the bank and strode back to the camp to build up his fire. Angrily he threw on more wood than he needed and built it high. Tomorrow he would take the slimy little brute back to the Nyols for a bit and put a fire in a dead tree for Merv. He would send Merv for some good maps of the Gulf and find that river with the falls.

In the night by moonlight the Yunggamurra sang, but not the love-singing. It sang softly of falling water and swirling bubbles, a song that held no magic but its own. All the same Wirrun raged at its cheek and longed to stride down and forbid it. He did not dare because the Yunggamurra sang so teasingly; he could only sit stiffly in the dark and listen, and watch the spirit play with reflected stars, and later try to sleep knowing that it still played there.

'Oh mate!' he groaned to Ularra's spirit, but this time no help came. The leaves whispered only with a sound like gentle laughter and in time Wirrun slept.

Peeping from her pool the Yunggamurra saw: the hero was sleeping beyond the range of speech with his power beside him. Did he truly think that power would hold her all this time and even while he slept? Because its magic guarded him even in sleep did he think his stone had memory and will? That it would obey him when he did not speak? He trusted to that; he did not know, he did not know!

But if he did not know what use in staying? She might stay for an age and the game never end. Or she might slip away, as she might have in all the times he left her free, and find some pool where no old thing lived and the fish were sweet. What would he do then? Would he think his power outworn and throw it away? Her laughter bubbled softly; but she did not go.

She chased and caught a water-spider. 'He will send me to my sisters,' she told it before she ate it. She smiled with joy and then was still with sadness; for he could not live among her sisters and he was not like other men. She slipped under water to catch a fish and came up again to sing to the moon: softly, not to wake the hero. She sang to him while he slept and when the song was finished broke into laughter. She had thought of a new game, a game to play with the hero.

She would not go; she would only lie on the water like foam and let it carry her. She thought how angry he would

be and laughed like bubbles and birdsong while the current
carried her out of the pool. As she slipped along under
shadowed banks to find a new hiding-place she wondered if
he would throw away his stone.

4

Wirrun woke early and remembered the song of the waterfall. He was surprised and a little disturbed to find that
while he slept he had forgiven the Yunggamurra for
speaking of Ularra. Forgiven or not, he would take it in
hand again and return it for a while to the dark as he had
planned. That would teach it to laugh at him - or rather, it
would give him time to fetch Merv and send or go with him
for maps of the Gulf.

He lit a small careful fire and cooked breakfast, keeping
away from the pool so as not to alarm the spirit before he
was ready. It was very quiet this morning; though he often
glanced secretly from under his brows not once did he see it
peep or play. He thought how he would take it back to the
cave ordering it to stay with the Nyols till he returned. It
would be distressed, of course - indifferently obedient as it
had been at first; but he would remember that there must be
pity. He would explain how soon he would be back, and
that he needed maps to find its country, and that he would
bring it back to its pool in the sun as soon as he could. And
when he did come back it would be glad and laugh teasingly
and sing about the waterfall . . . and be like mud and slime
to touch . . . .

And while he thought of this and frowned over his tea he
heard the singing.

It was a song of the flowing of weeds and the swimming of

fish: silver-sweet, cool, unmistakeable. And it came from somewhere down the creek towards the first camp.

He could not believe it at first. He thought the spirit was singing under water and that this confused the sound. But the sound was clear and sweet and true. He went to listen by the pool.

He ordered the spirit to come up from under the water. It did not come. That as much as his ears told him it was not there. It had left the pool. He stood rooted on the bank shaking with rage and dismay. He had gone into the dark to rescue this thing - treated it with care - sought to find its home! He raged at its ingratitude and broke off to curse, and raged again at himself.

How could he have been so blind, so stupid? To trust that the power would hold it for any time and even while he slept! He had never thought or questioned; he had trusted rather to the creature itself and its longing for its country. To forget it was an eath-thing, wild and lovely and free of evil! To bring such a thing into the light where unwarned men might hear it - and then to lose it! In fright he raged at the spirit again and then again at himself.

And while he raged a cool sweet song came floating up the creek, a song of the freedom of all Yunggamurra and the winding of rivers.

He could not stand there helpless with fright and dismay. He must recapture the creature. If he could find it and creep near - while it was still proudly taunting him with its freedom and before it found its way out of the gorge - if he could take it by surprise while it must obey the power, and order it back to its pool, then he would have time. Then he could return it to the dark till he found its country and never mind how it felt. Let it think it was sent away forever - let it play gallant and indifferent - let it crawl on its lovely silver knees and beg for pity. He knew it better now.

The Yunggamurra sang of sunlight and the slipping of currents.

He listened and tried to judge the distance and examined the cover along the creek. He chose the eastern bank where the hillside rose steep and rocky and the trees came nearer the bank. Then he began his stalking.

He went like a shadow and kept to the shade: creeping between rocks, sliding behind a tree, crawling through bushes. It was slow and he had to stop often to watch and listen. Above the old camp and its pool he chose a rock behind which to crouch, expecting a wait of some time. The creature was sly: it would be hiding as closely as he was.

There was no waiting. The Yunggamurra sat boldly on the bank on his side of the pool, its back confidently turned, combing its long dark hair with its fingers. Wirrun's anger softened: it was like a child, pleased with its own cleverness and sure it had won. Or like a bird that knew nothing of the hunter. He stood up very quietly to examine the hillside and ran stooping through shadows to a treestump below. From there he crept into a gully and went very softly down in the shelter of its bank.

From the mouth of the gully he sighted the spirit again. Still sitting openly in sunlight, back turned, combing its hair. While he watched it began to sing, a song of moonlit nights and the deep sleep of heroes.

Like a shadow Wirrun slid from the gully to the first of the river-oaks. Still singing the Yunggamurra slipped into the water. A moment later the song came from far upstream.

Upstream?

Patiently and slowly Wirrun repeated his stalking in reverse. His heart lifted to see the spirit in its old place where the water ran into its pool. Of course it had never meant to leave him until he had found its country; it had been thoughtless like a child but not sly or cunning. It waited for him now. He came out from the bushes.

The spirit laughed, waved, and was gone. He caught a silvery glint from under a bank lower down.

It was hard to admit that the thing might be playing with him. He frowned heavily, decided that his cover had been poor and took a more careful route back to the old camp. From there he heard singing lower down the creek. He knew that lower pool: its banks were high and well covered, easy to approach. With great care he worked his way down to the river-oaks by the creek; he could move more quickly and freely there and follow the creek itself down. He ran lightly past the pool at the camp.

A light splash behind him - a catfish landed jumping at his feet - a bubble of laughter and a ripple travelling the wrong way, upstream again.

He had to accept it: she was teasing him. Did she think she'd get away with that? Wirrun rubbed his hair into curls: at this rate she would. He was about to push the catfish back into water with his foot when he realised that it was now lunch time any rate, that he might as well catch up on food while he thought, and that while he had no knife there were matches in his pocket. He lit a fire and grilled the fish whole in the old way, and sat on a log to eat it in his fingers and think.

He thought of the creek as far as he knew it, of all its deep holes and shallow places. He thought of the Yunggamurra and how to make a Yunggamurra trap. After that he waited till he heard the singing again far upstream, trying to call him back. Then he ran as quickly and quietly as he could down the creek to the swamp.

He stepped lightly on firm ground around its margin to those stands of bamboo, the tall grass, and felt only one spasm of pain at the sight of the small burnt patch. The next moment he was calculating whether that patch could be seen from the creek. It could not; both before and behind it there were stands that reached farther into the swamp and hid the burnt one. He examined those two stands, listening for the singing as he looked. Soft boggy going - he and Ularra had avoided them for that reason though they reached so much farther into the swamp - but if he placed a dead branch or two between them he thought he might leap fast enough from one to the other.

Quickly, for he knew the speed of spirits and she would be wondering where he was, he found two dead branches and pushed and tugged them into the mud and tested them with his weight. With a smaller branch he made himself a hide in the stand of bamboo farther from the creek. Hidden between tall stems and shaded by drooping leaves he sat watching the place where the creek ran in and listening for a song.

She could not escape from the gorge without passing through the swamp, or pass through that without his seeing her; and if he were her game she would come because he was there. He thought with a pang of guilt that she was only playing, that she would not come this way to escape but only because he had drawn her. It could not be helped. She did not mean to be evil or dangerous but he must not leave her free till he had found her right place. He watched relentlessly.

A long time went by. He played the game of patience as his ancestors would have done: he never moved or forgot to watch but sometimes flexed his muscles silently to keep them ready. A frog leapt on his foot and away again; mosquitoes buzzed and stung; a small lizard stayed for a while on his hand. Over his head the leaves whispered of smoke and Ularra, and his spirit whispered silently back that it did not matter; the cure had failed but now as then he did not want to be cured.

He waited. In an hour he heard the singing close in the creek, a song of hiding and finding. He smiled. After half an hour he glimpsed her at the mouth of the creek, and after another half-hour glimpsed her again. In a while she stood straight, looking at the swamp with something like fear, her eyes old. She drew back and sang a little and was silent. He had to wait again, flexing his muscles.

Then she came. With bravado she walked light-footed over the surface of the swamp: a lovely sight but he only grew tense and ready. She turned his way, bright-eyed and honey-smiling. He waited while she passed the first stand of bamboo and neared the second; then he struck a match and put it to the dead lower leaves.

This was the one second that counted. At the first crackle he exploded across his bridge of branches and struck another match. From there he plunged muddy and leaping through the swamp itself and held her penned against two fires of tall grass.

They were leaping fires now and the smoke rolled from them. He thought she would come springing back in terror and he would catch her - he had even planned to hold the slippery creature by the hair. But she stood frozen, eyes huge, as if she were already caught and could do nothing. Smoke rolled over her and she writhed in it - she dreaded fire - he need not be crueller than he must. He came plunging to catch her in her panic, and wound the dark hair round his left arm and tried to draw her away. She only stood, her feet sinking now in the mud, her lovely silver turning to lead, coughing and writhing, gazing strangely at him and the fires.

'You did know,' she whispered and slumped against his arm.

What had he done? Blood pounding he grasped her, expecting a light floating weight and the slither of mud. But the grey slime had dried and hung in strips and the weight was human and alive. His blood stopped pounding and began to sing fiercely: the Mimi! She never could believe how little a man knew! *Fight it with the smoke of a tall grass* - how could he have known from that? With lungs aching and eyes streaming he carried the Yunggamurra deeper into the smoke. She lay with eyes closed, seeming dead but feeling alive.

He held her over the small licking flames and saw strips of dried slime fall away and burn. He watched with hard disgust something more horrible: a million tiny leeches crawl from the pores of her skin to fall into the flames. Her eyes were fixed on him again, dark with old knowledge and streaming with the tears of smoke. He gazed back stern and pitying, and they wept and coughed together while the smoke rolled, the leeches burnt, the flames sizzled in the swamp and died. She never fought. When there were only dead fires and lazy smoke he lifted her and kissed her and her lips were smoke-dried but soft and cool and clean. He was suddenly ashamed and bewildered.

Squelching in muddy boots he carried her to the creek and up to the first pool. Clothed and booted he walked deep into the pool and held her in water to heal her of the fires. The love-singing was loud in his mind: *are you not here?*

She and not he had come. He had always known, in spite of all pain and enchantment and evil, what he must do with the silver Yunggamurra. But the love-singing was drowned in a clamour of warning bells while he stood holding the living golden girl.

SEVEN

The Water-Girl

I

So he had known after all. She was clothed in flesh; the game was played. What was she now? What should she do?

Her body felt tight and hard, stinging from the terrible smoke. He held her in the water and she felt the current flutter as soft as ever on her skin. But she could not ride the current; she was as heavy as stone. The water flowed past and did not move her at all.

She shifted her legs and arms feeling their new weight and the man let her go. At once she plunged down under water to restore her burnt face and frizzled hair. That was bad, it was frightening. The man had to lift her again because she could not raise herself, and under water she could not breathe and could scarcely see. Had her water-country gone with her silver foamy self? Where were the fish? And the light precise weeds pointing the way of the current?

She had no country left; she must live in the world of dry sunny air. It was too much. She closed her eyes and mind and let her heavy feet move as they would while the man half-carried her a long way to his sleeping-place. There he wrapped her in something soft and laid her in the shade. It was easier to be heavy lying down. She opened her eyes again to watch him.

He was sitting on his pack watching her. He too was scorched by fire.

Neither had spoken at all. They were filled with the silence of time and old magic, of red plains and tall rocks and dark places. It was in their eyes too, and smoked the sunlight.

He broke the silence at last with a few mumbled words: 'I'll call you Murra . . . I'm Wirrun.'

That was a saying fit to break old magic. She lay and listened to it: that he was Wirrun and she Murra. Not a Murra or the Murra but Murra. She had never been so single before. She lay listening to the word while he fell asleep exhausted and until she slept too.

She slept through the rest of the sunlight and through evening into night. When she woke in the last of the moonlight he still slept; the man: Wirrun. He lay in the same place, tumbled on the earth like a child's stick-doll and sleeping like death. He had left the night to her.

There were shadows that sat in the moonlight and watched curiously. She saw and ignored them; she was very young and very old and enduring, and the night was hers. She threw off the soft wrapping with those new heavy legs and arms and lay working them: finding the strength of bone, the pull of muscle, the soft response of skin. She sat up, stood, walked in the moonlight. There were strength and balance to match the weight, and as she used them the weight seemed to drain away. She walked on sticks without breaking them - on grass without bending it. That was not like walking over water or lying on a current; but in the dry sunny world it would do.

Finding the rhythm of her body she swayed and danced - see! she was still slender and light and lovely! Her new darker colour belonged to the shadows of day and night as her old one had belonged to the water. She laughed a little and chased a bandicot. See! She still played! She was herself.

Herself. Murra.

The moon had gone and she was hungry. But she did not know the food of the dry world. She would wake the hero Wirrun and tell him she wanted food. She ran back, not bending the grass, to push him awake with her foot - and had to learn first to stand on one foot only, and then antici-pate the double warmth she would feel when her warm toe met his warm leg. And while she paused over these things she looked down and drew back her foot. She would not

wake him. He slept like death and was tumbled like a stick-
doll. She stole away.

She went back to the only source of food she knew: to her
old pool. There were fish and beetles and spiders waiting,
she knew where. But she was frightened by the water, twice
frightened. Once was because of the way her body had
trapped her when she went under water after the smoke.
Twice was because now water was wrong for her and her
sisters were fierce. He, Wirrun, did not know it; he had taken
her into the water for healing. But she knew.

She sat on the edge of the pool and wished for water and
fish but was afraid. The reflected stars made her smile: how
they would jump if she tried to catch them! She reached
down for one and fell heavily into the pool. And after all she
felt lighter in the water than out, and could stand up and
breathe.

It had happened, then; and her sisters were far away she
did not know where. She found that now she could ride the
water a little - go deep if she took the dry air down with her -
see when she learnt to understand what she saw. She played
water-games that were near enough to the old ones. She felt
the slither of a fish and caught it by habit and feel.

She came out to sit on the rocks and eat the fish and went
in again to catch more. When Wirrun woke at dawn she was
sitting in her old place above the pool and there were three
fresh catfish at his fireplace.

2

When Wirrun woke and saw the lovely flowing shape on the
rocks he would have believed the smoking was a dream if it
had not been for her colour darkening to his own - and for
the three catfish. He was astonished. That limp, stricken
doll of yesterday - already she had learnt to move and swim
and catch fish!

He was moved by the fish. Hadn't he dragged her, lost and

a stranger, out of her world and being into his? She should have hated him and instead she had brought him fish. He lay a while longer pretending to be asleep so that he could watch.

Still playing: combing the waterweeds with her toes. The eyes dew-lit, the smile still sharply sweet, movement as flowing, shape as slender as before. His heart turned over. Maybe she was a girl now, Murra, but still she was not like any human girl he'd ever seen. Lovely, gallant, enduring, and playful as a child. He could not bear the moment of knowing and loving, and got up to light the fire.

Murra at once began to sing about the heaviness of heroes clumsily tumbled in sleep. Her voice was as sweet as yesterday; and as teasing. It was enough to make any man grab her and drag her off into the bushes - except that he was almost sure she did not know it. His ears rang again with a warning like bells and he pushed a hand through his hair.

He had seen his friend changed and knew what it was to bear. He had been warned that there were all kinds of beasts and that there must be pity. It was he who had lit those fires and smoked the water out of the water-spirit; and now she was a stranger in his hands as Ularra had been. He must take care.

He had not meant to take revenge for Ularra; but it lay in his mind like a stone that the revenge was terrible already.

He cut into the song about the heroes with a carefully cheerful shout: 'What's got into these crazy fish, jumping out of the creek like that? Reckon they're safe to eat?'

She considered the question in some surprise and saw that the hero was teasing. She smiled with delight and splashed down into the pool. He smiled too at the splash: a person and not a spirit was swimming.

While the fire burnt down to coals he went down to the creek below the pool to wash himself and clean the fish. There were two immediate problems that he could already see: to clothe Murra, and to feed her with a breakfast cooked at a fire. For weightier problems he needed time; he would concentrate on these two first.

Murra swam down to the outlet of the pool and gave him a third. With her face floating in a cloud of hair she said soberly, 'I should be kept from water. It is the rule.'

'That so?' said Wirrun cleaning fish. 'Who says?'

Again she considered the question. It was a foolish one but she answered. 'It is I who tell you. Murra says.'

He smiled at her. 'If you shouldn't be in the water you'd better come out.'

She sighed, frowned, nodded. 'It is right.' She swam back to the rocks and drew herself out. He hoped his other two problems could be solved as easily.

When he called her to breakfast she came warily, watching the fire, keeping at a distance, yet not as nervously as he had feared. She watched with reserve while he ate but at first refused her own share.

'I have eaten already. While you slept and the fish jumped out of the creek.'

'Never mind. You can eat a bit more. Have a little bit.'

He offered the pannikin. She sat unmoved. He held it a little closer. She gave in, took a piece of fish in her fingers and put it whole into her mouth. She chewed with a thoughtful frown.

'Soft. Dry. The bones wander about.' She added sadly, 'But I must not eat it raw. It is the rule.'

'Why did you, then?'

'I was hungry and you slept. I do not know dry food. And my sisters are not here.'

'Tonight you can try rabbit stew.'

'It will be hard.' She sighed and repeated her experiment with the fish. Full of admiration at her good sense and tolerance Wirrun approached his second problem confidently.

'Better put that on,' he said tossing her a knitted cotton shirt from his pack.

She gazed at it without comprehension.

'Like this,' he pointed out, showing her that he wore one too.

She seemed bewildered. 'Do you not like me, then? Am I

not beautiful?' Since he only looked away with tightened jaw she argued warmly to convince him. 'I am beautiful, that is sure, for all the Yunggamurra are beautiful. There was never a Yunggamurra that was not beautiful.'

He broke in roughly. 'You're as lovely as the day and I like you very much. Put it on.'

She gazed at him with old eyes and made no move to touch the shirt. It seemed that there could be nothing about clothing in the rules. Wirrun tried an appeal.

'I like you so much I don't want other men looking at you. I'm jealous.'

She frowned severely. 'You give me no reason. There are no other men here.'

'But we won't be here forever - there will be men! There's one up there on the cliffs could be watching us now! You need to get used to things like that shirt while we're here.'

To leave the creek between the cliffs for a wider world was a new idea that clouded her courage, but she was not convinced about the shirt. She grew sterner.

'Jealousy can only insult me. Which do you deny in me? - honour or understanding or will?' And, as he looked puzzled, 'Tell me. Am I stupid, weak, or a cheat?'

She was none of those and he had no answer. He saw that he must give her a real reason but it was hard to find. 'It'll keep off the sun and the wind and the flies.'

She disposed of that easily. 'It will save my middle from these dangers. Must my arms and legs and face be chilled and bitten?'

Wirrun scowled. 'I'll get stockings for your legs if you like, and gloves for your arms and a hat for your face. Only I haven't got 'em here.'

She blenched but was not defeated. 'Because you do not need them. Then why this?' She touched the shirt scornfully with one toe.

Wirrun struggled. 'Look. Would you wear that in the river with your sisters? I mean, just say you wanted to: would you?'

She gave a short bubbling laugh. 'I would not.'

215

'Why not?'

'They would laugh and jeer and drive me away. Or tear it off.'

'Right. Well that's why you do have to wear it here.' He saw that she was turning that over in her mind and tried to complete the reasons. 'And because I do; and the only other way is for me to take mine off and I'm not going to. You changed to me and not the other way round.' Because he had still not made it clear he grew heated. 'Look, can't you see? If you're my kind I gotta think about you and take care. If it's the other way round it's easier to forget - think you can look after yourself. Can't you *see* that? Maybe it's stupid but it's true. Did I look after you like a person yesterday? Not me. I made a trap and caught you to keep other people safe.'

Murra gave a small defeated sigh and picked up the shirt. He moved to help her but she frowned and drew away. She examined the shirt for a moment looking sharply from it to Wirrun's own, and struggled into it with a wild waving of arms. She laughed like a magpie at this performance, wriggling inside the shirt to feel it as it fell loosely around her and laughing again when it tickled. Her long hair was still caught inside the knitted neckband. Wirrun, smiling, leaned forward and gently freed it.

That made her look sharply again. She fought her way out of the shirt and back into it, freeing her own hair this time. She took it off and put it on again, and went running down to the pool to lean over the bank and look at her reflection and laugh and laugh. The drooping shoulders of the shirt brought its sleeves below her elbows and its hem hung below her knees. She tugged at it and let go, watching it stretch and pull back. She smiled at its faded blue and poked at its softness with her fingers.

Wirrun watched, sad and smiling. What a shame; but he needed to have her in that shirt. She knew so little of the dry world - but he had made her a person. Very well; she must be treated like a person.

Murra pulled off the shirt and came back carrying it. While Wirrun banked the fire and cleaned up the breakfast things she watched closely and now and then put the shirt on or took it off. It was hard to work while she crouched there watching.

'What's it like being a Yunggamurra?' he asked to turn her attention away.

Her face stilled. She sat fingering the blue knitted cotton. 'It is to flow with the water and ride it; to be one strand among weeds, one voice in the singing. To rise to the sun or sink from the wind as the others do. To be no one but to be many, and to play.' She hesitated. 'That much I can tell. You must be Yunggamurra to know the fierceness of wanting.'

He did not think so.

'What is it like to be hero?' she asked.

He was surprised into an answer and more surprised at the answer. 'It's finding out if you are or not and never mind what they tell you.'

'And are you?'

He had thought so a dozen times and afterwards found he was wrong, but now he could say yes without pride of pleasure or doubt. What had it taken, since the day Tom Hunter came, to turn the name of hero into truth? Work, mainly. And the call of the wind. Ularra's need and sacrifice, Merv Bula's support. Ko-in's teaching and the Mimi's help. Hunger and dread fought off. Pity learnt. A long rugged road with a lot of helpers and more failures. There was no pride yet in being a hero.

Murra came with him to set traps for rabbits, watching sharp-eyed like a hunter and walking soft near the warrens, and he saw that the grass did not bend under her feet. She was not all girl, then; not yet any rate. The traps puzzled her, but when he explained she nodded quickly and seemed to find this way of hunting a game of suspense.

Between warrens she invented other games. Chasing birds was a failure; she frowned in discontent and Wirrun dreamed of taking her with him on the wind. Swinging from a low branch was good; he made her laugh harder by giving her a push. She would climb a tall rock and jump off, gasping with delight and terror. Wirrun jumped with her once. She laughed excitedly when he scrambled up beside her and laughed more at his heavy landing. Most of the time she wore the shirt but he was never sure when he might see her in her own shape, the shirt swinging from her hand or draped over her head and her eyes teasing. Once he had to pick the thing out of a sapling while she watched wickedly and pretended to have forgotten it.

She sat down often, missing the support of water; and Wirrun stood waiting while she rested, or perhaps showed her another of the dry world's foods. His restraint and shyness puzzled her. He smiled, but sometimes with pain - as if she had won the Yunggamurra's game and he had lost? She began to watch him secretly and kept the blue shirt on as often as she remembered.

When they had set traps and dug yams they returned to the camp to eat cold cooked fish. After that, while gold sunlight poured into the gorge and the cliffs hung blue-hazed from the sky, they lay or sat in the shade looking at each other and looking away.

Murra took the shirt off and quickly put it on again.

Wirrun picked a grass-stem and bent it into knots. In a careful voice he asked a question.

'What do you want to do now? - where do you want to go? Back to your own country?' He heard her quivering breath and found her looking at him almost in fear. He frowned. 'Well?'

'We cannot go to my country,' she whispered. 'You do not know the way.'

'If you want to go back I'll find it. Somewhere up where the sea's north.'

'West,' she whispered.

She had said north but he let that pass. 'Don't you want to go back and see your sisters?' She shook her head, staring as if he were some kind of monster. 'Why not, then?'

'Your friend is between us!' she cried. It was almost as though she howled again.

'Murra! No! You forget that, girl. It was an accident. Like a rock falling.'

'He is between us.'

'No, I tell you. He was at first - but not now. I swear.'

'You say it but you cannot show it.'

He smiled a little, brooding, and she watched him with old eyes. 'Ularra wouldn't come between me and a girl.' He looked at her straight and gave her the simple proof. 'You're wearing his shirt.' And, when she seemed not to understand, 'Would I give you that?'

She jumped up, tore off the shirt, ran to the creek and dived in. Going back to the water.

He could only sit and watch with the worry inside him like a stone. If Ularra stayed between them it was she who would keep him there; but what had he said to make her think it? And what could he do? He counted over the possibilities as he had done all morning while he watched her play.

He could drag her off into the bushes like the hungry beast he was - Murra, under whose feet the grass did not bend, whose joy was so sweet to him. The stranger, old and enduring and young as a child, lost in his dry country. And afterwards, what?

Take her back to the city or to some country town? Leave her alone all day in a one-room flat or the yard behind a pub? Take away her play and the freedom of waters and give her instead the dirty streets, a cotton frock and an old stove? No, of course he couldn't. It wasn't possible.

Take her back to her country, then? Saying, 'Thanks for a great time, kid, and don't you want to get a job somewhere near your sisters?'

Or just leave her, perhaps; here in the gorge, safe from the bewilderment of men. Men would be safe from Murra now. She could feed herself all right, and play with the water and the trees until she grew old and wrinkled. And perhaps in time she would find her way out of the gorge: Ularra's way.

There was no solution at all that he could see . . . .

3

For an hour Murra played fiercely in the water while Wirrun watched and brooded. For ten minutes more she played consciously, catching his hungry gaze and rejecting it. After that she climbed on to the rocks and sat cold and dignified and lovely; she was now almost as brown as he was. She began to stare at him defiantly, and at last she left the rocks and came striding back flattening the grass with angry feet.

She seized Ularra's shirt and pulled it on. 'I should be kept from the water,' she accused Wirrun. 'I have told you. It is the rule.'

His blood was pounding again but he was long used to that and could answer coolly. 'Stay out, then. It's up to you.'

'No it is not. It is you who should keep me from the water.'

'I don't keep people from what they want, water-girl. That rule seems like a pretty tough one to me. You've got a right to suit yourself.'

She gazed at him severely and sat on a branch. 'You know nothing about Yunggamurra.'

He was unashamed, being used to this sort of scolding from the Mimi. 'True enough. Never heard of 'em before. But you're not a Yunggamurra. If the rule says you shouldn't go in water, why do you?'

She pushed at a twig with her toes. 'The rule is hard,' she confessed, and added defiantly, 'But I cannot find my sisters, they are not here, they have lost me and cannot come! So . . . I am not afraid . . . . '

'Scared of your sisters? But you want your sisters! You wanted 'em bad enough yesterday any rate. What's up now?'

'Now,' she cried, 'I want to be! As everything that is wants to be! Each thing wants to be what it is and I am Murra. I want to be Murra.'

He was watching her from under heavy brows. 'And so you are. What else can you be?'

'Yunggamurra,' she whispered. 'That is what you should know.'

'Go on, then. You tell me.'

She hunched up a shoulder and spoke from behind it. 'It is a hard game, the Yunggamurras' game. The man cannot win. You think you have won because you have caught and tamed me - '

'Not me, water-girl. I don't hold with taming.' She peeped at him over her shoulder and fingered the blue shirt and he smiled. 'Some day I'll get something fit for you to wear. A rainbow, maybe?'

She brushed aside the teasing and faced him again crying, 'Some day! Some day I shall not be here to put on your rainbow! That is the game. My sisters will find me. They will call and call and I will hear and hear; and one day they will find me in water. They will catch Murra more surely than ever you caught Yunggamurra. They will take me back to the rivers and the games and I will be Yunggamurra again. You should keep me always from the water.'

There was silence for a moment. Wirrun broke it harshly. 'That's it, then. We better find your country and take you back.'

She threw back her head as if he had tried to hit her. 'But I want to be Murra! You have caught me and changed me - I have put on the shirt! Do you not want me? Do you not care?'

He almost did hit her. Eyes blazing he seized a dead branch and hurled it down to the pool. 'Of course I want you!' he roared. 'Bloody little fool! Of course I care! Haven't I followed your bloody singing half across the country and into the Dark? Haven't I watched you playing and left you alone while I tried to work out what was best?' He saw that she was bewildered, trying to follow what he said, and he sat down and fought with himself and whispered curses until he could speak calmly.

'Look. Water-girl. I do want you - it's eating me. But what

am I going to do with you? How can I keep you playing games?' And carefully, slowly, as he found the words, he told her about the world of men. About money. The Happy Folk. Jobs. Flats. About cities and towns and soft-drink cartons dancing in the wind on a pavement. About the People and how they lived, in settlements and on the fringes of towns. About the dry sunny world into which he had dragged her and how she might live better in it alone in the gorge than with him. And as he talked more passionately the ages of knowledge came back into her eyes and they were not dewy but moonlit.

She went to the heart of the matter. 'Do you like to live this way?'

'Like! No. It's the way men live.'

'But you are a hero with a power. Where is this money? I have not seen it. Here you set traps and dig yams and catch fish.'

'You can't catch everything you need in a trap.'

'No? Yet you have said that I might. What do you need more than I need, that you cannot catch in a trap?'

'Shirts. Traps. Other men. To walk over my country.'

'Is it wide, your country? Has it many fish and rabbits? Is it yours?'

From sea to sea . . . spread with broken fences and rusting wire for traps . . . rich in rabbits to be eaten and the skins sold . . . dotted with Inlanders needing wood for their stoves or a day's work now and then . . . . A rich country if your needs were small and you loved it. And his own.

'You have not told me. What more do you need that your country cannot give?'

He rolled over on his stomach and smiled at her tenderly. 'You.'

The moonlit eyes clouded. 'So you must go back to the money. For you have caught me in a trap and I will not stay.'

'If I knew you'd be happy I'd take a chance on that. If you were happy you'd stay, never mind how they called.'

'You followed my singing so far only because you would? It is easy to be called and not to hear?'

'Easy, no. It depends what you want and I wanted Murra. If there was even a chance you'd be happy I'd take it - that's just the ordinary chance of being alive.'

Now it was she who sat listening to something unheard. There was nothing to hear but insects, for the air was heavy with heat though only the cliffs were still gold in the sun. Perhaps she listened to those: to the strong silent singing of stone and the murmur of distance. Or perhaps she listened to a far-away waterfall.

'But there's not a chance,' said Wirrun, 'and it's no good me telling you. You don't know. You don't know being hungry or cold - or work - or getting old - '

'That is not the ordinary chance of being alive?'

'For me it is. It's my world and I can handle it. For you there's the river and your sisters and your games. That's too much of a difference; for me any rate. I can't drag you out of your own world into mine.'

Her eyes were as old as lizards and as soft as moonlight when she stood up. 'If you cannot that is all.' She pulled off the blue shirt and tossed it away and shook the dark hair till it flowed around her like water. 'While I am Murra,' she reminded him firmly, 'you cannot order me with your stone.'

His voice was rough. 'I don't want to. I just said.'

'And I cannot draw you with my singing.'

She turned and ran away over the grass, not bending it, and he heard her splash into the pool. He buried his head in his arms.

Are you not coming?
sings the bright water:
are you not coming?

It was barbed deep into him; he would never be rid of it.

The glimmer-bright water
alight with the glancing
of glimmer-bright eyes.

Knowing her and loving her had changed even his
memories. There was no longer any dread or magic in the
haunting; it was gay and teasing and alive, Murra and not
Yunggamurra.

> *Are you not coming?*
> *sings the dark water:*
> *are you not coming?*

An echo carried down from the cliffs. Wirrun rolled over
suddenly: an echo? And in his mind the singing had never
run so continuously.

> *The dark-flowing water*
> *like washes and ripples*
> *of dark-floating hair.*

He sat up. She was in her old place on the rocks, dripping
wet, leaning forward and singing, smiling her wild-honey
smile and teasing with her eyes; calling him out of his world
of money and jobs and flats, into her world of freedom and
the old ways of his People. When she saw his face she
laughed like bubbles and birdsong and slipped down into
the water.

Not draw him with her singing - what did she think he
was? Tugging off his own shirt he remembered that she
knew what he was as he knew what she was. She would
never be like any other girl; she was Murra, water-girl, half
spirit and half person. And some day she would hear her
sisters calling.

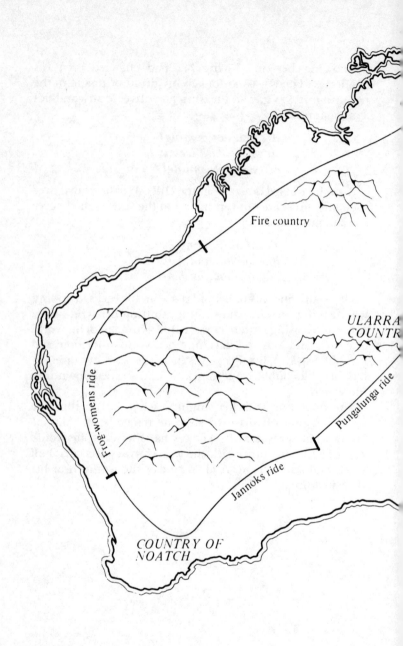

Fire country

ULARRA
COUNTR

Frog-womens ride

Pungalunga ride

Jannoks ride

COUNTRY OF
NOATCH

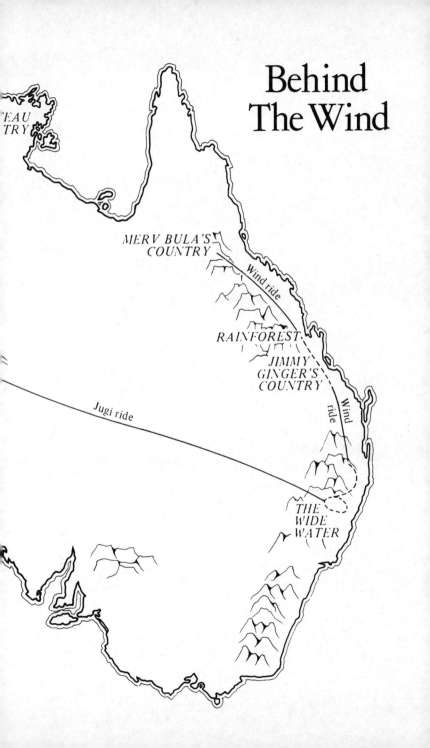

Behind the Wind

Author's Note

I could not have the temerity to invent the kind of experience an Aboriginal Australian might have in a meeting with death, or of such mystical processes as initiation at any of its levels. In section six of this story Wirrun's experiences with Wulgaru are heavily based on original accounts collected by Bill Harney and included in his book *Tales from the Aborigines* (Rigby, Adelaide). The events I have adapted from his two stories 'Mahlindji's Ride with Wulgaru' and 'How Bema Became a Doctor'; but for the appearance and characteristics of the monster I have adhered to first records as given in the story 'How Djarapa Made Wulgaru'.

ONE

A Thing with no Body

I

It was early autumn when Jimmy Ginger went after prawns.
Far away down the world the ice-winds had begun to probe
at the southern coast, and in the tropic north the Wet had
dwindled into a few sharp storms. The brassy sun was soften-
ing into gold but the warm sea held the memory of summer.
All down the long east coast of the old south land the white
race of Happy Folk still swam or ate ice-cream and drank
from frosty cans, while the sun toasted their white skins as
brown as those of the People. The only sign of autumn was a
scattering of more leathery tans: Inlanders on holiday too,
released from their farms at last. But the Happy Folk knew
so little of their white cousins that they did not recognise this
as a sign of autumn.

Jimmy belonged to neither of the white-skinned races; his
dark brown skin was leathered and tanned almost black. He
was one of the People, long in the land before these white
men ever saw it or were a race at all. He stayed away from
them in shy, sulky pride and did his prawning in the mouth
of a creek where mud and mangroves and mosquitoes made
the place his own.

Hidden among the mangroves was an old timber boat, his
to use when it wasn't wanted. He let his net fall heavily from
his shoulder into the boat. It was a pocket-net, with a wide
mouth to be tied between two stays and a long narrowing
pocket to drift along the tide; small as such nets go, but an
awkward weight for one man to handle. Jimmy was used to
it, and strong and active for his age; he manhandled the boat
between sharp mangrove-roots into open water, pushed off
and jumped aboard in one movement, and rowed a little

way frowning at the tide. The rusty rowlocks squealed.

In about five feet of water, near but not too near a belt of mangroves, two leaning poles were driven into the deep, soft mud of the bottom. Between them Jimmy tied his net by the ropes at its mouth, leaving enough slack to allow for the fall, and then the rise, of the tide. He sat for a moment watching the capped detergent-bottles that were his floats: seeing in his mind the mouth of the net gaping wide into the tide, the long pocket feeling along the mud. Then he took the oars, rowed back into the mangroves, stepped out and moored the boat.

He went ashore through mangroves and walked up a rise into banksias, above the mud and mosquitoes. He had left his lunch and two cans of beer up there where the honey-eater birds called rudely. To Jimmy a day's fishing or prawning meant a day alone in the bush. He liked company when the time was right: a quiet drink and a game of cards with friends, a night of talk and singing, or to watch young folk bouncing laughter off each other. But now that he was older he liked to come often to the scrub, to let the quiet flow into him and to remember.

He ate bread and cold mutton, drank one can of beer very slowly and left the other to keep cool in a spiky bush of heath. He watched birds and lizards, sang a little to himself in a heavy drone. He lay back under banksias to watch the silver undersides of leaves and the black wicked faces of cones and the blue shine of sky beyond; and in the warm shade he slept.

He woke aware and tingling, rigid except for the hair that lifted and crawled on the back of his neck. Something was near—something bad. He lay still to listen and look.

There was nothing he could see or hear—no snake's rustle or slither, no smoke or crackle of fire, no sound even of birds. Slowly, slowly, he stirred and raised his head: nothing but a grey spider on grey bark. And still every tingling nerve and creeping hair of Jimmy Ginger told him that something bad was near.

And that was very bad, for an unknown evil is one a man

can't guard against. Little by little, head turning and heart bumping, Jimmy sat up—stood—searched quietly near at hand. Nothing. He stood waiting, sure yet now not sure. Some old bad thing had been near, some menace that must have come to him out of the land itself in one of its dark moods. He had lived a long time with the land and the People and knew of things like that; but had it passed?

The colour of the sky between branches told him that the afternoon was going. He must not get trapped in this place by night and there was still his net; the tide would be filling. In a while he wiped his forehead and went to fetch his second can of beer. He needed it now.

It winked out of its bush, still cool enough for Jimmy. He parted the prickly branches with one hand to reach in with the other, grasped the can and saw through parted twigs the grey sandy soil beneath the bush. And the thing was there.

It was nothing that he knew. It had no body. It was just a pair of red-glowing eyes in some dark, rough sort of face. But the eyes looked at Jimmy, looked deep into him before he could move.

He sprang off with a yell and ran: down the slope into the mangroves, stumbling on roots and shoving his feet through risen water. He reached the boat, clambered or fell into it and sat shaking. The mangroves and the shadowed water enclosed him. When he could use his hands he pulled on the rope to bring the boat back to its mooring, fumbled with the knot to untie it, seized the oars and pulled in short hard jabs. When he reached open water he shipped the oars, wrenched open his can of beer and drank.

It had been bad all right, and worse because he didn't know the thing. The old stories told a man what he might see and what he ought to do, and Jimmy knew them. But he'd never heard of a thing like this in his country. He drank and shivered: lucky to be here, in the boat on the water with the old detergent-bottles floating near . . . but night would come and he had to get home.

He finished the beer, dropped the can with a clatter and roused himself to pull to each leaning pole in turn and unfasten his net. Then he began to haul it in. It came heavily, tugging against him; he had to put his mind to it and that was good. When he had it half in the boat, wet and heavy about his legs so that he could hardly move them, he glanced down to free his feet. And again the thing was there . . . lying in the bottom like some horrible crab . . . looking at Jimmy with those red-glowing eyes that he somehow knew a man should never see.

Jimmy gave an old man's hoarse scream and took a hobbled leap—overbalanced with the weight of the net—grabbed at it as he went overboard into deep water. The boat slid hard away into the current. Jimmy struggled and fought with his net while the boat with its shipped oars moved gently off on the tide.

Someone found it two days later stranded on the beach outside the creek, its oars still neatly shipped and an empty beer-can rolling in the bottom. It was a week before they found Jimmy Ginger bobbing in the surf, still tangled in his net.

The newspapers called it another fishing accident and mentioned the beer-can lying in the boat; but the People of that country shook their heads and talked quietly together. The weather had been calm all that week. They had known Jimmy well. He was not a man to drink too much alone, in the scrub or on the water, and not a man to tangle himself in his own fishing gear. The People found his death strange and troubling and told some of the old stories again when they were together at night.

2

Stories of Jimmy's death went from man to man among the People of his country, and up and down the coast to other eastern countries of the land. But none of them told of a thing with no body and with red-glowing penetrating eyes in a rough unfinished face. Nobody in the countries on that coast knew of such a thing. In all the east only one other man saw that face, and he did not speak of it or know of Jimmy Ginger.

He was a broad-shouldered dark-eyed young man with the heavy brow and the wide smile of the People. They called him Wirrun, though he had a white man's name among the Happy Folk in the town where he had grown up and worked. Now he had given up towns and jobs and cheap lonely rooms to live free in the old way with his new wife Murra; or as near the old way as they could come. They walked where they chose in the lonely back country and took what the land gave them of roots and fish and possum; took rabbits in wire snares that they could always replace from some broken-down fence; stayed a day by a creek where the fish were good or the weather called them to swim; and only now and then, when they might need something that had to be bought with money, would Wirrun look for an Inlander with a starved woodheap or a half-painted shed neglected.

Now they were walking a plateau-country under the north-pointing finger of the Cape; and they travelled east because Murra was afraid of the west. On the day Jimmy Ginger went after prawns they had found a deep gorge with a good creek in it; and it seemed to them both that this warm, sheltered stillness where the shadows would lie cool in the afternoon was a good place to spend a day and a night. They had set a few snares before they swam in a deep pool of the creek. When they were tired of swimming Wirrun lay and dozed in the sun on the bank while Murra knelt beside him and delicately plastered his head with mud. Her lovely face was sharp with mischief.

Wirrun stirred, and she grew still and alert as a bird. He muttered; turned his head; felt the weight of mud and woke and grabbed. But Murra had sprung away and stood laughing at him. He struggled up wiping trickles of mud from his eyes and pretending to be still stupid with sun and sleep; he knew already that barring accidents he couldn't catch her, but another thing he had learnt was when and how to try.

At the right moment he lunged, shouting "Got you!" But he had only succeeded in closing the distance.

She ran like a shadow, nothing moving under her feet, and he thudded after her, scattering pebbles. She doubled past him to a twisted ti-tree that hung over the creek and sprang at a branch. "Clumsy!" she called in a high sweet voice as she swung into the tree.

He knew what would happen—she would dive and hide in the water and be lost for half an hour. He flung himself at the tree and climbed. He was nearer than Murra had thought. She ran far out along a branch and he followed rashly. The branch sagged, cracked—Murra dived and Wirrun tumbled. The water closed over them both together. The shatter-and-crash of water rang through the gorge with the ringing of their laughter.

The mud was washed from Wirrun's hair.

They came out of the water, Murra bringing a fat cat-fish for when it should be wanted, and dried themselves again with a ragged towel. Wirrun pulled on his frayed shorts and fastened a belt from which hung a bag of netted twine with a grey-fur bundle inside. Murra drew over her head a man's shirt of knitted cotton, faded blue and long enough to hang past her knees; she lifted her long wet hair free of the neck and shook it.

Dressed, they went to inspect their snares. They had one young rabbit. Murra took it out with a hunter's cry of triumph, stroked the trembling thing with a gentle finger, broke its neck with a sudden quick twist and stood stroking the fur again. It was Wirrun who had taught her how to kill a rabbit quickly and painlessly, but he had to crush an impulse to take it roughly from her hands.

By now there was no sun left in the gorge.

"It'll come dark pretty quick down here," he said. "Do you want to take that poor thing back to the creek? I gotta find wood for a fire."

She nodded and turned back. She was bored by wood and suspicious of fire. Wirrun would light the fire and do the cooking, but she might clean and prepare the catch unless she found some other game to play.

He watched her go and began to hunt for firewood, throwing the pieces he found into a heap from which he could gather them later. There was a dark stand of she-oaks a little way off; fallen branches from those would make a quick, hot fire. He worked towards them.

They were tall old trees standing close, and between them it was already twilight. One of them was dead, half fallen and held in the branches of another. He ripped off long strips of the dead bark to act as a fire-starter and moved around it to look for broken branches. As he passed the torn-out roots he thought something glowed among them and bent to look.

Red-glowing eyes looked back.

Wirrun's face darkened and he stood up quickly. His hand had flown to the net bag at his belt. In a moment, still gripping the bag, he bent among fallen strips of bark and looked again.

The eyes looked back, knowing and menacing. There was no body. The clumsy face lay pressed against the soil.

Wirrun felt through his veins a flare of angry hate. He

felt in his palm the roughness of the netted bag, and inside
it the soft winding of possum-fur cord, and inside that the
hardness of stone and the stone was throbbing. He spoke to
the face.

"Get out."

It was gone. But he did not know where. In the darkness
of the oaks he stood frowning. He was no stranger to things
like this: secret shadows and shapes, earth-things that the
land had bred and few men ever saw. Wirrun had seen and
spoken to some and was wary of them all; good or evil by
chance, most of them, and knowing neither good nor evil.
But none had burnt him with sudden angry hate as this one
had. It made him careful.

He kept his hand still on the netted bag and strode into
the light of the late afternoon. Leaving his firewood where
it lay he went quickly back to the creek, looking with narrowed eyes as he went for the patch of blue that meant Murra,
safely there. He came on half running and when he reached
her began at once to stow things back in his pack. Murra stood
staring, the cleaned fish in her hands.

"Wrap it in leaves and give it here," he told her. "We're
moving out."

"But the sun has gone! Even from above it is going!"

"I know that—it'll be dark by the time we get up there. So
we better move. We're not stopping here."

She saw that there was a reason and ran to pull leaves
while he filled a waterbag at the creek.

The light drained away as they climbed out of the gorge.
A thousand miles to the west the land still lay in sunlight
but east along the coast it was dark already. That long coast
lay under stars with a pale ruffle of sea along its edge; wearing scattered brooches of lights where the towns were clustered, and here and there pricked with a light from an Inlander's home. But most of it, lying under the edge of
night, was in darkness.

It was a darkness that lived and moved, full of the small,
separate lives that hide by day: the flutter of moths, the

bumbling of beetles and the soft beat of feathers. Possums scolded in trees, bandicoots explored gardens for snails, wallabies swung silently over fences to investigate crops. And among them were inhabitants even older and more secret, the earth-things and powers and spirits of the land. And these were restless and angry, and some of them afraid.

Near the Cape one of them, an Anurra bouncing in pursuit of frogs, found in its way a thing that was a stranger— a thing with red eyes and no body. It bounced off again in sulky rage. Farther south in a scrap of rain forest a group of small man-shaped Dinderi stood gazing at red eyes among the ferns. Though the thing was a stranger to them too they did not order it off but grunted gravely to each other and went away and left it. A long way to the south a Dulugar, spindle-legged and hairy, found its mountain path blocked by a strange red-eyed face and flew off muttering among trees. Soon the eastern night was filled with angry mutters and whispers. Even old enemies whispered together like friends.

"Not of us," they whispered, and, "A dog-like thing, out of its place." And again, "Not our kind. A Man is needed." And as nights went by the whispers passed along the coast and grew.

"Where is the Hero, the Fighter of Ice, the Man with the power?" they whispered. "Where is the Hero?"

3

Wirrun and Murra had spent over a week in a gully, no more than a crease in the tangle of water-carved ridges that led to the coast. It was not a very good gully. Its trickle of creek fed only one small pool, and fish and yams were scarce. They stayed because Wirrun had come upon an Inlander who, like most, needed more help than he could afford. This one, caught in a late-summer accident of fire, was willing to pay a shabby passing stranger for a few days' fencing while he himself mustered several hundred head of straying stock; and as their way east brought Wirrun and Murra nearer to the countries of the Happy Folk Wirrun felt a need of money and accepted the job.

Murra did not approve. On several days she followed him from their camp to his work, within easy sight of the Inlander's white timber house; and since she wore only the old blue shirt that a white man would find outlandish, and since she put on her sharply teasing face and would not go away, Wirrun worked with one uneasy eye on the house and the other watching for a stranger.

Her reasons for disapproving were several. "I need not trouble to stay with you," she told him coldly, watching him work, "for you leave me alone to go and play with your crazy job and the money. You do not want me."

He could only mutter, "You know better than that," and hammer all the harder at a steel post. He could never appeal to her, or try to hold her with reminders of how alone he had been before she came or the sense of home she had brought. He could not remind her of his one friend lost— and nameless now, since the dead must not be named— drowned in a dark cavern far away so that Wirrun might live, and Murra too. But perhaps his face reminded her for she said no more on that line.

"Why do you need this crazy money?" she demanded in- stead. "You have told me it is finished, all this of the towns and jobs and money; and already you seek it again. Do we not camp where we please and take what we need? Why do you look for money?"

"To buy you a dress," he said patiently, having explained before when he first accepted the job. "That old shirt won't hold together another month—or my shorts either, come to that. One of these days we'll run into someone and sooner than you think. I won't have 'em looking at you like some- thing the cat dragged in."

She was indignant. "But for this I wear the shirt, that they will not stare—you have told me! Am I not beautiful in the shirt?" She dragged it off and stood in her own lovely shape.

"Put it on," ordered Wirrun sternly, his eyes on the house. "I don't try and teach you about catching fish. Don't you try and teach me about gear."

After a moment she pulled the shirt on again. "I wear it only to please you," she said grandly, "and not for any need. I am beautiful without your dress, a thing I cannot help, for I am Yunggamurra. To be Yunggamurra is to be beautiful when the cat drags you."

"To be Yunggamurra is to be tickled if you don't watch out. Any rate, you're not. You're my wife now." But he knew that in spite of his Clever Business, the magic with the smoke, she would always be partly Yunggamurra.

He had found her in a cavern deep under the ground, a Yunggamurra from some far-off river, a silver water-spirit with a song to trap men; carried off in a storm and lost and caught in the dark, no longer knowing where her country lay. He had brought her out, but since neither of them knew

her home he could not take her there; and so he had smoked
the magic out of her and made her a golden-brown girl and
his wife. For Wirrun she had put new gold into the sun.

He named her Murra. He dressed her in the old blue
shirt and she was lovelier than any human girl, lovely as
rain in sunlight or weed in water. He taught her tenderness
and she taught him laughter. He showed her the foods of
her new dry world, and how to set snares and roast yams in
a fire, but not the skills of hunting and finding; she drew
those skills out of the land itself and had done so for an
age before the coming of white men.

Even when she told him of the wicked Yunggamurra
game, and that one day her sisters would come to take her
away from him, he refused to be afraid.

"If you want to stop with me you'll stop," he said.

She looked at him with eyes as old as rivers or moonlight.
"You followed my singing only because you would? It is
easy to be called and not to come?"

He laughed, for now he was happy and had forgotten that
burning torment. He had only to watch her in the old blue
shirt running like sunlight over unbending grass, or sitting
alert by the fire she did not yet trust while the cloud of
dark hair moved of itself on her shoulders as if it still
floated, and he tingled with a delight he could never speak.
He said, "I'd be following yet if I hadn't caught up. I was
lonely for you, water-girl—needed you all my life."

Once, he could tell her; not again. After that he could only
watch and hope that the water-girl was happy. He had
watched her playing in creek after creek, all the water-games
she had invented to replace the games of her sisters. He had
seen the old blue shirt flowering high in the branches of
gums, turning him cold with fear while she invented tree-
top games. Wherever they stayed, even for a day, it was the
same: undefeated, enduring, Murra filled that place with
laughter and made it her own—and left it with pretended
indifference, looking back. No place, it seemed, would

hold to her; but she had seemed happy in all of them till now.

"What's wrong, any rate?" he asked her. "Don't you like it here?"

She lifted her head as if she were listening, and the dark hair moved on her shoulders. "I feel the west behind me," she said, and shivered.

Wirrun was glad when the fencing was done and he came back to camp for the last time with the money in good ready cash in his pocket.

Murra was there already, catching yabbies. He showed her the money. She poked it with a cautious finger and gave him a sly upward look. He snatched the money away and put it back safe in his pocket in case it should end at the bottom of the pool. She laughed and turned back to the water, dipping a rabbit's tail gently in to coax another clawed yabby within reach of her fingers.

Wirrun went to rake out the ashes of their old fire and lay sticks and leaves for a new one. He brought wood from a heap he had built in the shelter of stringybarks, lit his fire and set stones to hold a billy for boiling the yabbies. By then it was dusk; he could just see Murra at the top of the pool where the water trickled in, playing one of her water-games. It was an old one that she had played in many pools: sitting in the space between stones through which the water flowed, damming it with her body while it built up behind her, letting herself go with it at last to wash down into the pool. He smiled a little and went to bring more wood, taking his torch for it would be darker still among the stringybarks.

They were young trees. Leaves brushed his face as the twigs parted to let him through. He flashed his torch at the woodheap, reminding himself to add batteries to his shopping-list for the day when he reached a town. The torch-beam wavered as he went forward, making shadows jump aside and leaves flash silver-green. He stopped suddenly and turned the beam to one side: there was surely a shadow that had not jumped aside. His hand closing on the net bag at his belt, Wirrun spoke to it.

"What are you?"

The shadow moved. It was a shadowy woman-shape with horned shoulders, a shape he knew even before it spoke. It was the earth-thing Yaho, from his old country in the south. It said, "I come from Ko-in, Hero."

Wirrun relaxed. Ko-in: the ancient spirit-hero, the tall wise shadow that had sent him to find the netted bag he wore with its secret stone of power; Ko-in who had named Wirrun hero. Ko-in had sent this messenger before.

"What does Ko-in say?" he asked the shadow.

"That he must speak with you. He calls you to his country, to light your fire in the old place. Ko-in says that if you come fast you may come ahead of trouble."

"Hum," said Wirrun. "Maybe I don't travel as quick as trouble. It's a long way. Ko-in, now: he travels very fast. If he's in a hurry can't he come and talk here?"

"A time of trouble is no time for a Great One to be out of his place. But all countries are yours and your place is where you are."

"Hum," said Wirrun again, but he could not refuse a summons from Ko-in. "Tell him there's a lot of strange road between me and him and the winds don't always blow right but I'll come as soon as I can. It won't be under a week or two."

"The Great One knows you travel at a man's pace but he bids you travel safe. He sends a warning."

"That's something. Let's have it, then."

"Keep your hand near the stone of power—"

"No worries. Tell Ko-in I'm not a kid."

He thought the shadow gave a small malicious smile as it went on: "—and know always that you have mated with magic. It will swallow you or you will grow."

Wirrun frowned. "That's my worry. Get yourself back to Ko-in and say I'm on my way."

The shadow melted into others. Wirrun gathered his

armload of wood and went back to the fire. He thought of
the maps in his pack: east to the coast and south, it must be
a thousand miles—most of them fenced from now on, and
under the watchful eye of some Inlander. And what sort of
trouble worried Ko-in that he couldn't handle for himself?

Mated with magic . . . that angered him. He wasn't the
first. Sure, he didn't know the Yunggamurra or their country, but tales were told at campfires across the land of men
who caught and married water-spirits. But *keep your hand
near the stone:* Ko-in must know his hand was never far from
it. There must be some special danger that Ko-in dreaded;
something that did not keep to its own country as men and
spirits should do but lay all along Wirrun's road. He thought
for a moment of menacing red eyes that glowed in a face
without a body, but he put the memory aside. His own
quick angry hate had made him believe those eyes meant
something else. He had not told Murra about them.

He did not tell her, either, while the yabbies boiled and
she crouched near watching them turn red; or later while she
and Wirrun ate and talked about this summons from Ko-in;
or while they packed food and gear to be ready for the journey. He did not tell her about the face until much later. Yet
tonight, making ready to travel on east as she had wished,
her eyes seemed full of shadows and questions.

They left the gully next morning when the heights were
lit with early sun. They climbed up to those heights, for
even white men, if they had to travel this country at all,
knew better than to travel by the waterways and rugged
slopes. Wirrun drew down his brows against the sun and
tried to peer east, for he wanted to reach the coast by a
route as direct as gorges and gullies would allow and from
there to travel south by faster roads.

Even so early the wind pushed at them fitfully, for that
was a windy country, standing as it did above the coastal
plains and reaching away to the west. As the sun rose higher
and Wirrun could see east more easily, the wind rose too,
and pushed more roughly and pointed another way with

trees. And Wirrun began to look sharply and feel the wind, for the way it pointed was nearer to his true one: south-east. At last he stopped.

"This is a right wind, girl," he said. "Will we take it?"

She looked frightened for a minute and then excited. She had heard about winds from Wirrun, and had played in tree-tops that were bending as these did. She waited, watching him.

He opened the net bag that held the power and unrolled a length of the grey cord it was wound in. The end of the cord he tied to her wrist for safety, in case she should lose hold of his hand. Then he settled the pack on his shoulders more firmly and took a good grip of the net bag in one hand and Murra's own hand in his other and swung her round.

"Come on, now—turn round and run into it."

They ran hand in hand into the wind.

It took them and tumbled them and flung them above trees. They clung together breathless and laughing. The wind tossed them higher and spun them around, they rose into it like swimmers lifted on some enormous wave and hand in hand were carried away: south-east in sunlight.

TWO

*The Hero and the
Water-Girl*

I

Murra rode the wind with an instant skill that made Wirrun feel heavily earth-bound—her delight came to him through her fingers, throbbing like a pulse. In a moment she slipped her hand out of his and rode free on the lengthening cord of fur. Lifting like a feather she cried out: "I can see it—I can see it! The wind is a river!"

He too could sometimes see the stream and eddy of the wind as he had seen heat rising from a roof. Now he saw a Yunggamurra riding the stream: slipping in and out of currents, hanging like foam above depths, wrapped and unwrapped in her floating hair; and he saw with a pang that he, who lent her the power to ride it, could never fully share with her the river of the wind.

They crossed low over a ridge and she darted to the end of the cord, laughing like bubbles, to chase a startled magpie. She turned to wait for him, and he saw the laughter go out of her as she looked into the blue-hazed sky of the west.

He scolded her. "We're going ten times faster than we could down there. What are you scared of, any rate? Do you think your sisters'll come whizzing down out of the sky and grab you? They're water-spirits, aren't they? They'd be dried up into dust."

She looked at him gravely for a moment, then smiled. He reached for her hand and pulled her closer. "I wish you'd just forget about 'em. I told you before—if you want to stop with me you'll stop. People do what they want when they come right down to it."

She said nothing for a time but rode the wind beside him, looking down at the patterns of the land. When she spoke again it seemed not Murra, the teasing girl who had just chased a magpie, but something old and grave that spoke with warning.

She said, "Look below you, Hero. There is the land from which we are made, you and I, and does it not keep its own laws? Once it raised itself up and swallowed seas; they lie under it still. My kind remember them for we live long and remember much. It had proud rivers and tall forests then. See it now, this land, tired and old, worn down with sun and wind; for that is the law of lands. Am I more than the land? Must I not keep old laws? Look down, Hero."

He looked. The tired heights circled their secret valleys; stranded rivers vanished into hidden, guarded waters. The rough old rock was wearing into soil, the trees turned their grey leaves edge-on to the sun. He said soberly, "She don't give in, any rate; she creeps back another way."

Murra's eyes were as still and concealing as moonlight.

The day drew on. The country, grey-stubbled with forest, gave way to rolling grasslands with odd single peaks lifting out of them here and there. By late afternoon there were greener hills and sometimes, beyond them, a glimpse of the eastern sky low down, edged with a shimmer of sea. Wirrun had begun to watch for roads, for forest with water and a town near at hand. He could feel the wind beginning to fumble and had brought himself and Murra lower by loosening and tightening his grip on the stone of power.

They came down on a ridge with a road along its western side, a creek at its base and its spine clad in the rich dark green of rain forest. Wirrun had seen the roofs of a town under its southern tip: he could do his shopping early tomorrow while Murra waited safely in the forest.

They came tumbling into long grass near the road, Murra bubbling with laughter as she tried to stand. "I am too heavy!" she cried. "I have been too long in the wind's river and yet I saw no fish. Where were the fish?"

"Feathered fish," said Wirrun drawing her up. "I saw you go after a few." He took her quickly across the road, under a fence and into the forest.

They passed through its ragged edges of lantana and bracken and inkberry; beyond these the forest received them into stillness and a green water-light. Fern and fungus, moss-cushion and palm and downward-looping liana were posed as precisely as weed or sponge in a pool. Buttressed trunks stood close and soared high, beyond staghorn and crowsnest ferns clinging to upper branches, up and up to the green-lit surface of leaves. Murra walked between them wondering.

They went deeper in where a small plume of smoke would be lost before it cleared the forest canopy, and found a place with damp stones to build a fireplace and a springy bed of leaves to sleep on. There was no wood for a fire; all that had fallen was rotting with damp and green with moss. Wirrun left Murra to unpack what they needed for the night while he went back and forth the way they had come bringing wood from outside.

Murra curled up in a lap of great roots to feel the solemn height of the forest . . . and beyond it the strange eastern sea . . . and westward, reaching across the world, the old worn land over which they had come. It was one great quiet into which she sank, not hearing Wirrun come back and drop a load of wood in the leaves and go away. She let the quiet enfold her like water . . . and felt in it a trickle of something warm and needing . . . something small and simple and profound. Murra, the ancient hunter, smiled a little; she closed her eyes and went seeking, following that trickle of need.

A small thing, alive and old in the land. Driven by some warm dark need. A turtle—a snakeneck—working at a hole near the creek. Now she began to lay—her brooding satisfaction flowed into Murra too . . . When Murra opened her eyes Wirrun had brought another load of wood and was laying the fire.

"There will be turtle-eggs tomorrow," she told him.

"Good," said Wirrun to whom this sort of thing was no longer new. "I walk half a mile to get a bit of wood and you find turtle-eggs just sitting here."

She smiled and began to unpack, and then to cut up a rabbit they had brought.

They were both tired from the long day of sun and the pushing of wind at their backs. They built up their fire and put the rabbit on to stew, and while it cooked the dark came down in the forest while outside the sky was still streaked with red and gold. The dark brought curious rustlings, and small glinting lights like fireflies. Murra watched and listened sharply for a moment and then let her mind follow other sounds: the grunt of a possum, the screech and quarrel of fruit-bats in some fig. But Wirrun laid his hand on the power and spoke to the little lights.

"Come and talk."

They came slowly and unwillingly, little dark man-shapes that gathered at the edge of the light. It was their eyes that caught the fire and glinted red and yellow.

"What are you?" he asked them.

They answered in grunts with their eyes on the fire. "Dinderi, we." "Older than People."

He understood. They were claiming not only the age of all spirits but a precedence in the land. For a time that flowed back into dreaming, his People had lived in the land till it made them its own; and into their fears and dreams it had sent the earth-things. They and the People were related; they inhabited each other's lore and shaped and were shaped by it. But a few earth-things, like the tenuous Mimi of the north, were old beyond even the dreaming of the People—shaped, maybe, from the fears and dreams of long-forgotten men. This was the precedence that the little Dinderi claimed.

He offered them stew but they shook their heads though their eyes never left the fire. He made another guess.

"You want fire? Take some of ours, we got plenty."

But this too was the wrong guess. All the eyes darted fiercely at him and away, voices buzzed with anger.

"Ours, all ours!" "Plenty fire, we!" "You got ours!"

Wirrun was astonished. "*This* fire's yours?"

"All ours,". growled one of them again. "Older than People, we. Got fire. People came, got no fire. Stole it. Ours."

Wirrun considered. There were many tales of the coming of fire, but he was in the country of the Dinderi now and wanted no ill-will.

He said, "We thank you for fire. Take ours any time— it's yours."

They stirred, blinked at the fire now misting under ash, and in a little while drifted away.

"They are pleased," murmured Murra, having placed the direction of the fig tree. "I hear them whisper beyond the fire."

That troubled him. He sat staring into the dark for some time before he spoke. Then he said, "Don't you feel sad? Listening to 'em out there—and shut off? Don't you want to go back?"

To be a silver ripple on the water, he meant, a thing made of sunlight and rivers; to be one in the games, one voice in the singing; to live long and remember much.

She knew what he meant. "No," she said, "for then I had no name. There was nothing to name. There were only the Yunggamurra, all as one. But I am Murra, and she is the wife of Wirrun. And the fire is warm, and though you spoil the food with cooking yet it is sweet. I want to be here with you."

They sat in their separate silences, the shabby young hero and the water-girl in a blue cotton shirt, and each was suddenly alone. For he knew that with his gift of a name came other gifts that she must choose though she had no need of them: his gifts of cold and hunger and illness and age and death. And she, even while she chose them, knew that the choice was not hers to make; her choice was not allowed. So they sat apart and the dark whispered and listened.

In the morning they woke early and breakfasted on yams and tea. Then Wirrun left Murra alone again—for the last time, he told her—to find turtle-eggs and figs while he went to do his shopping. She watched with reserve while he went down the road with a long stride and a sack on his shoulder, for she did not trust this game of shopping. And he went like a child to a party, not only to end his worry about a blue-shirted beauty in the land of the Happy Folk but dreaming also of sausages and flour.

2

Wirrun followed the road down the ridge until he saw below the roofs of the town; and then he stopped. He had been away from them for so long that he had forgotten towns. It suddenly seemed that in a world where Murra lived these could not also be real. But there was the town, quite real, and he knew it well though he had never seen it before.

He went on down: to the hot black streets and hot white pavements that he knew. There it was, small but true to its kind—the shuttle of cars and people, the papers shuffling in the gutters, the shop windows brilliant with happiness carefully priced. It was a child's balloon, kept aloft by its own tensions, and he was a child going to the party. He found the supermarket easily since he knew it best of all and took his trolley and began his round of the shelves.

Flour, matches, salt, tea—and sausages; torch batteries, a comb; tough drill shorts, knitted cotton shirts, rubber sandals . . . he had reached the racks of cotton frocks and was suddenly timid. A girl should choose her own.

He chose two in shining cotton, one watery-blue and one golden-green, both hanging loose from shoulder-straps and each with a large square pocket that he thought might often hold yams or a dead rabbit. Then he remembered soap and a towel, and went back for them.

He had to pass a table of cheap, bright knick-knacks meant to be bought and given away, and he paused there to look and smile. He would have liked to bring Murra a gift—something extra—a moment of astonished delight that she could throw away later if she chose; but he thought that was more than he could manage. He grinned at the idea of bringing her a fancy tile, a china cat, a brass ash-tray, wooden salad-servers, plaster book-ends, a red-laquered trinket-box . . . Idly he opened the box. It was lined with mirrors. He bought it.

He was out of the store in half an hour, striding more slowly up the ridge with his sack heavy on his back and some of his money still in his pocket: a margin of safety in the countries of the Happy Folk. He had reached the rain forest within two hours of leaving it, and the day was still young.

Murra had dug yams as well as turtle-eggs, and cooked them in the last of the fire. She had gathered figs and lillipillis to eat along the way. She gazed in fascination at the packets and plastic-coated packages that emerged from Wirrun's sack, pushed an exploring finger into the sausages and chewed one end of the comb.

He offered her the dresses a little doubtfully. "Next time you can come and pick your own."

"Two!" she cried in bewilderment, and took them and sniffed at their colours and stroked their glazed shine while he explained why there were two and how the shoulder-straps worked and showed her the pockets.

"You did not say there would be pockets!" she cried, having envied Wirrun his. She tore off the shirt and began to pull the dresses on, one after the other. He left her to do that while he changed his own ragged shorts and shirt for new ones. By then she happened to be wearing the blue dress, so he quickly folded the other and stowed it in his pack with the old blue shirt. She looked at him sharply.

"You are new like rain. We are both very fine. Yet you say they will not stare."

"They can stare all they like now we're fine," said Wirrun. He reached into the sack for the package he had left till last and handed her the red-lacquered box.

"What is this?" she asked, not taking it.

"It's for you. It's a present."

She took it carefully. "Fire," she murmured, feeling the colour with her fingers and running one of them along the line of the lid.

"Open it," he said, and showed her how.

She lifted the lid—dropped it quickly—lifted it again a little way, peeped in and closed it again. She whispered, "Water . . . water and fire . . ."

"And you," said Wirrun; but she knew the face in the box was hers for she had often seen it looking at her out of water. She stood opening the box, peeping quickly and closing it again as if the water might run out, while Wirrun managed to store everything in his bulging pack. He lifted the canvas water-bag to strap it in place, found it empty and muttered with annoyance. He had once been carried far on his way by a wind, and set down in a wilderness, leaving most of his supplies and water behind. It was not a mistake he wanted to make twice, even though they were already late in starting.

"I will take your crazy bag to the creek and fill it any rate," said Murra, perky with the excitement of her red box and her new pocket.

Wirrun grinned. "Good girl. Wait by the fence. I won't be long. Just gotta stretch these straps a bit and make the fire safe." He passed her the water-bag and she went off between tall trunks, the bag in one hand and the trinket box in the other, singing softly.

Wirrun fought with buckles and straps a little longer, emptied the billy over the fire and raked it out for safety, hoisted the pack and shrugged it into place between his shoulders, and himself set off through the forest. The bulky pack was not properly balanced; he eased and settled it as he went, stumbling a little. The stumble turned him aside into walking-stick palms; he pushed through, regaining his balance—saw the narrow blunt-nosed head come swinging at him from the palms—yelled and leapt and swung as he landed to balance the heavy pack. The snake, a Brown, poured its long body between stones and fern.

Wirrun stood still for a moment to slow his pulse and his breathing, thankful that the snake, having waited for a heavy footfall to reach it, had struck only once and gone. A man didn't expect a Brown to behave in either of those ways, and hampered by his pack he could easily have been in trouble. In the cool and damp of the forest, perhaps the snake had already felt winter coming and grown lazy. The moment was over: he took a deep breath and saw, with a jerk of his nerves, other shadows moving in the palms.

Three or four small Dinderi were crouched there. They looked with grave unblinking eyes from him to something half hidden in moss and dead leaves. Wirrun's hand closed on the power: he saw only the glow of red eyes but he knew what lay in the leaves.

"Get out," he barked for the second time.

The thing with no body looked at him for half a moment, knowing and menacing. Then it was gone.

"Cheeky like a dog," said the Dinderi.

"Why didn't you send it off, then?" Wirrun growled. He saw that the Dinderi rejected this thing and therefore the forest was not its place. "Are you scared of it?"

They shook their heads. "Older than People, we," they said.

He did not pause to wonder what they meant; he was full of an urgency he had felt before. The thing had gone, he did not know where, and Murra was waiting at the fence. He went after her. But as he went he thought swiftly of other fearful things he had seen—men of ice, a stone monster, the old and terrible Bunyip and others more strange; and he wondered why this thing of red eyes and no body should chill him more. For it seemed less than they; clumsy and unfinished, a drawing by a child, a no-thing; yet it chilled and angered him.

Murra was waiting by the fence, opening her red box a little wider than she had dared to do before and peeping a little longer. "See," she said, giving him a quick glimpse, "I have caught a tree."

He grinned in congratulation and because he was so glad to find her safe; but there was a question in his mind that had to be asked if he could ask it. He lowered his pack over the fence and climbed through. It was a question he wished he need not ask while she felt the west behind her.

She gave him the water-bag and he strapped it in place and lifted the pack again. "Didn't catch a Yunggamurra in the creek, then?" he asked, pretending to tease.

She closed the box and looked at him, gravely surprised; for her sisters, who would one day come to take her home, were not a matter for teasing.

"No," he said quickly, "all these rivers over here flow east. Any rate, they wouldn't come themselves. Too far for 'em, little silver things like that. They'd send a friend, some other thing."

She considered what he said or else she considered him, and after a moment answered quite directly. "Their laws are for the Yunggamurra and no other thing. Only they will come."

He would have to think about that—and turn her away from thinking if he could. He told her about the snake and that too she considered gravely.

And now at last they were free to travel the white men's roads in the eastern country: clothed like any other couple and with a little money in case they might need the white man's power. They set off down the ridge on their long journey to Ko-in's country.

3

The green plains and valleys of the east were edged by hills and criss-crossed by roads. Little towns were strung like beads on the roads, and cars scuttled between; the coast was lined with holiday beaches. Wirrun and Murra avoided them all.

They kept among hills, using dusty country roads when they could but letting the highways lead them from a distance. This was Inlander country: cars were fewer, towns smaller and easy to avoid, houses could be passed at a distance. There was always a place to camp and food to be gathered. Sometimes the hills stood close, looking down at them with faces of stone or slopes of forest; sometimes they were farther off, blue and shadowed with purple, shifting a little stealthy and unseen. Sometimes the roads crawled over their sides, and Wirrun and Murra looked down from heights at green plains, east-flowing rivers, and the sea at the hem of the sky.

They were already a long way south since the wind had put them on their way, but still they had a long way to go. Yet they travelled fast. There was something abroad that hurried them on, melting the miles in front. Once they were lifted by another wind and carried far south in a day; often they stumbled on easier, straighter roads than those on Wirrun's map and were led by shortened routes; sometimes a car with a dark-skinned driver stopped to give them a lift. Murra as well as Wirrun noticed how they were hurried on and sometimes she was silent.

"What shall I do," she asked him, when a carload of the People had set them down after a drive of a hundred miles in two hours, "if this Grandfather Ko-in calls you to travel west? For trouble may be anywhere but all the land is west."

He frowned. "Not all—not Ko-in's, or the south countries. No use wondering any rate. We'll have to wait and see." But he did wonder.

The eyes of these People who drove them always caught and returned to the net bag on Wirrun's belt; they looked away in sudden awe and stole glances from under their brows at the lovely girl with floating hair who carried a red box. Sometimes they told an old tale of their country, or of strange things they had seen, and waited; and Wirrun, understanding, would tell them in return about tailed women in a cave or the icy green-eyed Ninya from under the desert. And as word spread among the People the way to the south grew easier: a driver watched by the road to take them on, or a woman waited in the evening to bring them to a meal in a cottage.

There were nights in shanties on the edges of towns when old men talked and young men listened; and Wirrun, who was hero but young like the others, was strengthened too. There were nights when Murra sang sharp and sweet like a bird of the green eastern countries: of rain sinking and roots spreading and of tall proud trees; and the People listened and were silent. And here and there along the coast there were nights when Wirrun heard at last the name of Jimmy Ginger.

The story was told again and again of Jimmy, that sober and capable fisherman who on a clear, still day had tangled himself in his own prawn-net and drowned; and whenever it was told the men sat waiting, their eyes on Wirrun. He could only shake his head—but his skin began to prickle at the name of Jimmy Ginger, and more than once he thought of the snake in the forest and the red eyes in the leaves, and of Ko-in's warning. He never mentioned the unfinished thing, the no-face; partly because he knew nothing of it yet and partly because he still could not understand his own dark anger. He had only a feeling that this thing was some-

how apart from others—there was some more knowing evil
in the eyes, a less innocent evil.

Those were good days and nights for Wirrun, at home
among the People; days and nights of a kind that he would
never know again. Yet as the journey seized them and hurried them on, the travellers clung more to their days and
nights alone. For it seemed that days and nights, like hills
and rivers, would not hold to them any more. All the wide
land was focused on the point of here, the immensity of
time was sharpened to the point of now. The hero and the
water-girl were glad of days when they walked alone on
some white man's land through brown seeding grass, and of
nights when they cooked what they had caught or gathered
at their own fire, and afterwards Murra begged to be told
again how Wirrun became the hero Ice-Fighter; for that
was a name she heard often, both among the People and
whispered beyond the fire.

He always hunched a shoulder when she asked him, for
she had heard the tale often enough and he was afraid she
was secretly laughing at him. But Murra would coax and
tease, tug at his hair, stroke him gently where the gills
would be if only he were a fish, struggle away from his
defensive tickling, till at last he gave in and told her again.

He told her how the land, threatened by ice, had called
on him to leave his job and fight against the Ninya; how
Ko-in had led him to find the ancient power of his People
where a dying man had hidden it long ago; about a great
stone monster worn away by time, and spirits and earth-
things of countries far from hers. And she listened soberly,
for these were things she understood.

"Truly you are a hero out of your time," she said once.

"Not me. It's the power. I'm only the man that holds it."

She smiled a little. "And what man held it first? Who
wound it in fur and hung it in a bag?"

"Eh?" said Wirrun. "That was a long time back. There's no
way a man could know."

"But others could, of my kind. They know this power and

obey it in all their countries. Yet they name it only from you: Ice-Fighter's stone."

Later, when they lay in a blanket under the stars, Murra would watch the sky unsleeping and listen to the whispers beyond the fire; and she would know that she too was known. The silver water-spirit from a country far away, turned to gold and browned by the sun, dressed in a cheap cotton frock from a chain store: these others knew her.

So the journey hurried them on, but when they could they clung to now and watched the blue hills turn. When they found a river quiet between the hills they stopped to swim or fish and keep the river there. They lingered in a valley to snare rabbits and preserve the valley. They crossed the border of two states among trees so grand and grace- ful that Wirrun was silent and Murra remembered when forests and rivers were new. South again they went, between tall hills crowned with rock that turned the wind aside, and there they found a river that travelled with them. They came on it again and again, its main stream or its backwaters, and knew it by its feel.

"It's the big one," said Wirrun. Here in the hills it looked as small as another but Murra, knowing rivers, eyed it with respect.

It met them in every valley, and when a ridge of hills took them eastward over the plains it opened broad full arms and enfolded the hills. Towns and canefields clung to it, it grew rank with the smell of dairies and sharp with the smell of the sea; but always there were lonely banks and swamps where the swamp-lights played, and the river led them through. They stood at last on a ridge with the river behind, and in front a sheet of water, miles across, that the river filled in passing. This wide water stretched away to the west where far hills melted into sky. White cloud fanned over it, stilled yet full of force. And Murra, with the dark hair moving on her shoulders, said, "If you must go west I will wait for you here."

"Have sense!" snorted Wirrun, for half the world lay

open to the west that she feared, and the clouds hurtled out of it like a great white explosion. "How could I go off and leave you here?"

She followed his eyes. "We will stay a little any rate and catch new fish, for this is sea-tainted water and sea-things live in it." She turned to him and smiled. "My sisters would never come into this water, it would burn them. It is not water for Yunggamurra but only for Murra."

They went down the ridge through stringybark and iron-bark trees and found a path through a fringe of swamp. They left their things under the oaks that cried thinly in the wind. The water was shallow and warm, not fresh and not salt. They went out through deep soft mud, laughing as it dragged at their feet, past beds of weed into deeper places. A flock of coot rose with a noise like the crackle of fire, peli-can looked on solemnly, and from over the water came a gentle argument of swans.

They found mud-crabs and chased eels and swam in the deeper channels with young sharks and other things of the sea. They caught mullet and bream and carried them back through the shallows. Murra gave a teasing call and vanished into a bed of weeds and was lost for ten minutes. He knew she was there, and that now she was nearly human and had to breathe, but he could not find her till she appeared again with a tangle of weed in her hair.

They took their catch to the shore and laughed again at the mud and tried to wash it off. The river-oaks trampled the risen tide under their roots. Wirrun and Murra went back through the swamp and up a small gully among lilli-pillis, and made a fire by its trickle of water to cook their fish. The afternoon grew close and warm, and after they had eaten they slept.

When Wirrun woke it seemed dark under the trees. He looked for a patch of sky: it was purple and green like an old bruise, and while he was still gathering his wits the thunder growled. He began to throw things into his pack, casting about in his mind for shelter. The trees stirred anxiously and were still again. The river-oaks cried and were silent.

"Murra!" he cried. "Wake up, girl! There's a storm brewing."

A fierce blue flash ripped the dark. Murra was up, seizing her red box and a packet of salt. She was suddenly still: her eyes aged and she stood holding the box and the salt. She dropped them and went running through the scrub. Wirrun shoved his pack under a log and went after her.

"Murra! Where are you going?"

She stood at the edge of the scrub looking down over the water, and her eyes were wide with fear.

"Murra, girl!"

She shrieked: "No—not yet—one small summer—" Then she was running again.

He ran too. The trees cried out and a great fist of wind shoved him back. A whiteness of rain came roaring over the water. Lightning slashed, thunder cracked, and he ran on. He could see Murra running through the swamp—the wind threw her green-gold dress back at him. He lost her in the shrieking oaks but he knew where she was: in the sea-tainted water, fighting through mud, making for the weeds.

He followed through the howling oaks into stinging rain and hammers of wind and on into churning water where the mud gripped his feet and he stopped. Which weeds? There was no sign. He too was afraid, for above the shout and shriek of the storm he began to hear another sound and he knew it.

There was a high, sweet singing in the heart of the storm He knew those voices, sharply sweet like wild honey. They had come for her, the Yunggamurra sisters.

He plunged deeper into mud gripping the power and shouting. "Get off—get off!" But the stone did not throb or the voices falter: they were too far and high, the power did not reach them. All the other voices of the storm were hushed, it seemed, and gave way to the singing that pleaded and charmed, the notes that came falling like leaves through the rain. He could not hear the words for they were not sung to him, but their sweet and sorrowful pleading burnt him. Yet the water-girl did not come.

He thought he could see wind-tangled hair flying in the clouds, and lightning-gleams on silver twining limbs. "Get off!" he called uselessly again, for the voices tore even him. But the water-girl did not come.

Then the singing wavered and broke, and the voices rose in a sound as wild and haunting as a man could hear. A wild lone howling filled the sky and wavered and mourned; it was as if a pack of dingoes ran through the storm. Wirrun was stilled and shivered. Then he saw.

Through the screen of the rain came a tall column of water, twisting, circling, its head leaning into cloud. It was brown with sucked-up mud and weed, fish flew in it and fell. Silver long-nailed hands reached down from the clouds and the Yunggamurra mourned and howled. He saw one small brown hand break up from the water, and the column reached for it and she was drawn up wrapped in the darkness of her hair and taken into the storm. The column swayed and shattered.

Wirrun came to himself waist-deep in water with his feet trapped in mud and knew it was useless to shout any more; she was far away. They had not come into the sea-tainted water; they had called her out to the deep channels with the young sharks. They had drawn her out of hiding— she had made her choice between now and forever.

In the heart of the storm she clung to her sisters for they were clever and cunning. Though pleading could not touch them they knew it would touch her: they had begged her— not to come home but only, for the sake of memory, to come nearer. Rolling in the wild wet turmoil of the storm she knew she had been right in the beginning. There was no choice; there had never been a choice.

THREE

The Death in the West

I

He had known all along, from the very first day; even when he refused to hear her warnings, he had known he could not keep her. A thing grown out of dreams and fears and time—out of water and sun and starlight—could not be tied to a wrinkled old age and death. Yunggamurra: that was the cruel and beautiful, vanishing thing that a man could not have. He knew it, yet he could not believe she was gone. Not yet, not really gone. Not forever.

She would escape from her sisters and come back. He sat on the ridge above the wide water and waited.

He watched all through the first night, flashing his torch from time to time so that she could find him. At dawn he told himself it was still too soon; she could not have come straight back, they would only have followed her. He ate cold baked yams and dozed a little in the shade—and woke with a start fearing she had come while he slept. When he had called and walked about in the open and found she was not there he thought of cooking a meal to have ready when she came. He took a possum from a hollow limb where he heard it scratching, and found dry firewood in the storm-wet scrub and made a fire.

When night came again he watched for a long time keeping the fire alive. Towards dawn he suddenly began to swear, and tore the cold baked possum apart and ate some. On the second morning he knew she would not come. He went on sitting where he was.

He was bitterly angry, holding the anger over something dark and terrible underneath.

In the evening he finished the possum and sat with his head on his knees, now and then impatiently reaching for something to throw on the fire. He did not look up when the leaves rustled over his head or when a shape dropped lightly down beside him.

The shape stood watching him, tall and commanding, a man of the People. It carried a firestick in one hand and wore a pattern of white pipeclay. It waited in silence for a moment and then spoke deeply.

"Greetings, Hero."

Wirrun looked up. "Ko-in," he muttered, and lowered his head again.

"Speak with me," the shape commanded.

Wirrun lifted his head for another moment and dropped it again. "Hi," he said.

The shape seemed to grow taller.

"Is it for this I leave my country in a time of trouble? Was it for this I hung that bag at your belt and called you hero? That you should sit here an empty mussel-shell, a nothing on a hill? Call back your manhood, Hero."

Wirrun's lips twisted into a kind of smile. "Yeah? And do what with it?"

Ko-in's eyes flashed. "The man who asks that is indeed an empty mussel-shell. I have called on you for help: is that nothing? Your friend lies nameless in the First Dark, a hero of your making unknown in his own country. Is that nothing?"

Wirrun stared sulkily at the fire. There was no answer to the second charge. To the first he growled, "You don't need no help. You got your own kind to help, and all the power you want between you. You can fix your own troubles better than what I can."

Ko-in snorted. "So says the Ice-Fighter to the one who made him and gave him help in his troubles. I have warned you, Hero—those who mate with magic are swallowed or they grow; there is no way between. And I do not choose that a hero of my making shall walk through the land an empty skin." He moved around the fire till he stood above Wirrun and spoke sternly. "I lay on you my need and the need of your friend. I give you a day to recall yourself—and to think if it is a small thing that brings me out of my country against my will. And when the sun lies on the hills again I will come back." He rose rustling through the leaves and was gone.

Wirrun sat on for a time, obstinately rigid. Then he shrugged, reached into his pack for a blanket, rolled himself in it and slept.

In the morning he looked for food and found nothing ready. He refused to trap or fish and made tea instead. When that proved not enough he gave in with irritation and used flour and salt from his pack to make a very bad damper, cooked too slowly in a fire with too much flame. He ate some of that and for a time moved restlessly about in the scrub, but he would not leave it. Even through its screen of leaves he could see, if he were not careful, glimpses of sleek still water, blue-grey, with a far shoreline of slate-grey trees beyond.

Yet as the day went on the scrub smothered him. He could not leave it and neither, he saw angrily, could he stay in it. He found himself thinking often of Ko-in and of the friend who must not be named but who was named in his heart: his friend Ularra. They invaded his mind, now one, now the other, in snatches of memory and echoes of words. Defensively he turned to his pack and began to stow away the things he had used. And at once he knew that this was no idle passing of time: he was packing to travel. He could not any longer sit idle in this poisoned place.

He packed sometimes fiercely and sometimes in confusion. A comb and a blue cotton dress he bundled tight and thrust hard into a rotted log. A faded cotton shirt he stared at helplessly and at last left it on the ground. He was fastening the pockets on his pack when his eyes caught a splash of red in dead leaves on the other side of the fire: the lacquered box. He reached for it to smash it . . . or shove it under a log . . . *see, I have caught a tree* . . . he thrust it deep into the last pocket and pulled the strap tight.

Now he could get away . . . but it wasn't time. He lay down and went to sleep again. When the setting sun struck low over the water and under the leaves of the scrub to light his face, he woke. By then he had come to some sort of terms with his deep and bitter pain. He could not see a life ahead but he could see a step.

A man had debts. He would pay what he owed his friend; and before he set out he would hear what Ko-in had to say.

He made fresh tea, ate more damper, and sat keeping the fire up and staring at it. Ko-in came silently down through the trees and stood watching. He had been there for some time before Wirrun saw him and called to him.

"All right, old friend. Sit down and talk. And make it good—I got work of my own to do."

"You are more right than you know," said Ko-in coming forward. He folded himself down cross-legged by the fire. "I speak to you not for my own country but for all the countries of the land." He waited.

"Go on," said Wirrun, waiting too.

"You were called once by the land and once by the People. Now I bring you the call of earth-things and spirits."

"I don't think I follow that," said Wirrun at once but politely. "The land—well, she calls who she likes and the ice was everyone's business. Maybe I was a sort of bridge between white men, People, earth-things, the lot. After that the People: well, fair enough; I was their own and who else would they call? But now it looks like you want me to handle your kind of trouble, the sort your kind could handle better than me if you wanted to. Why me? I don't follow that."

"How should you," said Ko-in tartly, "when the cord is not yet in your hand? I might claim the right of a gift for a gift—for my kind gave you help when you called. But I see you are not yet strong enough to remember your friends for their own sake; I must put the cord in your hands and close your fingers on it. You must answer the call of the earth-things because their trouble is of your making, not theirs. It is a trouble of man's making, a man of the People; and now it wanders and disturbs my kind."

Wirrun lowered his brow till his eyes were shadowed and looked darkly at Ko-in. "I still don't follow. What sort of thing can a man make that can trouble your kind?"

"A thing of power to rule him," said Ko-in looking darkly back. "A thing to be seen or unseen as it will, to go where the wind goes, to live from age to age. A thing to call men's spirits from their graves and take to itself the telling of right from wrong. An evil thing that calls itself death."

Wirrun's dulled mind had had no time to grasp at this. He was staring stupidly. "An—earth-thing? Made by a man?"

"No," said Ko-in strongly, "for earth-spirits grow from the land and know only its laws—as heroes grow from man's best self and know only that. There are earth-things that steal a man's spirit from its grave—that prey on living men—that bring sickness and death and fear and fire and whirl-wind—that are evil and yet know nothing of evil. This thing knows. It knows from its maker."

"It must know madness too, then," said Wirrun harshly. "What man would make a thing like that to rule him?" But his skin prickled. *This thing knows:* had he not seen an un-finished thing with fiery eyes that knew evil?

Ko-in smiled grimly. "A foolish man indeed, with a sing-ing too strong for him that he got from one a little wiser. A man hungry for power, who made the thing to serve him. A man too foolish to know that such a power would never serve but must rule."

They were silent for a while. Wirrun stared at the fire, trying to come to grips with a story so different from all he knew of the People's lore. Ko-in watched him.

"And see," he said in a moment, "how this thing takes its evil from its maker. It takes the power over life that he longed for, for to look at it is death to a man. It takes the greatness he sought, for it makes itself a judge of dead spirits and a maker of Clever Men. And as he made it, it makes others of its own kind to serve it. They are many and make trouble in that country."

Wirrun grunted in angry doubt. "I never heard of a thing like that in all the land."

"That is not strange for its country is far in the west, and there, where it was made, it must be borne like other fears. It is an old shame now and the land is very wide; only my kind still whisper of it. But now this hungry thing comes east. We have seen it, and not we only. A man is dead."

"What man?—how?"

"A man to be trusted, and one of the People. Taken dead from the sea, tangled in his own net."

In the fire Wirrun saw days and evenings that could not come again, and a worried waiting look in many eyes. "Jimmy Ginger," he said, and Ko-in nodded.

"Nothing outside its own country will endure this thing," he said sternly, "and none will meddle with it. A dog-like thing, a man's work, fit only for a man to master. We call on you, Hero: a man of power, and one to whom all countries are his own. The work is yours."

Wirrun frowned. "I don't know this thing—for all I can see, it makes no sense. There must be Clever Men in its own country; call on them. You talk about a gift for a gift, I reckon you've weighed that up on the wrong side. Your kind have cost me dear, man. Right now I wouldn't care if I never laid eyes on 'em again."

"And did you think," said Ko-in, "that if the great Ice-Fighter grasped at fire his hand would not burn? You should know, Man, that anger is a dog: its own ears are quick but its snarling stops its master's ears. We do not ask a gift, or for help. We call on you for rightness and the law. This is a man's work. You are the Man, the one fit to do it."

"I got work of my own, for one thing. For another, there's no man fit to do it. If this thing's come from far west right over here, it must be all over the land. How can a man cover that? It can't be done."

"When you journeyed at the land's call it gave you help. When you answered the call of the People they gave help. Are they earless, empty things that call you now?"

"You said they wouldn't meddle."

"Nor will they. But where they ask they also help and their footprints are in the whirlwind. Ask for no knowing or searching or doing; even your power will gain you nothing. But ask for yourself what you need and say only who you are. Ask to journey and you will arrive." Ko-in stood up. "Come, now. You have seen this thing yourself and yet you are alive: you must know you are the Man. And one dark angry sorrow has not killed all your spirit. You have work for your friend; that too lies west. Begin your journey for your friend and follow your own spirit from there. It may lead you on, and into many countries." He looked searchingly at Wirrun. "Even into the country of the Yunggamurra."

2

Wirrun rose slowly as if anger forced him up. He glared at Ko-in. In a moment he said tightly, "What's that mean? If it's a carrot for a donkey the carrot's rotten. You think I'm a fool?"

"I do not know," said Ko-in. "I do not need to know; the need is yours. But I would not send one I love on such a journey in any kind of need. Tell me, then: what are you?"

"I thought you had it off pat. Ice-Fighter, aren't I? Clever Man. The one with the power. That's what you said."

"That much I know. Beneath these stars and above these rocks it is very little. Are you no more?"

Wirrun clenched his hands.."I'll tell you. I'm a man. Of the People. It's all I want. It was you put the name of hero on me."

"Oh Man!" cried Ko-in. "And is that all your greatness? An axe falls on it. You are cut short. I am Man, I am hero, I am black—with every name an axe-blow. You see this fire? I see it in your eyes: a little fire, made small. All your names are yourself in the eyes of others; yourself made small."

"Forget 'em then," growled Wirrun, bitter and confused. But Ko-in seemed to tower and spoke with passion.

"I am hero, Ice-Fighter, Clever Man—with every name the axe falls, you are cut short! Poor spirit! Under all these blows how can it find the strength you need? Will you not speak for it? Will you not say what the stars will stoop to hear and the rocks answer?"

Wirrun only glowered again. But Ko-in was an ancient hero, one who had awed many ages of People; he could compel. Wirrun growled, "I'm—" and stumbled into silence. He could find no other name.

"When the need comes," said Ko-in, quite calmly now, "you may remember it." He laid a hand like a bat's wing on Wirrun's shoulder. "I give you what strength and rest I can. Take what you will and say where you will go, for word has been passed and they wait."

Dazed and emptied as he had been before by Ko-in, Wirrun reached for his pack. He had made no decisions and knew almost nothing of what he was supposed to hunt but the moment had caught him. Looking at Ko-in he said, "Take me . . . to old Tom Hunter, wherever he is . . . somewhere near Mount Conner."

Before he had finished speaking he felt a panting breath on his neck. He swung quickly to see firelight on leaf-shaped yellow eyes—on great white teeth and a tongue lolling red near his shoulder—on the shaggy shape of a huge black dog.

"Jugi!" he whispered, for he had seen one before at a distance and it had been dreadful then.

The dog crouched. Wirrun hesitated, then climbed on to its back, twisting his hands in the deep, strong hair. Its dog-smell was suffocating and the hair and body felt real, yet when it moved he felt no play of bone or muscle. There was only a gathering of power under him and a strong smooth flowing of himself and the dog through scrub.

He crouched down to keep leaves and twigs from whipping at his face and saw no more of the fire among the lillipillis or the scrub or the wide water. The power beneath him surged and flowed with a speed that blurred the pale new stars. They passed through evening into sunset down wide inward-sloping plains, and in a cupped red country hung with blue hazes they caught up with the hot gold glare of late afternoon. That was as much as Wirrun saw until he felt that surging power lean back into itself, and saw with the blood pounding in his head that they had stopped among ironwood trees on yellow rocks. The Jugi stood; he tumbled and slid from its back; it shook itself, gathered for a spring, and was gone. Wirrun fell back among rocks and lay there.

As the heat of the land's centre released its grip and began to rise he saw that he knew this place among the ironwoods. The Jugi had brought him not to Mount Conner but to a gap in ranges of jagged rock that walled a town. It must be here that he would find Tom Hunter, that steady man who had brought both Wirrun and Ularra here on the People's business—but it was hard to camp here now, where he and Ularra had camped. And it was a hard thing he had come back to do for his friend; he sat and thought about it where they two had sat before, while the hills of the red country turned apricot and gold in the sunset.

In a water-clear twilight he took his billy and went out of the ironwoods, side-stepping down the rocks to a wide dry river-bed below; for he knew that at this time there would be a few of the People somewhere along the river. He had been shown how to draw water from this river. He crossed its bed, grassed over between patches of sand, till he found where the old iron lid lay. It lifted back from a hole—it could not be called a well—dug only deep enough to reach the river's hidden water. He lowered his billy, glancing along the farther river-bank and up towards the town. A dark-skinned group, perhaps a family, watched him from the shade of tall ghost-gums. Lower down the bank and quite near, two small boys inspected him secretly while they pretended to gather wood.

He held up the billy and called to them. "Want a drink?"

They came, trying to stand behind each other, taking a few sips each from the billy while from under their long dark lashes their eyes travelled over him. Wirrun nodded towards the family watching from the bank.

"Your old man up there?"

They nodded.

"You give him a message for Tom Hunter. Tell him the Ice-Fighter's come." They stared at him. "Go on, now."

He waved them off and they scampered away like young

rabbits. Wirrun refilled his billy and covered the water again.

He strode back across the river-bed, climbed the rocks to his camp and lit the small fierce fire of the dry country to make tea. He ate the rest of his scorched dry damper with it, watching the fire and thinking, gathering together the threads of the story he had to tell so that the men of Ularra's country might understand his greatness; for Ko-in had hurled him like a spear into this work and he had to relive things that had been laid away.

It was painful remembering, and it held him so that he did not hear the tread of boots over rock or see the arrival of Tom Hunter. He only looked up to find the old man standing looking down: steady and dignified as always in his frayed trousers with an old waistcoat over his checked shirt, his grey-stubbled face and intent dark eyes catching the light of the flame. He carried a torch in one hand and in the other a white-wrapped parcel which he held out to Wirrun.

"Few chops," he said, but he did not smile.

Wirrun took the parcel uncertainly. "I'm not here on your business. That's done. I come to tell about him. Him that went with me."

"He's dead," said Tom. "We heard."

Wirrun knew they would have heard something since the journey had been their affair. The young men moving over the thousand-mile-tracks—from settlement to mission, to station or fishing-boat and back down the long roads—would have passed the news along.

"There's more," he said. "No one knows it all, only me. Are there men from Conner here?" For men drifted over many miles of sand and spinifex and mulga into this town.

"Jump-up," said Tom, "and I dunno who else. Enough to pass the word." He stepped back into the dark and flashed his torch.

Wirrun put more wood on the fire. He was cold, colder than the sharp desert night and the sharp bright stars. This time he heard the boots on rock, a number of them.

The men came out of the dark into his camp led by Tom Hunter's torch. They stood around the fire, a circle of dark eyes and faces catching the light. None of them smiled. He remembered some of the faces but looked only for Jump-up: older than Tom, more grizzled, his face deeply creased. Wirrun nodded to him. "You'll find a rock to sit on."

They all found places on rocks round the fire and sat gravely waiting. Wirrun knew that perhaps only two or three were men from Ularra's country near Mount Conner; the others had come to hear and support. But they came not only for Jump up and Ularra. They were the men who had called on him to quieten troubled earth-things wandering far from their own countries and to send them home; they came also to hear of that. He sorted the threads of his story and spoke.

"There was this singing got me. Out east before I come here. I never knew what it was. Never thought it was mixed up in your business."

They listened and waited. He told them in plain bare words how he and Ularra had found a cave; and the trouble was in it, and the singing too.

"Only he—he got himself caught too. Not the singing, not then. A different thing. She turned him." The shaggy hair, the long claws, the pleading eyes of the beast that had been his friend Ularra.

He told how in this need he had made a turning of his own and made the beast into his friend again. "It worked. Only he couldn't trust it. The beast—was too much for him. He couldn't forget . . ."

They shifted, in fear or pity. He told how he had left his friend safe, he thought, while he went into the cave and deep underground to find the singing, cause of all their trouble.

"But he knew, see. He knew I was sung. He came after me." Wirrun hunched closer to the fire. Himself and Ularra quarrelling in the ancient First Dark—bitter words—and the silver water-spirit with moonlit eyes singing them on. "He got past me—" Ularra's face in the water, so strongly at peace. "He knew—he let her drown him. To save me and be rid of the beast." He laid his head on his knees. "He was a hero."

The men were very still. After a moment Jump-up spoke. "Where is he?"

Wirrun lifted his head. "I couldn't bring him out. I did what I could." He told them that too.

"We'll do the rest," said Jump-up, and Wirrun nodded and waited. If they asked for the end of the story and the fate of the water-spirit he would have to say the words, whether they were understood or not. If they did not ask they could hear the words from someone else in time or perhaps had heard them already. The eyes were still grave and withdrawn. At last Tom Hunter spoke.

"What had to be done, you did it; the both of you."

The men nodded. He saw that they understood, and saw for the first time what drew them together against him. It was not anger or blame but awe: they were afraid of him. Three days ago he would have seen it with a bewildered sense of loss. Now he saw it wearily. Memory had drained out of him in the telling, leaving only something heavy and solid, a stone inside him.

"Where you going from here, then?" Jump-up asked after a pause.

"Eh?" said Wirrun; for he had already taken his one step and had made no more decisions. He stirred restlessly. "You know anything about a fiery-eyed thing that calls itself death?"

They looked uneasy and shook their heads. If he had been only young Wirrun who rode the wind and sent the ice-men home they might have said more. But he was an older Wirrun who had turned his friend from a beast back to a man and had seen dark things. The young men had not spoken to him at all.

"Don't anyone see it," he grunted; for they were all good men. Sound men, to be trusted. Men like Jimmy Ginger.

They saw his restlessness and rose to go. "Thanks, then,"

said Jump-up and they nodded. Seeing them turn away and Tom Hunter flashing his torch Wirrun found a sudden need and turned quickly for his pack, fumbling with a pocket. He spoke softly to Tom.

"See you in the morning?" He held up a little cash. "Bring a couple of cans."

Tom hesitated only a second, took the money and nodded, and turned away with the men. Wirrun listened to their boots drawing away down the rocks.

He had still made no decision. He felt only weary, dissatisfied and uncertain; and that Tom Hunter was a man who had listened at campfires in many countries of the west.

3

In the chill of that night Wirrun crept into his sleeping-bag: the first time he had used it since he and Murra lay in one blanket under the stars. He slept heavily but not well, dreaming of a death with red knowing eyes and waking before dawn with death in his mind.

Hunger and illness and age and death . . . *Truly you are a hero . . .*

. . . And is that all your greatness? An axe falls on it . . .

The stone inside him began to swell. If he were not careful it would turn into pain. As soon as it was light enough he shook himself free of the sleeping-bag and went down to the river-bed for water.

There were hours to be passed before Tom Hunter might come. He lit his fire, washed and shaved, changed to fresher clothes—making himself, if he had known it, a less awesome figure than he had been last night. He cooked and ate some of the chops Tom had brought. After that he sat avoiding memory, exploring his own dissatisfaction with the story Ko-in had told and what he had seen of the red-eyed thing; watching through the ironwoods the land gathering heat, the roofs of the town beginning to shimmer, the hills putting on their fragile, vivid blues.

At last he saw Tom coming down the river. He waited for the sound of the boots on rock and went to the edge of the shade. Tom carried a small sack that clinked as he walked. They nodded to each other and moved back to sit in the shade.

Wirrun said, "Thanks, mate. It's better here than showing up in town." Tom nodded again, reaching into his sack.

The beer in the dewy cans was still cool. Wirrun sipped it slowly; Tom drank and waited. After a minute Wirrun said, "You ever heard of a thing that calls itself death? Anywhere?"

It was easier to talk in daylight over a beer. Tom shook his head. "Spirit-chasers," he offered. "At graves. After dead men. There's plenty of them."

"I know them. You do the right things and you beat 'em. That's like—all the rest. I'm told this thing's different, you can't beat it. I never heard of anything like that." He sipped.

"There's one like that up north, round Katherine," said Tom. "They reckon a Clever Man made it a long time back and now it's got 'em."

Wirrun turned to him. "That's the one. Do they reckon"— he slowly turned the can in his hand, carefully approaching his own restless discontent with this tale of Ko-in's—"that it gets the lot of 'em in the end, then?"

Tom nodded and drank, wiping his chin afterwards. "Gets the lot and says which ones can go home. There's some gotta be cleaned up first with fire."

That was it: the incredible thing, the thing that fitted no lore of the People that Wirrun knew. He shook his head. "I know it's bad, I've seen it." Tom looked sideways at him and away. "But I never heard of anything like it."

"Worse because they made it theirselves," Tom suggested. "That's what we say." But Wirrun only nodded moodily so he emptied his can and opened another. They both brooded in silence. At last Tom thought of something. "I heard they got a thing out west, right down near them Stirling Ranges. I met a man once."

Wirrun raised frowning eyes. "Yeah?"

"He said they had something. I dunno much. A thing that gets after a man's spirit only there's one it wouldn't take. She was too bad for it. Would that be the same?"

"What's it called?"

Tom struggled. "I remember the woman best . . . Balyet, that's her. Young girl, pretty as a bird, caught lots of men. Two of 'em, blood-brothers, fought over her and killed each other. Worst thing that can happen over there, blood-brothers doing that. They wouldn't have this Balyet after that; wouldn't kill her and send her home. This—white thing—Noatch, that's it—it wouldn't have her either. Too bad for it. She's there yet. Calls little 'uns and young girls; puts her arms round 'em if she can get 'em, and they die real quiet." He glanced sideways at Wirrun. "Would this Noatch be any good? Too far, I reckon."

Wirrun gave a tight smile. "Not for me. They're taking me wherever I want. Do it under an hour."

"Ah," said Tom uncomfortably, but Wirrun didn't notice. He was thinking.

"This Noatch: what do they do for it? Can you remember if he said?"

Tom thought obligingly. "Fire," he said at last. "It's a cold thing, this. Goes to fire. Wants to get warm, or it's curious. You make a big fire, take it away from the little grave-fire. It'll go to the big one and the dead man gets away. No warmth, see."

"There you are, then," said Wirrun. "There's rules for it. Might take a look at it all the same." For he could not sit on among the ironwoods any more than he could have stayed in the eastern scrub, and he had not yet uncovered all his uneasiness about this northern death. He added, "I knew a man'd be able to count on you. Thanks, mate."

"Don't know if it's right," said Tom. "Don't you want this other can?"

"You have it. One'll do me, I'm not used to it."

"I'll go, then," said Tom getting to his feet, for he did not want to see Wirrun leave.

"No hurry—stay and finish the beer. I got all the time there is."

Tom stood looking down, and Wirrun could not see

whether his eyes held fear or pity. "You've gone too far ahead of us, boy. You got a bad job this time. We'll make a singing for you."

"You do," said Wirrun full of uncaring weariness. "That's what I need." He watched old Tom go out of the hot shade into the beating sun; watched to see him cross the river-bed and climb slowly up the farther bank. Then he saw to the remains of his fire and fastened his pack and hoisted it on.

As he did so he chose the words that would take him on the next journey. He did not want to face this white thing that might be a death; he wanted to observe it unseen, at least for a time. Somewhere near it, that was what he wanted. Gazing through trees at the river he said, "Take me to this Balyet."

The ground stirred: a small secret movement that rattled no stones. The river-bed was blotted out by a darkness. Something lay in it, something large and dark and coarsely textured with a fluid shape that might have been poured molten. Toes?—a foot? Wirrun's blood was singing and he clutched the power in reaction and the trees swayed and cracked as a great dark hand came down through them and closed over him. He was swept up above the broken trees into hot sunlight.

From the chest down he was gripped and enclosed in enormous fingers. He was swung above the river-bed and stared into teeth like white rocks. They opened and snapped, and through them came a laugh like a roaring wind. By staring up Wirrun could see the rest of the coarse-grained face. The Pungalunga shook its head, still laughing. Its body was an indistinct darkness going down into the river.

"Ice-Fighter!" it roared. "No fire-eyes round here, Man. Balyet, eh?" It held him firm and shaded against what must be its chest and took a step up on to the range. It paused there, and Wirrun looked down at fangs of rock with treetops between. Then the rushing journey began.

Swing and pause, swing and pause, half a mile at a swing with the wind drawing the air out of Wirrun's lungs till he could scarcely breathe. He saw and felt only the pitted-rubber skin of the Pungalunga, heard only the wind and once or twice a deep shaking grunt. Swing and pause, swing and pause . . . he was half hypnotised.

When the rhythm broke and slowed he was startled and stiffened. The Pungalunga came to a stand, grunted again and lowered its hands a little letting in the dazzle of light and the stroke of heat.

"Coming, Ice-Fighter," it boomed. "Soon here."

He gathered himself together and looked, and first he saw that the day was younger. Then he saw the miles of sand-plain, red misted over with the grey of mallee scrub, that reached away to a blur with the white dazzle of a salt-pan to the north. Moving fast towards him against the hazy distance a tall finger of red sand curled and beckoned: a willy-willy. The Pungalunga stood like a tower on a low granite ridge and waited.

When the whine and rustle of the willy-willy sounded near, it said, "Jannoks here. Hands over face, Hero."

Wirrun's hands were already there for he knew what that whirling column of wind and sand could do. The Pungalunga swung him forward; there was a confused moment when wind smote, sand stung, bony hands plucked and grabbed; then he was moving fast within a stillness, enclosed in the rustle and scream of the willy-willy. He lowered his hands and looked.

The funnel of the wind, dimmed by flying sand, was dark-ened by a funnel of dark bodies that swung and circled in it. Those nearest held him firmly between them: they were shapes like very old men, grey-haired and emu-footed. Now and then they peered at him with bright curious eyes but said nothing. Now and then, from high or low in the column or near at hand, they screamed with the screaming wind. He could not speak to them for the noise and speed and whirl-ing, but for safety he shouted into the nearest ear: "Balyet!"

The Jannok nodded. "That rubbish!" it screamed, and spat.

After a time the noise grew less and the light stronger. Between grey heads and brown shoulders he glimpsed sunlight and whirling leaves. The column wavered and shifted in shape and soon the old emu-footed men fanned wide on the wind, clustering about Wirrun in their centre. He saw that they blew over woods of mallee towards high rocky crags where the mist curled; and while he, who had ridden many winds, was wondering at their speed they set him down among the crags and whirled away. He was stumbling between rocks and sank down on one of them to rest.

He had come over more than half the land, catching up with the sun. He would not choose to be spirit-carried oftener than he must; he sat feeling only the turning of the world that was like stillness, and its quiet that was like the deep quiet of thought.

At last he saw that he was in a gully under steep walls of rock. It was shadowed and cool though sunlight fell down its farther wall; a wisp of grey mist drifted in it and was gone. He knew that Balyet, killer of children, must be near, and since death had refused her she must still be human; but he saw no sign. He went up the gully a little way to look but came back and sat down again. It was safer to wait where the Jannoks had left him. At last he grew impatient and shouted to her: "Balyet!"

At once the gully was alive and full of calling: "Balyet—Balyet—Balyet!" And it seemed to Wirrun that the voice could not be his own thrown back by the rocks. It was a softer voice full of something he could not name. Where he had only called, this voice now yearned. A trail of mist curled over his feet and drifted away up the gully.

Frowning he called again. And again, first here then there, the voice pleaded back: "Balyet—Balyet—Balyet—" With his hand on the power he saw that she was there, the woman who could not die; she fled up the gully and drifted down again.

She was so thinned by time that he barely saw her, scarcely more than a voice that cried back to others and her shadow no more than a trail of mist. Her shape was not old or young but only a woman's, wind-drifting. What he saw was the shadowed darkness of her eyes. He saw those dark shadows of longing and loneliness and he knew why she folded the children in her arms, and how she must wail with grief when they quietly died. He was filled with pity for this long punishment.

He saw her float unresting up the gully and come drifting down again. He thought the dark eyes fixed on him with sudden eagerness and that that was why he felt chilled; but then he saw they were fixed on something behind him, and he turned his head rigidly and looked.

There was the thing: a white shadow without shape or warmth or life, a wreathing of mist behind him. And though it had no eyes he knew it watched.

He had not guessed that the woman would follow the death so close. He had lit no fire.

4

The thing that was called Noatch lay like a patch of mist in the gully and watched. And even with his hand on the power Wirrun was afraid: it was as though a blind man watched. The mist curled and wreathed and changed, there was no shape to Noatch. It thinned into nothing and thickened into mist, the blind watcher never wholly seen. He knew from its ancient cold denial of life that the thing had no speech. It was a slow thing yet it had the speed to catch a flying spirit. As the Jugi had its monster-smell of dog so this thing had the monster-smell of fear and Wirrun was afraid.

Then the shade of Balyet flowed past him entreating; a woman as he was a man, and pleading to be denied life. In a flash the blind watcher was gone, leaving her to drift away down the gully with a wind-cry of despair. And again Wirrun was angry. He could not change the fate of Balyet; no man or hero could do that. But anger warmed him and called him back to life.

He was no naked helpless spirit seeking its home—he was a living man. If Noatch had any power over him let the power be seen. He was here at the call of earth-things and had faced worse things than this one. He had come to draw it near and watch it: to see if its refusal of one sad spirit gave it power over others and the right to call itself a death. He would not be put off because the thing instead had watched him. Tight-lipped he looked for fuel for a fire to draw it back.

He was reaching for a stick when again its dank cold reached him. It had come without drawing.

He straightened and turned. It lay along the high rocks of the gully like a mist dissolving at the edges and it watched. He went back to where he had left his pack and sat down; leaning against the rock, he watched too. He thought grimly that maybe this would unsettle the brute; it was more used to terror than to watching.

Yet it seemed a useless waste of time. He had seen already that Noatch had no likeness to the fire-eyed thing that had looked at him with menace, and watching it he could see nothing more. If there were questions to ask he could not frame them or Noatch answer them, even if it would. Still he looked, lying carelessly back on the rocks, and soon he saw there were other earth-things near it.

They were often hidden but always appeared again: man-shaped things, grey-haired and emu-footed like those that had brought him. Now and then they glanced at Wirrun with sharp, calculating looks, but always they watched Noatch and kept their places near it as it shifted and writhed. He thought they must follow and watch over it, and that such a thing would need these followers—creatures to give life to its denial of life.

And certainly these others could speak. If he had questions to ask he could ask them of these Jannoks . . . except that he knew they would not answer. He remembered the words of Ko-in.

Ask for no knowing or searching or doing . . . but ask for yourself what you need.

He'd do more than ask, he thought irritably. He'd make them answer if he could. His need was to know. He looked again at Noatch.

It drifted, twisted, changed and was the same, the blind watcher half-seen. Shapeless, colourless, warmthless . . . drawn to fire because it had no warmth . . . Drawn to colour, then, because it had no colour?—to shape because it had no shape? There was his billy, strapped to his pack: that was a shape. Almost idly Wirrun began to think. While he did it he sat up and fumbled carelessly with his pack. He could still feel a dank cold coming from above.

He had decided that the circle of the billy was a shape too natural and unending to draw a thing that curled like mist. A circle was the sky, a tree-trunk, a nest, the sun. Noatch had the land's great burning sun to warm it, a sun that cracked rock; but it came to a little man-made fire. He needed an unnatural shape, something straight-sided and sharp-cornered . . . He had one of the straps of his pack unbuckled; he reached into a pocket and drew out the red-lacquered box.

He played with it for a while, turning it this way and that. The hard bitter thing inside him stirred quickly but he would not let it grow into pain; he thought as quickly of Balyet and let his anger turn towards Noatch. He thought of the mirrors that lined the box and wondered if they might be useful. He remembered that Noatch was used to men's terror; it would hardly expect an invitation.

He shuffled his feet a little, looking for smoother rock; reached for a dead twig and carelessly chewed it; opened and closed the box, flashing its mirrored lid. At last he bent forward and set it down close by his left big toe, and while his body covered it, propped its lid slightly open on one end of the twig. The other end he pushed between his toes. Then he lay back in his old position and let his eyelids droop.

The box stood alone, straight-sided and sharp-cornered on rough rock. The sun that spilt into the gully lit its red to brilliance. Looking down between his knees Wirrun could see it there; looking sideways he could see up and down the gully. He could not see Noatch above him but soon he felt its cold increase. Yet he knew from an excited chittering of Jannoks that it was in the same place.

At little time went by. Wirrun kept his eyelids lowered and his ears alert. He heard the Jannoks twitter from farther to his right, and then from lower down. They seemed alarmed. He strained his eyes to the right, up the gully, and watched its rocky floor.

The white mist flowed into a hollow of rock and lay floating there, cupped and restless. The Jannoks moved about it crooning and coaxing. Sometimes it licked quickly at their claw-toed feet so that they chittered and leapt back. Its coldness rolled nearer: it lay against a rock close by. Wirrun lay still.

It moved again; it flowed over and around the box while the Jannoks uttered warning cries and Wirrun felt a cold sweat on his ankles. A wisp of Noatch curled under the lid— in a flash it was gone—inside the box? Wirrun, startled, jerked his foot hard. The lid of the box cracked shut and he jammed his foot down on it quickly. The Jannoks screamed in fury.

"I reckon I might give this to Balyet," said Wirrun sitting up with his hand on the power and his foot on the box. "Or will I take it north with me?" A huge cold anger came through the lid of the box and chilled his foot, but he thought the mirrors might confuse the thing for a while.

"Die! You must die!" shrieked the Jannoks.

"A good time for it," said Wirrun, "while the big boss is shut up safe and can't get after me. But you tell me a bit about that other death, the one up north, and I might let this one out."

"We tell you nothing, big-head!" they screamed. "That thing is your affair. Let the death out!"

Wirrun laughed. "You told me one thing already—this is no death." His leg was aching to the knee with cold. "Maybe it's your big boss but it's not mine. This thing can be fooled. A man can draw it off with a fire or shut it up in a box. What sort of death is that?"

They glowered at him and reached for the box. He dragged it closer and his hand was always on the power.

"What about this other one up north? Is that a real death —better than this misty-looking thing?"

They spat at him. "That rubbish. A man has made it.

But good enough for you, big-head. You will not shut that one up in a box."

"You never know," said Wirrun.

They sneered at him. One of them said, "Can you fool a thing made of your own worst parts? Your knowing of evil, your power, your greed, your fear—" The others stirred and muttered and that one fell silent.

"Hum," said Wirrun. "The best of me'll just have to be a match for the worst of me, won't it? What do I call this thing when I see it?"

Even that they refused to answer till he changed feet on the box like a man settling down to wait. Then they muttered, "Wulgaru."

"All right," said Wirrun, since he could think of nothing else to ask. He drew the power out of its bag and laid the fur-wrapped stone for a moment on the lid of the box. "Now I'll leave this box here while I climb out of this place, and when I'm gone you can open it. It won't open till then." He stood up, looking down at the box with a darkened face. "Tell your boss he can have it. Present from the Ice-Fighter."

They watched angrily while he strapped his pack, heaved it on and began to climb out of the gully. "Do not die in this country, Hero," they called after him. "Noatch will run fast for you."

"That's friendly," said Wirrun, and he climbed up into the sunlight to warm himself and rest; for though he had reached another place where he could not stay he had not found any purpose that called him on and had no wish for another spirit-journey.

He found a mountain slope studded with box trees, warm in the sun of mid-afternoon and looking wide over grassed plains below. He was not hungry but made a small fire and brewed tea, for his legs ached with the cold of Noatch and all his body was chilled. When the tea was made he let the fire die and sat drinking tea and sun together. He felt cold and weary in every bone, and a bitter sadness he could no longer hide from; and somewhere, somehow, a secret touch of comfort.

He had known before he saw Balyet that the law had no pity. He had known before he saw Noatch that death was no cold, blind spirit-chaser that a man could fool; that it was as the People said, an end and a beginning. He had proved no more than this and could not tell where the comfort came from.

His mind went back to Ularra, whose story he had told to the men of the Centre. No death and no spirit-chaser had caught that spirit, he knew; it had escaped from the ancient dark into the rustle of leaves and the whisper of grass. And it came to Wirrun that of the two of them, himself and Ularra drawn by the singing of the silver water-spirit, Ularra had chosen the better way.

FOUR

In the Country of the Yunggamurra

I

Of all his journeys the one to the north was most like a dream in Wirrun's mind. He called for it late at evening when the old sense of restless dissatisfaction had grown strong—when he must move somewhere and knew no other way to go. He was at once seized by a great man-thing whose head was hidden in shaggy white hair and beard so that only its eyes and nose could be seen, was thrust into a bag and hoisted to the creature's shoulder, and after that knew little more than speed and darkness.

He was brought out of the bag into starlit darkness and the smell of marsh, and was caught up again and carried for a long time through water. He felt only its silken tugging and sometimes the rougher grasp of weed and the suck of mud. Those who carried him seemed women from the waist up, but their legs were the legs of great frogs. Sometimes the darkness grew thick and close and the water's lapping rang hollow, and he knew they travelled by underground rivers; and so at last they reached a billabong whose shores dulled and glowed like a fire. When the frog-women drew him towards this glow he saw them clearly for the first time: their faces were as lovely as their large webbed feet and splayed and leathery knees were ugly.

A crowd of little men were gathered on the shore—he glimpsed long ears, big heads and bellies carried on stick-thin legs and saw that the ground of all that country glowed like fire. But the little men bore him fast, laid like a log along their shoulders, and soon he saw only the blur of leaves and stars and after that nothing at all.

It was still night when he felt grass under him where he lay under a great broad dome of sky pierced with stars. The lights of a car flashed by on some road not far away. He waited, dazed, but no earth-thing came; only something small and furry, warm with life, blundered against his foot and scurried off. He roused himself to pull out his sleeping-bag and crawled into it and slept heavily until morning.

Then he found he was lying in tall brown grass with polished stems that glistened in the early sun. A straggle of box trees and bloodwood crouched low on the plain to his left; behind him the dark green heads of native plum and the white railing of a bridge marked the line of some creek or river. The sky was still a broad, full dome, now blue. He knew only that he had asked to be set down "somewhere near Katherine" and the town could not be far away. He could think of nothing to do except to look for some breakfast. He had finished Tom Hunter's chops last night at the white-misted mountains.

He stowed his pack in a patch of grevillea, took his water-bag and went down to the river. It was a small stream but flowing well and its water tasted sweet. He filled his bag and walked along the bank looking for a deeper pool hidden from the road. On the way he found the trailing green of yams and dug several large tubers. He reached a pool well screened by banks and trees and stripped off and slid quietly in: if there were fish he knew he could catch them.

He caught two unfamiliar catfish under the banks, killed them and laid them by his canvas bag, washed the yams and himself, dried off in the sun and dressed. And all this time, though the river ran so quietly, he was haunted by a sound that he could not quite hear but that he thought was the calling of water.

He carried his breakfast back to the bark-littered ground under the straggling box trees, fetched his pack, lit a small fire and while it built its coals cleaned his fish and set stones to heat. Often he grew still to listen for some far-off waterfall and shook his head with irritation when he heard nothing but birds.

When he had eaten and repacked he sat impatiently wondering what to do now. He had arrived at the place he had chosen, in a country at least near the country of the thing he had been called on to find. What next? He had no plan to approach it, or to seek some power he might use against it; he had so far only resisted and avoided it and did not ask himself, even now, why he had come or why he did nothing. He only felt impatiently that he must do something next—and that here he was too close to the road for freedom—and that beyond this point he knew nothing of the country he was in. He took up his pack and began to walk.

He walked up the river, keeping it in sight since it was water and food in a strange land. It led him closer to looming cliffs of rock, yellow in the sun, ragged and scantily tree-clad, that seemed to wall the plain. He remembered that these would be outlying arms of the escarpment, the worn and broken edges of the high rock-country that was near. The wide-skied, tall-grassed, rock-bared country of the north soothed him as the quiet Centre did. Sometimes he stood still, losing while he listened for it the half-heard sound of falling water.

By late afternoon those walls of rock had closed in to east and west on the river. He had walked a long way under the pressure of the northern heat and was tired and ready to camp. And except that he had recognised the escarpment he knew no more of the country than he had when he began.

He remembered that far away in the east this red-eyed thing, this Wulgaru, had obeyed his power when he met it. In a moment of exasperation, perhaps with himself, he gripped the stone and called aloud: "Come on, you Wulgaru. I'm calling you."

Nothing happened. Remembering how it had lain hidden he set down his pack and went searching among scrub and rocks. He could find no trace of it: whatever the thing had done in the east it had not obeyed his power here. That shook him into thinking for a while.

He thought slowly while he chose a place to camp, caught more fish, this time with a line, set snares that he baited with raw fish, filled his water-bag and billy, gathered wood and made his fire. By then he had concluded that it would have served him right if he had succeeded in calling up trouble while he was tired and hungry and had no clear idea of where he was, or whether the thing he sought was in reach of his power, or even if he was in the right country.

While his meal cooked he argued that he was not going to find out much more about the country by crawling over it like a fly—or, judging from last night, carried at the speed of earth-things. He needed to see it fast and wide by his own means, and he had the means. And what was that cursed sound he couldn't hear?

While he ate he considered his means of travelling fast and wide, and tried to prepare his mind. It was a dangerous means, and especially in a strange country; but he had been given the whole of the land for his country; this country too was his.

In this land of burning distances his ancestors had lived for unknown ages; he was not the first who had needed to travel it farther and faster than a man can walk. His People had long ago learnt the way: to free their spirits in sleep. To travel in the spirit as a man does in dreaming and return to their sleeping bodies when the journey was done. It was a way to be taken only at need—to leave the body empty, unprotected, while the spirit went naked and at risk among others stranger and darker than itself. But Wirrun had done it once before.

When his meal was over he banked his fire between stones and drew over it ash and charcoal for safety and warmth while he slept. While he did this he tried to still his spirit to that deep aching pain, and his mind to thought and anger and doubt of Ko-in. He sat for some time holding between his hands the power wound in its cord, letting his hands feel it while his spirit reached out to feel the night: dark, moonless, with that star-pierced dome enclosing it and mischief stirring in it and shy things hiding and others brooding deep and slow.

He climbed into his sleeping-bag and lay with his hands still folded on the stone and his spirit still reaching for the whisper of grasslands and rivers and the strong proud silence of stone; and he said to them in his spirit, "I am here. All countries are mine. I claim you . . ." And he slept, and his spirit slid free and drifted up like smoke. He drifted over his sleeping body, a shadow of himself holding a shadow of the stone.

And the grasslands and rivers and the high stone country were spread out for him but he could not see them. He was seized on at once by the crying of a waterfall.

It called from somewhere far off, a fall that roared and in a little while faded and in another while roared again. It was a fall that had haunted his mind for more than a year: the mysterious hush-and-fade of water out of which had come the singing of the Yunggamurra. It possessed him.

He went seeking it: first to the river he had followed all day. Hovering over it he felt the life in it, and how in the Wet it came pounding down from the plateau to the plain; but now it came only trickling and had no fall that roared and faded. He rose higher, above the broken escarpment and north over the plateau itself.

Its age came up to him like the deepest notes of an organ he had heard in a cathedral, notes that had trembled in the cathedral's stone. The deep notes of age trembled in this stone, but he listened only to the call of water. It was stronger now.

The plateau was square-cut with joints, each deeply carved and tree-lined, each a river interlocked with others. He slid over great gorges in which trickling streams grew suddenly immense and heard gentle falls that a few weeks ago had roared and shouted. He sought only a river bubbling with sly laughter and wickedness, singing both sweet and sharp like wild honey, a fall that mysteriously shouted and whispered in turn.

And he found it. High on the plateau he found it carving its way out of spring-fed marshes and over the edge of the escarpment. Its fall did not shout or whisper but sprang in smooth curves from ledge to ledge till it ribboned down a long drop into the valley; but its hushing voice was the one that had called out of the old enchantment. Hovering over it he felt its slyness and its nurturing of ancient things and knew it with certainty. He had found the country of the Yunggamurra.

He hid among trees in case they felt his presence, and while he hung there the fall changed its note and began to fade. And his spirit fled on the breathing night. He could not look for he knew what he might see.

She was Yunggamurra now, a fragile silver thing among her sisters. He wondered with pain if he might not know her from the others—but he fled in terror that she might no longer know anything at all of him.

He sped over rocks as old as the world and over plains, not seeing where he went but only travelling fast, and the cry of a stone-curlew followed him. When he faltered and went heavily at last he thought it was because of his own terror and not from any evil in the night. He let himself sink into forest and hide among thin lancewood leaves.

Then at last he felt a darkness that was more than night and that dragged at him. He stayed close among leaves, waiting. The stone-curlew cried again. He heard wings in the darkness: not feathered wings but something strong and swooping that beat close. They came closer still—he crept deeper among leaves, and they parted, and the clumsy face with red-glowing eyes was looking at him.

If it had not come when he called, at any rate it had found his naked spirit now.

It hung like a mask among the leaves, grotesque and unmoving. Only the eyes were hard and bright and knowing, and they gazed into his. He gripped the power and drew quickly behind the cover of leaves.

A rush of air stirred the leaves as the wings swept by and circled and swept back. He waited for them to pass again, and while they turned he sped like thought to another tree-top and hid among new leaves. But the wings swept back as close as before or closer, and the leaves stirred and parted, and there hung the mask with the flame-bright eyes that looked at him.

To be hunted like this turned Wirrun's fear into anger. He held up the power and cried, "Keep off! I order you!"

The face did not move but the eyes seemed to dim for a moment. He shouted his order to the swooping wings, holding up the power to them, and they faltered and swept farther off. But when he turned back the eyes that a man should not see were flame-bright and staring again, and while he threatened the face with his power the wings swept back.

His anger blazed. With the power in his left hand he seized the mask-face with his right and turned it so that he need not see it. It screamed when he touched it and burnt like fire, but he was still himself, and the wings beat in fear, and the face felt as it had looked—a wooden mask, hollowed and empty. And since he should not look at it and would not let it go he held it like a mask before his own face and looked through its flame-bright eyes.

At once he saw the troops of dark wings like giant bats, and the spirits of dead men drifting and wailing below, and the land's dark mass spread out in rain-carved heights and valleys and swamps, and star-flecked rivers snake-gliding to the sea; but the dead were cowed weak things that had failed in life, and the land was wearing into nothing, and the rivers hid old and fearful things. He felt a bitter hardness that was not his own, and under it an anger that was his and fought to be free; and he clung with all his strength to the stone of power.

He came out of the treetops, masked behind the face, and

the bat-wings swept beside him and the spirits wailed and
followed; and the rustling night grew still as he passed. He
let his own anger carry him back to his camp with the fire
banked down and his body safely sleeping. Slender curious
spirits of rocks and caves drifted about it, and fled when
they saw the mask come through the dark.

He went quickly to his fire and uncovered it and dropped
the mask in. It screamed again and vanished, gone without
burning. Wirrun shivered and slid quickly into his body.
For a moment he felt it enclose him: the weight that pressed
him into his sleeping-bag, the beat of his pulse, the cool, even
flow of air in his lungs, and in his hands the softness of fur
that wrapped the hardness of the stone of power. In the
next moment he slept.

2

Wirrun slept only fitfully and woke before daylight, hearing clearly now the half-heard sound of yesterday. He remembered his spirit-flight looking through the fiery knowing eyes of the thing that called itself death and thrust the memory away with a shiver and an uneasy look at his right hand. The hand was not withered or damaged; its flesh had not held the mask-face. And after all his long journeys in search of this thing he felt only a smouldering anger that it had hunted him. His ears were filled with the calling of the Yunggamurra's river.

He lay in his sleeping-bag waiting for the sun, and the trouble inside him was no longer a stone but something that swelled and churned. He longed fiercely to go in his body to the river and to see it with his eyes, but he fought the longing and shrank from the thought of so much useless pain. His mind saw clearly that it could bring him nothing.

What could he do at the river? Only look and come away —if he were strong enough—and go on suffering as he suffered now. Could he catch her again with her sisters at hand and smoke her again into a golden girl? Maybe: and what then? At best a few more weeks of troubled, uncertain happiness, and after that—all of it over again. He clenched his hands. How many times could a man go through that gain and loss?

Or how many years could he live at the call of a river?

There must be a way—or how could she have come to him in the first place knowing what she knew? How could anything do that to a man?—how could Murra? By her own words she had known what must happen. He was flooded with memories of her playing in the water—swinging high in a tree—throbbing with delight on the wind—running over unbending grass and sitting distrustful by the fire with her dark hair stirring; of her coaxing and teasing, the tenderness of her singing and the courage of her laughter. Oh Murra—water-girl—could you do that to a man? There must be some other way.

And he saw that there was another way. There was Ularra's way.

He fingered the thought, and in a moment a feverish excitement took hold of him. That was the way: to stop running, stop suffering and require of her Ularra's peace. He would go in his body to the country of the Yunggamurra and see it with his eyes; and she who had known the end at the beginning would press him under the water with her long nails and give him that strong calm peace she had given to Ularra. She would remember; even slimed with the silver of the Yunggamurra she would know what she did. He would not think that now she might have forgotten and would drown him like another man.

He thought instead with the fever mounting that now his body must travel to the river, and his burdened restless spirit knew the way, and the river called. He thought he could find it in a couple of days of hard walking—or in a moment if he called for earth-things to carry him. But his troubled spirit rebelled at that; as soon as the grey light was strong enough he began to prepare for the walk.

Pleased with his calm good sense he caught fish for breakfast and more to take with him wrapped in a wet shirt; for a man must eat if he wants to walk hard under the pressure of the northern sun. He dug more yams and collected his empty snares; made his fire, cooked and ate breakfast, filled his water-bag and rolled his pack. As the sun was rising he set out to find a road, for his spirit had seen that a road was near.

He struck first a track and then a highway north-east along

the plain. He walked it for most of the day with the sound of the river in his ears. He saw none of the speeding traffic till a grey van overtook him and the driver, a man of the People with a face pock-marked with old scars, offered him a lift. It was a silent drive for the driver too was a silent man; but sometimes he cast a sidelong look at the haunted figure beside him.

When they reached a town Wirrun thanked him briefly and climbed out listening for the river. The drive had saved him a day's walk but he could get farther on before night; he chose a road north. At dark he camped where he was on a hillside, relying on the water he carried. The crying of the river was clearer now. Through the exhaustion of the day and the heat he felt a hard triumph, and he climbed into his sleeping-bag and slept.

But he slept badly. Whenever his mind sank deep enough to loose its hold his troubled spirit struggled to get free on some business of its own. Again and again he was jerked awake, dreaming of bat-wings or drowning and hearing the waterfall rush and fade. Towards morning he slept more deeply and woke late at last in full sunlight. The river was still calling. He ached and did not ask whether it was in mind or body or spirit.

Doggedly he ate and drank and rolled his pack. Doggedly he walked and listened. He was soon finished with roads and followed fainter and fainter tracks, and sometimes blundered through trackless shining grass that hid logs and rocks and for all he knew snakes, or through low straggling forest where the trees posed awkwardly and his feet crunched on thin curled sheddings of bark. Sometimes as he stumbled on he talked to his dead friend.

"Only her, mate . . . none of those others . . . she'll know me all right."

"Peace, mate, a man's gotta have peace."

"No good to a man . . . a bit of slime, you said."

The call of the waterfall was clear and even, hushing gently in the heat. The sun had gone down when he stopped short knowing that he heard it with his ears and not only from within. The fever of excitement rose strongly and called back his mind.

He looked for the fringe of trees that would show him the river so that he could follow it up to the fall—but a stab of cunning stopped him from making that mistake. He put his hand on the power and thought more clearly: they would feel him near, he must keep away from the river. He was going of his own choice to the one Yunggamurra who would hold him under the water with her long nails—oh yes, she'd remember, she'd know. He would not be drawn against his will to the whole band of sisters.

He looked instead for the line of the escarpment, moving the net bag on his belt to keep the power between him and the river. He reached the fall at dusk and quickly unwound a length of grey-fur cord and laid it in a wide circle near the river. He stayed within the circle.

The fall hushed steadily on, still bright in the dusk. His spirit knew it well and curled and cringed somewhere near his belly but he did not feel it. He sat on a boulder within a screen of leaves and watched the water build its unchanging curves at the lip of the fall, spring in its smooth leap over rocks halfway down and fall in plumes into the pool below. Already, in watching it, he found a kind of peace and reached for his water-bag and drank. Dusk brightened into young moonlight and the water gleamed.

A moment came when he gripped the power and grew tense: into the hush of water had come a sound that rang like drops in a cave and he knew it was laughter. It led his straining eyes to the lip of the fall and in a little while he saw them: a gleam of silver limbs and a shine of dark hair in the light of the young moon.

He saw them gathered above the fall, a line of them across the river. They were laughing as they twined their arms together and laid themselves across the flow. The hush of the waterfall changed, faded, its gleaming curves flattened and its plumes wavered and fell; there was only a whisper of water. Above it the laughter grew, the line of silver bodies strained and struggled, their dark hair washed over their shoulders as the water behind them mounted and trickled past. Suddenly the straining line broke—hung wavering—and on a leap and roar of released water the Yunggamurra came spinning and tumbling over the fall into the pool below. The waterfall built its curves again and hushed steadily on.

He had seen what made it mysteriously roar and fade and the pain was like a blunt stone knife, for he had seen the game before. Fierce and proud and enduring she had played her sisters' game alone; one Yunggamurra sitting between stones in the trickle of a tiny creek, letting herself be carried a foot or so down into a pool and never speaking of what she remembered.

When he recovered he saw that the sisters had climbed the wet rocks of the fall and reformed their line at the top. He crouched in leaf-shadow in the circle of the power and fingered the tightness of waiting as a fisherman fingers his line. The voice of the fall softened as its water fell. Above it the laughter bubbled and rang and the Yunggamurra twined and struggled to hold to each other and their eyes shone like stars. The line strained, broke, wavered on a wall of water, and was flung in a debris of moonlit gleams down into the pool. With the power in his hands he sprang forward and shouted before they could flash away.

"Wait! Stay!"

She would know him, she would know—

All their startled faces turned to him. In a moment they were huddled on rocks on the far side of the pool—but they were ordered and could not go. A hero with a power had come on them and the proud Yunggamurra lifted their heads and howled. He saw their sharp claws scratch at rock like angry crabs, and their gleaming throats pulse and their dark wet hair twine about them. They were all as lovely and dangerous as moonlight and water and he could not tell one from another.

"Where is she?" he shouted. "The one you brought back in the storm. The one that was with me."

The howling died and they turned to him all their indifferent faces, all their old, moonlit eyes. The moment built into a wave like the one they had built in the river.

"Murra!" he shouted. "You know me whatever you are. Come out of that, girl!" They gazed at him. "Where is she?" he roared.

They answered at last in cold sharp-sweet voices. "Gone. She is lost and gone."

Seven—he knew there should be seven—feverishly he counted them. There were six.

"Gone? Lost? How lost? You took her back!"

Their eyes were indifferent, absent. "We do not know how or where. We cannot sense her. She is gone and lost."

The moment broke and crashed over him. He stumbled away from the river and left them: the proud Yunggamurra defeated but untaken, shamed. Their howling followed him and grew fainter, and at last he fell into a thicket to lie.

The moment had flowed away and left him stranded.

She was gone; the land kept its inexorable laws. Ularra's way was not allowed to him. He saw at last he had not come in love and despair seeking peace, but only in anger and seeking revenge; dragged there by no enchantment but his own.

3

They were clever and cunning, her sisters. They clung about her in the wildness of the storm, entangled and bound her in their hair, enmeshed her in arms and legs and filled her ears with singing of her lost river-country. They carried her down into streams and leapt up again in new storms. They bathed her in mud till her skin softened and paled, till her silver slime grew again and tiny leeches crept back into her pores. From storm to river and river to storm they brought her across the land, and sang with joy of the lost Yunggamurra found and how far they had travelled—farther than in all the ages—to bring her home. There was laughter and singing wherever she turned, there was always a slime-soft hand in hers and an arm about her waist till at last, as in the old days, she could not rest alone. And so, in a short time at the speed of earth-things, they had her back.

She sank with them into her own remembered river. There were the great yellow cliffs standing over it, and the palm and plum and wild passionfruit hanging. Its water was softer than any, its fish sweet and lively, its waterfall leapt and called. Under quiet banks the tresses of weed moved together like voices in song. Combing her hair with her long clawed nails she wondered how she had lived so long away: how it was that she had not broken like a bubble or dried into dust with loneliness for her sisters and longing for her dear and only river. For they were herself and they made her real.

It was a thing she could wonder in the midst of a water-game, while her laughter joined with the others and her

voice called or sang with theirs. She did not wonder alone
for she could never bear to be alone. That was a darkness,
and silence was a danger on the edge of it. Her sisters knew
it too: they were never apart and never let the silence hang
—except sometimes for a moment, looking at her. Then,
when she hurried to break the silence that she could not
bear, there were secret knowing glances and a tiny smile
passing from mouth to mouth.

One day, seeing that, she broke off the song she had begun and let the silence creep back for a moment while
she looked at her sisters. How many had been taken as
she had, and turned with smoke and taught to know tenderness? She could not remember, the ages were so long, but
she knew some had. Was that how they learnt the danger
of silence and the darkness of being alone? Was that why
their smiles were small? She had no time to think about
it then, for the silence grew too long for the others and
they broke it with a game; but she let the thought lie in
her mind.

There came a day when all the water-games were played
and the sisters looked for a new one. Then again they
glanced at her and the little smiles went from mouth to
mouth. One of them cried, "I know a game! Quickly, bring
me a white stone!" and she gave the Yunggamurra a little
push. So the Yunggamurra dived quickly to find a white
stone, and when she brought it back the others were gone.
They had left her alone.

And first she called them in fear but they did not come,
and then she flashed to and fro to look for them, chattering
empty words to keep the silence away. But the darkness
was pressing closer, the darkness of being alone; and suddenly it pounced and caught her, and it was shaped like a
great dark cavern with a glint of water in it. The Yunggamurra stopped her frantic search and was still, for she
knew that cavern. She had been alone before: long alone,
and in a very deep old dark. In her stillness she sank, and

the river washed her under its banks and she lay there and let memory wash her too.

It could not be for long for her sisters would not let her win their game and came to find her, calling in anxious voices and smiling little smiles. But memory runs fast and she had time enough to learn what darkness lay beyond the edge of silence. It was sorrow.

After that she learnt to play a secret game of her own: to slip away for a moment between rocks and laugh when she was found—to tumble and spin a little longer in the waterfall and climb a little slower to the top, to play and sing with the rest and yet to be alone; to gather moments. And if she kept the memory close every moment brought her something.

Sometimes it was the beauty that the land hid under its rocks, the secret sparkle of stone. Sometimes it was the shimmer of the eastern sea or a glimpse of dark faces dreaming while she sang. Most often it was one dark face, sober with care but breaking into the warmth of a smile; memories flew like leaves in the wind about that face. Once, with a slash of pain, she saw it darkened with loss and staring up into storm.

Once a moment brought a question: did her sisters who had been taken play this secret game as she did? Watching she did not think so; they kept the group whole as if each truly lived in the others. They sank or rose, sang or played as one, and only she was a fraying at the edge of the group. She could not know how it came about that she was changed from every Yunggamurra of them all: that in all the ages of their being—free in the river or taken to the dry world and taught to know tenderness—only she had been shut away alone a long time and learnt to know herself. She had learnt while the land held her shut in its great fist with the pale spiders and ancient crumbling bones. For others too there were lost faces and sorrow waiting to pounce. For her there was also herself.

She had never time for such thinking but little by little

she gathered materials for thought. In an age or two, perhaps, she might have threaded the moments together into
thought. They only tumbled through her mind like a
handful of pebbles on the day the man came with the gun.

On that day all the Yunggamurra were in the pool above
the fall. They were restless and tense and did not play, for
they heard the crack of the rifle and the shrieking and crying
of birds and knew there were men about. They heard these
sounds often: it need not mean that the oldest game, the
Yunggamurra game, was beginning. The men might not
come near the river, or they might be too many, or white
men. It need not mean that the game was beginning—but it
might.

The bad old game of the Yunggamurra did not come
often in these days. Their hunger for it kept them sharp-
eyed, waiting. They heard the rifle-crack high on the escarpment: he had climbed! He would go to the marsh for
the water-birds, and that was near! They quivered and
grew still. He came closer; they could sense that this was
truly one man alone, a man of the People. Their sharp eyes
softened and glowed. The one who had been lost quivered
and tensed as eagerly, softened and glowed as cunningly,
as they all did. It was the game!

With the others she drew herself on to the rocks and sat
languid and lovely combing her hair. Her voice yearned
as sweetly as theirs in the drifting notes of the old love-
singing. She softened her smile and lit her eyes as they did,
and swayed to the singing and longed for him to come.

Are you not coming?

He heard, was caught, came nearer; they drew him on.
Their voices had never been so sweet and magic.

And then the moments of memory went tumbling through
her mind and she saw in the river the shadow of a drowned
face and heard her own voice crying *your friend is between
us!* And the man came closer and she knew she would not
drown him.

Still she sang and swayed a little longer, for this was her

dear and only river and her sisters' life was hers. They saw the man among the trees, they all leaned forward in longing, and quietly she slid into the water like a ripple and let it carry her away. She did not see herself doing this or think what it meant or where it would lead. She only thought, "I will not drown him," and drifted away.

She went over the fall like foam with the singing still in her ears and was spun and tumbled into quiet water. She found a current and rode it down like a glimmer. Where two branches of the river met she turned south into the second thinking only of some place to hide—they would not easily sense her for all this water was alive with the sense of Yunggamurra, but they were swift and cunning finders. She knew a small crack between rocks where she had sometimes stolen a few of her secret moments. She found it and slipped through into a tiny dark cave: only a hollow that held a puddle of stale water from the Wet. She huddled in it.

And now she had more moments than she had had since the First Dark and she began to think. And first she saw that of all the Yunggamurra sisters only she could stay so long in this silent lonely place. And next she saw that she could not refuse the Yunggamurra game and still return to her sisters; she would be forced to play it another time.

Then she saw quite suddenly that after all there had been a sort of choice and she had made it: not between earth-spirit and woman for that choice was not hers, but between her secret self and all that was sweet for a Yunggamurra. Slipping over the waterfall she had slipped away forever. Where should she go?

She might find a way into the deep caverns where she had been lost before, and learn to bear again the First Dark and the land's old bitter water . . . Or in the cool night she might travel over land and find some water where no old thing lived—some place where deep rocks had moved and a spring broken through. But in every country she must pass she would be an intruder, out of her place and in danger; she must always watch.

It was a hard thing, to choose her secret self and be alone . . .

She chose to travel over the land at night; and if she could find no new water she might find a road deep into rock. When a bright-polished moon hung in the sky she climbed quickly out of the river and began her journey.

She travelled easily at first. The ground was hard to her mud-soft feet, sticks and twigs scraped at her protective slime, but the Wet was not long over and the waters were still many. She easily found small waterholes in which no old thing lived and in which she could lie by day and be healed. There were still frogs in plenty, and small fish and water-beetles and weed; she was not hungry. In spite of that, land-travel was not her kind of travelling and the distances were great. She went slowly, circling in search of some water that was not linked to her own river or the rivers of others, that was not inhabited by any old thing like herself, that would out-last the Dry.

She was very lonely—a small silver thing that crawled over the vastness of the land and had no time to play; but she had been lonely in a darkness without moon or stars or shadowy trees and she bore it. She was often afraid and remembered how to hide.

The shy Mimi who lived within the rocks did not worry her. Though they saw that she wandered they avoided her as she avoided them, and frowned at a distance or retreated into rock. The small powerful Podji-Podji over whose underground homes she trespassed were only curious; they were free of the sunlight and not angered by a water-spirit straying at night. But the Nabeado water-girls drove her furiously from their river; the Mormo of the caves were of many kinds and not to be trusted; and she often sensed older, darker powers strange to her, and knew too well that she must not meet them.

South over plains she went, circling and searching. Once or twice she thought she had found a way down underground

to the old water, but when she sank into it this water
was too hot and bitterly stinging for her. And the days went
by and the small surface waters began to dwindle and dry.

South and east were the dry lands where she could not
live. North was her own country from which she fled. The
Yunggamurra turned west.

Almost at once she sensed her own river that had turned
south and west too. That made it harder to keep to her purpose, harder to spend a day in the mud of a shallow lagoon
under water-lilies. For one day she weakened and sought
her river: it brought news of her sisters far away upstream,
and she knew it carried news of her downstream away from
them. She rested and recovered and ate sweet fish, and yet she
could not sleep. The water tingled with knowledge of the
Yunggamurra, and she had always to start up and test it in
case they were too near. That day gave her strength to
leave her river yet again.

And now the waters dried fast, and only a few rock-pools
held. She could not travel far from those or rest safely in
them and began to feel stretched and thinned, like a bubble
ready to burst. There were nights when she circled aimlessly,
not knowing what purpose drove her on.

So it was that one dawn she found herself on the bank of
a small drainage dam that held only a puddle. Uncertain
which way to turn she slipped wearily into the puddle to
rest awhile; and when the sun was strong and the water
turned to mud she woke in despair. There was no water
near that she knew. She looked hopelessly about and saw
only a hillside of boulders where at least there was shade.
She dragged herself there and crept into shadows between
boulders and slept exhausted.

The sun moved on. In the afternoon she lay in sunlight
on rock and did not feel it; the bubble was stretched very
thin. Though her ear was pressed to the rock she did not
hear sounds within it: a deep *boom-boom* or a strange high
humming that rose and fell. The last of her grey slime dried

and fell away in strips. A million tiny leeches wriggled out of her pores and were shrivelled on the rocks. In another moment she would dry into dust.

But in that moment a strange figure came out of the hill: a figure like a man half-crouched, with a sharp and beaky nose and with eyes screwed up against the light. It lifted the frail Yunggamurra in its arms and carried her into the hill, humming as it went like the wind in long grass and walking *boom-boom* through deep dark caverns. And though she was almost dust the Yunggamurra stirred and moved her dry lips, for the stuff of which she was made felt a presence very old and very great. And the shy kind spirit, He-of-the-Long-Grass, went booming and humming along his hidden ways: sharp-nosed and crouching—forgotten and discarded by men—and richly beautiful.

She woke in a pool of sweet water that came trickling in a stream through caverns. There was daylight, but dim and cool; it came through a pot-hole above where twisted roots gripped the rock. She looked and felt and slept again. The next time she woke she saw cakes of ground grass-seed left on the rocks above the pool. She looked at them in awe; for she was a Yunggamurra who had drowned men but he whose vibrations filled the cavern had fed and cared for men while they remembered him. She was awed that his pity should extend to her but she ate a little and slept again.

In a few days she was strong enough to take up the task of living alone: here, in this one pool that He-of-the-Long-Grass had given her. She would not follow the trickling stream up or down; the small fish that darted through her fingers and away down the stream, the spider or lizard that scuttled off into the dark, had escaped into sanctuary for she would not take more than she was given. Sometimes she caught the vibration of booming footsteps or a humming voice and lay still. Sometimes when all the rocks seemed quiet she sang a little, of memories or great rivers or of herself alone.

She saw that she was golden again: her silver slime had gone and there was no rich mud to bring it back. "In time it will come again," she murmured.

At night she often climbed through the pot-hole to feel the wind and the dark spreading land and to look at stars. In time she ventured far enough on the surface of the land to gather figs and a little wild honey and a moth or two. Once she found yams and dug them excitedly and took them back to her cavern; only then did she realise with disgust that they were raw and too hard to eat.

"I can make fire," she said—and sat astonished listening to the words; thinking of the play and shift of red-and-yellow light in her cavern, of a dark face lost and the warmth and company of fire. But she did not make it. To the Yungga-murra fire and smoke are a choking fear. She buried the yams in the soil again.

One night she sat in a tree above her pot-hole in the rustle and sway of wind, looking wide over the land by moonlight while the wind billowed the long shining grass. She was singing of the land that was old by day and young by night, when suddenly she quivered and was still. The wind brought a tingle of knowledge that took away her breath and all her strength: she could not believe it and she could not move.

But it was true, he was near and the wind brought him nearer, he who was at the core of all her memories, whose brown face looked upward in the storm. He could not be near this hidden place on the far side of the land, but he was: his spirit, his sleeping spirit. In a flash she had slipped from her tree and into her cavern. She did not venture out again for two nights.

They had endured what had to be endured, he and she. They had been made and broken and it could not be borne again. But afterwards she made a small fire in her cavern and sat far off in a corner to watch while the dark hair moved on her shoulders. She stared hungrily till the flicker died away and left her eyes shadowed.

FIVE

The Grave-Trees

I

Wirrun, stumbling away from the howling of the water-sisters, fell into a thicket and lay there. The stars moved towards morning; in time he stirred, and sometimes rolled his head from side to side, and at last stiffly sat up. He was dusty, red-eyed, stubble-chinned. He had driven himself hard in his pursuit of shadows. He felt beaten with whips of weariness and loss. But he was himself.

He drank, ate a little cold yam, rewound the cord of the power. Then he stood up, hoisted his pack, and by starlight began to pick his steps away from the country of the Yungga-murra.

No loss, he told himself. If she could do it . . . giving up all she'd had and loved since the land was made . . .

At some time in the night, for one fierce eager moment, he had told himself she had gone back to him: back far east to find him again. But he knew it was not true. The game was too cruel, they could never win. They were trapped in the net of old laws and old magic—but while he had sat screaming in anger and self-pity she had looked for the secret way that the net left open. He should have known it: had he not seen her, lonely and indomitable, making each place her own?

As for him, he was only a man. He could not match her, old and lovely and terrible spirit, but at least he was through with screaming. He could escape into work—instead of using it to escape only from place to place. *You have mated with magic* . . . And it had nearly destroyed him, true enough.

But Ko-in had not known its forbearance or the strength of its independence.

While he stumbled on in the starlight he turned his mind back over the way he had come. And first he remembered the echo-woman Balyet whose very shadow was faded to a wisp of mist; and he was suddenly cleanly glad of the work he had to do and of that unconquerable strength he had once named Murra. They would not fade away into an entreating mist, not himself or the silver water-spirit.

His bushman's eye, reddened and weary, still noted the escarpment looming dark against a paling sky and set a course while his mind followed another trail. The great black dog: its flowing speed and the feel of its rough hair. The old man Tom Hunter, forbearing too—*you've gone too far ahead of us, boy*. Noatch, that was all a man need fear and yet was not evil; the frog-women and the little big-ears of the fiery country. So much help, yet he had not managed to grasp his work. He had still no plan or purpose, he was still drifting.

The sun rose and began to probe down with heat. A flight of black cockatoos flashed their red tail-bands. The tall brown grass shone like silk, the stunted misshapen trees held their awkward poses. He kept to their shade when he could, rested now and then as the heat strengthened, and found the rough tracks of wheels to follow. He was thinking at last of that night when his body slept while his spirit went hunting and was hunted instead; he had not thought of it since but he shivered now to remember his flight looking though the eyes of the mask, and of how it had screamed and vanished in the fire.

In the afternoon his track became a gravelled road and brought him to some creek or river. He stayed by it during the worst of the heat: refilled his water-bag, stripped off and cooled in the stream, caught two small fish and cooked them at a tiny fire, ate and rested and thought. From time to time his ear caught the distant sound of a motor travelling at speed; his road would soon bring him to the highway. This gave him a satisfaction that he had to examine before he understood: he wanted to reach the highway before night so that he could make an early start along it tomorrow. He was going back to that camp where his body had slept while his spirit was hunted. He had remembered that in a game of man against spirit the man had not much need of plan or purpose since he could not make the rules or even know them. He could do no better than be in the right place and meet what came, and that camp was as near as Wirrun could come to the right place.

He would hunt again and invite another hunting, and now that he knew it he felt stronger.

When the heat was more passive he moved on and reached the junction with the highway before sunset. There was no water in sight for a camp so he turned into the highway and walked on hoping to find water before night. A car overtook him speeding south, and a great massive low-loader creeping and labouring north to the new mines. He walked on the grass verge for safety and comfort.

He was frowning as he walked; his eyes watched for a river, his ears noted the motor coming from behind, but his mind was dark with the memory of sweeping wings and of dead men drifting disconsolate. He did not notice the grey van pass till it stopped ahead and then reversed back towards him. He had only begun to see it when the passenger's door swung open and the dark-skinned pock-marked driver leaned across.

"Where to this time?" said the driver.

Wirrun stared puzzled. It took him a moment to remember that someone had given him a lift on this road when he travelled north, and to guess that this must be the same driver. He nodded as though he remembered the man.

"You must live round here. I'm just looking for a camp. Happen to know if there's water handy?"

The driver swung the door wider. "Dump your pack in

the back," and when Wirrun had climbed in and slammed the door, "There's a mudhole or two but good water's farther south. Heading far?"

"That far any rate, if you are. Thanks."

The driver nodded and started the van. Wirrun settled wearily into his seat, glad to watch the level monotonous miles flash by; glad too that the driver's jaw looked as though it were used for chewing rather than for talking. In the red glow of sunset they reached the town where last time they had parted.

"Wanta stop?" asked the man.

"Not if you're going through. Don't fancy a night in town."

The driver's jaw tightened in what might have been a smile. He had rarely seen a man less likely to enjoy a night in town. They went on south, and in the twilight the white rails of a bridge glimmered ahead.

"This do?" said the driver nodding towards the dark treeline of the river.

"Great," said Wirrun with appreciation. "A good long start for morning. I'd never have made it." He half-turned the handle of the door waiting for the van to stop and let him out, but the driver only changed gear and swung off the roadway into long grass.

"Mind if I share it?"

Wirrun was confused for a moment. He would have preferred to camp alone, but this was a man of his People and one who had twice helped him on the road. Moreover, it began to look as though the man had driven out of his way to do it. He said, "Glad to have you," and frowned a little in embarrassment. "I got nothing much for visitors, though. I was going to do a bit of fishing."

"Too dark by the time you get bait," said the driver climbing out of the van with the key in his hand. "I got plenty." He opened the rear door, passed Wirrun his pack, took out a roll of blanket and a large battered cooler, slammed the door and headed for the fence. "Derby's the name," he said over his shoulder.

Wirrun hoisted his pack. "Thanks, Derby. Mine's—"

"I know," cut in Derby pushing his gear under tightly strained barbed wire and holding out a hand for Wirrun's pack. "Know one or two of yours," he added while he spread the wires with a hand and a foot.

"Oh." Wirrun's hand brushed the bag at his belt. "Yeah." He climbed through the wires and held them for Derby in turn, took up his pack and reached for the cooler. It slid from under his hand.

"You get that pack unrolled while you can still see," said Derby firmly. "You oughta shut them eyes or you'll bleed to death." He strode towards the shelter of the low scrub and Wirrun followed, meek and strangely shaken.

It was clear that Derby was supplying the meal and taking charge of the fire and cooking. Wirrun made the only contribution he could by bringing water from the river. Its shadowed pool and curving line seemed familiar, and so did the straggling line of a boxwood tree lit by Derby's fire. He saw that this was the place where the little big-ears had left him when they brought him north. That was luck. He had been brought to the river that was his road to the country of the red-eyed mask.

Derby, already shaking sausages in a pan, received the water with a nod of thanks. "Nice and quick," he said, referring to the sausages. "Fireplace all ready, stones and a bit of wood and all." Wirrun was heartily glad that his fireplace had speeded the cooking but he did not yet explain. After so many scrappy meals of fish and yam the smell of the sausages filled his throat, and when Derby's brown hand reached for eggs to add to them he went away abruptly to unroll his pack.

"Grub's up!" called Derby at last and Wirrun went slowly back. Two plastic plates were generously filled with sausages and eggs, another with buttered slices of bread, and the billy was in place on the fire. Derby took up his knife and fork and went to work. He did not speak or glance at Wirrun till the plates were all empty and the tea brewing. Then he ventured a sideways look and asked a question.

"Where to tomorrer?"

"Eh?" said Wirrun. He gave up the unreasonable hope of polishing his plate any cleaner with another slice of bread and answered the question. "Cross country for me from here. Up this river." He saw Derby's face grow wooden with surprise and added, "I never knew till just now. But this fireplace with the stones, that's mine; spent one night here and never saw the place from the road. You brought me luck, Derby. From here it's up this river a day's walk, in under the escarpment."

Derby poured two mugs of tea and gave another sideways glance. "In to the old graves," he said.

Wirrun's head jerked. "Old graves? I never saw any."

"Me either," said Derby. "Wouldn't want to." He settled back and blew on his tea. "The old hands know. They don't say much in case of tourists and that—there's some'd sell their own grandfather's bones for money."

"They must know too, though. Don't see how you'd keep it from any of the men of the country."

"It's all going now, old places not been used for a long time. You gotta do it right by the white man's law."

Wirrun sat drinking tea and thinking. Maybe it was all going now but he would bet that none of the men of the country would spend a night in the old burial grounds. That would be looking for trouble in the place where trouble lived; for where would a death, a spirit-stealer, live but in a burial ground?

"What's there?" he asked.

"The usual for these parts. Cave where the bones get left in the end. Bit of scrub—lancewood, I reckon—where they'd make this place up in a tree for him to lie on first."

"I know that any rate," muttered Wirrun, for his spirit had been resting in lancewood branches when its hunting began. He had drifted unknowingly into the burial trees among the helpless drifting spirits of an older dead; no wonder he was hunted. Not until Derby reached for his empty mug did he see that tidying up had begun and move to help.

"Not you," said Derby. "Into your blanket. You'll want an early start. It's near done anyhow." He had refilled the billy from a jerrycan and now poured hot water over plates and mugs. Wirrun looked on helplessly. "Get on," said Derby. "It's my stuff, I'll clean it."

That left no option. Wirrun could only mutter, "Thanks, mate. My lucky day."

"See you tomorrer," said Derby.

But Wirrun at any rate did not see him. Weary with driving himself through the heat, freed from obsession and fully fed for the first time for days, he fell at once into heavy sleep and did not wake till the sun was high. By then Derby and the grey van were gone leaving a collection of goods near Wirrun's pack: a carton of eggs, two packets of bacon, a can of baked beans and one of meat-balls, and a plastic-wrapped tray of chops. With them was a note pencilled on torn brown paper: "Cant use it dont waste it D."

Wirrun had grown unused to the luxuries of bacon and kindly despotism. He shook his head and took himself down to the river to wash and fetch water. After that he breakfasted on eggs and chops, wrapped those left over in a wet shirt buckled into a wet canvas pocket of his pack, stored the other supplies inside the pack, buried the remains of his fire, and headed up the river towards his next camp.

2

It was good to be travelling with the river again, from shade to shade under paperbark or ghost gum with the cool of the water at his right hand. At midday Wirrun stopped to brew tea and rest, his eyes wandering often to the far high shoreline of the escarpment. By sundown he came between its closing arms to the camp he remembered and found his old fireplace and brewed more tea. He sat drinking tea and looking about: he would find some heavy stones and build a cool storehouse in the river for his precious supplies; there would be fish in the river, yams along the bank, possum in the scrub. Yet he looked with tingling nerves at this good camp, for it was in the country of the evil thing and he did now know where his danger might lie.

He found himself thinking with an inward twist that Murra would have liked it here. The river was shallow and gravelly under its shade, but it must take water from the plateau in the Wet and somewhere there would be a deep pool gouged by a fall. He saw no lancewood or any sign of old graves and did not look for them. That would be a matter for careful search if a man needed to undertake it; they would not lie near the river. But he felt them in the huge unbroken silence.

The silence brooded, heavy and aware. The dark scrub did not watch but knew it was watched; and the watcher was that high jagged line of broken rocks that made up the escarpment and the plateau. They stood shoulder to shoulder but alone, aloof from the scrub and from small living things that battled with Wet and Dry and strove to live. There were never, Wirrun thought, rocks that spoke more clearly of the age of the world, the loneliness of space or the small accident of life. They were the scarred and broken planet Earth journeying through the sky; what was carried with them they only watched.

He felt this aloof proud watching in the days that followed. Circling about his camp to look for old burial grounds, sitting at night without fire and alert for the brush of wings or the glow of red eyes, he would feel the watchful brooding and grow tense with his hand on the power. It was always the watching rocks; nothing else troubled him though he invited trouble.

Sometimes, holding the power, he sternly called for Wulgaru. Nothing answered. The power never throbbed in his hand. He began to doubt that he had found the right country and to fear that on that other night his spirit had travelled farther than he knew; but as often as he doubted his eyes would narrow in puzzled thought and he knew the answer was not so simple.

For one thing, he knew now where the country of the Yunggamurra lay and it was not far; on the night of his hunting his spirit had travelled only from here to there across the plateau. Perhaps when he fled from the waterfall he had gone out of his way, but he had come easily back to his camp. More important: even if he had missed the country of Wulgaru and the evil was not here, that did not explain the emptiness of the country.

Not only did he fail to find this Wulgaru: he found nothing. It was not natural. He could not believe that nothing lived in the river, that nothing of the Mimi type came into the rocks, that no small powerful wrestlers hid under them. There should have been times when some curious earth-thing came near, some little sly spirit of the place, and made the power throb in his hand. He could only think that they kept away, or were kept away, for some reason that he could not understand; and out of the very emptiness of the country came a puzzled conviction that was a sort of hope. He thought he had found the country of Wulgaru sure enough, and that he was being avoided.

To test it he risked his naked spirit again and hunted the mask-face in sleep. For three nights he sought it in a wide circle: hanging above the plateau, floating in tree-tops, slipping low over the grass, testing the moonlight and the dark towards morning after the moon had set. He found the lancewood scrub again and saw among its branches the rough platforms where dead men had been laid; but even here nothing moved. Wherever he went the stone-curlew cried and the night lay still. Except once: for a moment that shook him more than Wulgaru could have done and sent him back in panic flight to his trembling body. For on that night, caught between terror and longing, he glimpsed the one spirit he must not see—the water-girl.

His spirit, questing for earth-things and powers of any sort, felt at first a tingling in the air and then a throb in the shadow-shape of the stone. He went questing on down a hill-top slope of grass and under trees taller than those of the plains. In a little while he heard singing—the downward-drifting notes, the voice haunting and sharply sweet—and he wanted to call to her and knew he should go and could not do either. His spirit quivered like flame and was drawn on by the singing.

He caught words about the tall grass shining by moonlight and the land that was old by day and young by night; and he glimpsed her high in a tree and shining gold as the moon with the breeze wrapping her long dark hair about her. The song broke—she slid down from the tree and vanished and Wirrun fled too. They had found their ways out of the net and must not be caught again.

He lay in his body and trembled because she was near and had fled and because he had gone too close and could not go closer. He thought wonderingly, "Gold . . ." and forced his mind away and talked aloud, putting roughly into words a set of questions about the evil of Wulgaru. He brought the questions back to the surface of his mind and buried under them the comfort of her nearness and her singing; and a new idea of the river that flowed by his camp.

In the morning he recited his questions again and, having put them into words, rolled up his pack and made ready to leave for a time. Some of the questions had followed him across the land and still he could not answer them; he needed a man of the country. He was going back to that highway along which all men of these parts travelled, and if the People he met were not of the right country he would send a message to Derby.

The way from his first to his second camp had become familiar. He knew the shady stretches and what point to aim for by midday; it left his mind free for the questions he could not answer. Why was he being avoided? It could not be that this Wulgaru—this worst of evils, made by men and using its knowledge of them to enslave them—was afraid of a man with a power. Since it was made by a man it could not be among the First Things or the great dreamings; yet it had lived and ruled since the land was young and must have faced many men like Wirrun. He could not believe that it feared him, for that would surely make nonsense of Ko-in's tale and of Wirrun's mission.

And yet . . . it tied in with Wirrun's own feelings of doubt, of uncertainty and dissatisfaction. For this was what he had always felt—what he had tried to tell Tom Hunter, why he had journeyed west in search of Noatch—that the mask-face, though it chilled and angered him with its knowing evil, was somehow not enough. To anger and disgust the spirit-world, to justify Ko-in's tale and Wirrun's journey, there surely had to be more. Something was missing.

He remembered that he had seen this thing three times and had thought it not a terror of men but an evil. Once it had struck at him with a snake; twice he had ordered it off and it had obeyed. Only when he met it in the spirit, and it a hunter of spirits, had it seemed to defy him—and even then he had seized and made off with it and had escaped. And now, in its own country, it avoided him. To make this thing a ruler of men there had to be more to it. Something was missing.

He reached the camp by the highway while the sun was still above the horizon and made use of it to set up his camp for a day or so. He built up a useful woodheap, dug yams and fished for both dinner and breakfast. By dusk he was ready for an early vigil next day, and lit his fire and set stones to heat for grilling fish. He was breaking more wood when a pair of headlights came sweeping on to the bridge spotlighting the white railing; they faltered on the bridge, came on slowly, then turned aside and stopped.

Wirrun hunched his shoulders and muttered: some fire-ban must have been imposed and this warden or policeman was investigating. He was determined not to eat raw fish for lack of a fire and kept his head down as the fence-wires twanged and footsteps approached.

"Want a lift?" said a familiar voice at his shoulder.

Wirrun swung round incredulous and stared from under lowered brows at the firelit pock-marked face of Derby.

"Saw your fire," said Derby. "Just wondered." His jaw was tightened in the way that meant he was grinning.

"Me too," said Wirrun. "You got a job driving up and down this bit of road?"

"Yep," said Derby. "Job watching out for you."

"Yeah? And who pays you for that?"

"No money in it. Worse luck. Tommy Hunter sent word. Every man and his dog's gotta use this road. I was to watch out and help when I could. Hang on till I fetch my gear."

He strode off into the dusk, and Wirrun pushed yams into the coals of his fire and set his whole catch of fish to grill. The van's lights reached for him as it turned off the road-way to park. Derby came back with his roll swinging from one hand and his battered cooler in the other. He glanced dubiously at the fish and opened the cooler.

"Brought a bit of tucker. Seeing you're a long way from a store."

"Fine," said Wirrun, "but this time you eat with me. Food of the country. Good while since you ate that."

"Good tucker as long as there's enough. Everyone eats fish."

"There's plenty," said Wirrun with an inward grin. He felt he owed Derby something for keeping his own council in so tight-lipped a style and mentally checked the supplies in his pack. Four grilled lizard-tails to add to the fish; for afters a few young pandanus-nuts and a handful of dry woody wild apples which were nothing like apples except perhaps as to their worms.

"Where you heading?" said Derby.

"Here. Looking for you."

"So where to?"

"Back again, now I've seen you," said Wirrun taking his revenge. "That's if you know the country. I want to talk to a man of the country. So you can stuff that ignition-key you know where and lubricate your jaw for talking."

"About what?"

"If you heard from Tommy Hunter you oughta know. About this . . . Big-Cap of yours, mostly." In courtesy to Derby he would not speak the name of Wulgaru into the dark.

"Ah," said Derby. "I'll get a bit more wood."

"There's a fair heap under that old bloodwood. Use that." Wirrun reached into the cooler for plates.

Derby set to work to lay a second fire.

3

Wirrun, serving his dinner of fish and yam and lizard-tails, was glad of the cool of night but knew that in any case a second fire could not have been helped. The powers of another country, or the small earth-things of the place, may be talked of at night by one fire; for a Big-Cap like Wulgaru, and in its own country, it is wiser to talk between two. He made no comment but handed Derby his plate and set the billy to boil. Neither did Derby blench at the lizard-tails but reached for the salt and ate with calm enjoyment.

"I'll let you off the fruit course," said Wirrun kindly. "And there's still a bit of sugar left for your tea."

Afterwards he cleaned up and put away while Derby lit his second small fire and brought more wood to have at hand. They sat with their mugs of tea between the fires and blew and sipped.

"What you wanta know?" said Derby.

Wirrun was silent for a while. Derby was a good man, he thought; but so were Tom Hunter and the men of the Centre, men who had accepted him once as a hero and as a comrade too. He had had to tell those men too much and he had lost them. He did not want to lose any more good men to fear or because he had gone too far ahead of them. He wondered for a second if this was what life had made of him now—a lonely man isolated by fear; lost to his friends by being too far ahead, lost to his love by being too far behind. He turned away quickly from the thought and chose his words.

He said carefully, "They're dodging me, keeping out of

my way. All of 'em. There ought to be others besides this—thing of yours. There's nothing, all empty. I can't come to grips."

Derby frowned at the fire. "If you can't I don't see me doing better."

"But I want to know why, man—I want to know what he's up to."

"You need better than me," said Derby. "The others—the small rubbish—they'd be doing what they're told, wouldn't they? But what *he's* doing—" He shook his head. "Only—" He glanced sideways. Wirrun waited. "Only," said Derby uncertainly, "it looks good, don't it? If he's dodging? Must be he can't trust himself."

And Derby was a man of the country, one who sat between two fires to talk about Wulgaru in the dark.

"I heard he was a terror," said Wirrun.

"He's that."

"But you're telling me that in all the time he's had, all the time there is, he's never been faced before? Never met a man like me and can't handle it? Is that what you're saying?"

Derby tossed a stick on the nearer fire. "Maybe there never was a man like you. Don't know, do we? Maybe it's because you're a stranger. Not one of his own."

"Hum," said Wirrun. "Only it's been over east lately—you know that?"

"Not to say know. Heard something."

"Cheeky as a snake, not acting scared of strangers. That's why I'm here. It's your Big Cap and no one else can take it from you, but they're not having it over east."

"That's it, then," said Derby. "Why he's dodging. Hasn't got himself in charge over there yet. When he has he can handle you. That'll be it."

"Hum," said Wirrun again. He remembered that in the east the mask-face had obeyed his power but that here in its own country it had first hunted and then avoided him. "How big is this thing, then?"

Derby leaned over to make up one of the fires. "Big enough. There's those say he's only bad for bad men and for good ones he's good. Good or bad he's got 'em in his fist."

Wirrun frowned. Here was this judging of good and bad again: how could it be allowed to Wulgaru? As far as he knew there was no such judgement. There was only the law: safety or disaster for all. And men who broke it, who risked disaster for all, were punished in life by other men. He thought of those greatest powers who gave the law, whose names were spoken in secret by those who had the right. They had sometimes punished men on earth, but even they did not sit in judgement on the dead: was Wulgaru greater than these? He asked the question aloud. "Is he a Big Sunday?"

Derby shifted restlessly. "Different kettle of fish, isn't it? He made nothing. Only Clever Men; he makes them sometimes."

Wirrun nodded for he had been sure of it. They would never have sent him against one of the secret, sacred beings of the country. "So who put you in his fist? Where does he get his power over a man's spirit?"

"Where does he get it? He's got it, that's all. He takes it. There's others do the same."

"Man," said Wirrun impatiently, "I know about them. I been and looked at one on purpose. And if there's anything the same as this I don't know it yet. These others, they're hunters, that's all. Like a chicken-hawk. They might get hold of you or they might miss, depends how quick you are and if you do the proper things. But this of yours—there's no proper thing you can do. It don't hunt, it takes—and it takes the right to say if you can go home! Who gives it that right? Do all the old ones, the dreaming ones, give in to it over right and wrong? Because if they do it's the biggest of all and a sight too big for me."

Derby sat frowning at the fire, following Wirrun's argument. Wirrun waited tensely; this question, he knew, was

one key to his helpless uncertainty. At last Derby turned to
him, puzzled but doing his best, and picked up one phrase
of the argument.

"If you can go home: he don't say that. That's out of
his hands."

Wirrun breathed heavily. "All right, then, what does he
say? What does he judge you for?"

"To get born again, of course. They all will, only some
he'll hang on to for a good long time and clean up a bit
first."

"Glory be," said Wirrun blankly. He must have been only
half-awake sure enough. He had forgotten that every one
of the People had at least two spirits and some of them
three; that one of these was a man's own self and found its
way to his right home; and that just as his body dissolved
into earth and lived again in other forms so a second spirit
stayed on earth to be born and live again. He had confused
these two, the inviolate self and the earth-self; he had seen
this Wulgaru as a man-made barrier standing between men
and their dreaming. Instead it was only, like so many others,
a tormenting hazard of his earthly life. No wonder Derby
watched him in frowning surprise.

"Well," he said, "that cuts him down to size. I got hold of
the wrong end talking to Tom—I needed a man of the country. Only . . ." He paused again and Derby waited. He
had to wait some time; long enough to feed the fires again.

At last Wirrun spoke as if he were carrying on an old
argument. "Look. I've seen this thing. Three times."

Derby gave his sidelong look. "You oughta be three times
dead."

"I got protection," said Wirrun with a hand on his belt.
"But maybe you're right, and that's what ties me up. I
don't reckon this thing's big enough for all the fuss. Nasty,
I'll give you that. But no bigger than others I've seen and
not as big as some. I don't reckon it's worth all I've heard."

"I don't reckon you've seen him then," said Derby solidly,
and Wirrun was startled. "What've you seen?"

"What I was sent after," Wirrun declared; and he gave Derby a short account of the fate of Jimmy Ginger, of his own meetings with the no-thing, what he could remember of Ko-in's account, and the time he was hunted in the lancewood scrub. Derby listened, brooding over the fire, but at the end he shook his head.

"Not him. Not his own self."

"You telling me that Ko-in and his sort wouldn't know?"

Derby shook his head again. "Same thing really. These faces, they'll mean the same. Little bits of him that he's sent out; the ones he made, that he uses. But it's not like seeing the Big Boss his own self."

"Glory be," said Wirrun again. It was another thing he might have worked out for himself if his mind had ever been properly on this job. "I shoulda talked to you a long time ago."

Derby grunted in a satisfied way and after a moment ventured a comment of his own. "I been thinking. No wonder they're dodging you, man. That last time with the wings, that would've shook 'em up. You handled that right."

"Eh?" said Wirrun. "I was a fool, man. Not thinking right. Still don't know how I got out of it so easy."

"I reckon you do," said Derby. "That's the way with this lot—take a tough line and act hard. That's the only thing ever works."

"Is that right?" said Wirrun dubiously and had a sudden feeling that it was. He would never want to do it again, but in some way he did not yet understand it was as well to have looked through the kindled eyes of the mask—to have seen the dead drifting disconsolate, the land wearing away and full of fearful things, the small harmless spirits fleeing.

"You want any help?" said Derby. "There's others standing by."

"Tell 'em thanks but they sent me the right man. I see my way now. I'll be getting back early and—drag this thing out somehow. I just gotta think of something."

"Hit the sack, then," Derby suggested, "and think on your

feet tomorrer. You'll take the tucker I brought, it was got for you."

"Glad to—but no more worries, tell 'em. I been taught by experts, I don't starve in the bush."

Derby's jaw tightened again. "I seen that. Only bush tucker needs time. You might be short of it. Get off, now."

Wirrun yawned, nodded goodnight and made for his sleeping-bag. He felt released, his mind clear, and knew that he would sleep. He drifted off while he looked at Derby, still sitting hunched between the fires.

He woke in the dark between moonset and dawn, and rolled his pack and stowed away the bagful of provisions he found near it. Derby was heavily asleep, rolled in his blanket between the fires that were dead but not yet cold. Wirrun did not disturb him but only groped into the cooler to make sure that it still held something for his breakfast. Wirrun himself would breakfast by daylight somewhere up the river. He went quietly away.

It was slow walking in the dark but he had not started early for the sake of a quick journey. He had wanted to be away and alone, to be moving in the right direction and thinking as he went. When the sun rose he took time over breakfast and washed in a pool. He sat out the heat of the day beside another. There was little to be gained by reaching camp before dark.

He did reach it before sunset, and stripped and cooled off in the river again. By then he knew the source of that hard anger he had always felt against this Wulgaru: that with all the arrogance of its maker, and with no other power than evil magic and the helpless fear of men, it dared to take to itself this right of judgement. And he knew what tough, hard line he was going to take with the thing, by what means he would try to force the thing to face him. Now that he knew its limits he did not care why it avoided him—whether for Derby's reason or some other of its own. While it did avoid him he could do nothing; it must be made to face him. If it would not come to him he must go to it.

He knew only one place that the thing might call its own: the lancewood scrub. There would be others—the burial cave if he could find it, and if he must find it he would. But the lancewood scrub with its burial platforms he already knew, and that place too Wulgaru must claim as its own. Wirrun had found it empty like the rest of the country; he had been avoided there too. But if he occupied it, made it his own, stayed in it night after night, then one of two things must happen. Either Wulgaru, avoiding him, must lose this ground and accept defeat by a man or it must face the man and claim the ground.

He thought it would face him in time. A man-made thing, taking its power over man from man himself, could not afford the defeat; it would be known throughout the land and in Wulgaru's own country. It must face him.

He thought of moving his camp into the scrub and gave up the idea. In his camp a man has to sleep. He did not know his enemy and would keep his attack direct and simple; he would sleep and eat here as he had before and in the safer hours of daylight. The nights he would spend awake in the scrub. At sunset he dressed, made a small fire, ate and drank, tidied the camp and put out the fire. When the line of the escarpment was sharp against the green-glowing sky and the moon low in the east he went out of camp north to the lancewood scrub.

He went carefully with a hand on the power but it gave no sign. The stone-curlew cried and the powers of the country drew away as always. The last daylight drained from the sky as he neared the escarpment; he felt its heavy brooding and nothing else. He reached the lancewood scrub and went into its moon-patched darkness. There was nothing; it rejected him. Yet the place itself weighed on him for he was a man of the People; and he remembered the wailing spirits he had seen in it. He was glad of the small torch in his pocket, brought for the deeper darkness of the scrub.

He flashed the torch only once or twice as he found his way in, stopping often to look up into sparse leaves black against the sky. Soon he found what he was looking for: a heavier shape among the leaves, a platform where some dead man had been laid till his bones were ready for the cave. He sat down under that tree for the rest of the night.

In such a place he had no need to fight off sleep; he was tense and aware. He unwound a length of cord from the power and let it lie loose on his knee, kept a hand on the stone to receive any warning, and made himself sit relaxed like a man at rest. Now and then as the hours went by and the moon passed over he stood up and moved about a little and sat down again. Nothing else marked the hours; he expected nothing. It would take more than one night to stir Wulgaru.

At dawn he went quickly back to camp and washed and ate and slept. He woke in the afternoon, attended to firewood and water, cooked his evening meal and set out at the same time as before. This time he carried a blanket and water, both for comfort and the appearance of it.

He went to the same tree, sat there as before, and the night passed just as the first had done. By the third night, with the moon beginning to wane, he was growing accustomed to the lancewood scrub and sometimes even dozing for a moment.

On the fourth night he was jerked out of a doze by the stone throbbing in his hand.

4

If the throbbing of the stone jerked him suddenly awake
at least he woke alert; he made himself limp again at once
and felt for the cord that lay loose on his knee. From under
his eyelids he searched the scrub, turning his head with a
restless sleepy grunt. He could find no red-glowing eyes but
the stone throbbed more strongly and his muscles secretly
tensed.

At last he saw, on a branch just above him and much
nearer than he had expected, a shadow too dark and too
regular in shape. It was so near his head that he sprang in
reaction even while he shouted, "Stop! I order you!" He
had grabbed at the shadow and looped his cord about it
before the words were out.

There was a wild wing-beating struggle like the struggle
of a giant moth and the feel of something like thin dried
leather. He looped it with more cord, pulled it tight and
jerked his hands away. Then he pulled the torch from his
pocket and flicked it on.

Small red eyes glared at him between dark enwrapping
wings. The thing lay on the ground at his feet; it stirred
and stilled as the light caught it. There was a wizened skull-
like face between the leather wings.

"You belong to this Wulgaru?" said Wirrun.

It hissed at him.

"Did belong, more like," said Wirrun. "That's my power
holding you now."

The winged thing jerked a little inside the loops of cord
and was still again.

"I could keep you now, if I had any use for a thing like you." It hissed at him again. "But I haven't so I reckon I'll send you back to Wulgaru. This time, any rate. But you tell this Wulgaru not to send any more things like you against me or they mightn't be so lucky. I came here to have a few words with him but I find he's moved out. So I'm moving in. You tell him if he wants to talk about that he better come and face me under these grave-trees; himself, tell him. He needn't send any more big-eyes or bat-wings. But he better come soon, you tell him, before word gets out that I've taken over his grave-trees."

He did not order the creature with his power for he knew it would carry all it heard and saw back to Wulgaru; it had been sent for that. He began to toss free the loops of cord and wind them in; the creature jerked against the cord and lay still. When the last loop fell away it beat its wings furiously, seemed to struggle from the ground into the tree above, rustled for a moment among the leaves, then reached with its wings for the darkness and swept away. Wirrun smiled grimly and sat down to wait out the rest of the night. But he did not doze again.

For another two nights he sat under the grave-trees and felt their desolation and the country's withdrawal. The stone-curlew cried ahead of him as he came and went. He told himself that such a Big Cap as Wulgaru would not easily accept a challenge from a man; it needed time. He thought a great deal about the meeting that must come and how a man could take a tough line with Wulgaru itself—but until he knew what it was that he had to meet the thinking was wasted. Sometimes for comfort he thought of the river near his camp and that deep-laid feeling that it flowed from the water-girl to him. So near to the plateau it must, he thought, receive water from those heights; at least in the Wet and for some time after. Yet in all his wanderings in this country he had not heard a waterfall or seen a wet face of rock. Underground, perhaps . . . some fault in one of those giant gorges . . . she had seemed to vanish into the ground. It was a refuge she would know and understand.

Alone under the grave-trees night after night, with some great trial ahead that could not yet be seen, his mind gave up the memory he had buried. Gold . . . she had surely been gold . . . as when she first came through the smoke. But if some other man had caught and turned her the old Yunggamurra laws would be working again; her sisters would know where she was and would come for her. In all the time she had crawled through caverns, lost under the land, they had left her alone; only when he found and turned her had they come to take her home. Alone, then . . . an escaped Yunggamurra alone and turned to gold . . . a freed Yunggamurra? Freed by whom and from what?

On the third night after his capture of the winged creature he was so lost in these thoughts that he did not feel the faint throbbing of the stone. It was pulsing strongly before he was roused to that or the heavy chill that pressed him down. Then he tried to spring up but the cold wrapped him as his cord had wrapped Wulgaru's creature; he could make no move except to tighten his hand on the stone. And wings were beating in the trees.

He saw red eyes like firesticks in the dark, a great number of glowing eyes crowding close as the wings swept near. He could not speak to order them away. Voices hissed at him: they were close at hand.

"Dead man. Can't move, can't speak. All men dead here. This man can't speak, can't know, this dead man. This man got empty ears."

He thought he was truly dead and knew nothing of himself, but his fingers were closed on the stone. And suddenly a great tall shape stood among the others but not near or distinct; he saw it as a faint green glow, like a toadstool that glows in the dark or the glow that lights and fades in a dark moving sea. This shape spoke, and its voice came down like the sound of wind in a tall tree.

"Who waits for Wulgaru under the grave-trees? Say what man you are."

And he thought he was no man; that he was dead and had no answer. The leather wings swooped by his face, the fiery eyes shone close, and behind them the tall shape glowed green.

"Say what you are," it called again.

And suddenly in Wirrun's mind another great voice spoke with passion: *Poor spirit, will you not speak for it? Will you not say what the stars will stoop to hear?* And he opened his dead lips and answered.

"I am." Again he could say no more—yet as he said this he knew himself. "I am!" he cried more strongly. The wings faltered and the fiery eyes flickered; the green glow pulsed. But Wulgaru spoke again like a tree and ordered him.

"Say who you are."

"You know that," said Wirrun grimly through the crushing cold that still held him down. "Ask who I'm from."

The shape of Wulgaru laughed a great sneering laugh. "I know that too! From shadows and nothings, things that creep like beetles out of the land and are bound by its law."

"And that's the law they send you. It's too big for you, mate."

The shape laughed again. "A law of beaten sand and crumbled rock and dust carried on the wind, a law of lost water and dead seas. What is that to me? I take my law from the living and knowing, from Man—I take it and make it my own. What is the land to me?"

Then Wirrun was angry for he had looked through the eyes of the mask and seen for himself the lies of Wulgaru. His anger melted the cold and he sprang up at last and faced the green-lit shape. It dimmed and gathered itself again; the red-glowing eyes hung near it and the wings rustled among leaves.

"Big words for a thing that a man made out of a tree!" shouted Wirrun. "I'll tell you what the land is to you—

outside this country it throws you off like an old dead dog! Here you belong to the men that made you, and as long as they give it to you this is your place. Stick to it. I'm ordering you. Where I come from men don't give up their law to a man-made thing like you."

"Do they not?" The voice was softly mocking. "Then Wulgaru has lost his ears and must hide in a cave among bones. I dreamed that where you come from men give up their law for man-made things far smaller than Wulgaru. Do they not give their children man-made toys instead of love? And kill themselves every day in man-made fun? And give away their law for man-made power and man-made empty hate? I thought I saw this. Poor Wulgaru: he dreamed that in the east men threw away their law and begged for him."

"And who did you dream gave you the right to say so, you bit of tree?" The shape shone green with anger and Wirrun clutched his stone. It took all his strength to speak so boldly, but his mind tightened like his fingers and clutched at what he knew: that Wulgaru had avoided him and that only boldness would do.

And Wulgaru answered calmly, even kindly. "Man gives me the right for who else could? What else is there?"

"Not me," said Wirrun. "I give you nothing. So if that's your right there's a hole in it."

"It is a hole I must bear, for who would seek rights over Wirrun of the People, Ice-Fighter, Peace-Bringer, a man born Clever? His greatness sets him apart from men."

And is that all your greatness? An axe falls on it . . .

"You're selling me short," Wirrun retorted. "It's not on account of the big names that I throw you off. I just spit on you because I am."

At that the anger of Wulgaru broke through. "A little reason! Because you are. Because the winds blow this way or that, the flower falls or fruits, the cicada sings or dies in the shell. Only for that?"

"For all of that."

"Only for that you stand under my grave-tree and order me? You have strange dreams, little stranger."

"No stranger," said Wirrun shortly, holding hard to his strength. "If I never stood here before I stand here by right. I've been given all the land for my country. And I see you don't turn me out. Took your time to face me, didn't you?"

"I don't face you now," said Wulgaru sharply. "If I faced you, Little Am, you would not speak so loud. You would be a skin-and-bone fellow, one of the poor sort that wail about you now if I could show them to you."

"I've seen 'em."

The green glow dimmed and gathered itself again. "It is my kindness to the hero Ice-Fighter that I do not face you."

"And is that what I'm to go back and tell 'em? That Wulgaru's a terror for dead men but he was too kind to face one live man? There'll be one big laugh all over the land. Every tree and rock and swamp and claypan'll be laughing at the kindness of Wulgaru. Any rate I won't be going back for a bit, I reckon. I like it here. I'll just be camping in this bit of scrub till your kindness runs out and you ask for your grave-trees back. And then, if you promise to keep yourself and your brood at home, maybe I'll let you have 'em."

He quailed inside and clutched the stone for Wulgaru roared his answer like a storm-wind among trees. "Face you, you half-made thing—face you! But will you dare face me? You talk-talk-talk like a cockatoo and hide away inside your flesh but will you come out of it and face me? Will you face me truly, in your spirit, eh? Or will they laugh at *you* across the land?"

Trembling as he was, Wirrun forced his voice to be strong. "I'll face you any way you like. Say how and when."

"Ah!" breathed the shape; and yet it was silent for a while. When it spoke again there was neither anger nor triumph in the tree-tall voice but a tone almost of sadness, like the west wind among she-oaks. "You have claimed this country as yours, you shall face me like a man of the country.

124

When night comes again you shall sleep at your own fire with the bag you wear, and the power within, to guard your sleeping flesh. But your spirit shall lie unguarded up there in the branches where other men have lain; and you shall be brought to face me truly, and I will destroy you."

He did not know how he could meet this test but only that he could not avoid it—and that he would not be parted from the stone for he did not go into battle in order to lose. He said, "It's me you're supposed to be facing and not some other man. Where I go the stone goes: its outside with mine and its spirit with mine. But I'll give my word not to use it against you. If you destroy me that's that, I can't do more. But if you don't you stay in your own place ever after, you and all your sort. Give me your word for that or it's off and I'll carry on the way I am." He waited grimly and when no answer came shouted, "Come on, Wulgaru. A Big Cap like you, you can't be scared of a bit of quartz on one man's belt."

It answered sombrely. "You speak what you do not know, you and your little stone. If I do not defeat you still I must destroy you; you cannot face me unchanged. But I will take your words as you meant them: if I do not destroy you like another man I and mine will keep to our place for always. It is agreed."

For a moment the scrub was hung with glowing eyes and beaten by the sweep of wings. Then it was still, the cold drained out of it and the shapes all gone; there was only the heavy silence of the grave-trees, dark branches and thin leaves against the sky, and the darker shape of the platform of the dead on which Wirrun must lie.

5

Wirrun went out from the grave-trees and sat unsleeping under the stars. They were paled by the pale gold of moonlight but the edge of the scrub hid the moon. At first Wirrun was weak and shaking, for to face even the veiled shadow of Wulgaru had cost all his strength. Later he was heavily weary but far from sleep. His mind shrank from the test to come and could find no way to withstand it; it seemed that some force beyond himself or Wulgaru, some tide as deep and quiet as the moonlight, had lifted him and brought him to this night.

He remembered Jimmy Ginger washing in his net, and the snake that was set in his way, and how against all reason his defiant spirit had seized the mask, and the old and bitter view he had seen through its eyes. That had been Wulgaru's view; he had seen with Wulgaru's own eyes; he sat with his brow drawn heavily down and tried to turn that view on himself and the struggle. He could see nothing clear. He felt only that deeper tide sweeping them on and a sense of loss and of power turned knowingly against itself. He did not know what that meant, unless it were aimed at his stone.

He thought of Noatch, thief of souls and hungry for warmth, trapped in a red box lined with mirrors; and he knew that he could invent no trap for the wise and knowing evil of Wulgaru. He thought of his body left empty and asleep in the country of the enemy, and he shivered again. That was the danger to be dreaded. His spirit would be alive and aware and could meet what came according to its strength; but if they destroyed his senseless body while he was away he would have no earthly escape. That must be guarded against; he thought the threat or warning of it lay in the last words of Wulgaru.

At daylight he rose and turned back to his camp and nothing peeped at him as he went. There was only the old land stirring, setting itself against the sun for one more day. He thought that if he must be destroyed he would choose to have it here, under the aloof and watching rocks. He found himself looking on at his own life as men are supposed to do in drowning: none of it easy, much of it hard and bitter, but all of it enriching. He would not give it up easily.

He could never choose Ularra's way—that had been a lie told by angry self-pity. He could choose only life and more of it, lived more freely. More of day and night and rocks and tall, remembered trees, of singing recaptured and dark hair seen again; of wind-riding and friendship and fear. It was good to be sure of it before he met Wulgaru. He was thinking this when he came in sight of his camp and saw smoke rising from his fireplace.

He told himself he should be wary but there was that sense of being lifted and carried on to some unavoidable end. He knew who had lit his fire and sent the smell of bacon wafting towards the escarpment; and when he reached the camp it was indeed Derby's scarred face that looked up from the frying-pan. It was like the chime of a bell to see him there.

"Still spying on me," said Wirrun, his voice ragged from weariness.

"Few stores in case you're running low," said Derby. "See you got those bleeding eyes again. Breakfast's ready."

Wirrun sat down and accepted bacon and eggs. "You been walking all night?"

"Yesterday," Derby explained. "Smelt your fire and got in just on dark. You were out."

They shared bacon and eggs in silence and Wirrun savoured the luxury of the sharing. When they both sat with their mugs of hot tea he said, "Planning to leave right away, are you?" and grinned to see Derby frowning at the fire.

"Thought I'd give it a day or two," said Derby at last. "Man of the country. Might be some good."

"Too good a man to waste," said Wirrun. "This is no place for a man of the country. You're leaving right away."

"What's on then?" said Derby postponing argument, and Wirrun gave him the barest outline of the night past and the one to come. Derby wasted no time on the unforeseeable but went straight to the point that could be foreseen.

"It's not a thing a man can do," he said roundly. "The rest can come at you asleep while you're off busy with the Boss one."

"It's not a thing I can leave," said Wirrun.

"You need someone standing by. I know the business, what there is."

"Sure you do but I'm not trusting it. I got safer plans. No knowing how long this sleep-journey might take, and a man on guard'd have to sleep himself sooner or later. I'm not risking it any rate—I want to see you round again and not be tied up worrying. If a man of the country was wanted he'd have been sent, but they sent me. You finish your tea and take your pack and get off down that river."

"Not me," said Derby solidly and they drank in silence a while longer.

"Man," said Wirrun at last, "you've been more good than you know—what I needed most you've just given it to me. But I reckon I know where to go for help. Now you do what's gotta be done, same as me."

Derby frowned again but found nothing else to say. He said nothing till the camp was cleared up and he stood with his pack on his shoulder ready to leave. Then he said, "Make a smoke if you need me. And for god's sake get some sleep."

"I'll do that," said Wirrun, "and thanks, mate."

He watched Derby slouch away down the river; whatever might happen, there went a man who would know a bit about it. Enough for word to pass. When he had gone Wirrun himself took a last look at the fire for safety and, leaving his pack where it lay, turned away up the river.

It was hard to find from the ground, by daylight and with only his eyes, what he had seen once by moonlight as he floated above. But he thought the upper course of the river might set him on his way, and with the escarpment so near he should soon know. The heat was beginning to swell but the flood-scoured banks of the river, hung with paperbark and ghost gum, made their own shade. He kept to the reaches of sand and gravel in the river-bed; almost at once it became a series of wide shallow pools and flowed partly under its bars of gravel and sand.

Between paper-wrapped trunks and under screens of drooping leaves the mosquitoes hummed. The river-bed was narrowed by rocks, widened and was narrowed again. He reached the outlying hills near the escarpment and still there was no whisper of falling water. A deep pool ahead was partly hidden by two twisted leaning gums; he pushed through the leaves and saw beyond them a hillside. There was no more river.

It had gone underground.

The broken rocks edging the farther end of the pool were not damp but wet, and above them rose the hill. Now that his eyes saw it he knew that his spirit had seen it before. He filled his water-bag, rested for a moment, and went out into the heat and began to climb.

It was a tough steep climb up the broken hillside. It was hard to believe that above there could be tall trees and slopes of brown grass. But when he came between high rocks on to the hilltop he saw that it sloped gently away to grass and distant trees; some trick of winds or circle of harder rock had built up a sandy soil here instead of tearing it away. He went on down the slope.

An ocean of silence flooded the world and drowned the plains below; small sounds of birds and insects floated in it for a moment and washed away. Wirrun thought he heard a song dropping into it note by note; he wandered on from shade to shade with his hand on the power, hearing but not hearing the sweet clear notes and sometimes murmuring as he walked.

"You know it's me, girl, but don't be scared . . . It's all over, can't be helped, you said we couldn't win . . . I wouldn't take away what you've got, I just need a bit of help. If you don't like it you just say . . . Only I can trust you, see, a man can count on you . . . Let me come, water-girl, just the once . . ."

He drifted on murmuring to the enormous silence, seeing trees that his eyes had never seen before and unable to choose between them. But the power tingled a little in his hand and the notes he could not hear trembled in the silence and he knew she was near.

Then the power began to throb, and looking quietly about he saw that after all he was watched and heard. A figure went with him from shade to shade watching secretly behind tree-trunks and rocks, rustling after him in the long grass. He could never fully see it except that it was bent and awkward, and that sometimes a sharp awn of grass moved and became a long sharp nose; and at first he wondered if some evil jailer had shut the water-girl away. But his spirit rejected that idea with conviction, and his memory of her singing by moonlight denied it too.

At last he found himself returning again and again to one tree and stood and looked at it. She had vanished into the ground . . . to the underground stream . . . There seemed to be no opening a man could see, and if there were he could not enter. He must wait till she came. This place was hers, it was her peace and safety; he could not go in unasked.

And suddenly that bent and awkward figure stood at the base of the tree and he saw it fully. It stood half crouched, wearing a broad belt of hair, and looked at him earnestly with eyes squinted against the light, its long nose as sharp as any grass-awn. And in its watching squinted eyes he saw the watching remoteness of the rocks and the immensity of the silence and the old patient endurance of the land; but he saw them caring, and he went without question to the spot to which the figure pointed and found a pothole and climbed through.

He fell on to sand and into dark coolness. He could see nothing yet, but he knew the Yunggamurra was there and spoke humbly to the dark. "Don't be scared. Don't be angry. I was going to wait but I was sent."

There was no answer.

"I'll go if you say. Any rate I won't come back. Only I wish you'd listen first."

He heard her voice a little way off: "Who sent you?"

"Bent up; sharp nose; squinty eyes; a Great One but gentle." He was beginning to see in the dimness of the cavern.

"He-of-the-Long-Grass," she murmured. "He was a dreaming once."

"You can feel it." She was crouched at the far end of the cavern, glimmering softly gold with the dark hair moving on her shoulders. She wore her only defense, that look of cool indifference that had always moved him. He spoke with a broken tenderness that he could not help.

"Water-girl. Don't worry. We couldn't help it, we had no chance. Man and spirit, it's not meant to be; I know that now. Only I needed you so bad, you're all a man can trust."

She cried, "You cannot trust me! Have I not played the Yunggamurra's game? I gave you happiness and broke it— you cannot trust the Yunggamurra!"

He smiled. "You always told me only I never listened. And the happiness was worth the breaking. But there's nothing else I want to trust like I trust you, that's something still between us. And if I'm wrong I won't complain."

She looked at him in silence for so long that at last he pleaded. "This old one, Long Grass; he's not like most. He's a looking-after sort."

"That is his beauty. Even a Yunggamurra knows it."

"He wouldn't have sent me if it wasn't right."

She said, "Tell me your need."

So he told her how Wulgaru had come east and he was sent to keep it in its place; of all that had happened in the forest and how his spirit must go out of him to meet and withstand Wulgaru. And her eyes widened in fear and were moonlit and darkened by turn, but Wirrun was too troubled and weary to notice.

"So they get two chances to my one. If the Big Boss gets hold of my spirit I'm done; but while that's going on there's the rest of me asleep and the others can have a go at that, and then I'm done anyway. It wins even if I win."

"I do not think Wulgaru means such a trick, but there are other chances. You wish to sleep safely watched?"

"If you'd do that for me, water-girl—if you'd let me sleep here and stay by till I wake—then I'd go off sure. And after I'd forget I ever saw you again."

"And if Wulgaru wins? If I stay by and never see you wake?"

He frowned. "I never thought of that . . . Would this Long Grass help? Get rid of me for you? Find you another cave?"

"Oh Man!" she cried in pain and anger.

He was cast down, troubled and still frowning. After a moment he raised his eyes and found hers watching him. They sat at opposite ends of the cavern and looked at each other while the small clear stream trickled from him to her and away into the darkness.

"Gold," he said at last. "What happened to your silver?"

She stirred restlessly. "It will grow again in the right mud . . . It was the sun. I was caught among rocks. I was too dried to use my senses."

He nodded. "Well, with gold you can have the sun and the water too. I've seen your sisters. They don't know where you've got to. You don't want to go back?"

"It is hard to be alone. But I keep my own self."

He nodded again. "And you're free."

"If I were caught again they would find me and bring me home."

He smiled. "And you'd run off again. And find another place. And keep your own self. You don't need them any more, or Wirrun-and-Murra either. You're free. And now, while I can still keep awake, I better do the same. Find another place to sleep."

"You will wait," she said, "while I bring grass. There is no other place. You will sleep here."

He could not speak. He only drew away to leave room while she climbed the rocks to the pot-hole above. In the corner where he now stood there was a blackening of the cavern wall. With a bushman's instinct he looked for and found the little heap of charred wood and ash, and stood looking at it while he waited.

Only weeks ago she had sat by his fire drawn and yet distrustful; a human girl who had not outgrown her Yunggamurra dread. But here, a Yunggamurra again and alone in her cavern, she had made her own fire.

In the Cave of Wulgaru

I

Wirrun waited with nervous irritation in the cavern. It was past midday already and his body, strained by the fearful night under the grave-trees, ached for sleep; whatever waking time was left he did not want to spend waiting alone while that golden ripple of a Yunggamurra gathered a mound of grass. This was the last chance of his life to be with her a little while, to hear her speak and look at her again. He could have gathered grass for himself—tired as he was, he could have slept on broken boulders.

While he was thinking this the light in the cavern blinked and brown-gold grass came spilling through the pot-hole into a great mound beneath. After it came the Yunggamurra, bouncing lightly into the grass with a bubble of laughter. She climbed out of it still laughing; he could see her planning to turn the pot-hole entrance into a game.

"Leave it," he said shortly. "I can sleep on rock."

"He-of-the-Long-Grass sends it," she said severely. She fished in the heap for a woven-grass bag. "And these." She gave him the bag and he saw that it held flat scorched cakes of coarsely ground grass-seed.

"It's early yet," he said fretfully. "I just want to see you for a bit before I sleep."

"You see me now. Eat."

"I'm not hungry."

"That is not important. You bring me your human self to care for and I bring you the help of the Long Grass. Sit there and eat."

He sat and chewed unwillingly at the hard grass-seed

cakes and watched her body gleaming in the dimness as she carried bundles of grass into a corner for his bed. The little river slid over its rock and its water rustled softer than the grass.

"A man needs to be more than a man," he grumbled.

She tossed her head and was wrapped in hair. "And the wind blows and the sky is blue and the sun will rise tomorrow. You are weary beyond sense. You must sleep soon, for while sleep is heavy it keeps the spirit in."

She came out of the darker corner and sat watching him eat. "Weary or strong," she said, "you must listen a moment. For if the powers of this country have avoided you you cannot know them."

"I thought I did," he said grimly remembering the night.

"There are others. I do not speak of small earth-things, my own kind, but of older and stronger powers. There are those whose work is joined to the work of Wulgaru. If, as it seems, he was unwilling to face you he may call on the help of these others."

Wirrun frowned. "What others?"

"Some are called Moomba. They look like men but they draw the life from men. Wulgaru waits for the shades of the dead; these send them to him. Watch for the Moomba."

"It's supposed to be only him and me and that was bad enough. Well . . . what else?"

"There are those that guard the law. If it is broken they too may send men to Wulgaru."

He frowned again. "I'm no law-breaker."

"You know where in this country a man may walk and where is forbidden? What foods may be eaten in what season? You are free of this country as any man born here, that is known; but if Wulgaru seeks to trap you are you prepared?"

He was silent.

"Watch for Kurakun, shaped like the smoke-hawk. Its business is with marriage. Watch for the Lundji, great black dogs that nose out law-breakers and destroy them."

"I'm used to dogs any rate. Is that the lot?"

"Only one more word before you sleep. There are powers in the land that are guarded against by fire or by water, and some by the beating of weapons and loud noise; some fear a kind of stone or wood and some may be sung. Against Wulgaru there is only one guard and it is harder than the rest: it is courage. If you can meet him calmly and boldly you can save yourself. And so I have no fear for you."

Wirrun gave a twisted smile. "That's one of us any rate. I'll do my best."

"Sleep, then."

"Not yet, water-girl, there's time yet. I'll never talk to you again. Sleep can wait."

"No, it cannot. I will not sit by and see you lose because sleep held you too tight. Go to your bed, Man, while the Yunggamurra sings."

Wearily he knew she was right. His eyes turned to the scorch-marks on the rocks: hiding alone, she had made a fire in memory of him. She had taken him into her safe and secret cave, fed and advised him and promised to guard him. Now she reminded him of what they were: he man and she Yunggamurra, the cruel and beautiful and vanishing thing that a man could not have. He went at once and lay on his bed of grass.

"You better try and sing me up some of this courage," he said giving himself the last word.

"If you needed it you would not be here," she retorted taking it from him; and she sang no song of courage or power but only of the grass whispering in the wind and a tiny lizard hiding. And within a minute he slept.

The Yunggamurra sat like a lizard herself, not near but alert in her stillness. She sat while the water whispered in the cavern, while the day moved on and the sun set and the light from the pot-hole faded. With eyes that had long ago learnt to see in caverns she watched unmoving; and at last she saw the man's sleep change.

His body stirred, loosened and relaxed. A mist flowed out of it and hung for a moment and gathered itself. She saw the spirit-shape of the man Wirrun. He seemed to stand in air just above his sleeping self and to reach high up in the cavern with the shape of the power still hung at his waist; and he looked at her steadily with love and gratitude and perhaps farewell, and the Yunggamurra stood up and looked back.

They did not speak though they knew they might have done, for they were still man and earth-thing; since the barrier of his flesh was put aside they set silence between them. But she lifted her chin with the free, fierce pride of the Yunggamurra and showed him her moonlit eyes full of faith, and he smiled and bent his head and rose up out of the cavern. Then she sat on the rocks by his sleeping form and watched again and sometimes sang.

Wirrun hung in darkness under the stars for the moon would not rise for many hours. He knew the dark did not hide him but he felt hidden and was glad. Yet for safety he turned away from the lancewood scrub and circled east and north over the plateau before he turned west again. So he came over the edge of the escarpment and down into the scrub.

Nothing followed him; he was avoided still. Nothing brooded in the lancewood scrub but its own heavy stillness and waiting dark. He drifted low through trees till he found the one he knew and rose to the dark shape in its branches. The platform was made of saplings tied in place with red-ochred string. Broad sheets of papery bark lay on it. Wirrun did not fully know the proper ways of the country, but after a moment's pause he crept between the sheets of paperbark and lay covered.

The bark weighed him down as the cold had done before. There was nothing to come between him and his fear: no throbbing of blood or tightening of muscle or deep-drawn breathing. He had not known how a man's body, responding to fear, can shut him away from it. Now he was alone with fear. Shadow-hand on shadow-stone he looked for help.

No help came. He had received all that could be given

and must manage the rest for himself. But in a while he found strength. It crept into his spirit mysteriously, hidden in scraps of memory and whispered in many voices. Wind-journeys over the land that had once been young and swallowed seas . . . *Am I more than the land?* Majestic flooded gum trees in the east, white ghost gums in the Centre, twisted and stunted gums of the north . . . *See, I have caught a tree!* Dark faces authoritative with age, quiet and waiting like the great rocks . . . *You've gone too far ahead of us, son.* The great black dog flowing under him, the Pungalunga rearing out of the river, the Jannoks spinning in the willy-willy . . . *A man of power . . . you are the Man . . . Maybe there never was a man like you.* The wildness of a storm over the water, and voices singing and howling in the storm . . . *You cannot trust the Yunggamurra!* . . . *But there's nothing else I want to trust.*

From these scraps and more his spirit gathered strength. The unknown was terrible, the fear would grow, but he would meet them as boldly as he could . . . *And so I have no fear for you.* And as he gained this foothold on fear he felt the cold of Wulgaru through the heavy cover of bark, and the stone throbbing in his hand, and heard the branches rustling a little way off and knew he was looked for.

2

With the sweep and hush of wings through the trees came the
rustle of leaves and the creak of branches: they were working towards him by some plan, going from one to another
of the dark quiet platforms where dead men had been laid.
The waiting was bad but it did not test his courage, for
the bark cover and the heavy cold weighed him down and
he could not move. He heard them in the next tree, in the
next branch. His cover was lifted, red eyes flared and a
word was spoken.

"One."

He was covered again. The grave-tree was silent.

In time a scuffling and muttering broke out below. The
tree trembled and began to sway, not the branches only but
the whole tree. He felt himself lifted, lying on his platform
under the bark: the tree itself was rising.

He would not lie like death and face his fear unknowing.
Anger stirred him to move a little; the bark slid aside and
he looked into the dark. And first he looked up through
branches to the stars.

They blazed white and very near: not the stars men knew
in these days but those men had always known, a cold white
blaze in the sky. He was carried so near that it seemed the
soft black sky might drape and smother him. In a spasm
of fear he turned his face aside and looked down.

The trunk of the tree reached far down out of sight. The
lancewood scrub was gone. By the light of the terrible stars
he saw a wide and dreary plain. It shimmered a little like
the magic waters of the desert, and gathered on the plain

he saw the crowd of the dead. Shoulder to shoulder they stood and covered the plain for they had been gathering a long time. They stood listless and drooping, and as the grave-tree passed over they raised hopeless faces and looked up. Their faces filled him with terror: ghost-whitened faces of the People but all now without hope or pride, for these were the dead that Wulgaru judged evil. Some wore the scars of their manhood, some wore red ochre in beard and hair, but all were lost. He saw one alone and bewildered staring up from a tangled fishing-net.

Suddenly the sky rang with a sound of clapping, regular and rhythmic, and a great voice began to chant. And on the plain the dead began to dance, shuffling and swaying to the freakish call of tap-sticks and songman. The grave-tree was gone like a dream. Wirrun stood on the plain among the dead and their weary despair wrapped him as the cold had done. They flowed past him following the tap-sticks and the song and turned their darkened eyes to him and called in empty voices that he must come. He went with them, drawn by the calling and the music, and saw great rocks darkening ahead and in them the mouth of a cave. The crowd of the dead flowed into it taking him with them.

He passed between cleft cracked walls of sandstone and saw painted on them a thousand years of dreaming: animals and men, ancestors and beings not to be named. Some were faded into ghostly shapes like the crowd that led him, some were kept bright and clear through all time. Mystery-beings in mystery-dress gazed down from huge dark eyes, but the crowd of the dead bore him under these and deeper in beyond the starlight. He saw ahead the changing light of a fire and went on with the others into a wider cavern. And at last, by the wavering light of flames, he faced Wulgaru.

It sat sprawled on a stone in the firelight. Its head and body were cut from a tree-trunk, its arms and legs from branches. Its joints were round river-stones tied with red-painted string. Its face was a clumsy mask like those he had seen before but greater and more terrible. Wirrun's hand went to his belt and he tried to draw into his being all the strength of the stone, for the thing called Wulgaru was roughly made but with a fearful power.

It sprawled on its stone as if to let him look and the timid dead drifted back against the cavern walls. Wirrun stood free of them at last. He saw perched behind Wulgaru a great grey falcon, the smoke-hawk Kurakun, and crouched at each side a monstrous black dog, the Lundji, with red leaf-shaped eyes and their red tongues lolling. But he could not look at them for Wulgaru suddenly opened its jaws and snapped them shut with a sound that rang in the cavern. Then it lifted its head and looked at him, and its eyes blazed white like the terrible stars.

"I welcome you," it said in its great voice like a windy tree, "Man of the east who mated with the Yunggamurra of the west." Behind it the smoke-hawk stirred and lifted its wings but Wirrun had no fear of the smoke-hawk.

"I've been told," he answered as boldly as he could, "that if a man mates with magic he's swallowed or he grows. Maybe you'll swallow me, Wulgaru, but you haven't done it yet. I've got time to grow."

The smoke-hawk settled and the mask of Wulgaru smiled. It spoke again as if for the first time.

"I welcome you, Man of the east; you who have come through the secret cave and seen what the law forbids."

The two great dogs sprang up, stiff-legged and snarling. The black hair bristled on their shoulders and the rattling of their snarls echoed in the cavern and grew.

"I came by the way I was brought," said Wirrun, "and I had the right. The whole land knows all countries are mine and this one too. That's why I'm sent."

But the dogs stood snarling and Wulgaru said, "There are degrees of manhood. Not all our men have the right to see that cave. Where are the marks that show your right?"

"I need no marks. I take the right from those that sent me."

Then the snarling rose and the great dogs leapt and he knew that if he were torn in pieces he must not show fear. He saw their red eyes and red mouths, and since he could not use the power and had nothing else he lunged out with an arm against the dogs and waited for the crunch of teeth.

But the dogs faltered, ears and tails flattened. Their red eyes were angry but they would not attack and at last slunk back. Wirrun tried not to show bewilderment, but he spread his fingers and stared at the hand that the dogs would not bite.

A single hair lay in it, a long coarse hair as black as the Lundji's. A hair of the Jugi. It had been entangled in possum-fur cord or rough bark twine since he rode away from Ko-in on that great black dog—or it had come into his hand by spirit means—it did not matter. He held it out to Wulgaru.

"There's the mark of my right," he said grimly. "From those that sent me."

The white fire of Wulgaru's eyes blazed for a moment but it spoke as calmly as before.

"I welcome you, Man of the east whose living spirit comes before its time into the cave of the dead."

Then the crowd of the dead raised a howling and screeching and broke towards Wirrun in a wave from the cavern walls, all their darkened eyes staring at him and their ghost-white hands reaching to claw and tear him. They were more dreadful than the dogs but still he must be bold: he took a great leap forward and grasped the shoulder of Wulgaru and stood close between the monster and the snarling Lundji. And as the howling dead hung back he shouted to them.

"There's one of you there in a net. Let him come out."

The crowd of the dead wailed and drifted and stared with their empty eyes; but in their drifting a way opened and the ghost stood there that stared hopeless and bewildered from its tangled fishing-net. And Wirrun was filled with anger and swung round to accuse Wulgaru.

"This was a man from the east. He's got his own dreaming. If he's broke your law that's because it wasn't his.
What's he doing here?"

Wulgaru's eyes blazed again. "He is mine and so he is
here. What is he to you or his dreaming to me? I took him,
and those I take must follow my law."

"There's a bigger one. You and all these know it: a man's
got a right to his own dreaming. If he leaves it and comes
here that's his risk—but this man died in his own country and
there's a road waiting for him over there. You set yourself
up over right and wrong, you turned your dogs on me for
breaking the law. Well now I name you, Wulgaru, breaker of
the law. I call on all the powers of this country to send
this spirit home. And what are these Lundji dogs going
to do about that?"

The cavern was filled with a wild outcry but the fire, that
had burned bright though it was not fed, sank low. Wirrun
only heard the angry baying of the Lundji, the beat and
flurry of wings, the fearful crying of the dead; he saw only
their whirling shapes and the white fire of Wulgaru's eyes.
And in the midst of this fury and flurry the voice of Jimmy
Ginger cried, "Home!"

The fire sprang high again. The Lundji and the smoke-
hawk and all the crowd of the dead had gone and Wulgaru
sat unmoved. "You have won a ghost," he said with a sneer.

"I've won something, then," said Wirrun stoutly in the
face of his disappointment.

The sneer vanished and Wulgaru laughed a little. "And
did you hope to win more? To see me torn in pieces, say?
Must I teach you victory?"

Wirrun only gazed sternly back. He would not be fooled
by any trickery of words; he was not yet a victor for his
spirit was still held to Wulgaru and he knew it. Wulgaru
laughed again.

"Should the law of the country be torn in pieces when the
law of the land is made whole? You have finished your work,
Man. For if the powers of the country take from me the

ghost of the eastern dreaming how can I hold any other but my own? You have turned my country on me. It will hold me to the law for all time."

Wirrun gazed in doubt and hope into the star-white eyes of the mask. He thought that truth was in them, and something darker that filled him with dread. He waited.

"And now," said Wulgaru in its voice like the wind in trees, "since you have laid your hand on me we fight. And we shall find out who and what you are."

The cavern was filled with the echoing rhythm of tap-sticks. Though the crowd of the dead was gone Wirrun saw that other man-shapes stood against the sandstone walls. And he knew them for the Moomba who drain the life out of men.

3

Wirrun's spirit was heavy with fear for he saw that no light live spirit could win a fight with the great log-shape of Wulgaru. If courage was his only defense he had lost already, but he seized the vanishing tail of courage and made himself stand straight and look bold.

"If you destroy me," he said, "you'll send my ghost home."

"Yourself you have made it sure. But if a man claims all countries where is home?"

That was a cold question that Wirrun could not now face. "We'll find that out too," was all he said.

The monster smiled. It stood up clumsily and began to shuffle and stamp to the tapsticks, loose-jointed and grotesque. Wirrun watched grimly. It came to him that Wulgaru was showing itself man-made and clumsy to catch him off his guard. He was not fooled; he knew power when he saw it.

"Come," said Wulgaru and danced away out of the cavern. The Moomba went after it tapping to its dance and Wirrun followed.

They went through the dark passage and under the painted eyes of the outer cave and on to the plain. The terrible stars were gone and it seemed daylight. Wulgaru's stone-jointed arms swung loose and crashed the tops off trees. It snapped its jaws in time with the tapsticks and sent parrots screeching away. Now it seemed too powerful for any live thing to approach and he thought he could only try to use the lightness and speed of his spirit.

"Here," said Wulgaru at last, and the tapsticks were silent

and the Moomba stood aside. "The ground is clear and level. Does this place suit you, little Man? I would not have it said in the land that Wulgaru defeated the Ice-Fighter unfairly."

If he was being taunted he would not rise to the bait. He said only, "One place is as good as another."

Wulgaru smiled again and turned to face him. "Are you ready, then, Hero?"

"Ready as I'll ever be," said Wirrun alert and watchful.

Without any further word the thing lunged at him. He whirled aside and let it pass. It brought up with a crash against a tree that rocked and swayed.

"You will not fight?" it said politely.

"I'm not a tree," said Wirrun. "I use what I've got." He side-whirled again and reached quickly for a fallen branch. At the third pass he managed to thrust the branch between the thing's wooden legs. It fell with a crash that rattled its joints and sprang up again.

"Ah," it said, and reached out an arm as quick as light and drew him close.

Water, he thought desperately, I'm water; he made himself inert and fluid and slid down out of its grasp. But in a moment it had him again.

They fought like two spirits, both light and lightning-fast, a slippery sort of wrestling in which Wirrun held his own for a while. In a moment they fought like two strong men; they fell and sprang and grunted and struggled while dust rose about them and one reached for a stone or another a stick. That too changed in a flash and they fought like man and power; and Wirrun found himself helpless, held unmoving, weakening into nothing even while he fought to fight. And from very far away the voice of Wulgaru reached him as solemn and sad as the wind in she-oaks.

"For though I am man-made, a bit of tree, yet am I death. You cannot meet me unchanged."

Defeated, he slid away into some long winding dark.

Yet he would not submit. Darkness contained him but

from within it he knew the sun still beat down on the plain and the dust had not settled. Hands seized him and he knew they were the hands of the Moomba. Now he could see again: they slid him into a grass-woven net and hoisted it into a tree and set him swinging. And while he swung gently to and fro they sang with great sweetness.

He was weary, weary . . . he had journeyed over the land . . . hunted and been hunted, watched many nights under the grave-trees, entered the secret world of the dead and set free the captive ghosts. Victory was his . . . he had earned the right to sleep . . . he slept . . .

The darkness was real and immediate and smelled of old death. The net bound him close and he could not move. The darkness was a cave and all around, in every crack and niche and hollow of worn sandstone, were the pale skulls and bones of men. They were so still; they forced themselves on him out of the dark with their powerful, oppressive stillness.

He knew he was in that darkness beyond the painted cave, bound as other men had been and laid in the last burial-place of these People. He was laid here by the Moomba and could never escape. The heaviness of death smothered him and nothing came between him and his fear.

He could not bear this fear—he must escape it. He struggled for life, for his memories of days and night, the love of Ko-in, the trust of Ularra, the faith of the golden Yung-gamurra. And as he set these things between him and fear he saw that in the very fear itself he was still himself. He was not yet nothing. He knew himself.

"I am," he whispered stiffly.

The heaviness of death lifted a little.

"I am."

The air moved and sweetened as if a breeze had stirred it.

"I am . . . I am . . ."

The bones of the dead were pitiful: neat puppets made for children, broken and untidy now.

"The bit of me here, it's spirit. They can't make bones out of that."

He found that he could move a little, enough to loosen the net. It opened easily. He slid free.

At that same moment in another cave, in her own cavern where the river ran, the Yunggamurra stirred and stilled. There was a change. She leaned near the sleeping body of the man and the dark fall of her hair came over him. She hesitated, touched him lightly with a finger, lifted her head and howled softly. The cavern walls howled very softly back.

The Yunggamurra rose and went quickly to the farthest corner of the cavern and crouched inside the dark fall of her hair. She waited and listened still but she did not go near the man or look at him again.

4

Wirrun stood in the cave of death and breathed air with the burnt-honey sweetness of gum-blossom. The lost white bones of the dead were pitiful yet they had strength; disjointed fingers lying here had painted those dark eyes in the outer cavern. He felt tall and strong, not smoke-drifting or dream-seeing like a man in sleep but more fully alive than he had ever felt, and he strode towards the inner cave of Wulgaru.

It was good to move so surely over the uneven rock. He went into the firelight and found Wulgaru sitting where he had sat before with the Moomba around him. When they saw him they laughed aloud and thronged about him rubbing their hands over their own bodies and his, exchanging sweat in the business of friendship. He felt no awe or triumph but stood looking over their heads at the great tree-trunk body and mask-face of Wulgaru. It spoke to him graciously.

"I welcome you, Man, great-grandson of my maker. Sit by my fire and talk to me."

The Moomba laughing and nodding moved aside but Wirrun still stood and looked at Wulgaru; and again he was filled with a sort of pity. For this was another puppet, more clumsily made but with strength and not yet broken. He saw that truly it took its power from men; it had none but what they gave it, no wisdom but what they taught it, and in evil or good was only obedient to them.

"You've not destroyed me, then," he said.

The mask smiled and the eyes burnt white like the terrible stars. "I have not destroyed you with fear or your own evil. I have not destroyed you like another man."

"We had a bargain," said Wirrun.

"It was made good when you sent the eastern ghost home."

"That's reasons and argument. I don't trust to them." He laid his hand on the shape of the stone. "I kept my word and never used this against you, but now it's over I got the right again. I speak for the powers of the land and I order you and yours to keep your own country from now on for all the time there is."

"You may order without the stone or the land's old beetles. Do you not also thank me?" Wirrun was silent. "There have been Clever Men," said Wulgaru, "who thanked me for their making."

Wirrun smiled. "If I'm Clever I was born that way. No thanks to you." For he would not teach the creature any more power.

The eyes blazed white again but the voice said only, "You say true. Go, then, and find out who you are and where is home. I fear I shall not see you soon."

Wirrun gave one nod of farewell to Wulgaru and one to the Moomba and turned to go. Behind him the tree-voice murmured wistfully.

"Yet I think you may thank me."

Wirrun did not look back. He did not look again at the small lost bones in the second cave or, since he did not have the marks, at the paintings in the first. He strode light and easy out of the cave into country he knew, under the edge of the escarpment.

It was bright with the day's last sun and fell steeply away to wide grasslands and scrub. He could see the mouth of the valley where the river ran in between outlying arms of the escarpment to his camp. That other dreary plain was gone, the plain where the crowd of the dead had danced and he had fought with Wulgaru—yet when he thought of it it was there for a moment, shimmering at the edges like vanishing desert water.

He climbed strongly into the air and travelled over the known country. He wanted to shout with the power and fullness of living, with joy that his work was done and his battle over. He wanted to see the Yunggamurra's eyes turn to moonlight and to hear her sing a song of heroes. And before he crept back into his puppet body and put his flesh between them—before he went away at last and left her safe and free—they would look at each other again. They would know that in spite of all laws and all time they loved each other and were truly man and wife.

With the speed of spirits he came over the hill, found the tree and the pot-hole and slid into the cavern. It seemed to be empty but he knew she was there and shouted impatiently.

"Water-girl! Come out of that! Where are you?"

She came glimmering out of the dark and stood with hands folded and head bent. "I am here, Great One."

He laughed enormously. "You knew, then? You saw? It was just like you said only worse! I was scared right through. Oh, girl!" He stretched till he seemed to fill the cave and still she stood with bent head, and he laughed again at her pretended respect and thought how small and fragile she was and how lovely. "I'm starving," he boasted. "Any more of those cakes left?"

She looked up very gravely. "You are hungry?"

"I could eat a horse."

"The dead," she said, "are never hungry."

He frowned.

"You travelled fast and well?" she asked earnestly. "Was the sun warm? You heard the birds and smelled the honey?"

"What's wrong, girl?" he asked. Her eyes were dark. Without knowing he did it he took her hands in his. "Don't be scared. Everything's fine. Tell me what's up."

"See!" she cried. "You breathe deep! Your hands are strong and warm."

"Yours too. What's up?"

She swung away behind her hair. "You cannot trust the Yunggamurra! You have won and I have failed! Go and see."

He tried to draw her with him but she pulled back; so he went alone to the corner with the bed of grass and looked down at Wirrun sleeping. And he saw he was turned into stone.

"So the Big Cap won after all," he said dazedly. "He's destroyed me." But he knew it was not so. Even this moment of shock could not blunt his freed mind; he knew he had been changed as ancestors and heroes and lesser men before him had been changed. The land was silently peopled with them; among its ancient rocks their stone bodies lay in warning or in promise while they themselves lived on; behind the wind as the old men said. Now he too lived behind the wind. He had grown out of now into forever.

But he felt a great tearing pang that he had lost the companionship of men, and of desolation that he was free and homeless, a being without a place. And behind him, as if in answer to that, he heard the Yunggamurra sobbing. He turned away from the blurred and coarsened shape of himself and went to her, where she sat weeping within the dark fall of her hair.

He sat near and drew her against his shoulder as he would have done once, and laid his cheek on her hair. "Now then, girl," he said gently teasing, "you never did that. I got a lot of faith in you but this was something bigger. Nothing you could help. Bigger than you and Wulgaru both."

She went on sobbing.

"Come on, now. Some people'd be *glad* if a friend of theirs got turned into a hero forever."

"But you did not choose it!" she cried. "You have lost your old self and you set me to watch!"

"And you went off playing with the wind and singing to the grass, *I* know, and when you got back there was this red-eyed thing turning me into a rock. Well I'll just have to beat you, I reckon. A man's gotta beat his wife now and then."

The Yunggamura gave another sob or two and fell silent. Wirrun was silent too; the silence lengthened. There was only the rustle of water over rock, and some fragment that fell into it with a small clear *plink!* of surprise. When they had both listened for some time to Wirrun's last words he lifted his head and laughed again; not largely this time but deep and quiet.

"I gotta hand it to him," he said. "He did win. And I shoulda thanked him. Girl dear, do you think your sisters'd steal his wife from a proper forever sort of hero?"

She smiled a secret Yunggamurra smile in the darkness of her hair. "Surely," she said, "he would spring up into the storm and take her back?"

"And beat 'em off with whips of lightning. Or follow them to their only river and call her out of it. That's if she was the right sort, one that'd come with him. She'd have to be the sort that broke free on her own and got turned a bit by the sun. A gold Yunggamurra."

"Surely," she said peeping wickedly, "a proper hero would take no other sort? For a man must take the Yunggamurra he can catch but a Great One may choose."

"Is that what the law says?"

"The law of the Yunggamurra is for men and not for Great Ones."

"Well," said Wirrun, "I don't know how great but I travel very fast on air. And I could still eat a horse only you don't like horse. Will we go east to the sea-tainted water and catch a fish for breakfast?"

She considered gravely. "May we cook it on a fire?"

"Dear girl! But here's your own place, with your own river and all. If you leave it something might steal it from you."

She lifted her chin with the old fierce pride. "Nothing would dare. Have you no place in the east, and would you lose it?"

"When a man claims all countries home's everywhere."

"Then let us go east and find the morning and ride it west! There are rivers and hills and forests to see again."

"And winds and waterfalls to ride."

"And strange old things to peep at, and stones that grow and sparkle in dark places!"

"But I tell you I'm hungry, girl—"

"That is not important. If there are no fish there will be turtle-eggs or a rabbit."

So the hero and the water-girl went from the cavern up into the green evening sky; and a shy stooped figure, that had seen one of them turned gold and the other to stone, nodded gently and watched them go. But where they went only the land knew.

In time, as word spread down the long roads, most of the Ice-Fighter's story was put together and told; but its ending changed from place to place and often it only drifted into silence. For in the Centre, and in the high country under the Cape, and below the great northern escarpment, there were men who claimed that the story was not ended and the Ice-Fighter was still around. He had been seen, they said, sitting at a campfire in the evening and talking with a friend—but when a stranger came near he went away quickly, and the man who was left at the fire only shook his head and would say nothing.

The old south land lies like an open hand under the stars. They shine more brightly there. They tell their stories to every kind of man and the stories change from country to country. So one group is the Southern Cross here, and there a black swan flying from a spear; another is Orion's Belt, or again it is the sisters of the eagle. But one group keeps its name through many stories: it is called the Seven Sisters.

Under the escarpment these seven are the Yunggamurra. They were human once, sisters who broke the law and were changed in punishment; the cruel and lovely and vanishing singers of the river. The stars too are veiled in shifting

darkness like the Yunggamurra in their hair. They gleam
and vanish as the sisters do and are very hard to count. Few
men see that now there are only six.

The seventh Yunggamurra has broken free and roams
the land with Wirrun.